Praise for Kat Martin

"Filled with suspense, action and sizzling scenes, the pages of this book practically turn themselves."
—*Bookpage* on *Beyond Danger*

"The kind of taut, edge-of-your-seat action you crave from a suspenseful book."
—*Bustle* on *Beyond Reason*

"Martin whips together unforgettable characters and a high-octane plot with more twists and turns than a street in San Francisco . . . As the suspense unfurls at a breathtaking pace, readers will be captivated by this tale of drug dealers, foreign terrorists, bloody violence, and hot, steamy sex, all leading to a shocking ending. Martin's fans and newcomers alike will enjoy every moment of this thrill ride."
—*Publishers Weekly*, STARRED REVIEW on *Beyond Reason*

"Intense mystery and sensual love scenes will lure readers into this novel and not let go until the final page is turned."
—*Publishers Weekly* on *Against the Wild*

PIVOT

KAT MARTIN

ALEXANDRA IVY

REBECCA ZANETTI

ZEBRA BOOKS
KENSINGTON PUBLISHING CORP.
www.kensingtonbooks.com

ZEBRA BOOKS are published by

Kensington Publishing Corp.
119 West 40th Street
New York, NY 10018

All Kensington titles, imprints, and distributed lines are available at
special quantity discounts for bulk purchases for sales promotion, pre-
miums, fund-raising, educational, or institutional use.

Special book excerpts or customized printings can also be created to fit
specific needs. For details, write or phone the office of the Kensington
Sales Manager: Attn.: Sales Department. Kensington Publishing Corp.,
119 West 40th Street, New York, NY 10018. Phone: 1-800-221-2647.

Zebra and the Z logo Reg. U.S. Pat. & TM Off.

First Printing: April 2020
ISBN-13: 978-1-4201-5114-5
ISBN-10: 1-4201-5114-2

eISBN-13: 978-1-4201-5115-2 (eBook)
eISBN-10: 1-4201-5115-0 (eBook)

10 9 8 7 6 5 4 3 2 1

Printed in the United States of America

AGAINST THE HEART

KAT
MARTIN

Chapter One

"This isn't enough, dammit! Come on, Meri, I know you've got that money squirreled away someplace and I want it. If you know what's good for you, you'll get it for me now!"

Meriwether Jones forced herself to stay focused on Joey Bandini's face and not the escape she was planning to make, not the car, packed and waiting for her and her daughter in the parking garage under her apartment.

"I don't have any more money, Joey. Mrs. Vandermeer wasn't a wealthy woman."

"Bullshit. Besides what she had in the bank, I bet that old biddy had money stuffed in her mattress."

"She had some savings when she died, and she made sure I got the money. But it wasn't all that much." And what she'd had was almost gone. Mrs. Vandermeer had been her foster mom. As the woman grew older, Meri had become her caregiver. As soon as Joey had seen the older woman's obituary in the paper, he had reappeared in her life. He'd been harassing her, demanding money, certain Mrs. Vandermeer had left her a lot more than the small inheritance she'd actually received.

Meri had paid him, hoping he would leave her alone.

Instead, she was out of cash and Joey was still the bloodsucking leech he'd been before.

When she'd checked her savings that morning, she'd had five hundred dollars put away for the trip: four hundred in twenties in her wallet and an emergency hundred-dollar bill tucked into the hideaway spot behind her driver's license.

Then Joey had appeared at her door, grabbed her purse, and stolen all the cash, leaving nothing but her credit card with a three-hundred-dollar limit, and her hideaway hundred-dollar bill.

She looked at Joey, who kept counting the twenties over and over as if they might multiply in his hand. "Four hundred bucks? That's chicken feed. I know she left you plenty. Where's the rest, Meri?"

"I got eight thousand total, Joey, just like I said. I spent some of it taking care of Lily. Most of it I've given to you."

"I told you to cut the crap. You've still got plenty and I need it. If you don't get it for me, you know what's going to happen."

A chill slipped through her. He was going to find a way to get to Lily. He had threatened to take her daughter away from her—one way or another.

"Leave Lily alone."

"You want me to leave her alone? Get me that money."

Meri looked at Joey. Five years ago, the night she had met him, Joey Bandini, with his dark hair and long-lashed blue eyes, had been amazingly handsome. If she didn't know him the way she did now, maybe she would still think he was.

But Meri saw the destruction his alcohol and drug abuse had caused, the slackness in his features, his pale skin, and the hollows in his cheeks. She knew he was a lowlife who would do anything to get what he wanted.

She took a calming breath. "Okay, I'll get you the money. But the bank is closed on Sunday. I won't be able to get the money until tomorrow." It didn't matter what she told Joey. She wasn't going to be there when he came back to collect. "Meet me here at noon. I'll have the money for you then."

"I'll be here at eleven and you better have at least a couple of thousand. You don't, Lily comes with me."

Meri suppressed a shudder. It was hard to imagine that the man standing in front of her was Lily's father. Amazing how just one night—one stupid night—could change your life forever.

"I said I'd get you the money. Now get out of here and leave me alone."

Joey tucked the roll of twenties into the pocket of his black leather jacket. "Tell Lily her daddy sends his love."

Turning away from Joey's grinning face, Meri walked back into her apartment and firmly closed the door. Trembling as she stood at the window, she watched until Joey and two of his no-good friends got into Joey's beat-up Ford and disappeared.

Unfortunately, tomorrow they'd be back for the money she didn't have. Her girlfriends had tried to get her to call the police, but Meri didn't trust the cops, hadn't since she was a teenager, shunted from one foster home to another. Back then, a lot of her problems had been her own fault, but even now, trust didn't come easy.

And the hard truth was, Joey was Lily's father—DNA would prove it. Meri didn't know what the police might say about that and she wasn't sticking around to find out.

"Lily, honey, come on. It's time for us to leave." Her four-year-old daughter came running out of the bedroom. Lily had the same dark hair as Joey, the same blue eyes, but any other sign the two were related was in Joey's drug-hazed brain. "Go get your travel bag and let's go."

"Okay." Lily raced back to her bedroom and grabbed her red wheeled bag with a ladybug on the front. Meri grabbed the handle of her carry-on. The bags were the last two items she needed to load into the car.

In minutes she was on her way, driving her old, reliable Chevy Malibu out of Riverside, then hitting the I-15 freeway heading north. Though she had a possible destination in mind, with her money now mostly gone, she would have to be flexible. She wasn't completely sure where she was going to end up, just somewhere out of California where Joey couldn't find her. The I-15 was closest to her apartment. She could change the route as she went along. It didn't really matter. As long as she wound up somewhere Joey couldn't continue to harass her and Lily.

She was on her way as far as the money in her wallet and her credit card would take her, on her way to a life somewhere else.

Meri just prayed wherever it was, it would be far enough away to disappear.

Ian Brodie took the Argonne Road exit off the freeway, east of Spokane. The road took him north, into the open Washington countryside. It didn't take long to reach the rural, ten-acre property where he had been raised, the two-story farmhouse his father had been living in for the last thirty-five years.

He pulled his dark green Jeep Cherokee up in front of the white two-story, wood-frame structure and turned off the engine, just sat there for a while. He'd moved out right after high school, gone to college in Seattle where he'd majored in police science, then become a cop with the Seattle PD. He'd left that profession years ago, taking a job as a private investigator for one of the local security firms. Now he owned his own very successful business in Seattle, Brodie Security, Inc.

As busy as he was, Ian didn't get back to Spokane all that often, hadn't seen his dad in nearly two years.

Guilt slipped through him. He should have returned a lot sooner. But since his mother had died five years ago, his father had changed. Daniel Brodie was little more than a shell of the man he'd once been. These days he was bitter, sour, and most of the time, downright unpleasant.

Ian looked at the wood-frame house. The place had deteriorated since the last time he was there. The white paint on the door was peeling, the front yard needed mowing, the rain gutter above the porch was hanging loose. He had figured the house would be badly in need of repair and had taken two weeks off to get the work done.

He had called his father, a little reluctantly since he was afraid his dad would tell him to stay away.

Climbing out of the Jeep, he headed for the door, trying to ignore the dread churning in his stomach. The front door was unlocked, the way it always was. Daniel Brodie didn't believe in locked doors. Ian had tried to tell him that times had changed, but his dad refused to listen.

Daniel Brodie lived in the past and it looked like he always would.

Ian walked into the house, calling his father's name. "Dad! Dad, it's me, Ian!"

"I'm in the den!" his father yelled back, not bothering to come out and greet his only son. Ian steeled himself and walked in that direction.

Only one set of curtains had been opened in the living room, which was dark and smelled airless and musty. The furniture hadn't been moved or cleaned since before Ian's mother had died, the same burgundy overstuffed sofa, same maple coffee table, same crocheted doilies on the tables and the arms of the chairs, the cotton thread no longer white, but yellowed with age.

As he passed the kitchen the smell of rotten food hit him, making his stomach churn. A stack of half-eaten TV dinners sat on the kitchen counter, along with a three-foot stack of dirty dishes.

Ian silently cursed. The place was a screaming mess, far worse than he had imagined.

He continued into the den, found his dad sitting in his favorite dark brown Naugahyde recliner, his feet up, newspapers strewn all over the floor.

"Hi, Dad."

Daniel cast him little more than a glance. "'Bout time you showed up. How long has it been? Two years? Three?"

"Two years. And you're right, it's been way too long."

His dad grunted. At sixty, his hair was completely gray. He'd been a tall man, six-two, an inch taller than Ian. Now he was stoop-shouldered, his face too thin, and somehow he looked smaller. The white bristles on his cheeks said he hadn't shaved in days.

"You want a beer?" his dad asked. He was watching a football game, blue eyes the same shade as Ian's glued to the screen.

"No, thanks." Ian blew out a breath as he glanced around the dismal room. "Listen, Dad, like I said on the phone, I'm here to help you get the place in shape. I'm going to carry my duffel up to my old room, put on some work clothes, and get started."

His father just shrugged. "Suit yourself. You always have."

Ian let the remark slide. After all, he deserved it. But he was here now and he wasn't afraid of hard work.

Two hours later, when all he'd managed to do was repair the rain gutters around the perimeter of the house and pick up the trash in the yard, hadn't even begun the job of cleaning up inside, he decided he could use some help. There was plenty he could be doing outside while a cleaner put the inside of the place back in order.

There was a supermarket in a shopping center down Argonne Road, he recalled. He hadn't been there in years, but he remembered the bulletin board just inside the door that held cards and notes left by people who were looking for work. They were usually locals, trustworthy folks. He'd start his search there.

Ignoring the unpleasant odors inside the house, he went back into the den. "You need anything from the store, Dad? I've got an errand to run. I'll be right back."

"Get a couple of those TV dinners. We'll heat them up for supper."

Ian's stomach rolled. "I'll get something, I'll be right back." He left the house and stepped outside, trying not to sigh in relief. At least his room was the same as he'd left it the last time he was there. He'd opened the windows to air it out, but the bed was made, the floors clean. A little dust didn't bother him.

Ian slid behind the wheel of the Jeep and headed back down the road to the grocery store. Maybe he'd get lucky and find an experienced woman who could help him get the place in order.

Ian sure as hell hoped so.

Chapter Two

Meri was almost out of gas. Her credit card was maxed out and she was almost out of money. Worse than that, she was almost out of ideas.

"I'm hungry, Mama. Can I have a candy bar?" Lily sat in her booster seat in the back of the old brown Chevy. They'd been stopping at food marts and fast food restaurants along the freeway all the way from California. At the last stop, Meri had bought Lily a chocolate milk and a packaged bologna-and-cheese sandwich. But that had been hours ago.

The child had slept for a while, but she was only a little over four and she was getting tired of the endless driving. They'd traveled over thirteen hundred miles so far.

Meri had a friend in Portland, a girlfriend she'd met at her last foster home. She and Michelle had stayed in touch and Michelle had said there were plenty of jobs in the area. Meri had spoken to her as she had driven north and Michelle had convinced her to head in that direction.

Meri had hoped to make it all the way there, but only a few gallons were left in the gas tank, and she didn't have enough money to fill it. When the fuel light came on, she took the first off-ramp, Argonne Road.

"Mama, I'm hungry."

There was a Safeway up ahead. Food came first. Meri pulled into the parking lot of a small shopping center that included the grocery store, a Rite Aid, and a row of smaller businesses.

Taking Meri out of her booster seat, she took the little girl's hand and headed toward the store. There was only a ten-dollar bill in her wallet, but it was enough for a snack and a small carton of milk for Lily.

Meri started for the door, which opened automatically, and the two of them walked inside. The first thing she noticed was the bulletin board. Dozens of cards and notes had been pinned up there, addresses and phone numbers of people looking for various types of work.

She could do just about anything, from waitressing to secretarial, bookkeeping, cleaning, cooking. She'd even worked as a trainer at a Riverside gym. But even if she left her cell phone number, she couldn't wait around for someone to call. Either she had to keep driving or find a place to stay. Maybe she could find work in Spokane. It wasn't that far away.

She decided to leave her number on a slip of paper just in case, and began digging around in her purse for a pen. That's when she saw him, the handsome blond man with the brilliant blue eyes who was intently studying the board. He was over six feet tall and broad-shouldered. Worn, faded jeans hugged a set of very nice buns. He was carrying a notepad, she saw, jotting down phone numbers.

He didn't look like a serial killer, so Meri took a chance. "Are you looking to hire someone?"

He glanced down at her and she felt a jolt when those cool blue eyes fixed on her face. "Actually, I am. I'm looking for a housekeeper."

"Well, there's a coincidence. I was just getting ready to put my number up on the board. I'm very good at housekeeping."

"It's really more of a cleaning job," he said.

She thought of the ten dollars that was all she had left in the world. "I can do that. I don't mind hard work and I'm very efficient."

Lily tugged on the hem of her T-shirt. "Mama, I'm hungry."

"In a minute, sweetheart." She turned back to the man, desperation mixed with hope. "I'd do a good job for you. I'm a very hard worker."

Those cool blue eyes ran over her, taking her measure. She was five-foot-six, not too short, and after her job as a trainer, she was in excellent physical condition.

"I was really looking for someone older," he said.

"I'm twenty-eight. That's old enough to clean a house."

His mouth edged up. He had a very sexy mouth. Funny . . . she had never thought of a man's lips that way.

"I see you have a daughter," he said. "What would you do with her while you're working?"

Her insides knotted. She really needed this job. "She'd stay out of the way, I promise. She's very well behaved— aren't you, sweetheart?"

Lily started jumping up and down. "I'm hungry. I'm hungry!"

Meri lifted her up and propped her on a hip. "If you'll be good, I'll get you one of those orange-vanilla ice creams you like. But you have to be quiet until Mama finishes talking to this nice man."

Lily started nodding, visions of ice cream dancing in her four-year-old head. "Okay."

Meri set her back on her feet. When she looked at the

man, she could read the amusement on his attractive face. "As I said, she's usually well behaved," she said. "You wouldn't even know she was there."

His amusement slowly faded. "I'll be honest, Ms. . . . ?"

"Jones. Meriwether Jones. People just call me Meri. This is my daughter, Lily."

"I'll be honest, Meri. The house is a real mess. It's going to need hours of hard work to get it in shape. I think you'd be better off—"

She caught his arm, stopping him mid-sentence. "I really need this job. I promise, if you hire me, you won't be disappointed."

His gaze traveled from the reddish-brown hair she had braided into two long plaits, paused at the pink T-shirt that read I AM WOMAN, moved down over her jeans to her pink canvas sneakers. He looked at Lily, who stood quietly now, big blue eyes a little lighter than his, staring back into his face.

"All right, fine. You're hired. But my father lives in the place and he isn't going to like having a kid in the house. You have to keep your daughter away from him."

Her heart was thumping. This could be the answer to her prayers. Or at least to her immediate prayer that she could earn enough to get to a city where she could find a real job. "That won't be a problem. He won't even know she's there."

"I guess we'll see."

"How far away is the house?" Meri thought of the Chevy and wondered if she needed to use some of her remaining ten dollars to put a gallon of gas in the tank.

"Not far. Just up the road. How soon can you start?"

Her stomach growled. She'd been feeding Lily, but she was afraid to spend her last few dollars on food for herself.

"If you have something there to make sandwiches, I can start today. In fact, I can start as soon as I get there."

The man pulled out his wallet and handed her a couple twenty-dollar bills. "Get some bread and meat and whatever else you need. You don't happen to cook, do you?"

She started nodding. "I'm a very good cook. I took cooking lessons. For a while I wanted to be a chef."

One of his dark gold eyebrows went up in what could have been relief. He handed her another twenty. "Get something to make for supper. You can eat with us if you want."

Did she want to eat supper with two strangers? Her stomach growled again. Oh God, did she. "It won't take me long. I'll get the groceries and follow you home."

"All right. Fifteen minutes. By the way, my name's Ian Brodie."

"Nice to meet you, Mr. Brodie."

"Ian works."

"Nice to meet you, Ian. We'll be right back." Grabbing her daughter's hand, she hurried into the grocery store. Sixteen minutes later, she was through the checkout line carrying three plastic grocery bags of food, out the door into the parking lot.

The bad news was, there was no sign of Ian Brodie.

Ian sat in his Jeep waiting for Meriwether Jones. He should have hired someone else. Some big strapping brute who could tackle a dirty job like the one in his father's house. But Ian was a sucker for a woman in trouble, and he'd been a cop long enough to know this one surely was.

He could read the desperation in her face, and the fact that she was so pretty only made it worse. Along with her mahogany hair, golden-brown eyes, and fine-boned features, she had sexy, feminine curves in all the right places. He'd felt a kick the moment he'd laid eyes on her.

Add to that, she had a kid. Ian had a weakness for kids, and Lily, with her big blue eyes and angelic face, was a real cutie.

He saw Meri emerge from the store, holding on to an armload of groceries, Lily hurrying along beside her. In a pair of jeans, a neon-green T-shirt, and pink sneakers the color of her mom's, the little girl licked an orange 50-50 bar. Meri halted just outside the door, surveying the parking lot in search of him. Even from a distance, he could read the fear in her face.

Opening the car door, he stepped out and waved. "Over here!"

She seemed to sag in relief as she hurried toward him and handed him the grocery bags, which he loaded into the back of the Jeep. She carefully counted back three one-dollar bills, gave him twenty cents in change, and a receipt for the food.

"That's my cell number." She pressed a slip of paper into his hand. "In case we get separated in traffic."

"I won't lose you," he said, looking down at the money she had so carefully returned, a good sign, he thought. "I promise."

Meri just nodded. He watched her as she hurried to her car, loaded Lily into the kid's seat in back, then went around and slid into the driver's seat.

Ian kept the old car in his rearview mirror as he drove back to the house. He wasn't looking forward to the confrontation with his father, but what was done was done.

He'd given Meriwether Jones a job. He didn't know her story, didn't know what kind of trouble she was in. In time, he'd figure it out. Investigating people was what he did. In the meantime she'd be working for him.

Ian hoped like hell he wouldn't regret it.

Meri wrinkled her nose at the smell as Ian held open the front door of a white two-story house surrounded by open fields. Walking past him, she towed Lily into the entry.

"Mama, it stinks in here."

Heat rushed into her cheeks. "That's why we're here, sweetheart. To help Ian get the house cleaned up."

Ian glanced around, rubbing the back of his neck, a little embarrassed, she figured, seeing the house through a visitor's eyes.

"When my mother was alive, it was spotless," he said. "She died five years ago. My dad never really got over it. He isn't much of a housekeeper."

That was the understatement of the year. "You want to show me around?"

"First, let me introduce you. Dad's in the den."

She followed him into a small, wood-paneled room off the hall. An old-fashioned TV was playing a game show, she saw. The room looked like something out of the seventies, with dark brown shag carpet, and a brown vinyl sofa, chair, and recliner.

"Dad, there's someone I'd like you to meet. This is Meriwether Jones and her daughter, Lily. Meri is going to do some cleaning and cooking for us."

He just grunted. "I thought that's why *you* were here. You said you were going to get the place cleaned up."

"I am. But there's plenty to do outside. Meri's going to take care of the inside."

Another grunt. "Suit yourself. Long as she doesn't come bothering me in here."

Ian turned in her direction. "Meri, this is Daniel."

"Hello, Mr. Brodie." The room was so dim it was hard to see exactly what he looked like. Tall, she figured, since his son was. Silver hair reflected in the light of the TV screen.

He made no reply.

"Say hello to Mr. Brodie, Lily."

She looked up at him, her eyes big and solemn. "Hello, Mr. Brodie."

He pushed the handle down on the recliner and sat up in the chair. "She's got a kid? How's she going to clean while she's tending a kid?"

"We'll let her worry about that," Ian said, heading for the door. "Come on, Meri. I'll give you a tour."

Thankfully, Ian left the den, leading them into the hall and up the stairs.

"The room I'm using is relatively clean and there's a TV in there. Lily could watch cartoons while I show you around."

"That'd be great."

Ian led her into one of the bedrooms. Football wallpaper covered the walls, and there was a full-size bed. It looked like the room of a high school student. Gold athletic trophies—swimming, tennis, and football—lined the bookshelf. A canvas duffel sprawled on top of the old-fashioned quilt on the mattress.

"I just got here," Ian said. "I hadn't had time to unpack."

"This was your room?"

"Yeah. Mom never changed it after I left."

Curiosity moved through her. You could tell a lot about a person by the space he lived in. She wondered what the room would tell her about Ian Brodie.

He walked over, picked up the remote and turned on a small TV, set it on the Disney channel. Meri lifted Lily up on the bed in front of the screen.

"You stay here. Mama's going to work for a while. I'll make you a sandwich and bring it up, okay?"

Lily nodded, her eyes fixed on the cartoon characters on the screen. "Okay." Besides watching cartoons, her favorite pastime was coloring, or playing with her Kermit the Frog hand puppet. Meri made a mental note to get the toys out of the car.

"I'll show you the rest," Ian said. "Then I'll show you where the cleaning stuff is kept. It's bound to be there, since Dad clearly hasn't used it."

She smiled and followed him out of the bedroom. A quick tour of the upstairs included a total of three bedrooms and two baths. Except for the master, where Daniel Brodie slept, the upstairs wasn't too dirty. She figured not too many people had stayed there over the years, so the doors and windows had remained closed. Still, the rooms were musty, dusty, and the linens all needed washing.

The living room was dank and cluttered, but had seen little use. She paused in the dining room to admire the lovely old mahogany table with its eight high-backed, tapestry-upholstered chairs, and the beautiful matching sideboard with a silver tea service on top.

"This was my mother's favorite room," Ian said softly, reaching out to run a finger through the dust on top of the table, exposing the mirror-like sheen underneath.

"It's beautiful." She looked up at him. "It will be again, Ian. I promise you."

He smiled. It wasn't one of the wary smiles he'd been giving her. It was a smile that lit up his face and made her breath catch at how amazingly handsome he was.

"My mother would like that," he said.

Meri just nodded. Her mouth felt dry. Her heart was hammering. It had been years since a man had attracted her. Not since before Lily was born. She had learned the hard way what could happen when you let your physical desires rule your head. The only good thing to come from that night with Joey was Lily. Meri would always be grateful for her daughter.

She glanced away from Ian's sexy smile. "Where's the kitchen?"

"This way." He led her into a once-white room whose walls were now closer to gray. White curtains trimmed with faded red hung at the windows, and the white Formica counters were piled high with dirty dishes.

"Cleaning won't be enough," she said, appraising the dreary room. "It needs to be painted." The whole house did, but she wasn't sure she should say that.

He nodded. "It's pretty bad. After you put things away, I'll come in here and get it done."

"You're going to paint it yourself?"

He grinned. "What? You don't think I can handle the job?"

Her gaze cut to the powerful biceps stretching the sleeves of his dark blue T-shirt. She had a hunch Ian Brodie could handle just about anything.

"I guess I just figured you could pay someone to do it."

"I enjoy the exercise."

Her gaze ran over his impressive chest and wide shoulders. "Where are the cleaning supplies?" she asked, forcing her gaze away.

"Some of the stuff is under the kitchen sink; the rest is in the mudroom." He showed her where to find everything then they returned to the kitchen.

"Now that you've been here and seen what you're facing, you still want the job?"

It wasn't what she'd planned, but it would get them moving again. "Yes."

"All right, then, why don't you go ahead and get started? I'll be outside working in the barn if you need anything."

As he headed for the back door, she turned to the gigantic stack of dishes in the kitchen sink. She was supposed to cook supper, but no way was she handling food in a kitchen this dirty.

Fortunately, she'd bought a couple more prepackaged sandwiches at the grocery store, one for Lily, one for herself. She tipped her head back and listened, heard cartoons playing on the upstairs TV.

Lily had spent a lot of time with babysitters or in day care while Meri was at work. The little girl had a vivid imagination and with only a few toys or a coloring book could entertain herself for hours. Meri took the sandwich and a glass of milk upstairs, went and got the toys out of the car and took them up, then came down and set to work.

She had a job to do and it was a big one.

For the first time, she realized she hadn't even asked how much Ian Brodie planned to pay.

Chapter Three

Daniel Brodie started switching the channels on the TV in the den. Dammit, he hadn't had this much commotion in his house in years. And he didn't like it.

This was his home. He hadn't asked these people to come here and bother him. He hadn't asked his son to come home.

He clicked the tuner, put on one of the ESPN channels and started watching an old football game. The Seattle Seahawks had lost to the Atlanta Falcons, but he didn't mind watching it a second time. It had been one helluva game. And he didn't have anything better to do.

"Whatcha watching?"

He jolted at the sound of the small voice right next to his recliner, turned to see the little girl with the dark hair and big blue eyes standing there staring up at him.

"Go away. I'm trying to watch the game."

"My mama watches football sometimes. Who's playing?"

He frowned. What the hell? "Seattle and Atlanta. Now go away."

"I watch, too, sometimes. Can I watch with you?"

He didn't know what to say. She was a kid. No way would she sit still during the game.

"Can I?"

He looked into those big blue eyes. "I don't care what you do."

"I need a chair."

She needs a chair, he silently mimicked, but kept the sarcastic words to himself. He remembered his son when he was that age. Kids always needed something. He glanced around the room. There were a couple of folding chairs around the card table in the corner. Some of the guys used to come over and play poker, but that was a long time ago.

When she didn't just leave, he grumbled something under his breath a kid shouldn't hear, sat up in the recliner, and roused himself enough to get to his feet. He looked at the folding chairs, but they were hard as hell to sit on. He turned and caught the arms of the overstuffed chair, dragged it over next to the recliner so she could see the TV.

"You wanna sit? Sit."

She wouldn't stay long. Kids her age didn't watch football. He'd humor her until she got tired of sitting there and left him alone. As long as she kept her mouth shut and didn't bother him, she could stay.

"Thanks," she said and climbed up into the armchair.

It was halftime before he realized she was still there. When he looked over, the little girl was sound asleep.

Ian hammered a nail into one of the stall doors, swung it back and forth a couple of times to make sure the hinges were working, then moved on to the next stall.

When he was a kid, his family had owned horses. One of the mares had foaled, and his father had given him the palomino colt for his sixteenth birthday. He and his dad hoped to use the little stud for breeding.

His father had wanted to raise quarter horses, at least a few, and the stallion that Ian named Sunny had impeccable bloodlines. Ian calculated Sunny would be fifteen years old now. As he worked in the barn, he almost expected to see the horse out in the pasture, running like fire over the fields. But his dad had sold the stallion after Ian's mother had died, along with the mares and colts they were raising.

With Emma gone, Daniel had no more interest in the horses he had loved or anything else. And Ian had been busy with his own life. At the time, he'd just started a new business, chosen a different course, one he had never regretted.

He hammered in another nail, looked up to see Meriwether Jones running toward him. With the sun glinting on the ruby strands in her dark hair, damn she was pretty. "What is it?"

"I can't find Lily. She isn't in your room."

Ian dropped the hammer and started back toward the house, Meri hurrying along beside him.

"She never does this. She always stays where I tell her."

They shoved through the back door together, walked through the mudroom. It took a moment for him to register that the dishes were all washed and put away, the countertops wiped clean. He caught the scent of Lysol as he made his way toward the stairs.

"Lily!" he called out. "Lily, where are you?" They went upstairs and searched his bedroom, then the other two upstairs rooms and both baths. No sign of Lily.

His worry kicked up as they headed back downstairs and he strode into the den. "Dad, Lily is missing. Have you—"

For a moment, he couldn't speak. Lily was sitting in the

overstuffed chair, which had been pulled up next to his father's lounger. She turned when she saw them and smiled.

"We're watching football," she said, returning her attention to the screen. "I took a nap but I'm awake now."

Meri started forward, but Ian caught her arm, stopping her where she stood. "Lily's okay," he said softly, easing both of them back out the door. "My dad would never hurt her and . . . I can't believe he's letting her watch TV with him."

"He must be really lonely living out here all by himself. From the looks of things, you don't get out here very often."

He felt a fresh slice of guilt. "I live in Seattle. I own a business there."

She looked down at his left hand. "You have a family?"

He shook his head. "I've been too busy to think about that sort of thing." Her eyes found his and he felt that little jolt of awareness.

"I imagine you're the kind of guy who plans everything," she said. "I was that way once. Then Lily came along and things changed."

"Stuff happens," he said, wondering what had happened to Meriwether Jones.

She looked back into the den. "If you think it's okay to leave Lily with your dad, I'd better get back to work."

His gaze followed hers. "Maybe she'll be good for him."

"Maybe." With a last glance at her daughter, she headed for the kitchen. Ian followed her, took another look around and was amazed to see how much she had accomplished since her arrival.

He walked over and opened the fridge, which was sparkling clean and filled with the groceries she had bought earlier. The stove top was clean. He could smell the self-cleaning oven hard at work.

"So . . . what's for supper?"

Meri turned. "I bought a roast. I found a Crock-Pot in one of the cupboards and put it to work. As soon as I get the oven clean, I'll put some potatoes in to bake."

His mouth watered. "That sounds great."

"I was wondering . . . since I won't be finished cooking and cleaning up until late . . . there's a room and bath off the kitchen. It's being used for storage now, but it wouldn't be hard to clean out. I could . . . you know . . . stay here tonight with Lily and be ready to go to work first thing in the morning. After I cook breakfast, of course."

The lure of a homemade breakfast had his mouth watering again. Being a bachelor, he didn't get many home-cooked meals. Still, the implications were worrisome.

"I guess that means you don't have an apartment or anywhere else to stay."

Her chin hiked up. "I didn't say that. I just thought it would be easier if I stayed here."

He knew she wasn't being honest. And she knew he knew. But she had her pride, and Ian wasn't about to take it from her. "Sorry. I didn't mean to insult you."

"I just got into town, you know? It would just be more convenient, that's all."

A helluva lot more convenient for her. Ian had no doubt Meri and Lily would be sleeping in Meri's old car tonight if he didn't let them sleep in what had originally been built as a maid's room.

"I think you're right," he said. "Staying here would be easier for all of us. When you get to a stopping spot, come get me and I'll help you empty out the room."

The relief in her face made his chest feel tight.

"All right." She turned away from him. "I've got some other stuff to do first."

Ian nodded and left to return to the barn. When he came back three hours later, the maid's room was empty, the cardboard boxes inside stacked neatly in the garage. The floor was scrubbed clean; even the windows had been washed.

When he walked back into the kitchen, he found the table set, the aroma of roasting meat in the air.

"I was hoping you wouldn't mind helping me move one of the mattresses down from upstairs."

"We'll bring down one of the beds and set it up."

"Just the mattress is enough."

"You need a bed."

The sound of footsteps cut off any argument. Ian looked up to see his dad standing next to Lily.

"I'll give you a hand, son. That's a man's work, not a woman's."

Ian worked to keep his eyebrows from shooting up. He didn't argue. Things were happening in this house that should have happened a long time ago.

"Come on, Dad. Let's go."

Every night, Meri fell into bed exhausted. But also proud of the work she had done. Housekeeping wasn't a career choice, but she was earning money and stashing it away. Ian paid her every day. She and Lily had a place to stay and she wasn't even paying for food.

And her little girl was happy. The third day they were there, Ian insisted Meri and Lily come out to the barn to see the litter of kittens he had found.

"The mother cat lives here," he said to Lily. "Keeping the mice away is her job."

"Can I hold one?"

"Not yet. They're still babies. But it won't be long before they're old enough. Then you can hold one."

Since Lily had never seen a newborn kitten before, she was enthralled. Every day after, she went out to the barn and just sat there watching them nurse and sleep.

One afternoon, after stripping the beds in the rooms upstairs, Meri tossed the sheets into the washer, then walked outside to dump some trash. Hearing Ian and Lily in the barn, she found herself walking in that direction.

This time of year the weather was warm. In jeans and a T-shirt, Lily sat on a clean pile of straw Ian had placed in the stall with the kittens. He was standing at the rail, his arms draped over the top.

"Lily's a beautiful little girl," he said as Meri walked up beside him, his voice as smooth as honey and just as warm.

"Thank you."

"Dad isn't ready to admit it, but Lily's the best thing that's happened to him in years."

"She likes him. She's never had a grandfather. I guess she sees Daniel as kind of a substitute."

"He's promised to take her over to Mrs. Peterson's. She's the widow who lives on the property adjoining ours. One of her mares just foaled."

"Lily would love that."

Ian shook his head. "I can't believe it. Dad hardly ever leaves the house anymore."

"Maybe once we get everything cleaned up, he'll be more active. Maybe he'll even want to have people over again."

"Maybe. I don't know. Heddy Peterson used to come by and see Dad once in a while, but she finally gave up on him."

"Well, she's going to see him tomorrow when your dad takes Lily to see the foal."

Ian's beautiful blue eyes came to rest on her face. "Maybe you'd like to see it, too," he said softly, and the bottom dropped out of her stomach.

Oh dear Lord. That sexy voice, combined with those amazing blue eyes, was the problem. She was getting the house in order, just as she'd promised. Ian was paying her a more than fair wage, and she was saving money, getting in a position to move on, to get to Portland and find a job. Not as a cleaning person, but maybe a secretary or a book-keeper.

She was good on a computer, good with numbers, and she had done that kind of work before. Everything was going smoothly. Except that she was growing more and more attracted to Ian Brodie, and that wasn't good.

Ian didn't know anything about her, didn't know she had been raised in a series of foster homes. Didn't know about Joey and that she'd been stupid enough to get pregnant by a loser like him.

Ian was a successful businessman. He owned a security company in Seattle, he had told her. A guy like that didn't want a woman with a child and a shady past.

At least not for more than a couple of nights in bed.

Meri had to think of Lily. Getting involved in any way with Ian was out of the question.

"It's nice of you to ask," she told him. "I wish I could go, but I have too much work to do."

Before he could try to persuade her, she turned and walked out of the barn. Her heart was pounding, her thoughts in a jumble. All she had to do was look into that handsome face, imagine running her hands through that neatly trimmed pirate-gold hair, and her insides grew warm.

Dear Lord, the man was going to be trouble. Meri shook her head. She'd been attracting trouble since she was five years old.

Chapter Four

Ian watched Meriwether Jones walk away. With a will of its own, his gaze traveled over the round bottom hugged by her faded blue jeans. His mouth edged into a smile at the pink sneakers on her feet.

In the week she had been there, everything had changed. She had the house cleaned—all but the dining room—the upstairs rooms stripped and ready to paint, which he had hired a crew to do and planned to start tomorrow morning.

Dinner was no longer a morbid affair of frozen TV dinners eaten in the dark in front of the TV. They ate in the spotlessly clean kitchen around the old claw-foot oak table, good wholesome family meals like spaghetti, and stew, and chicken and dumplings.

One night, he picked up some steaks to grill outside, which turned into more work than he had expected since the grill hadn't been used in years. When he lifted the lid he found the whole thing greasy and rusted.

But cleaning it was worth it. The steaks were great and the look on Meri's face when she took a bite of medium-rare fillet, obviously a treat, made him glad he had gone to the extra trouble.

While he'd worked on general outdoor maintenance, like mowing the lawn, trimming the hedges, and pulling weeds, Meri had worked miracles inside the house. He admired her tenacity and grit. He admired the way she took care of her little girl.

He admired a lot of things about Meriwether Jones. He also found her sexy as hell. He tried not to think of the perfect little ass filling out her jeans, the way her breasts plumped under her T-shirts. He desperately wanted to see those long, mahogany braids unbound, wanted to run his fingers through the fine, silky strands.

Instead of her work clothes, he wanted to see her in a sleek satin nightgown. Then he wanted to strip her out of it.

He wanted to take Meriwether Jones to bed and it was driving him crazy.

Fortunately, Meri had enough sense to realize what a mistake it would be and stayed away from him.

Hell, he was only going to be in Spokane a couple of weeks, and the hard truth was, he wasn't interested in a relationship. He worked long hours and rarely had time for female companionship.

Which wasn't to say he didn't have a lady or two he took out on the occasional date or called once in a while for a sleepover. He liked sex, and just because he was busy didn't mean he did without.

Still, there was something different about the desire he felt for Meri. It was a yearning deep in his bones. Every time she smiled at him, he felt a little kick.

He didn't understand it. Hell, he'd never felt anything like it.

And he sure didn't know how to deal with it.

And there was Meri herself. He didn't know anything about her, except that she was in trouble. If he was back in his office, he'd run her name, see if she had a criminal record. When he thought of the way she was with Lily, thought of the amazing mother she was, he had a hard time imagining it.

And the truth was, even thinking about digging into her past felt like a betrayal.

He was staying at least another week. He had help coming in to paint the upstairs but he planned to tackle the kitchen himself. Maybe he would just ask her what she was running from.

Whatever it was, it couldn't be good.

Maybe if he gave her a little more time, Meri would come to trust him enough to tell him.

As long as she didn't trust him enough to wind up in his bed.

In the end, they all went to see the foal. Maybe she was a little overprotective, but Meri didn't really know the Brodies well enough to let them take off with her little girl. In her heart, she believed father and son were exactly what they seemed, good men who had problems to solve, just like everyone else.

The little bay foal named Dolly was darling, and of course Lily instantly fell in love with the filly.

"Look, Mama, she likes me." The foal butted her tiny head against Lily's hand, then nickered softly when Lily started petting her. "Can I have a horse, Mama? A baby one like Dolly?"

"We'll be living in the city, honey. Horses need lots of open space to play in."

"But I want one." Her face puckered up. It looked as if she was going to pitch an old-fashioned crying fit, which was rare and never worked, but Meri guessed this was a high-stakes wish, and Lily figured it was worth a try.

Ian must have recognized what was coming because he stepped into the breach, scooping Lily up against his chest.

"Mrs. Peterson loves visitors. I'm sure you can come out and visit Dolly anytime you want." He glanced at the short, silver-haired woman who stood next to Daniel at the fence.

Mrs. Peterson smiled and nodded. "Anytime, sweetheart."

Lily's eyes lit up and Ian put her down again. "Can we, Mama?"

"For now, why don't we just enjoy Dolly while we're here?"

The foal neighed and Lily returned her attention to the tiny horse, satisfied at least for the moment.

"She's such a sweet little girl," Mrs. Peterson said, smiling down at Lily with a soft look in her eyes.

"Thank you."

"I remember when my daughter was that age. Seems like only yesterday. Ashley's all grown up now with kids of her own."

Heddy looked over at Daniel, who seemed to be looking everywhere but at the woman beside him. "I'm glad you came over, Daniel. It's been way too long." There was something in her eyes, something Meri recognized.

Daniel just nodded. He was an attractive man, she realized, now that he was standing a little straighter, had gotten a haircut and shaved.

"We'd best be getting back," he said. "Ian's got the painters coming in tomorrow morning." As Daniel started back down the road toward the farmhouse, Mrs. Peterson turned to Ian.

"I'm so glad you came home. I can see the difference in your father already."

"I should have come back sooner. I won't stay away again."

Heddy Peterson smiled, but her gaze strayed toward the man walking off down the lane. Another woman attracted to a man she couldn't have.

Meri understood completely.

Taking Lily's hand, she walked next to Ian back to the house. Once they got there, Ian took Lily out to the barn to watch the kittens. Meri walked into the kitchen just as her cell phone rang.

Pulling it out of the pocket of her jeans, she looked down at the caller ID but didn't recognize the number. She pressed the phone against her ear. "Hello."

"Hey, baby, I guess you forgot our appointment."

Her stomach curled. Nausea rolled through her. "How . . . how did you get this number?" She'd changed it after Joey had conned one of the girls in the secretarial pool where Meri had worked as a temp into giving it to him.

"You can't keep secrets from me. You should know that by now."

Her mind spun. Only a few people had this number. Her friends knew what Joey was like. No way had it come from one of them. "What do you want?"

"You know what I want, you little bitch. I want that money old lady Vandermeer left you."

"I don't have it, Joey. It's all gone. I tried to tell you that."

"You're lying. You packed up and left so you wouldn't have to give me my share. You think I couldn't figure out where you were headed when you left? Your friend Michelle Peach was with you the night we met. Remember? She said she was moving to Portland. She wasn't that hard to find. Me and Kowalski paid her a visit and we had a little chat."

Dear God, Joey was in Portland! And he was with that big bruiser friend of his, the one he called Ski. "You and Kowalski . . . you didn't hurt her?"

"All I did was slap her around a little. It's your fault. I wouldn't have had to do it if she'd given me your number the first time I asked."

She couldn't think of anything to say. Her heart was hammering, her palms slick with fear.

"Where are you, you little bitch? I spent a fortune in gas driving up here. I had to sell some of my personal stash to get enough money to make the trip. I want it back."

"You . . . you should have stayed in LA."

"Bullshit. Michelle says you changed your mind about Portland, says you're taking the kid somewhere else. I want to know where the hell you are."

Meri hung up the phone. With shaking hands, she hurriedly pressed Michelle's number, ignored the frantic beeping of Joey calling her back. Michelle picked up on the second ring.

"Are you okay?" Meri asked.

"I'm okay. That bastard scared the hell out of me, but I'm fine. I had to give him your number to get him and that big behemoth to leave."

"Oh God, Michelle, I'm so sorry. Are you sure he didn't hurt you?"

"He slapped me a couple of times. I hit my head when I fell, but I'm okay. I didn't want to give him your number, but—"

"No, you did the right thing."

"Don't come here, Meri. I told him and that bald creep I didn't know where you were. Since it's the truth, I'm pretty sure he believed me. But, Meri . . . Joey's crazy. He's taken too many drugs or something. He isn't thinking straight."

"I just talked to him. Will you be okay?"

"I'll be all right. I told him if he came back and bothered me again, I'd call a friend of mine who's a federal agent. Raider's like family. He'd be here in a minute. Joey could tell I meant it. Besides, it was obvious you weren't here."

"I'm changing this number," Meri said. "Once I have a new one, I'll call you."

"Take care of yourself, Meri. And take care of Lily." Michelle ended the call.

With trembling hands, Meri turned off the phone so Joey couldn't call her again, then she sank down heavily in one of the kitchen chairs.

You're safe, she told herself, trying to calm her nerves. *Lily's safe. Everything's going to be okay.* Joey had called, but there was no way he could find them. As long as they were in rural Spokane, they were safe.

Still, she couldn't stop shaking. She gasped when she looked up to see Ian standing in the kitchen doorway, his jaw set, his face as dark as a thundercloud. She wondered how much he had overheard.

"What's wrong?" he asked.

Meri forced herself to smile. "I . . . ah . . . saw a mouse. Silly, I know, but those things really scare me. Sorry."

Ian didn't look convinced. "You're shaking. Are you sure that's all it was? If something's wrong, you can tell me, Meri. You can trust me to help you."

She took a steadying breath, managed to control her voice. "I was talking to one of my girlfriends. The mouse caught me a little off guard. I'm fine."

Ian's eyes remained on her face a few seconds longer;

then he grabbed something in the mudroom and stalked back out of the house.

Meri took a deep breath. She still had a job, still had a lot of work to do.

And she refused to let Joey Bandini interfere in her life again. Meri grabbed the broom and started sweeping.

Ian carried the wrench he'd been looking for back to the barn. He didn't know if he was more angry at Meri or whoever had been on the other end of her phone.

Dammit, why didn't she just tell him? He could help her if she would only let him.

With a frustrated sigh, he walked over to check on Lily, who sat in the stall with the kittens. She seemed mesmerized by the tiny little gray-and-white creatures, content to watch them for hours on end.

Satisfied that she was okay, he returned to the tack room he had been cleaning, putting away old saddles that needed oiling, headstalls, reins, and miscellaneous feed bags and water buckets. The smell of hay and manure brought back memories of his youth, a time when he had imagined working with his dad to raise quarter horses. At least a few of them, more a hobby than for the money they might earn.

At the moment those memories were overridden by the scene he'd stumbled onto in the kitchen, which refused to leave his head. He didn't know what had happened, but he'd seen Meri turn off her cell phone, seen the pallor of her face.

Someone Meri didn't want to talk to had called, someone she didn't want to talk to again.

As much as he hated to go behind her back and check on her, Ian figured it might be in her best interest if he did.

Maybe the trouble she was in had nothing to do with something Meri had done, and everything to do with someone who intended to do something bad to *her*.

He'd give it another day, see if he could get her to talk to him. If he couldn't, he'd phone his office, get one of his investigators to do some digging for him.

Ian found himself walking back out of the barn over to his Jeep. Though he owned the company and rarely took cases anymore, he was a licensed private investigator, and as such, licensed to carry.

His Glock nine mil rode in a locked compartment in the center console. He couldn't leave it lying around with a child in the house, but the gun safe was portable. He could make sure his weapon was loaded and in easy reach if he needed it in a hurry.

Ian carried the gun safe into the barn.

Chapter Five

The painters arrived the following day. Ian put them to work upstairs while Meri did a last-minute check of the kitchen to be sure it was also ready to paint. Lily was in the den watching cartoons with Daniel.

Meri found herself smiling at that.

She felt better this morning, more optimistic. So Joey had been looking for her. So what? Michelle didn't believe Joey would be back to bother her again. He hadn't found Meri and he wasn't going to.

She took a last look around. The ratty old kitchen curtains were down, everything was put away or draped with a cloth. Ian was on his way out the door to buy the paint when she caught up with him.

"Ian, wait!"

He turned and smiled down at her. "What is it?"

The man was so handsome, for a second she forgot what she was going to say. "I was . . . just thinking. I know the kitchen was white when you were a boy, but with all the white cabinets and counters, it's going to look awfully stark in here. How would you feel about a soft, butter-cream yellow? I think it would really warm the place up."

He glanced around the room, probably seeing it as it had been when he was a kid. "My dad would probably have a fit."

She shrugged. "It was just an idea."

He gave her one of his charm-you-out-of-your-knickers smiles. "Come with me to the paint store and we'll take a look, see if it would work."

She hesitated. She shouldn't go with him. She didn't trust herself where Ian was concerned. Just looking at him made her heart beat too fast. Yesterday she had seen him with his shirt off as he worked in the yard and, dear God, the man was ripped. A sweat-slick chest banded with muscle, broad shoulders, a trim waist, six-pack abs, and powerful biceps.

Last night she'd had an erotic dream about him. Since she'd never experienced the hot rush of passion she'd known in the dream, it was insane.

"Come on," he urged, grabbing her hand and tugging her toward the door. "Lily's in the den with Dad. She'll be fine till we get back. We'll pick out the color together."

She flicked a glance toward the den. They would only be gone a few minutes. She let him pull her out of the house and help her climb up in his Jeep. As she clicked her seat belt in place, she could still feel the imprint of those warm, hard hands around her waist.

Thinking what those big hands had done to her in her dream, heat rushed into her cheeks . . . as well as other places she firmly ignored.

She started talking about the house. "It's really coming along, Ian. I think your dad actually likes the way it's shaping up."

"You've done a great job, Meri. I couldn't have asked for more. In fact, I was wondering if you might want to stay on after the house is finished. You know, keep doing what you have been? Cooking and cleaning for my father?"

She shook her head. "I appreciate the offer, but I'm planning to move to the city, get a secretarial job or something."

As the Jeep moved along the road, Ian flicked her a sideways glance. "What city do you have in mind?"

She'd been planning on Portland, but that was now out of the question. "I don't know. Lately I've been thinking I might go to Denver. I hear it's really pretty there and if I start looking on the Internet ahead of time, I should be able to find a job."

"Seattle's nice," he said blandly.

But Ian lived in Seattle and she needed to stay away from him at all costs. If she didn't, she was going to end up in his bed. She wondered if he was one of those guys who was into making conquests. If she slept with him, would he be down the road the next day?

She didn't want to find out. She knew how much a breakup could hurt. Joey was the stupidest thing she had ever done, but falling in love with Matt Sawyer had been even worse. Matt had made a complete fool of her. He'd spent weeks seducing her, finally scored, and dumped her three days later.

She wasn't making that kind of mistake again.

"I'm thinking Denver," she said more strongly. "I don't have enough saved yet, but in a couple more weeks I will. That should give you time to find someone else to take care of your dad."

He just nodded, returned his attention to the road. In the paint store, he surprised her by picking up a paint chip the exact shade she'd had in mind.

He held up the soft-butter-yellow chip. "How about this?"

She loved it. "What about your dad?"

"What do you say we brave the lion and take our chances?"

Meri laughed. "I say yes."

So they bought the paint, got back in the Jeep and started home. "I was wondering, Ian . . ."

He cocked a dark gold eyebrow. "I think I see more trouble on the horizon."

"What if we got some curtains to match the color of the paint? Maybe some placemats or a tablecloth? It would really finish off the room."

Instead of answering, Ian wheeled the Jeep around and headed for the Bed Bath & Beyond they had passed along the route.

Twenty minutes later, they walked out of the store with kitchen curtains, two tablecloths, two sets of placemats, and some yellow-and-white terry cloth kitchen towels.

"Oh, it's going to look wonderful," Meri said.

Ian cast her a glance. "Let's hope my dad thinks so." But he was smiling.

Meri smiled back. She couldn't wait to see the curtains up and everything in place, couldn't wait to see how the room finally turned out.

While Ian finished painting the kitchen, the crew at work upstairs finished the entire second floor. The bad news was, the whole place smelled of paint fumes. There was no way they could stay in the house while the work was being done.

"What are we going to do?" Meri asked. "It's not that cold—maybe we could all sleep in the barn."

Ian laughed. "My barn-sleeping days ended a long time ago. We'll take rooms somewhere for a couple of nights.

I'll get on the phone and call around, find us a decent motel."

A knock at the front door interrupted him. When Ian walked into the entry and pulled it open, he found Heddy Peterson standing on the front porch, a foil-covered glass pan in her hands.

"I saw the paint trucks parked out front. I figured with the house torn up, you wouldn't be able to cook tonight, so I brought you a ham-and-cheese casserole."

"Come on in—if you can stand the smell." Ian took the casserole dish from her hands and led her farther into the house.

Heddy wrinkled her nose at the fumes. "My goodness, this is worse than I thought. There is no possible way you can spend the night in here."

"I was just about to start calling motels, see if I could find a place for all of us to stay. The painters think they can finish by tomorrow night. Once they're done, we'll air the place out and move back in the next morning."

"If you want to leave, go ahead," Daniel grumbled as he ambled toward them down the hall. "I'm staying right here."

"It's dangerous to breathe this stuff, Dad," Ian said. "It shouldn't be a problem to find a couple of rooms for the next two days."

"Don't be ridiculous," Heddy Peterson said. "Your mother was my friend. She would roll over in her grave if I didn't insist you spend the night at my house. I have plenty of room and I'd love the company. Now . . . when you've finished working, just get what you need and come on over. I'll put the casserole in the oven and it'll be ready whenever you are."

Daniel stepped in front of her. "Did you hear what I said, woman? I'm staying here."

Heddy didn't back down. "Ian told you it's dangerous. You're staying at my house, Daniel, and that's the end of it."

He scowled, but then a smile of amusement slowly curved his lips. "You always were one stubborn woman, Heddy Peterson."

She blushed. Ian couldn't believe it. Heddy and Emma Brodie had always been close friends. But after his mother died, Heddy seemed to look at Daniel a different way. There were a few times Ian had thought that his dad was seeing Heddy in a different way, too.

If he had been, he had ruthlessly squashed any chance of a relationship. Looking at the two of them now, Ian had a hunch he knew why.

"We'll stop work a little before dark," he said, "get showered, and come on over."

Heddy reached out and took the casserole from Ian's hands. "I'll have supper ready," she said, turned and walked out of the house.

"Stubborn damned woman," Daniel grumbled, his gaze still on the place she had been. In her late fifties, Heddy was an attractive woman, small but buxom, with short silver hair, clear skin, and a face that was mostly unlined.

"She's a good woman, Dad. You always liked her. What happened?"

Daniel looked up at him. "Nothing happened and it isn't going to. I was married to your mother for thirty-five years. I loved her something fierce. She's still right here, you know?" He pressed a hand over his heart. "Even now that she's gone, it doesn't seem right to look at another woman."

Ian just stood there. He'd been right. Guilt was the force keeping his father away from the woman next door.

He watched his dad walk away, glanced up to see Meri standing in the doorway.

She smiled as she came toward him. "I've never believed in that kind of love. The kind your father and mother had. The kind that lasts forever."

"Yeah . . ." Ian's throat felt tight. "Dad always said, when a Brodie falls, he falls hard."

"I think he likes Mrs. Peterson more than he lets on."

"So do I. It's been five years since Mom died. Maybe Dad'll figure out my mother would want him to be happy."

"Maybe," Meri said wistfully. There was something in her voice, something that made his chest feel tight. When she looked at him, he felt that funny little kick.

Ian cleared his throat. "The painting crew is at work in the den. I'm going to start on the living room. I want to get as much done as I can before we quit for the night."

"Why don't I pitch in and help?" Meri asked. "There's nothing else I can do till the house is finished."

"You know how to paint?"

She shrugged. "I can do pretty much anything."

Ian's gaze drifted over her. He couldn't help imagining her naked, moving beneath him in bed. "I'll just bet you can."

Meri blushed, just like Mrs. Peterson. He found it charming, then realized it actually wasn't. He had to stop thinking about Meri that way. Told himself firmly that he would.

The furniture had all been moved to the center of the living room, a tarp spread over it so nothing would get ruined. For the next two hours, he and Meri worked side by side, painting the living room a nice soft shade of rose, the color it had been before.

"I like your mother's taste. This is a really pretty shade and it looks great with the burgundy furniture."

"You didn't much like the white kitchen."

"It was okay." She grinned. "Yellow looks better."

Ian's mouth edged up. "The kitchen's still partly draped, which means my dad hasn't noticed yet, but sooner or later he will."

Meri groaned. "Don't remind me."

Ian laughed and they went back to work.

Chapter Six

That night they stayed at Mrs. Peterson's house. Meri called her Heddy now, as the older woman insisted. Heddy had installed Meri and Lily in one of the upstairs bedrooms, put Ian in a second room, and his dad in another. It was a big, roomy old house in excellent condition. Unlike Daniel, Heddy maintained her home very well.

Since it was so late when they arrived, they ate at a table in the kitchen, a big open space like Daniel's, this one painted a pretty robin's-egg blue. Heddy had fixed a salad and homemade Parker House rolls to go with the casserole. A big slice of chocolate cake appeared for dessert.

"This is soo good," Lily said, getting thick chocolate frosting on her mouth. Ian leaned over and wiped it away with his napkin, smiled and tweaked her nose. Lily laughed. Watching Ian with her little girl, Meri felt a clutch in her chest.

Don't even think about it, warned a stern voice in her head. *A man like that isn't for you.*

After supper was over, Meri helped Heddy with the dishes, then put Lily to bed upstairs. But Meri had too much on her mind to sleep.

The doors to all the bedrooms were closed as she

walked down the hall and descended the stairs, wandered out to the stable where the little bay foal stood in a stall with its mother.

Moonlight slanted in through the open windows of the barn, illuminating the interior, which smelled sweetly of fresh-cut hay. Watching the mare with her baby, Meri found herself smiling.

At the sound of footsteps, she turned and saw Ian walking out of the shadows. Moonlight shone on his pirate-gold hair and his eyes were a fierce shade of blue.

Meri's breath caught. She told herself to make an excuse and leave, but her legs refused to move.

"I guess you weren't sleepy either," he said in that sexy, seductive voice she heard in her dreams.

"I was a little keyed up, I guess, being somewhere new."

"It'll only be for a couple of nights."

"I don't mind. Mrs. Peterson is really nice."

"Yes, she is."

A soft nicker came from one of the stalls farther down the line. Ian tipped his head in that direction. "Come on. Meet Sunny."

She let him guide her deeper into the barn, toward a stall near the door opening onto the open pastureland beyond. A beautiful golden palomino stood inside, his long blond mane and tail freshly curried. Clearly Ian had been the one to do the work.

"He used to be mine," he said a little gruffly, stroking the horse's velvet nose. "Dad sold him when Mom died. I never knew Heddy was the one who bought him until I spotted him in the field when we were here looking at the foal."

"She never said?"

"I was almost never around back then. First I was in college; then I started working. I had my own business by the time Mom had a heart attack and passed away." Ian smoothed a hand over the horse's muzzle, scratched between his ears. Sunny rubbed his golden head against Ian's hand.

"I think he remembers you."

He smiled. "I raised him from a colt."

"Maybe you could buy him back."

Ian shook his head, but she thought she caught an instant of regret. "I'd have to leave him here. Unless Dad got interested in horses again, it wouldn't be fair to Sunny."

Meri glanced back at the beautiful golden palomino. "It must have been great having a horse of your own."

"It was," he said. "I was a pretty fair rider in my day. I thought about doing a little rodeoing, but Mom thought it was too dangerous." His mouth edged up as if he were amused by some inner joke.

Meri wondered what it was. Her mind sifted through the possibilities, but when she looked at him again, his focus had shifted away from the horse and he was looking directly at her.

"I can't stop thinking about you, Meri," he said softly. She felt his big hand on her cheek, gliding gently down to tilt up her chin. Then he was bending his head, covering her mouth in the gentlest of kisses.

Her heart started racing, her stomach fluttering like the wings of a bird. He tasted like chocolate frosting and strong, sexy male, and when he kissed the corners of her mouth, ran his tongue along the seam of her lips, coaxing her to open for him, she couldn't resist.

Meri moaned as she went into his arms and Ian deepened the kiss, stirring the warmth she felt inside into a roaring blaze.

"Ian . . ." she whispered, clutching the front of his shirt, then sliding her arms up around his neck.

"Meri . . . God, I want you."

But he didn't press her the way another man might have, just kissed her softly, one way and then another, kissed her and kissed her, until her insides burned and her womb grew damp and achy. Ian nibbled the side of her neck, then returned to her mouth, kissing her as if he had all the time in the world.

As if she were something to treasure, not something to plunder. Meri kissed him back, letting the heat pour through her, letting the yearning build. Dear God, she had never been seduced with such tenderness, never been so tempted to give in to the wild yearning he stirred.

Never been so tempted to let him take her where he wanted, give her the pleasure each of his hot kisses promised.

Instead, he let her go, stepped back so they were no longer touching. The rush of cool air stirred an aching sense of loss.

Reaching up, he touched her cheek. "I'm sorry, honey. I didn't mean for that to happen."

She swallowed against the lump that rose in her throat. "I'm sorry, too." Sorry she'd given in to the desire she felt for him? Or sorry he had stopped instead of taking his tender seduction further?

"I'd better go in," she said, fighting to control the tremors still running through her, the longing to go back into his arms.

"Good night, Meri," he said.

Her heart squeezed. Deep down, she knew it was time for her to leave.

"Good night, Ian." Turning away from him, she hurried out of the barn.

* * *

Ian watched Meri until she disappeared out of sight. He could still feel the imprint of her breasts pressing into his chest, her slender body fitting so perfectly against his. The taste of her still filled his senses.

It had been years since he'd wanted a woman the way he wanted Meri. Maybe never. He still couldn't believe he'd been able to stop. In another few minutes, he would have pulled her down into a bed of straw and taken her. He would have ruthlessly plied her sweet body with kisses, stroked and touched and relentlessly seduced her.

He hadn't planned it. Had gone out of his way to make sure nothing like this would happen. He didn't want to hurt Meri. It didn't take a genius to realize she had been hurt enough already.

But the moment he'd kissed her, the moment he had tasted those cherry-red lips, run his fingertips over the smooth planes and valleys of her face, held her in his arms, he'd been lost.

Even in her jeans and sneakers, she was a sweet demon in his blood, a sensual little witch he couldn't resist.

Ian sighed into the darkness. Beyond wanting her, he admired her. More every day. Which only made his need for her worse.

He had to stay away from her. Had to make sure what had happened tonight didn't happen again. It was only fair to Meri.

Thank God, he would soon be leaving. Or Meri would be leaving. The farther they got away from each other, the better for them both.

Unfortunately, there was no way in hell he was leaving until he was sure Meri and Lily were safe.

Ian silently cursed.

* * *

"So what about it, Dooby? Did it work?" Joey pressed his cell phone tighter against his ear, blocking out the Portland street noise outside the fleabag motel room he and Kowalski were staying in. "Were you able to track her? You said you could find her with GPS. You said it would be a snap."

"Cool it, dude. I said I could find her, but she turned off her phone. All I had to work with was the last call she made."

Joey shifted the phone to his other ear. After he'd left Michelle Peach's apartment, he'd found a cheap place to stay till he could figure his next move. Then lightning had struck and he'd thought of his old juvenile detention buddy, Dooby Brown.

The skinny little runt owed him for protecting him when they were kids. Dooby had done well for himself since then, becoming some kind of tech wizard. Fortunately, he still got a thrill out of an occasional detour into the wrong side of the law.

"She's somewhere east of Spokane, okay? I tracked the call to a cell tower near exit 287. That's as close as I can get unless she starts using her phone again."

Joey violently cursed.

"Are you sure she has the money?" Dooby asked.

"Hell, yes! That old lady put Meri through junior college. When she died, the old bat owned a house and a car. She treated Meri like a daughter. She probably left her everything. And since I'm the father of Meri's kid, she owes half of it to me."

Dooby laughed. Joey didn't know why. It made perfect sense to him.

"Good luck, dude." Dooby ended the call.

"He figure out where she was?" Kowalski asked. He was fiddling with his gun, a big semiauto Walther PPK that made Ski look even more badass than he was.

Joey didn't much like guns himself. Just watching Kowalski dicking around with his flashy piece made him nervous. Still, the kind of business he was in required he have protection. Joey owned an old, banged-up Ruger he had bought off the street. He kept it in the trunk of his car, but if he had to, he knew how to use it.

"Put that thing away before you shoot yourself," Joey said.

Ski pointed the weapon in Joey's direction. "If I shoot someone, it won't be me." He lowered the pistol and shoved it back into his holster. "Besides, we might need it, you know? If you want her to give us the money."

Joey nodded. "Yeah, maybe." Using his smartphone, Joey pulled up a map that showed the route from Portland to Spokane. He'd paid his Verizon bill with some of the money he'd gotten from Meri, figuring he'd need a phone on the road when he went after her. If Meri was still anywhere near exit 287, he'd find her.

Joey thought of the tweak he'd had to sell and worried what would happen if his supply ran out. His hand balled into a fist. The longer it took him to find Meri, the more he was going to enjoy paying her back for the trouble she'd caused.

Chapter Seven

The house was finished. They had stayed an extra day at Mrs. Peterson's so that the carpets could be cleaned, along with the sofa and chairs in the living room and den. Everything was shipshape.

While Lily went out to watch the kittens, Meri worked with Ian and Daniel to put the rest of the furniture back in place. Everything was ready, except for the dining room.

Though the room had been painted the original shade, a lovely sea-foam green, Meri had insisted the furniture remain draped until she could get the beautiful mahogany sideboard and table, the high-backed chairs and silver tea service, polished to the mirror-sheen the pieces deserved. She planned to have everything finished by tomorrow at the latest.

By lunchtime, the only thing left to do was rehang the pictures, which they would get to as soon as lunch was over.

"Soup and sandwiches!" she called out to the men, excited for Daniel to see what she'd done in the kitchen. The stark white walls, white-and-red curtains were gone. The room looked warm and welcoming in creamy butter yellow.

"Lunch is ready! Come and get it!" Yellow curtains

hung at the windows, the oak table in the middle of the room was set with yellow ruffled placemats and matching yellow napkins. Yellow-and-white kitchen towels hung at the stove.

She was grinning when Ian and Daniel walked into the kitchen.

Ian smiled.

Daniel stopped cold. "What have you done?"

Meri's smile slipped away.

"How dare you!" Daniel shouted. "This was Emma's room! How dare you change it!" His face was red, every muscle in his body vibrating with anger.

"Dad, take it easy. It's just a room. Mom isn't here anymore."

Daniel drilled his son with a glare. "What do you know! You don't know anything about it!" Storming out of the kitchen, Daniel disappeared into the mudroom, then slammed the back door as he stomped outside the house.

Meri looked down to find Lily pressed against her side. "It's all right, sweetheart. Mr. Brodie just got a little upset. Sometimes change is hard."

"Why is he mad?" Lily asked, looking up at her with a worried expression.

"Because he loved his wife very much," Meri said. "When she died, it made him really sad. Changing the kitchen reminded him of her and made him feel sad again."

"I'll talk to him," Ian said, and started for the door.

"Let him go, Ian. Daniel was right. You can't really understand the way he felt about her."

Ian's gaze remained on the mudroom door. Then he sighed. "I'll give him some time."

Meri nodded, pasted on a smile. "Why don't we have

some lunch? Chicken salad sandwiches and homemade cream of tomato soup? Lily, that's one of your favorites."

The little girl looked up at her. "I'm not hungry. I feel sorry for Mr. Brodie."

Meri wasn't hungry anymore, either, and Ian wore the same unhappy look as her daughter. "Tell you what. I'll put the soup back on the stove, and we'll eat a little later, okay?"

"Okay." Lily headed for the back door. "I'm gonna go watch the kittens."

"All right, but don't bother Mr. Brodie."

"I'm going to hang a few more pictures," Ian said as the little girl disappeared outside.

"I'll help you," said Meri.

Covering the sandwiches with plastic wrap, giving everyone a little time to settle down, she and Ian went to work.

"Mr. Brodie?"

Daniel looked up from where he sat on a bale of straw in the barn. "Go away. I'm not in the mood for conversation."

Ignoring him, Lily walked over and plunked down right next to him. "Please don't be mad at my mama. She worked really hard to make your kitchen pretty. She thought you would like it."

"Well, I don't. And she had no business changing it without my permission."

"She looked really sad. I think she's sorry."

He grunted. "She oughta be. All of you coming in here, changing things around, changing a man's life. That isn't right."

Lily picked up a piece of straw and waved it through

the air like a magic wand. "Your house was really dirty. You needed to get it clean and Mama helped you. It looks a lot better now."

He glared down at her, into blue eyes the same shade as his and Ian's. He tried to frown, but the hell of it was, she was right.

"It's my house. If I wanted it dirty, that was my choice."

"Did you like it better dirty?"

He tried not to smile. He liked it spotlessly clean the way Emma had always kept it. "No. I didn't like it dirty. I let things go and I shouldn't have." He sighed. "The truth is, your mama and my Ian set things right. I'm glad they did, even if it means I have to change, all right?"

Lily started smiling. "I like it better clean, too."

He just nodded. His chest was no longer squeezing down the way it had been.

"So you aren't mad anymore?" Lily asked.

He should be. Ian and Meri had taken a lot for granted when they had started messing with his things. But it took a lot of effort to stay angry. Somehow he just couldn't muster the will. "No, I'm not mad anymore."

"Good. 'Cause I'm really getting hungry. Mama made sandwiches and soup. She makes really good tomato soup. Let's go eat." She jumped off the bale of straw and held out a tiny hand. Daniel reached down and took it, stood up and let her start leading him back to the house.

The hell with it, he thought, and lifted her up against his chest, set her on his shoulder the way he used to do Ian.

He was smiling when he walked back into the mud-room, ducking through the doorway so Lily wouldn't hit her head.

"Where is everybody?" he called out as he walked into the kitchen. "We're hungry!" Daniel set Lily back on her feet just as Ian and Meri hurried through the kitchen door.

"Daniel, I'm really sorry, I didn't mean—"

He held up his hand. "Yellow looks better. Let's eat."

It was peaceful out here in the country, especially at this time of night when everyone was in bed. In Bellevue, where Ian lived in an apartment not far from his office, there was always something going on. Which suited him just fine. He liked the hustle and bustle of city life, liked to interact with the men and women who worked for him, liked the challenge of running a company of his own.

And Seattle was really more of a town than a city, kind of the best of both worlds. He didn't have a lot of time off, but that was his own choice. Once in a while, he liked taking a date to a movie or going out to a fine restaurant.

Still, he missed the quiet out here in the country. It was a good place to get away from the stress of running the business, away from the traffic, if only for a while. He'd promised himself he wouldn't stay away as he had before, and it was a promise he meant to keep. Not just for his father's sake, but for his own.

Stepping off the back porch, he headed for the shadows behind the barn, a towel slung around his neck. There was a man-made pond out in the pasture. His father had built it and had a well dug to keep it full. It had been used for watering the horses.

As he approached, he saw the big sycamore tree near the edge. As a kid, Ian had tied a tire on a rope to one of the lower branches. In the summer, he and his buddies would swing out and drop into the water.

The tree was still there, but the tire was gone. Just the rope hanging down, rotted and forlorn.

The pond was still full, though. Tossing the towel onto the grass, he sat down and jerked off his work boots, pulled his T-shirt over his head, unfastened his belt and unzipped his jeans, slid them and his boxers down over his hips. Naked, Ian waded in and sank down till the water came up to his neck.

For a while, he just paddled around, enjoying the cool liquid against his skin, remembering the fun he'd had back when he was a kid. He'd brought a girl out here once when he was in high school. With his folks in the house, nothing much happened; they'd just made out for a while. He grinned, remembering it was the first time he'd gotten to second base.

A memory returned of Meri's soft breasts pressing against him. He tried to imagine the exact shape, the color of her nipples, how they would harden when he cupped them. But he hadn't gotten that far and the image wouldn't come.

Better that way, he thought.

Something moved in the shadows. He knew who it was without seeing her, realized she must have been there a while, been watching when he undressed. It made him go hard beneath the water.

"Want to join me?" he asked, certain she would say no. Half of him praying she would, the other half throbbing with the need for her to say yes.

"I don't think that's a good idea."

Relief and regret rolled through him. "I'm about to come out. You better turn around."

"Why should I?" she teased. "I've already seen everything."

He thought of the fierce arousal that rode against his belly. "Not everything," he said gruffly. "I want you, Meri. That hasn't changed."

"Oh! Okay . . . I-I'm turning around." He heard her feet moving as she turned away from the water. Ian started sloshing toward the shore. He grabbed the towel he'd brought from the house, dried off as best he could, and pulled on his jeans. At the buzz of his zipper sliding up, Meri turned and stepped out of the shadows into the moonlight.

Ian couldn't breathe. In the soft light of the moon, her long braids were streaked with gold, her face dusted with silver. Her cherry lips looked as smooth as the petals of a rose.

His loins clenched. He started getting hard again. Sweet God, she was beautiful.

"We'd better go in," she said, but she made no move to leave.

Ian walked toward her. "What were you doing out here, Meri?"

"I saw the pond one day when Lily and I were watching the kittens. I wondered how it would look in the moonlight."

"It's just a reservoir, not very deep, but it does look pretty at night."

"I needed a place to think. I figured maybe . . . out here . . ."

He stood close enough to smell the fresh-scrubbed scent of her, ached with the need to touch her. "I know you're in some kind of trouble. Tell me why you're running, Meri. Let me help you."

Her eyes, a warm golden brown, widened in alarm. "What makes you think I'm . . . I'm in trouble? How do you know I didn't just want a change of scenery?"

"Where did you live before you came here?"

She glanced away, bit her full bottom lip, made him want to kiss her.

"Tell me, Meri. You can trust me."

She swallowed. "Riverside. That's east of LA."

"I know where it is. Was that where you were raised?"

"Mostly."

"Were you working there?"

"I was working for a temp agency, doing a little of everything . . . secretarial, bookkeeping, receptionist, stuff like that. It didn't pay much, but it was work I enjoyed."

"So why did you quit?"

She shrugged her slender shoulders. For a moment he didn't think she was going to answer.

"A problem came up with Lily's father," she finally said. "He wanted money. I didn't have it, so I left."

"Do you owe him money? Because if you do—"

"I don't owe him anything!"

"He can't force you to give him money. That's called extortion, Meri. I saw a lot of that kind of thing when I was with the department. It's against the law. If you'll let me help you—"

Her head came up. Wariness crept into her features. "What does that mean . . . 'when you were with the department'? What department are you talking about?"

"Seattle police. That's how I got into the security business. I told you that."

"You didn't . . . didn't say you were a cop. You said you owned a security firm. I was thinking more like home alarm systems."

"We have people who can do that. Mostly we do private investigation, personal protection. Security background checks. Things like that."

He didn't miss the tremor that ran through her. "I need to go in. I've got to check on Lily." She started to turn away, but Ian caught her shoulders.

"Let me help you, Meri."

She pulled away from him. "The house is almost finished. In a day or two I'll be leaving. Let it go, Ian. Please."

Turning, she walked off into the shadows, heading back to the house.

Ian watched her go. His insides were twisting, churning with the knowledge that he had been right and Meri was in trouble.

He had to do something. He'd waited long enough. He had to find a way to help her.

Whether she wanted him to or not.

Joey moved off into the shadows, a smug smile on his face. He'd found her late that afternoon. Stupid woman had parked her car right in front of the house. Once he'd figured out exit 287 off Interstate 90 was Argonne Road, he'd had a place to start.

First he'd gone south, but that had turned into shops and businesses and led nowhere. He'd worried maybe she'd just been filling up her gas tank or getting something to eat when he'd phoned, but he'd come too far to give up. He'd taken his time, driven till Kowalski started complaining, and he figured he'd gone far enough.

Then he turned around and headed north, driving back across the freeway to see what was up at that end of the road. The open country made it easy. A few miles north of I-90, in front of an older two-story white house, he had spotted her old brown Chevy.

He'd found a place to park down the road out of sight and just as dusk was falling, he and Ski had walked back to the house to check things out.

He'd seen her and the kid inside, seen the old man with the silver hair. He'd watched the two of them hanging stuff on the walls and setting things back on tables. It was clear the house had recently been painted. Everything was newly cleaned and repaired.

Joey wondered who the people were and how Meri knew them. He didn't think she had any relatives, but maybe he was wrong. When Meri went in to cook supper, he and Ski had left for a while, driven back down the road to get burgers and fries. He'd needed a little boost, so he'd taken care of that with some of the tweak he had left, felt better now that he had.

They'd gone back to the house after dark.

He'd waited a while, watching the occupants through the windows; then his blood got to pumping when he'd seen Meri walk out of the house and head into the darkness behind the barn. He and Ski had followed. He'd been about to approach her, give her a little of the treatment he'd given her friend in Portland, when he'd seen the man approach.

Joey hadn't noticed the guy before, but he got a real good look at him tonight. Over six feet tall and buff. A muscle jock if he'd ever seen one. And the look on Meri's face when she had seen him naked.

Joey leaned over and spit into the dirt. Made him want to barf.

"I think your old lady has the hots for that dude." Kowalski stood next to him in the darkness, watching first Meri, then the muscle jock, walk back to the house and disappear inside. "I'm surprised they didn't get it on right there."

"Shut up."

"What are we gonna do, Joey? I ain't got any more money and you don't either. I bet you don't even have any more rock to sell."

"I told you to shut up."

Kowalski fell silent. He was dumb as a stick, but he could be useful. As they reached the car, moonlight shined on the big Polack's bald head, glinted on the earrings in his ears. Kowalski looked like a real badass, and he was even tougher than he looked.

At least he could be when he got riled. Joey was smart enough to know exactly how to use Ski's considerable talents.

"In case you forgot," Joey said, "that bitch has plenty of dough. You saw what they've been doing—fixing up the whole damned house. She's probably been paying for it with my money."

"Yeah, you're right. So what are we gonna do?"

"I got an idea. Even if it turns out Meri doesn't have any money left, I bet the old man or her boyfriend does. Did you see that fancy Jeep parked in the driveway? Those cars don't come cheap."

"You're right, Joey."

"Yeah. All we gotta do is take our time, figure out a plan, then go for it. Somebody's got money." Joey looked back at the house, watched the upstairs light go out.

A slow smile spread across his face. "Somebody's got money," he repeated. "And I'm going to have something they want bad enough they'll be more than happy to give it to me."

Chapter Eight

Meri spent her last day working in the dining room, cleaning and polishing the furniture and the beautiful silver tea service. Even the glass chandelier over the table sparkled and gleamed.

She had told Daniel and Ian she planned to leave in the morning. Both of them had tried to talk her into staying, but her mind was made up. Every time she looked at Ian, her heart hurt.

Stupidly, she had let herself fall in love with him, and it was a crazy, ridiculous thing to do. Ian had never hinted at any sort of feelings for her, nothing, at least, beyond the physical attraction he felt, and even that he had determinedly avoided.

If she stayed, she was going to get very badly hurt and worse than that, so was Lily. Her little girl was falling in love with Ian and Daniel, too. If Meri didn't get her daughter away from there soon, leaving the men was going to turn into a terrible trauma for Lily.

Meri sighed. Tonight was their last night in the house, and though her heart felt heavy with the thought of leaving in the morning, she wanted to make this last night special.

With Daniel's permission, she set the long mahogany

table with Emma's best china and sterling silver, got out the old-fashioned pink-stemmed glasses that went with the set, and put candles back in the silver candelabra she had found in the sideboard.

The room looked beautiful. No one had seen it yet, but she was sure Ian and Daniel would be pleased. She had also cooked a special supper of old-fashioned roast chicken, biscuits, carrots, and potatoes. The food wasn't fancy, but she had learned that it was a meal Emma had cooked for them, and it was one of their favorites.

She had taken one last risk and asked Daniel if she could invite Heddy Peterson.

"She was very kind to Lily and me," Meri said. "I'd like to include her, if you wouldn't mind."

Daniel's smile came slow, but it spread across his face. "One more change, Meri, honey? Is that what you're thinking?"

She blushed, knowing he had read the truth in her face. "I was thinking it might be good to have a friend again."

Daniel nodded. "You could be right. Invite her if you want. I'm not sure she'll come, though. I haven't treated her too well these past few years."

But Meri was certain Heddy would come, and when she had phoned, the older woman had enthusiastically agreed.

"I'll bring my famous rum and chocolate chip bread pudding. I got the recipe from Emma years ago. Daniel always loved it."

"That would be perfect, Heddy."

As soon as everything was ready, Meri went upstairs to change for supper. She dressed Lily in the one nice outfit she had packed for her, a pretty little sky-blue chemise dress with a ruffle around the hem. She brushed Lily's dark hair and helped her into her best shoes, a pair made of shiny black patent leather.

"I look so pretty, Mama." Lily twirled in front of the full-length mirror in the corner, her dark, chin-length hair whirling around her face. "I like wearing pretty dresses."

Meri felt a twinge. Silently she vowed that in the future, she would spend some of the money she earned to buy her daughter new clothes.

"Why don't you go downstairs and watch TV with Mr. Brodie?" she asked. "I'll be down in a few minutes."

"Okay." Lily headed for the bedroom door and Meri went to work on herself. Unbraiding her loosely plaited hair, she brushed it till it gleamed, then swept it up in a twist and secured the heavy mass with a clip, letting a few strands escape beside her ears.

Running out of time, she slipped into the only good outfit she had brought for herself. A short black skirt and pink satin blouse. She belted the outfit with a wide silver belt, added a pair of dangly silver earrings, and slipped her feet into a pair of very high black heels.

She checked her image in the mirror, pressed her hands against her stomach to calm her nerves. She was only staying one more night. She wanted to look good for Ian, wanted him to see past the jeans and T-shirts she had been wearing since they'd met, to the woman she was underneath.

With a last glance in the mirror, she summoned her courage and headed downstairs.

His father sat at the head of the table, with Heddy next to him on one side. Ian sat across from Meri, who sat next to Lily. Since the moment he had walked into the dining room and seen the polished mahogany table set with his mother's most treasured possessions, caught the glitter of silver and her beautiful antique stemware, the evening had taken on a surreal quality.

Now as he glanced around the room, Ian felt as if he were looking into some preordained future, some skip in time that showed him the family he was meant to have.

Since he'd entered the dining room and seen Meri waiting for him, he hadn't been able to take his eyes off her. She'd looked beautiful in jeans and a work-stained T-shirt. She was stunning in pink satin and high heels.

As she and Heddy served the meal, he had to force himself to follow the conversation. Every instinct urged him to haul Meri out of her chair, toss her over his shoulder like a caveman, and carry her off to his bed.

He had the weirdest feeling his father was experiencing some of the same primitive urges. Heddy was wearing an ankle-length cream lace dress, the bodice cut low, exposing her ample cleavage. Five years without a woman was a long time for a man as virile as Daniel Brodie. He was practically salivating as he looked at Heddy.

And the looks she was casting his way said if he had the courage, she was his.

"So what do you think, son?" Daniel asked. "Maybe having a couple of horses out in the pasture again might be a good idea. They'd keep the grass from getting too high."

With his eyes fixed on Meri, Ian had missed some of what his father had just said. Was his dad really thinking of getting horses again? He could hardly believe his ears.

When he didn't reply, but just kept staring at Meri, she stepped into the breach. "I think it's a great idea," she said.

"So do I," Heddy added, smiling. "There's an auction the end of next month. I hear they have some very good brood mares coming up for sale. Maybe you could find one you'd like to breed."

"I wouldn't mind raising a couple more colts," Daniel said, taking a sip of wine from one of the old-fashioned pink-stemmed goblets.

"I love colts," said Lily.

"I think it's a great idea, Dad," Ian finally said, forcing himself to concentrate on the conversation. "Who knows, you might even make some money."

Daniel smiled and nodded, apparently pleased with the notion.

It seemed like a blink before Heddy was serving her famous chocolate chip bread pudding, along with the rich dark coffee Meri had brewed.

Then supper was over and they cleared the dishes together. Meri and Heddy washed while Ian dried, and Daniel put the dishes back in the sideboard, Lily keeping up a running dialog as he worked.

"My, it's really getting late," Heddy said with a glance at the antique oak clock. "I walked down instead of driving. I wonder, Daniel, if you would mind walking me back home."

Their eyes met across the kitchen and the air seemed to sizzle between them. "I could do that," Daniel said. "Let me get my jacket and your wrap." His father flicked him a glance. "Don't wait up. We might watch TV for a while."

Ian bit back a smile. "Have fun," he said, wishing he was going to have the same kind of fun with Meri that his father was going to have with Heddy.

Standing next to her mother, Lily yawned. "I'm sleepy, Mama."

"Come on, honey. Time for bed."

"I'll carry her up," Ian said. Scooping the little girl into his arms, he carted her up the stairs, with Meri right behind him. She held open the door for him and Ian carried Lily over to the bed and set her on her feet.

He bent and kissed her cheek. "Sleep tight, kiddo." His gaze went to Meri and the longing inside him stirred. For a heartbeat neither of them moved.

"I . . . umm . . . need to get her undressed and ready for bed," Meri said, ending the moment with a dose of reality.

Ian just nodded. "Good night," he said. What he wanted from Meri, he couldn't have. Not without feeling guilty.

Meri looked as if she wanted to say something, but instead just shook her head. "Good night, Ian."

He walked out of the room and softly closed the door. Tomorrow Meri was planning to leave. Ian still hadn't figured a way to stop her.

Heading down the hall, he went into his room and closed the door. It was late and the house was quiet.

It didn't matter. Ian knew he wouldn't be able to sleep.

Lily slept in the twin bed a few feet away, but Meri was wide awake, her mind whirling with images and memories.

Tonight had gone exactly the way she had planned. The setting, the food, Daniel and Heddy. Even the way Ian had stared at her all evening, as if she were the only one in the room. He'd complimented her on how beautiful she looked while his gorgeous blue eyes told her how much he wanted her.

She hadn't anticipated how much the desire in his eyes would make her want him, too.

Meri wasn't a fool. She knew Ian wasn't interested in any kind of relationship. He had never pretended he was. But she was in love with him and nothing she had experienced had prepared her for the soul-deep yearning she felt for him. Feelings Meri knew deep in her heart she would never know again.

Shoving aside the covers, she sat up in bed and pulled her long white sleep-tee over her head and tossed it away. She had taken the combs out of her hair, but hadn't re-braided it. Maybe she had been planning to go to Ian all along.

She grabbed her pink flannel robe, wishing it were silk, shrugged it on and headed for the door. Feet bare, naked beneath the robe, she padded quietly down the hall.

As she glanced back over her shoulder, she considered knocking on Ian's door, giving him some warning, but the sound might wake Lily and she didn't want to take the chance.

Turning the knob, she quietly slipped into the bedroom. The curtains were open, moonlight streaming in to softly light the darkness. She could see Ian lying in bed, his muscular chest bare, the covers pushed down to his waist. She saw that his beautiful blue eyes were open and watching her as she entered his room.

She didn't speak and neither did he. For several seconds, she just stood there, giving him the chance to send her away. Instead, he swung his long legs to the side of the bed and stood up completely naked, started walking toward her without the least embarrassment. With a body as amazing as his, she didn't blame him.

"Meri . . ."

A little sound escaped from her throat as he drew her into his arms and his mouth came down over hers in a long, taking kiss, a kiss that seemed to brand her as his.

One of his big hands sifted through her hair, gliding through the strands, spreading the wavy mass around her shoulders.

"Like silk," he said. "And fire." Ian kissed her again, a

deep, burning kiss that sent heat spearing out through her limbs. His lips traveled to the side of her neck, pressing softly, trailing fire wherever they touched.

"I need you," he whispered. "I need you so much."

She reached up and cupped his cheek, felt the roughness of his late-night beard. "I need you, too, Ian."

Gently, he stripped off her robe, then stood back to look at her. "God, you're beautiful. I tried to imagine what you'd look like this way, but I wasn't even close." Kissing her again, he lifted her into his arms and carried her over to the bed, settled her in the middle of the mattress and followed her down.

"I've dreamed of this," he said between soft kisses that turned deep and erotic. "I've wanted you since the first time I saw you."

Her heart squeezed. She loved him so much. "I only have tonight. I want to spend it with you."

Ian kissed her long and deep, and everything inside turned hot and liquid.

"I should send you away," he said, "but I can't. Not tonight."

"I know." She had known from the look in his eyes at supper that if she came to him tonight, he would make love to her.

She felt his big hard hands cupping her breasts, taking their measure, testing the weight, urging her nipple into an aching bud. His mouth followed his hands, his tongue gliding over the crest, nipping and tasting, making her skin feel stretched tight, sending warm moisture into her core.

She was hot. So hot she began to shift restlessly beneath him on the bed. She could feel his erection pressing between her legs, thick and hard, demanding the warm, welcoming heat of her body. She parted her legs, heard

Ian's quick intake of breath. He kissed her deeply, taking his time; then he left her for a moment, returned and began to ease himself inside. Meri arched upward, taking him deeper, wanting more, eager to feel all of him, eager to be joined with him, if only for tonight.

"Meri," he whispered, claiming her mouth in a wet, erotic kiss as he buried himself in her soft, slick heat. "I've wanted you for so long," he said. "It seems like I've been waiting forever."

Meri bowed beneath him, taking him deeper still, feeling the hot rush of pleasure, the building need.

Ian groaned. "I want to please you," he said. "I want to make it good for you, Meri."

Her fingers dug into his powerful shoulders as he started to move. Just the words, letting her know that she mattered, that she was in some way important to him, were enough to send a burst of heat rolling through her. She arched upward, moving in rhythm to his heavy thrusts, their bodies aligned as if they had been designed for each other.

He began to move faster, deeper, harder. "Come for me," he said. "Please, Meri." And the soft command sent her over the edge.

She cried out his name as sweet pleasure tore through her, a rush so hot and pure she closed her eyes, wishing she could hold on to the moment forever.

She felt Ian's muscles tighten, knew a second sweet rush of pleasure as he continued to drive in and out, heard the low groan deep in his throat as he reached his own powerful release.

Long seconds passed, their hearts beating in unison, their breath mingling in the darkness. When he started to lift himself away, she clung to him, refusing to let him go.

Ian kissed her one last time. "Sweet Meri," he said. "My beautiful sweet Meri."

Closing her eyes, she turned away, thinking how much she loved him, knowing how lonely she would be without him, praying Ian wouldn't see the tears that tracked down her cheeks.

Chapter Nine

Morning sunlight streamed into the kitchen. Ian flicked a glance at his father, who stood gazing out the window, watching Meri on her way out to the barn to get Lily. Her car was already packed with the meager possessions she owned. Ian had been trying all morning to find an opportunity to talk to her, convince her to stay.

"So you're just going to let her go?" Daniel asked darkly. Ian wasn't sure what time his father had come home from Heddy's, but it was late, sometime early this morning. By then, Meri had returned to her room down the hall.

"You think I want her to leave? She's in trouble, Dad. I knew it when she came. I don't want her to leave any more than you do. I want her to stay here where she'll be safe."

Ian dug out his iPhone, showed his father the email he had received that morning from LA. "I ran a background check, started doing some digging. I didn't like doing it, but I was out of alternatives."

"What is it? Is Meri a criminal or something? Because if that's what you're saying, I don't believe it."

"She isn't a criminal. From what I can tell, she's exactly what she seems. She was born in San Bernardino. Her folks were killed in a car wreck when she was ten. After that, she was raised in a series of foster homes. She got in trouble a couple of times, shoplifting once, vandalism—though she claimed she was trying to stop the kids who were actually doing it."

"Sounds like our Meri."

He looked down at the email message. "At sixteen, she was sent to a foster home run by a woman named Eleanor Vandermeer. Apparently the two of them connected. Vandermeer helped her get through high school and two years of city college before Meri went off on her own. She was working as a bookkeeper for a guy named Arthur Battistone, an attorney in LA, when she got pregnant. She was twenty-three."

"If you called LA, you must have been talking to Ty."

Ty Brodie, one of his cousins, was a PI in Los Angeles and damn good at his job. Ian had a lot of Brodie cousins scattered around. The men tended to be ex-military, or work in some kind of law enforcement. And with all of them, family came first.

"I talked to him. He sent this email an hour ago. According to Ty, a guy named Joey Bandini is listed as Lily's father on her birth certificate. One of Meri's friends said he was a good-looking guy she met on a too-much-tequila night, a one-night stand she's regretted ever since—except for Lily, of course."

"So this is the guy giving her trouble? This Bandini fellow?"

Ian nodded. "Apparently Meri and Mrs. Vandermeer stayed close over the years. When she died six months ago, she left Meri a small inheritance. Bandini showed up a few weeks later. According to this friend Ty talked to, Bandini figured there was a lot more money than there actually was and started harassing her, threatening to take Lily away from her if she didn't give him more of the cash she'd received. Meri took off. Spokane is as far as she got before she ran out of money."

"So she's running from this Bandini. What's his story?"

"A total loser. Drug user. Got out of jail about a year ago for selling crack cocaine. He's got a record for assault but it's always been against women. I guess Meri figures if she can get far enough away from him, she can have a normal life."

"You've got to stop her. You've got to help her before this guy hurts her, maybe even hurts Lily."

Ian's gaze went to the window. "I need to talk to her, but I'm afraid if I push her, she'll run again, and I won't be able to find her."

"Why don't you just marry her? You're in love with her. I can see it in your face every time you look at her. Or maybe you don't think she's good enough for you."

Ian felt the words like a knife in the heart. "Her past has nothing to do with it. I'm just . . . I'm not ready to get married. I've never even thought about it."

"You don't think you could be faithful to one woman?"

He thought of Meri in his bed last night, how right it had felt, how perfectly they fit together. How he wanted her again right now, right this very minute. The idea of sleeping with another woman made his stomach burn. "That isn't it."

"Then what is it?"

"It's not that simple. Marriage is a lifetime commitment. It isn't something you rush into."

A woman's high-pitched scream interrupted whatever his father might have replied.

"Meri!" Ian bolted for the mudroom, slammed out the back door and started running toward the barn. Meri raced toward him, braids flying, her face as pale as last night's moon.

"Ian! Ian, he took Lily! Oh God, Ian, he has Lily!"

Ian felt the words like a physical blow. He caught Meri hard against him. She was shaking all over, tears streaming down her cheeks. "Bandini, right?"

She wildly nodded.

"We'll find her, Meri. I promise you, we'll find her." Dammit, he should have acted sooner. Now if something happened to Lily . . . Ian refused to think of it. He'd find Meri's sweet little girl, bring her home safely. He wouldn't fail either of them again.

"He-he wants money." Meri swallowed, her fingers trembling as she pressed a piece of paper into Ian's hand. "I found this in the barn. He wants fifty thousand dollars. Oh God, Ian, I don't have that kind of money. What am I going to do?"

Daniel spoke up from beside her. "You listen to me, young lady. Ian and I . . . we aren't going to let anyone hurt your little girl. You hear me?"

She buried her face in Ian's chest, her tears soaking through the front of his T-shirt. He ran a hand over the top of her head, felt the silky strands beneath his fingers, thought of the way she had looked with her hair unbound last night.

If this was happening to another woman, he might think it was a con. But he had no doubts about Meri, a truth that hit him squarely in the chest.

"We'll find her, honey," he said. "Finding people is one of the things I do."

"I don't know what . . . what he'll do to her, Ian. She'll be so scared. Joey hates kids, and if she cries . . . oh God, if she cries . . ." A sob escaped and he pulled her back into his arms.

"Listen to me, okay? We're going to get her back, just like I said." He looked down at the paper, read the words out loud. "'Fifty thousand. I'm Lily's father. I deserve it. Midnight tonight. No police. I'll call and tell you where to meet. Joey.'"

Meri looked into his face. "He . . . he's crazy. He thinks because he's Lily's father, he should get half the money I inherited from my foster mom. But it wasn't that much and now it's gone."

"You're talking about Mrs. Vandermeer."

She blinked up at him, for the first time grasping how much he knew about her. "How . . . how did you know about Mrs. Vandermeer? And Joey? How did you know about Joey?"

"I ran a check on you, did some digging. I gave you a chance to tell me yourself. When you didn't, you left me no choice."

Angry heat flooded her cheeks. "You had no right, Ian. I haven't done anything to you. I didn't deserve to have you prying into my past."

"I wanted to help you. I still do."

Embarrassment washed into her face. Her gaze slid down to the pink sneakers on her feet. "I didn't want you to know the kind of life I've led. I wanted to leave while you still believed I was the person you thought I was."

Ian caught her shoulders, forcing her to look at him. "This doesn't change anything, Meri. It just helps me understand you a little better."

She shook her head. "I wish you hadn't done it." She wiped away the wetness on her cheeks. "But I'm too scared to stay mad at you." When she tipped her head back to look at him, he couldn't resist bending down and very softly kissing her.

"It's going to be okay," he said.

Daniel cleared his throat, letting them know he was still there. "Let's go into the house. We've got plans to make."

* * *

"The money isn't a problem." Daniel walked into the kitchen, a canvas satchel in his hand. He dropped the bag in the middle of the round oak table.

Meri stared up at him. "You . . . you've got fifty thousand dollars in that bag?"

"What the hell, Dad? You keep money like that here in the house? Don't you know that's dangerous?"

"With all the trouble in the world, it could be dangerous *not* to have emergency money around. Better to be prepared. Haven't you heard of the 'doomsday preppers'?"

Ian just shook his head. "Well, I guess that's one problem handled."

Meri reached across the table and covered his father's hand. "I'll pay you back, Daniel. I swear it. I'll work here for free for as long as it takes, or I'll get a job somewhere else. I'll pay back every cent. No matter what I have to do."

Daniel squeezed her fingers.

"With any luck," Ian said, "Joey isn't going to end up with the money. We'll have a little reception waiting for him. Once Lily's safe, we'll take him down. He won't be a threat to you anymore."

Meri sat up arrow-straight in her chair. "No police. I know you were a cop, Ian, but I can't take the chance, not with Lily's life at stake. I trust you and Daniel. I'll do whatever you say, just don't bring the police into this."

Ian looked over at his father, waited for his reaction.

Daniel leaned back in his chair. "If this were Seattle, where you knew people you trusted, I'd be inclined to call the cops. As it is, we'd be running blind. Bandini might find out, do something stupid. I think Meri's right. We should handle this ourselves."

"How we going to deliver the money?" Ian asked. "We can't send Meri in there with guys like these. There's no way to know what they'll do."

"I'm bringing him the money," Meri said. "If I don't, there's no way he'll let Lily go."

Ian's jaw went tight, though from the start he had known there was no keeping Meri out of this, not with her daughter's life at risk. "I don't like it, but I get it. You can make the drop. But you do exactly what I tell you. Exactly. Understood?"

He could tell that didn't sit well by the subtle squaring of Meri's slender shoulders.

"This is what I do, sweetheart," Ian reminded her. "You need to listen to me on this."

Her eyes connected with his. He recognized the moment she decided to trust him. "You're right. I'll do whatever you say." She bit her lip. "But . . . there's something else you need to know."

Ian cast her a frustrated, what-else-haven't-you-told-me glance. "Go on."

"Joey isn't alone. He called me from Portland. I have a girlfriend there. That's where I was headed when I left LA. Joey figured it out and got there first. I talked to Michelle after the call. Joey hit her, forced her to give him my cell number. He mentioned he was traveling with this friend of his, Bart Kowalski. Joey calls him Ski. Joey's a real creep, but Ski's big and he's bad. He's dangerous, Ian. Just thinking about him with Lily . . ." She broke off, blinking back tears, swallowed and glanced away.

Ian's gaze swung to his father. "How's your weapons and ammo situation? You still got our hunting rifles in the gun safe?"

Daniel nodded. "Remington 308 and a Winchester

.30-30 locked up out in the garage. Haven't been used in years. Need to get them out and get them cleaned."

"Ammo?"

"All we need. I've also got my sidearm, Smith and Wesson .44. It's locked in the drawer next to my bed. And you got your Glock, right? That's still your weapon of choice?"

Ian nodded.

Meri's face went pale. "You aren't going to kill them, are you?"

Ian grunted. "Much as that idea holds a certain appeal, that isn't the plan. Getting Lily back safely is the objective. But this is kidnapping, Meri. Joey and his buddy aren't getting away with it. Once Lily's safe, we'll be taking the men into custody, turning them over to the police."

"But the guns—"

"If these guys aren't armed, we won't have to use them. If Joey or his buddy starts shooting, that's a different story." Ian's hard gaze zeroed in on her. "You don't still have a thing for this guy, do you?"

Hysterical laughter burst from Meri's throat. "I never had a thing for Joey. He was good-looking and I was lonely. That night I thought, you know, other women do this kind of thing, why can't I?" She shook her head. "One stupid night. That's all it was. I've been paying for it ever since."

Ian stood up from the table. He gently squeezed Meri's shoulder. "You're done paying, Meri. And so is Lily. This is about to be over. Make sure your phone's turned on." He glanced at his father. "Come on, Dad, let's go."

Ian and Daniel spent the rest of the afternoon cleaning, checking, and loading their weapons. They poured five gallons of gas into Meri's car from the can his dad kept in the barn, and continued planning their strategy.

Daniel Brodie was a former marine. He might be a little out of shape, but he was gun-savvy and he was smart. Ian trusted his dad to back him up when the time came.

And he had a hole card up his sleeve. What his dad had said about knowing someone on the Spokane PD had reminded him of a detective named Gray Hawkins he had worked with in Seattle. Family problems had forced Gray to move to Spokane. He'd been on the job here a couple of years.

Ian phoned him, told him he and his father were going into a situation that might require some backup and asked his friend to help.

"If this goes sideways, I need you to step in. There's a kid involved, so her safety is first and foremost."

"Are you sure you want to handle it this way, Ian? We could bring in some of our people, call in SWAT, do whatever it takes."

"Too risky. This guy is completely unpredictable. For now, I just need to know you'll be ready."

"You know my ass is on the line if you screw this up."

Ian just grunted. "Then I guess it'd be better if I didn't. I'll let you know the location as soon as I've got it." He signed off before Gray had time to ask him any more questions.

Now that they were ready, the waiting began. It wasn't until ten p.m. that Bandini called to give Meri the drop site. She put her cell on speaker as Joey talked.

"You got the money?" he asked.

"I've got it. Put Lily on the phone, Joey. I need to be sure she's okay."

"You can talk to her tonight."

"Joey, please . . ."

"Shut up and listen. There's a place called Sekani Park. It's not that far from the house you're in. There's a parking lot on East Upriver Drive, sits right on the water."

Ian knew where the park was. He'd been raised in the area. He nodded to Meri.

"Okay," she said.

"Be there at midnight. One more thing. I see any sign of a cop or those two jokers who live in the house, and you'll never see your kid again. You got it?"

Meri's face went pale. "No police. No one but me, I promise."

Joey ended the call.

Ian swore foully. "I can't wait to get my hands on that bastard."

"Promise me you won't do anything until we get Lily."

Ian's chest went tight. He reached out and touched Meri's pale cheek. "Lily comes first. You don't have to worry about that." His jaw hardened. "Then Joey Bandini is going down."

"I want my mama. I wanna go home."

"Didn't I tell you to shut up? I'm your father, okay? You're supposed to do what I say."

"You're not my father! Ian's my father! I want to go home!"

"Ian's some joker your mother is screwing. Now shut up before I put a piece of tape over your mouth."

Lily's face puckered up as tears threatened to surface.

"Do it, and I swear to God you'll be sorry."

She turned and pressed her cheek against the wall, managed to keep from crying. Where was Mama? Where was Ian? She knew Ian wasn't really her daddy, but sometimes she pretended he was.

She didn't know this awful man who had grabbed her out in the barn and carried her away. She had seen him talking to her mom a couple of times, but that didn't mean he was her father. And she'd never even seen the big ugly man with no hair.

"Look, your mother's coming to get you tonight. Okay? She'll be taking you home." He glanced away. "And good riddance," he mumbled.

"What time is it?" asked the big ugly man.

"Eleven o'clock. Time to go."

"You think she'll bring the money?"

"Like I said, if she doesn't have it, her boyfriend or the old man'll give it to her. That house is worth a lot of dough. Fifty thousand shouldn't be that hard to get hold of."

Lily listened, but she didn't really understand what the men were talking about. All she knew was she wanted her mama to come and get her. And she wanted to go home. She wanted to see the kittens and she wanted to be with Ian and Mr. Brodie.

Lily closed her eyes and said the prayer she and her mama said together every night before they went to bed. "Now I lay me down to sleep. I pray the Lord my soul to keep." She recited the rest of the prayer and added at the end, "And, God, please help me get back home. Amen."

Then she started to cry and hoped the men wouldn't see.

Meri watched Ian and Daniel prepare. It was clear the men knew what they were doing. They were father and son, but beyond that, Daniel had been in the military and Ian had been a policeman, and a private detective, he'd said. Ian had told her they both knew the park fairly well, remembered the parking lot along the river. And they had used Google Earth to get a closer look at places with good vantage points.

The plan was for Daniel to go in on the high side of the road, climb to the spot they had chosen, and cover her as she met with Joey in the parking lot. Ian would park out of sight a ways off, drop down on the south side and move along the riverbank, cover her from below.

Once Meri had given Bandini the money, the exchange had been made, and Lily was safely out of harm's way, he and his father would take the men into custody.

Meri looked at the clock on the wall above the sink in the kitchen.

Midnight was getting close.

But thinking of her little girl and what could be happening to her, she found the hour wasn't nearly close enough.

Chapter Ten

A waxing moon slid in and out between the clouds, casting enough light that Daniel should be able to find his target, not enough that he and Ian would be easily seen. The night was quiet except for a slight, temperate breeze that drifted through the dry grass and branches of the cottonwoods lining the Spokane River.

Ian checked his watch as he moved along the river-bank, careful to stay out of sight below the walking trail at the water's edge. He was getting close to the parking area. By the time he reached his location, Daniel should be in position deep in the cover of the pines on the opposite side of East Upriver Road.

Headlights moved along the ribbon of asphalt winding through the park. Meri signaled to turn, letting him know she was there, and pulled into the empty parking lot. She stopped close to the riverbank, killed the engine, and turned off her headlights, sat in the car to wait.

Only a few minutes passed before another car approached and pulled off the road into the lot from the opposite end. An old, rattle-trap Ford stopped thirty feet from Meri's brown Chevy.

Both front doors of the Ford swung open and two men got out of the car. Ian recognized Joey Bandini from the picture he had seen in the file—roughly six feet tall, slender and black haired. The other man was big, thick through the chest and shoulders, his bald head gleaming in a patch of moonlight shining down through a hole in the clouds.

Something else flashed for an instant in the darkness. *Sonofabitch.* Both men carried semiautomatic pistols in their hands.

Ian's tension ratcheted up another notch. Dressed completely in black, his face darkened with grease paint, he moved silently, Glock in hand, staying low and out of sight.

He had spoken to Hawkins as soon as he had reached the park. Though he hadn't told Meri, Gray had convinced him to have a team on standby, ready to go in as soon as Lily was out of danger. The police would be waiting, set to go on Gray's command.

Ian moved through the shadows along the water, slowed, and elbow-crawled to the top of the bank. Using the base of a tree as cover, he positioned himself and sighted his pistol on Bandini. His dad would be focused on Kowalski.

Ian could hear them now; Meri was talking to Joey. She was still twenty feet away from Bandini, following Ian's instructions.

"I have your money, Joey. Where's Lily?"

Bandini turned to Kowalski, tipped his head toward the car. "Get the kid."

Kowalski shoved his pistol into the waistband of his pants, lumbered over, and opened the back door of the Ford. There was a brief scuffle as he tried to drag Lily out of the car and she refused to come.

"Lily! It's Mama! Do what the man tells you!"

"Mama!"

"Mama's here to get you. Just do what the man says!"

Lily settled down and Kowalski pulled her out of the back seat. Meri winced at the brutal grip he had on her small arm, and Ian clenched his jaw.

Meri held up the canvas bag. "It's all yours, Joey. Fifty thousand dollars. Just let her go."

"You think I'm stupid? Toss it over here. I'm not letting the kid go till I know the money's in the bag."

Meri tossed the canvas satchel toward Joey. Kowalski sauntered over and picked it up, unzipped the bag as he lumbered back.

"You were right, Joey. She brought it. There's a lot of money in here. Give her the kid and let's go."

"Lily—come to Mama. Just start walking, sweetheart. Time to go home."

The child had only gone a few paces when Joey stepped forward and caught her arm, dragged her back against his chest. The gun gleamed in his hand, and Ian's control slipped.

If Bandini harmed a single hair on that little girl's head—

"You know, Meri, maybe I didn't ask for enough," Joey said. "You got your hands on fifty thousand without a hitch. I'm thinking maybe you could get me fifty more."

"Are you crazy, Joey? I borrowed that from a friend. He isn't going to give me anything more."

"By friend you mean the guy you've been putting out for? Your bedroom skills must have really improved if he was willing to fork up fifty grand for a piece of ass."

Ian clamped down on a surge of fury. It took sheer force of will to keep from squeezing the trigger and putting a slug in the center of Bandini's chest.

Meri took a step in Joey's direction and Ian's heart rate kicked up.

"Let her go, Joey," she said. "I mean it."

"You don't tell me what to do, bitch! You never did." He slung an arm around Lily's thin shoulders. Ian could tell how scared the child was. "You want the kid, come and get her."

The look in Bandini's eyes said he wanted more than money. He wanted payback for some imaginary wrong he'd suffered because of Meri. She started walking toward her daughter, and Ian bit back a curse.

"No, Mama!" Realizing Joey's intention, Lily slammed her foot down on Joey's boot, which only made him smile, but as she moved, her body jerked, her head shot up and cracked into Joey's chin, causing him to bite his tongue.

"Motherfuck—"

Joey's grip faltered, Lily took off running toward her mother, and a gunshot echoed from the top of the hill. Both men spun toward the threat and started shooting. Daniel's second round hit Kowalski in the leg and he started firing madly toward the unseen man on the mountain.

Joey whirled and aimed his pistol at Meri, and Ian pulled the trigger on his Glock, putting a round in Bandini's shoulder, slamming him backward, the gun flying out of his hand, disappearing into the darkness.

Hovering protectively over Lily, Meri ran till they reached the safety of her car, climbed inside, and ducked down out of sight.

Kowalski was down, grabbing his bloody leg and moaning. Ian was on him, kicking the gun away, rolling him over, jamming his hands up behind his back and tightening a pair of nylon ties around his thick wrists. He moved to Bandini, who lay flat on his back, gasping for breath, cursing and bleeding, but hurting too badly to cause him any more trouble.

Daniel appeared, rifle in hand. He swung the stock up against his shoulder, aiming the barrel downward, covering the two men on the ground.

"I'm shot!" Bandini whined. "I need a doctor!"

"If I had my way," Daniel growled as he grabbed the canvas bag full of money and slung the strap over his shoulder, "I'd just dump you in the river and let the fish take care of you."

Bandini moaned.

Adrenaline still pumping through him, Ian pressed the send button on his cell phone, heard Gray's voice on the other end of the line. "Time for the cavalry," he said. "They're all yours, Detective Hawkins."

At the first sound of sirens echoing in the distance, Ian turned and strode toward Meri. She came out of the car and flew into his arms.

"Ian! Oh my God!"

He kissed the top of her head, held her close against him, felt a wave of relief stronger than anything he had ever felt before. "Lily okay?"

Meri nodded. "She's fine."

"It's over, honey. The police'll take care of Bandini. You don't have to be afraid anymore."

Meri clung to him, and as his hold tightened around her, a sense of rightness settled over him. Things were changing in a way he hadn't expected. His life was changing, but in these last few moments, he had realized he ready for that change.

He felt a faint jolt as Lily's small body collided and she wrapped herself around him. Ian reached and lifted her up against his chest. "You okay heart?"

Lily nodded. "I knew you and Mama woul

Ian kissed her cheek. "You were right, baby. Everything's going to be okay."

When Lily nodded, he set her back on her feet. Meri took hold of her daughter's hand and released a shaky breath.

"Thank you, Ian. I'll never be able to repay the kindness you've shown us. Thank you for everything."

Ian caught her chin, leaned down and very softly kissed her. "I love you, Meri. You don't owe me a thing."

Meri spent the night and all the next day at Daniel's. The police had been there, taking report after report. A doctor had looked at Lily and found her to be okay.

Meri had spent almost no time with Ian. Instead, she moved around the house as if in a daze, wondering if he had really said he loved her.

And if he had, did he love her in the same way she loved him? With all her heart and soul?

She had to ask him and yet she was afraid of the answer, afraid to let herself hope there might be a future for them. A future that included Lily.

It wasn't until that night after supper that she sought him out. "Ian, I . . . I need to talk to you."

He nodded, his gorgeous blue eyes on her face. "We definitely need to talk. I'll be leaving in a couple of days and there are things I need to say, things we need to work out."

Her eyes burned. He was going to offer her the job of taking care of his father, try again to persuade her to stay here, where he believed she would have a good home. As much as she cared for Daniel, she needed to make a life of her own. And she had hoped, in some tiny part of her heart, that she meant as much to him as he meant to her.

"Let's walk out to the pond, okay? It's nice and quiet out there."

She just nodded. Her heart was squeezing. She should have left as she'd planned. If it hadn't been for the police and their reports . . .

He stopped in the shadows behind the barn, drew her into his arms and kissed her. She could feel the tears welling, tried but couldn't keep them from slipping over onto her cheeks.

"You're crying." Worry darkened his features. "Why are you crying?"

Meri swallowed past the lump in her throat. "I can't stay here, Ian. And I'm not sure your father even needs me anymore. I think Heddy will take very good care of him. I think they'll be perfect for each other."

"So do I."

"You do?"

"Yes, I do."

She brushed at the wetness on her cheeks. "Then what . . . what did you want to talk to me about?"

"Do you remember what I said last night?"

She remembered. The words were etched into her heart. "You said . . . you love me. I understand you probably didn't mean to say that. Things were happening. You were worried about Lily and me."

"I meant exactly what I said. I love you, Meri. I want you and Lily to be part of my life."

Her throat closed up.

"Do you love me, Meri? Because I'm over the moon in love with you."

"Oh God, Ian." Meri threw her arms around his neck and clung to him, just hung on and let the tears roll down her cheeks. "I love you. I love you so much."

She felt his muscles relax as relief slid through him. Ian

eased her away enough to kiss her, then dug into the pocket of his jeans and pulled out a blue velvet box.

"I wish I had time to do this right. Propose to you over some fancy dinner in Seattle, but I'm afraid you'll slip away from me, and I couldn't stand for that to happen."

He opened the box and held it out to her. "This is my mother's wedding ring. Dad wanted me to have it. Will you marry me, honey? I love you so damned much."

"Oh, Ian, yes! Yes, I'll marry you." Her hand shook as Ian slipped the ring on her finger. The small, perfectly cut diamond looked just right on her hand.

Ian kissed her, a long, slow, deep, heart-shattering kiss she felt all the way to her soul.

"Meri . . ." he whispered, holding her in his arms as they stood there looking at each other in the moonlight shining over the water.

"Are you sure, Ian? Are you sure this is what you want?"

"Honey, nothing I've ever done has felt as right as this." Ian brought her hand up and kissed her ring finger. "Let's go in and tell Dad and Lily." He smiled. "But don't be surprised if they already know."

Meri laughed as they walked hand-in-hand back to the house.

Epilogue

They were living in Seattle, Ian back to work at Brodie Security. Since his main office was in Bellevue, he and Meri were looking at homes in the area.

They were married. Meri had no real family and he hadn't seen any point in waiting. His own family had turned out in force for the wedding. Even his cousins, Dylan, Nick, and Rafe had flown down from Alaska.

Once he got his head on straight, it hadn't taken him long to figure out what he wanted. To realize his dad was right—he was in love with Meriwether Jones, and she was the perfect woman for him. Seeing her face up to a pair of vicious thugs like a lioness protecting her cub had only intensified his feelings.

As far as he was concerned, he couldn't get the woman to the altar fast enough.

A lot had happened in the weeks since their marriage; first and foremost, Kowalski and Bandini were both in jail. Besides the kidnapping charges both men faced, turned out Kowalski was wanted for armed robbery in Los Angeles, and though Bandini had accepted a plea bargain, he wasn't getting out of prison anytime soon.

Ian smiled. Meri was working as his bookkeeper/receptionist/secretary, and generally running his office, which was great. She was enjoying the job and she was good at it. She could set her own hours so she had plenty of time to be with Lily.

Plenty of time to be with him. He grinned to think of the hours they'd been spending in bed, how many times he'd made her late for work in the mornings, how she would blush when he teased her about it.

He had already filed to adopt Lily, and though it wasn't official, he was certain the paperwork would go through fairly quickly. Lily already called him Daddy. Daniel had insisted she call him Grandpa, which, every time she said it, made him smile.

Daniel and Heddy were an item. Heddy had insisted Daniel take down the fences between their properties so the horses, including the new ones his dad had purchased, could roam free.

As a wedding gift, she had given Sunny to Ian and Meri. Though the stallion would be staying at his dad's place, it was one of the best gifts he'd ever received.

Everything was going smoothly. And though Ian loved his wife and being married, he was glad to be working. He ran a private security firm. In a city the size of Seattle, he had plenty of business, and he liked the people he worked with, particularly liked working with some of his family.

Two of his best PIs were his cousins. Ethan and Luke Brodie were men he could count on. Down the road, he was thinking he might even open another office.

For the moment, however, he was content.

Ian checked his watch. It was six o'clock. Meri had left at five to pick up Lily. As Ian headed for the door, he smiled. By the time he got home, Meri would be starting supper. Lily would be watching for his car to drive up.

He was heading home to his family.

Ian could hardly wait.

SHAKEN

Rebecca Zanetti

Chapter One

Tough love had never been her thing.

Not in her wheelhouse. No matter how many shrinks, friends, or boyfriends had told Michelle Pamela Peach to write off her mother, she just couldn't do it. Refused to do it. Which was why she found herself at her small kitchen table, across from her mother, staring at the screen on her computer tablet. "I only have two grand, Jayleen." She'd stopped calling her mother "mom" after she'd been kicked to her third foster family at the age of nine. They were both okay with that fact.

"You must have more money than that." Jayleen leaned forward, her wiry frame engulfed by the tight tank-top and Daisy Duke shorts that were two decades too young for her. "You're a famous, um, graphic novelist. Right?"

"No." Michelle snorted, her gaze moving to the adjacent living room, where she'd hung a poster of the cover of her first comic book. "I'm a struggling comic book creator. One who works as a waitress to pay the bills." Maybe her superheroes would someday pay out, or maybe not. Either way, she drew and wrote for herself and waited tables to be sure she had a home. One with bright colors, clean surfaces, and plenty of food. The necessities. "I can give you half of my savings."

"No." Jayleen's bloodshot blue eyes widened, and her already pale face turned an even lighter shade. The sores along her neck, from her latest bout with meth, had finally healed, and she'd stopped twitching. Being clean for more than a month was a good sign. "I owe them money. A lot of it. If I could just get free of them, I'd be okay."

Michelle's heart kicked, but she swept her hand out at the small apartment. "Look around. I have secondhand furniture and live in a small place in the center of Portland. I use public transportation, and when I want highlights, I buy a box at the dollar store. But I'll give you all my savings." She mentally calculated how long it would take her to build up a nest egg again and then stopped counting. Her tips weren't that great. "Will that help?"

"That's not enough." Jayleen's gaze raked her. "You're obviously eating well."

Ouch. Whatever. Michelle had always been full figured, and that was fine with her. "Not all of us end up on a meth diet," she returned quietly.

"Touché, Michelle. Or Chelle. Or Pam. What are you going by these days?" Jayleen's bony shoulders dropped.

Michelle sighed. One of the benefits of moving from foster home to foster home, between bouts of living with her mother, was that she'd been able to reinvent herself each time. She'd gone by many variations of her names. "Michelle. I've used my real name for the last decade. At least." It shouldn't hurt that her mother didn't know that fact. It really shouldn't. So why did it?

"Okay. Michelle." Jayleen sucked in air, her expression brightening. "What about credit cards? You have good credit, I'm sure. You can get a loan on those."

Michelle's stomach ached. The woman didn't care if she put her daughter in debt for life. "Do you really owe people money?" Or did she just want cash for more drugs? Could go either way.

"Yes." Jayleen pounded a fist on the polished wooden table. "They'll kill me. For real this time."

Michelle shut her laptop and scrubbed her hands down her face. "How much do you owe?" She'd avoided the question long enough.

"Twenty-five thousand," Jayleen whispered.

Michelle's head shot up. "Seriously?" There was no way she could get that kind of money. "Why would they give you that much without security?"

Jayleen blanched. "Well . . ."

Oh, crap. "You were dealing." Nausea rolled in Michelle's stomach. "You had a stash and you stole it."

"It's not my fault," Jayleen said. "I'm an addict."

How Michelle hated those words. She didn't have a response, didn't even have a chance to speak.

The front door burst open, and two men rushed inside. The bigger guy, a six-foot-six bald man who looked like he'd just escaped from Rikers, smoothly shut the door.

Michelle froze in place.

Jayleen cried out and pushed back from the table so fast, her chair tipped over. She landed with a loud thump and rolled over, crab walking backwards until she hit the side of the refrigerator. Terror filled her eyes, and she made a small whimpering sound, curling her legs up to her chest.

The shorter guy smiled, his blue eyes gleaming. With his dark hair and lashes, he had probably been good-looking before the obvious ravages of alcohol and drug abuse had slackened his features and hollowed his cheeks. "Hello, Michelle. Remember me?"

She blinked. Shock grabbed her, and she held herself perfectly still to keep from shuddering. "Joey Bandini.

I didn't recognize you." He *had* been very handsome years ago, but now he didn't even look like the same man who'd charmed her friend Meri for a night, way back when, and impregnated her. "What do you want?"

"Well, now." He moved past the soft beige sofa with its bright yellow pillows, toward her. "You're even prettier than I remember. I should've gone home with you instead of that bitch."

Oh, this wasn't good. She cut a look to her mother, who was still cowering against the loudly humming fridge. A chill ticked down her spine, but she kept her expression calm and her body still. "That's a kind thing to say, but I'm wondering why you kicked down my door. You could've knocked." How was she going to get them out of her place? "I don't have any cash, Joey." Too many people wanted money for drugs from her. This was crazy.

"Oh, sweet thing, I don't want money from you." He reached the other side of the table and leaned toward her, his breath smelling like rotgut whiskey. "I want to know where that lying Meri is. Tell me, and we'll be gone."

Meri? The room spun and then settled. "Not a chance," Michelle snapped, anger rising almost to the level of the fear thundering through her.

Jayleen finally spoke. "Wh-who are you?"

"Oh." His smile might've been charming at one time. "I'm Joey Bandini, an old friend of Michelle's."

"I haven't seen you in years," Michelle muttered before she could stop herself. Bandini had had a one-night stand with one of the few friends Michelle had kept in the world, Meriwether Jones. They'd had a beautiful little girl, and Meri had dumped his ass, quite rightly. "I have no clue where Meri or Lily are, Joey." It was the truth. Well, kind of.

"They're on the way here, and we both know that. She

always wanted to move to Portland, and I heard you two met up again at the funeral last month." Joey's face lost its remaining hint of charm. "She has my money, and I want it."

Why did all of these fools look for the easy way to live? Michelle flattened her hands on the laptop. One of the nicest foster mothers of all time, Mrs. Vandermeer, had died and left a small amount to Meri. Her friend needed it for little Lily, and Michelle had been happy for her, although so sad at the passing of Mrs. Vandermeer. "I talked to Meri right after the funeral, and there was only eight grand. Most of it is gone."

"Bullshit," Joey responded. "That old lady was loaded."

Jayleen sat up. "Loaded?"

Heat flushed down Michelle's throat. "No. She was not loaded, for Pete's sake. She was a nice lady with a small, very small, amount of money. Meri isn't hiding cash from you." She had to get these apes out of her apartment. She'd scream, but both of her neighbors worked nights. How loud could she be?

Joey's eyes turned beadier. "I bet you're pissed the old broad didn't leave you any money. Right?"

Michelle's eyebrows shot up. "No. Not at all." It was the truth; she hadn't even considered the idea. "I was only with Mrs. Vandermeer for a few months." Then her mother had gotten clean—briefly—and carted her across the country, where she'd finally landed with Miss A in Kentucky for a wonderful three years until she'd turned eighteen. "Meri and I kept in touch as pen pals. That's all."

"She's coming here, so stop lying to me." Joey tilted his head toward Jayleen. "I'll give you a grand if you tell me where Meri is."

Jayleen stopped whimpering, and her gaze narrowed.

"I don't know, but Michelle will tell you. It's for a grand, Michelle. Come on."

"I don't know," Michelle blurted out. She had to get hold of Meri somehow and tell her to avoid Portland.

"Bull." Joey leaned over the table and slapped Michelle across the face so quickly she didn't have time to duck.

Pain ripped through her cheekbone, and her muscles bunched to leap across the table at him. He was several inches taller and definitely heavier than Michelle, but she'd rather fight than cower. She gripped the edge of the table for balance.

"I wouldn't," the bald guy by the door said, licking his lips.

She couldn't take them both, and Jayleen was useless. Joey moved to hit her again, and this time she had a chance to duck.

He snarled. "Kowalski? Grab the old lady."

The bald guy pushed off the door and moved toward Jayleen.

She cried out and stumbled to her feet, pressing her hands out as if she could keep him away from her. "Please, Michelle. Help me."

Oh, this was so bad. Michelle stood. "I really don't know where Meri is, but I can give you her phone number." She'd be sure to call Meri first and tell her to ditch the phone and head away from Portland. "It's all I have, Joey."

He held up a hand to halt his henchman. "Dooby Brown is back in Seattle, and I can have that geek trace the phone number," he murmured to the bald guy.

Jayleen gasped. "Dooby Brown?"

Joey straightened. "You know that dorky computer nerd?"

Jayleen frowned, her face going slack in an innocent

expression that had never fooled Michelle. "Um, the tweaker from Seattle who sometimes distributes Kicker for the Third Street Boys?"

Joey's left eye twitched and his hands started to shake just enough to show he was in withdrawal. "No. Different guy, who doesn't deal Oxy. He's just a small-time hacker several of us use once in a while. Shut up, now." He glared. "Number?"

Michelle rattled off the phone number. The second Joey left, she'd call Meri. It was a decent plan. She really didn't have any other option.

"Thanks." Joey looked around and his gaze dropped to the tablet. Again, with those surprisingly fast reflexes, he whipped it off the table. "I'll take this."

"No." Panic grabbed Michelle, and she jumped around the table, reaching for the tablet with both hands. She'd put all her money into the device. Her latest comic was on it, and she hadn't had time to back it up yet. More importantly, her work wasn't all that was on there. "Not a chance."

Jayleen stayed against the fridge, watching the tug of war, while the Neanderthal near the door chuckled.

Joey finally twisted his body, wrenching the tablet free and sending Michelle crashing into the table. Her temple impacted the edge, and she went down, stars flashing across her eyes. Joey laughed. "Kowalski? Let's go find my money, and then maybe we'll come back here for a visit. I've always liked a chick with spunk."

Michelle gulped down bile and tried to focus, her ears buzzing and her butt on the ground. She grabbed a chair leg for balance to keep from falling over. "I have friends in the Homeland Defense Department, dickhead. I'm making that call next."

Joey snorted. "Right." He turned and headed past the couch for the door. "I'll be in touch."

Kowalski opened the damaged door, gave her a gap-toothed smile, and then followed Joey out.

Jayleen looked over. "You okay?"

"No." Michelle flattened her hands on the chair seat and forced herself to her feet. It took several minutes of deep breathing before she could be sure she wouldn't fall again. Did she have a concussion? The room swirled around, but she couldn't wait any longer. She drew out her phone from her back pocket and dialed Meri, quickly telling her old friend to stay away from Portland. That loser Joey had already called Meri, but her friend assured Michelle she was safely away from Oregon.

Good.

Michelle hung up.

"Well." Jayleen edged toward the door. "I guess I'll be going." Her gaze had an odd gleam in it.

"Where?" Michelle tried to concentrate.

Jayleen smiled. "I know where to get the money I need. Don't you worry." She skipped out faster than Joey had.

Disaster. Now her mother was going off to do what? Michelle tried to concentrate, but the world started spinning again. She dialed another number to leave a message for the man who was the closest thing to a brother she'd ever had. "Raider? I think I'm in trouble. Call me." The phone fell from her hand as she dropped to the floor and let darkness take her.

At some point, she woke up, feeling somewhat better. So she crawled to the sofa and levered herself up to sleep the rest of the night away.

The screech of tires outside awoke her around dawn. Groggily, she sat up. Heavy footsteps pounded up the stairs outside. There was no way Raider had made it from DC that quickly, was there? The door flew open once again.

Nope. Wasn't Raider, but another man from her past.

The one she'd tried to forget every day. "Well, crap," she muttered as he overwhelmed the doorway. This was all she needed.

Chapter Two

Michelle shook her head and then winced as pain forced her to blink. Ah. Blinking. That would work. She did so several times, but the muscled body in front of her didn't disappear. It had been worth a try.

"You alone?" Evan Boldon, gun out, edged toward the bedroom, his gaze sweeping the area.

"Yes." She pushed her curly hair away from her face, knowing she looked a mess.

He finished scouting the entire apartment before replacing the gun at the back of his waist. When he returned, he seemed bigger than ever. He stood over six feet tall, and his chest had always been broad, but he'd filled out in the years they'd been apart. Had gone from a fit boy to a tightly muscled man. His thick black hair curled over his ears, and those greenish-blue eyes had darkened a few shades, holding a seriousness they'd lacked as a kid. "You okay?" His voice was even deeper than before.

"I'm fine." Except that Evan Boldon was now in her apartment. It was a lot easier trying to forget him when he wasn't right in front of her. "I take it Raider called you?" Oh, she was going to kick his butt next time she saw her pseudo big brother. They'd all spent time at Miss A's foster home, and those ties stuck for life, so she really shouldn't be surprised.

"Yeah." Evan wore jeans and a faded green T-shirt . . . and cowboy boots. That was new. "Raider is undercover, but he'll be here as soon as possible."

"That's okay. I was kind of in a panic when I called him." She tugged her now wrinkled T-shirt into place over her leggings. Why couldn't she get her head to clear?

Evan moved closer, sitting on the sofa. His scent hit her first with the familiarity of first love. Cedar and a wonderful mint. Every time she was in the woods or even near somebody chewing gum, her memories flashed to him. It wasn't fair. He leaned closer, his gaze focusing and then hardening. "What happened to your head?" He reached out and smoothed hair away from her aching temple.

She swallowed, her body no longer in pain. Desire flushed through her, heating every nerve, catching her off guard. From day one, even when they were only teenagers, she'd reacted like this to him. "I'm fine," she coughed out.

His chin lifted while his eyelids half closed, giving him the look of a predator much more dangerous than he'd been before. "Did somebody hit you?"

She barely hid a shiver at his tone. This was too much to handle. "Shouldn't you be fighting, worlds away?" He'd become a marine at eighteen, and they'd lasted together until they'd turned twenty-one, when she just couldn't handle the constant danger he lived in any longer. It had been six years without him, and no other man had come close. "Why are you here?"

"Raider called and said you were in trouble." He leaned back, out of her space, as if sensing she needed distance. "Who slapped you?"

Yeah, that was Evan. A dog with a bone. "Some druggie

taking my—" Panic slapped her, and she jumped up. "My tablet. Oh God." She strode away from the sofa, her mind spinning. "Okay. Those jerks needed money. They'll pawn it." She had to start investigating pawnshops right away. But what if they didn't pawn it? What if they found the materials on it? Her stomach rolled over. No. They'd pawn it. "I have to find it."

Evan stood, towering over her without meaning to do so. "A tablet? We can get you a new tablet, Peaches."

The familiar nickname nearly made her sway in place. Man, she'd missed him. "You don't get it." She whirled around, her breathing uneven. "My latest comic is on it, and it's going to be featured at Comic-Con. If I turn it in next week." The newest edition of Agent Nebula had taken her months to create, and yes, her hero smelled like mint and cedar. Darn it.

Evan straightened. "Don't you have pages around here you could copy?"

Rolling her eyes actually hurt, but she accomplished the act anyway. "I draw everything on the tablet, Evan. Many of us do." She had to start trying to find that tablet, but she couldn't stop looking at Evan. He'd grown up nice, and that tough-kid look had turned into a badass-man one.

"Haven't you backed the work up?" His dark eyebrows slashed down.

She nodded. "Well, kind of. It's been a while, but I have some of it on Dropbox." Not enough. She'd gotten caught up in drawing, as usual, and had not been practical. "That's not the only problem. I have a copy of *Malechi Three* on there. The one that won't be released for a month." *Malechi Three* was one of the top comic books right now, and if it was pirated, her friend would lose hundreds of thousands . . . and probably his publisher.

"Seriously?" Evan's eyebrows lifted. "*The Search for Matredomi*?"

Oh yeah. Evan had been way into comic books, and they'd shared that love for a while. In fact, he'd introduced her to the medium. Had her whole life been influenced by him? "Yes."

"How did you get that?"

She sighed. "George Tribini and I are friends, and he gave me an early copy. We critique for each other once in a while." Which might lead to George's downfall. "I have to find that tablet." And stop salivating over the hot man in her living room. They'd broken up for a reason.

"Speaking of which, who nailed you and took your tablet, Michelle?" He crossed muscled arms.

She ground her fist into one eye. "It doesn't matter. Getting it back is what counts." Since she'd warned Meri, her girlfriend would be safe, making Joey Bandini irrelevant. Unless he kept the tablet. "This is a disaster." She looked for her phone. "I need to call Raider." Maybe he could do a trace or something on Bandini.

"He's deep undercover," Evan said. "It was a risk for him just to call me. Now tell me what's going on."

Frustration heated her from head to toe, and she forced herself to focus. Evan was in front of her, with a gun, dressed like a civilian. "When did you get back to the States?"

A muscle ticked in his jaw. "Two years ago. I left the service, established myself, and wanted to get settled down before . . ."

She took a step back, her breath quickening. "Before what?"

"Finding you. Looks like I have."

* * *

The panic in the woman's deep blue eyes wasn't exactly reassuring. Evan held his ground, letting his words sink in. After they'd broken up, he'd done his duty with the Force Recon unit until injury forced him to take a second look at his life. He'd loved being a marine, but he'd reached that point where he wanted a home and a regular life.

He had those things now. But something was still missing.

He had to know if he and Michelle were the real thing, although those rumors about her dating George looked to be true. While he hadn't been a monk in their years apart, no other woman made him feel an iota of what he felt for her. But they'd been young, and feelings were intense at that time of life. Whether it was the real thing or not, they had a past, and he was going to help her. One way or another.

"You're not a marine any longer?" Her voice wavered.

"Once a marine, always a marine," he responded instantly. "I'm no longer active duty, if that's what you're asking."

She took another step back. "I didn't know."

"It took me a while to get my feet under me." That might be an understatement. Sometimes the nightmares still forced him to go running until dawn, but he was definitely better. Although this wasn't the time to discuss it. "If this was a robbery, why haven't you called the cops?"

She blushed. "Long story."

"I ain't leavin' until I hear it." He tried to keep his voice calm, but it roughened anyway. He had no plan to leave if she was in danger.

Her chin was still delicate . . . and stubborn. "Fine. An asshat named Joey Bandini took the tablet because he's chasing a friend of mine, who seems to be in a safe place now. I didn't call the cops because Bandini is the father of my friend's child, and she seems to think he might try for custody. I disagree, but she's the mom, so her opinion trumps."

Evan would check out Bandini as soon as he had the full truth. "He slapped you?" Once he found the guy, he'd take out some of his frustration on the deadhead. That seemed okay.

"Yes, but I'm fine." She edged closer toward the bedroom, looking delicious in a tight shirt and form-fitting yoga pants that hugged her firm thighs and curvy ass. "Now, thanks for your help, but I've got this covered."

He almost laughed out loud. Instead, he let a slight smile curve his lips. "What else, Peaches?"

Pink bloomed across her high cheekbones. Man, she looked good. Eyes bluer than any stone he'd ever seen, long, curly black hair, delicate features. She'd filled out in all the right places, too. "Fine. My mom was here, and who knows if she has warrants out on her or not."

His amusement morphed right to irritation. One of their main fights was over her willingness to take crap from that junkie. "You're still in contact with Jayleen?" He'd never forgotten how soft-hearted Michelle could be.

She stiffened. "Yes. She is my mother."

"That woman has never deserved the title." Last time he'd seen Jayleen, she'd tried to shake him down for money and then had hit on him for the same reason. Michelle definitely deserved better, but since he'd never had a mother, he couldn't really blame her for wanting to keep in touch with hers. But giving a junkie money was a mistake. "How much did you give her this time?"

Michelle's sweet jaw firmed. "Nothing. She's clean now, Evan. Finally."

Right. That would last. Not. "Wait a minute. She was here after you were hurt? She left you?" His chest heated.

Michelle's gaze dropped. "Yes." Then she stiffened, her head snapping up. "I figured Joey would pawn the tablet. Maybe Jayleen thought the same thing." Michelle turned pale. "I have to get that tablet before she figures out what is on it. The woman thinks I'm some famous graphic artist, and if she finds my new comic, or if she finds George's, she'll . . ." Michelle bit her full bottom lip. "Who knows what she'll do to get money." Then she focused on him again. "I can handle it, however. I've got this covered, Evan. Go back to your life."

"No." Yeah, being near her again had sent his blood moving like he'd run a 10K. "I'm not going anywhere." He pulled out his phone and sent instructions for his deputy, his one deputy, to run a check on Joey Bandini. Then he texted another number, this one given to him by Raider in case he needed federal help while Raider was undercover. "I'll see if we can track Bandini and find your tablet."

She was cute when irritated. Or was that frustration? They looked the same on her. "You are not coming in here and taking over," she muttered.

He just had. So why fight about it? "You used to like it when I took over," he rumbled.

Her eyes flared. Very pretty blue flashed hot and bright. "Yeah, and then you left."

"I had a job to do, and I did it." Not for one second did he regret his time with the military. Even when the nightmares tortured him into the dawn hours. "You just couldn't stand all the risk that went with it, and I actually understand that. Never held it against you." After her crappy childhood, he couldn't blame her. He'd faced death more than a few times, and he was grateful to be alive. But alone. He was tired of being alone. "I'm home now. For good."

She crossed her arms. "That's great for you. Good luck."

He'd forgotten how stubborn she could be. What was he dealing with here? "Are you seeing anybody? I read on a blog somewhere about you and George?" She wasn't wearing a ring, so no fiancé. There could be a boyfriend. Made sense. Michelle was a beautiful sweetheart with a sharp wit and impressive talent. Full of curves, she was all lush woman. He'd purchased copies of every one of her comics through the years. "Is there a guy around?" If so, why had she called Raider instead of the boyfriend?

"My love life is none of your business." She spoke through gritted teeth.

Okay. Maybe not so smart if she really thought that.

Her phone buzzed, and she yanked it from her table to answer. "Hello?" Her eyes widened. "No, Jayleen. Wait a minute. That's crazy. Just tell—" Her eyes closed and she set the phone down. "She hung up."

The skin prickled on the back of Evan's neck. "What did she say?"

Michelle opened her eyes. "Just that she has a line on getting a lot of money. I think she has a bigger score in mind than my laptop. Who knows. Whatever it is will be illegal and probably dangerous. We both know that."

Jayleen would have no problem dragging Michelle right into danger with her.

Evan drew his wallet out from his back pocket and flipped it open to reveal his star-shaped badge. "Well, then. I guess we have a problem."

Chapter Three

Even his truck smelled like him. Michelle settled back onto the leather seat of the old but well-kept vehicle. A truck that Miss A would've called a workingman's truck. She smiled at the memory and then crossed off another entry on her list of pawnshops. She sighed.

"There are a lot of pawnshops in Portland, Peaches," Evan murmured, flipping on the windshield wipers as a light rain began to fall.

She tried not to notice how strong his profile looked in the cocoon of the cab as he drove intently down another back street. "I know, but Joey needed a fix. I recognized the signs, and he'll want money as soon as possible." She hoped. If he'd taken the laptop out of the area, she was screwed. She should probably call George with a warning—maybe after checking a few more pawnshops. They'd only looked at three so far. "Let's just stay away from the well-known ones that would ask too many questions about the tablet."

Evan cut her a sideways glance. "Familiar with the criminal aspect of pawnshops, are we?"

"Of course. Jayleen has pawned everything you can imagine." Her stomach ached. "In fact, that was always a sign that she was using and I was about to end up in another foster home." Though she'd been lucky with some of her placements, that was for sure. "Let's check this one out next." She pointed to the next shop on her list, which was outside of Portland in one of those neighborhoods with litter on the street and bars on home windows.

"Sure." Evan peered into his side mirror and switched lanes to head onto the interstate.

The rain increased in force, splattering loudly against the slightly fogging windows. She rested her head back and closed her eyes, her temples still aching.

"Here." Evan's arm brushed hers, and he opened the jockey box.

She opened her eyes to see a bottle of Advil next to a black gun. Nodding, she took the bottle and dropped two pills into her hand, tossing them back without water. She replaced the painkiller in the glove compartment without touching the weapon, and shut it. "You're a sheriff." The badge had been a surprise.

"Yeah. Small town in Eastern Washington an hour from Spokane." His lips tipped in a half smile. "Great place. Lots of pasture, farms, fishing, and wildlife. You'd like it."

She'd probably love it, but she knew him. "You can't be happy in a quiet place." One of the reasons he'd liked being a marine was the action. His temporary tranquil life wouldn't last.

"I am," he said quietly.

He couldn't have changed that much. People never did. Oh, they tried, but she'd learned long ago that the true nature of a person remained the same. Truth be told, she'd loved Evan and hadn't wanted to change him. Well, maybe a little, but she'd given up that dream years ago. "Are you seeing anybody in your small town?" Now why the heck had she asked that? And why had her lungs decided to hold her breath? Geez.

"No." He sped up to pass a logging truck. "How about you?"

"Yes. Well, kind of," she blurted out. Going on two dates was kind of dating somebody, right?

"Kind of, huh? Is it George?" Evan's hands remained loose on the wheel. Broad, wide hands with long fingers and an interesting scar across the knuckles of his right hand.

"No." She chuckled. "George and I are just friends. I started dating somebody else. Well, sort of."

"That doesn't sound serious."

She crossed her arms. "It's personal."

He turned fully her way then, his eyes darkening. "I took your virginity, baby. We are personal."

Her spine straightened even as her abdomen warmed. Her nerves short-circuited in a way they hadn't in years, throwing her off guard. It didn't help that he was beyond sexy-looking in the dimming light. "I believe I took yours, too," she sputtered.

His grin transformed his rugged face from deadly to charming in less than a heartbeat. "That you did. Nicely done, too."

She coughed up a laugh, her body relaxing. "You are impossible."

"So you've said. More than once." He turned back to the road. "We're half an hour away from the next shop. Lay your head back, shut your eyes, and let the Advil go to work on that headache."

"Stop bossing me around," she muttered, putting her head back.

"I've been hit in the head more than once," he countered easily. "Trust me. You'll feel better soon."

She closed her eyes. "Obviously you've been hit in the head. A lot."

He snorted. "Smart aleck."

She tried not to smile, she really did. The drumming rain, warm truck, and inherent safety surrounding her lulled her into a light sleep. The only time she'd felt truly safe in her life was with Evan. How had she forgotten that? As tranquility took her under, she returned to being fifteen years old again, arriving at her new foster home. Her fifteenth, to be exact.

She stood in the parlor of a charming blue, two-story home on a quiet street and scrutinized the tons of framed pictures of bunches of kids on the mantel, beyond the floral sofa and cushy-looking chairs. The wooden floor gleamed, and no dust was apparent on the tables; the place smelled like fresh flowers, not cleansers.

"Come into the kitchen and call me Miss A," her new foster mom said, moving past the clean room.

Michelle gingerly toed off her too small and too dirty tennis shoes and left them by the door, scrunching her toes in their threadbare socks to hide the holes before following Miss A. The woman was about two inches shorter than Michelle's five-foot-four and dressed in nice white linen slacks and a purple silk shirt—both with no wrinkles, somehow. How did she stay unwrinkled in the Kentucky summer humidity?

The cheery kitchen had lovely yellow walls, tons of appliances, granite countertops, and several windows that faced a large backyard with flower gardens, a rope swing, and what looked like a volleyball court.

"What kind do you like?" Miss A asked, sweeping her hand toward several plates of cookies. "Those are chocolate chip, those are oatmeal, those sugar, and those peanut butter."

Cookies. Real, homemade cookies. They smelled delicious. Michelle's stomach rumbled. "Um. I like them all."

"That won't do." Miss A bustled toward a cupboard and took out a blue plate. "Have one of each and let's see. I love a good taste test." She placed one of each cookie on the plate and gestured Michelle toward the round oak table with a vase of roses in the middle. "I love to cook and experiment."

Michelle hung in the entry way, hesitating.

Miss A set down the plate and turned, her dark brown eyes softening. "It's okay, Michelle. You're welcome here and everything I have is yours. No tests, no right or wrong answers, just you." Her black hair, streaked with gray, was piled up on her head; light, classy makeup covered her dark skin. She was the prettiest and most natural woman Michelle had ever seen. "You're safe here. I promise."

Warmth overwhelmed the caution inside Michelle, and she moved toward the cookies.

The back door banged open, and three teenaged boys boisterously tumbled inside. Her gaze caught on the first one and she couldn't look away. Black hair, blue eyes, big and fit. A sparkle filled those eyes.

He moved toward her, snatching a cookie off her plate. "Hi. I'm Evan."

She could only stare.

Miss A sighed.

"We're here," Evan said, enticing Michelle back to the present. She looked over at her first love, seeing the boy who'd become a man capable of fighting and defending. The one who loved action, even back then. Being near him was just too much.

Evan switched off the engine and watched a mangy dog run across the empty street ahead, spraying mud from puddles. He turned and surveyed the dilapidated pawnshop, which was flanked by two boarded-up businesses. An empty lot, littered with fast-food wrappers, extended wide on the other side of the street. "How did you even find out about this place?" he muttered.

Michelle pushed unruly hair away from her face. "I googled it."

Huh. All right. He reached past her for his gun and tucked it in the back of his waist. "How about you stay here in the truck and I go inside?" Oh, it was going to get him smacked, but he at least had to offer.

Her frown was adorable and hit him dead center in the chest. "Not a chance."

That's what he'd figured. He tried really hard not to focus on the fact that she'd be doing this alone if Raider hadn't contacted him. How much had she done alone in the years he'd been gone? After returning home to the States, he'd had to work on himself, on the night terrors, before he could reach out to her—to any of his family. Was he ready? He wasn't sure, but right now they had more important things to worry about. "All right, but let me lead."

She shook her head, and all of that beautiful hair moved. "My tablet, my problem." Tugging down her mellow-yellow sweater over formfitting jeans, she pushed her door open and darted into the rain, her brown boots splashing up water.

He sighed and exited the vehicle, hurrying around to reach her. Together, they walked through weeds and up sagging steps to a dinged metal door. A sign above the door said PAWN, but the A was missing. The door opened easily, and he stepped inside a dusty showroom with surprisingly secure glass cases forming a square around the space.

A guy of about thirty scurried out of a back room, eyeglasses on his narrow face, his bony body covered by a striped blue and yellow collared shirt and sagging cargo pants. "Can I help you?" He pushed the glasses up his nose.

"Yes." Michelle stepped gingerly over the uneven wooden floor to reach the glass case, which held several cameras and a couple of sparkling necklaces. "I'm looking for a tablet with a case cover of various comic figures. It would've come in late last night or earlier today."

The guy's gaze flicked to Evan. "You're a cop."

"Yep," Evan agreed. "I'm here for the tablet and nothing else. Don't care what you have going on." Not to mention that he was way out of his jurisdiction and had no authority here, but the other guy didn't know that. "We'll pay for it." He'd do almost anything to ease the panic he kept glimpsing in Michelle's pretty eyes.

"I wish I had that tablet, I really do." The guy scratched at a pimple on his neck. "If you give me your number, I'll call you if it comes in."

Evan narrowed his gaze, remaining silent. The guy started to twitch nervously and grabbed a rag from his back pocket to rub across the glass counter, which was already clean.

Michelle looked at him, back at Evan, and then to the guy again. "We really don't care how you got it. Are you sure you don't have it?"

"I don't." The guy's Adam's apple bobbed. "Really wish I did."

Ah. Evan lowered his chin. "I take it we're not the first folks to ask about it?"

Michelle stiffened, and he placed a reassuring hand on her shoulder. The sweater material was soft and warm beneath his fingers, and he kept his touch gentle.

The guy looked at them, his chest sunken in. His eyes were bloodshot and his movements twitchy. He kept moving as if he couldn't stop himself, wiping down the glass cases. "Yeah. A lady came in and asked for it just a couple of hours ago, but I don't have it. I'm tellin' you the truth, man."

Irresponsible Jayleen. Evan set his stance. "Did she ask you for anything else?" He ignored Michelle's indrawn breath at his question.

"No," the guy said, his gaze flicking down.

Liar. "Did you sell her drugs?" Evan kept his voice level.

The guy looked up, his pupils dilated. "Nope. I don't sell drugs." He held up a bony hand as Michelle began to speak. "Even if I did, which I do not, that lady didn't have any money. So no."

Probably the truth. Evan smiled then, and he almost enjoyed the guy's audible gulp of a swallow. "Okay. Then give us the same list you gave her—the one with pawn-shops not found in the phone book or on Google. We'll leave you alone."

For now, anyway.

Chapter Four

Michelle picked at the pepperoni and pineapple pizza in front of her, her body tired and her head still aching. They'd searched eleven more pawnshops the rest of the day, coming up empty.

"We have a dozen more so-called shops to check tomorrow," Evan said, finishing off his third piece and looking way too at home across her small kitchen table.

She ate another bite, her senses tuning in to him. With his size, he usually overwhelmed most spaces, but it was more than that. His personality, his heat, and that naturally wild gleam in his eyes, automatically drew attention. Even sitting still, happily munching pizza, he looked like a cougar barely leashed. Or a bear. It was hard to pick an animal for Evan.

His dark eyebrows rose. "What are you thinking about?"

"Animals." Heat flared into her face, warming her. "I'm thinking about getting a cat." Oh, she was such a liar.

"Hmm. Cats are nice." He looked around the pristine kitchen. "Remember that old tabby we found and brought home to Miss A right about when we both were leaving?"

Michelle grinned, taking another bite. "I do. Raider was back visiting, and didn't he give the cat some Latin-sounding name?"

"Yeah. You and I just called him Fred. I think that name stuck." Evan chuckled. "I wonder how many pets Miss A has adopted through the years? I heard last month she had a couple of kids bring baby porcupines without a mama home to her."

Michelle winced, relaxing for the first time that day—probably thanks to the red wine she'd opened to go with the pizza. "I talked to Miss A last week, and she said the quills were becoming a problem already." Miss A could handle anything. Even two of her kids falling in love and then splitting up. How many times had Michelle cried on Miss A's shoulder after Evan had left for his last tour of duty? She'd stayed in Kentucky for a couple of years after Evan had left before heading to Oregon for a fresh start. Miss A had said things would work out however they'd work out. "I'm happy, Evan," Michelle murmured.

He sobered, his gaze darkening to a midnight hue of blue. "Without me."

She nodded. "Yeah. Without worrying so much all the time whether you'll make it home and who you'll be when you do." It hurt her to say the words, but she'd never been able to lie to him. Had never wanted to.

To her surprise, he nodded. "I get it and don't blame you. I worried about who I was last time I came home, which was why I decided to find another path. I've done my duty." He looked around the kitchen. "I know I told you I was done before, and I even tried to make it work."

"You weren't done." That had lasted almost a month before he'd gone back to his unit, most likely very much needed. She'd never begrudged him his path. "It's okay if you're never done. You are who you are." Letting him go had hurt more than she'd thought possible, but she was okay now, although she wouldn't put herself through that pain again. She had no doubt his sheriff job was temporary, much like the mechanic job he'd taken way back when, before the lure of the marines called him back.

His broad chest lifted in an inhale, which he slowly let out. "You've made a nice home here."

Had she? The apartment was warm and comfortable, and she had plenty of room to work on her comics. Did it feel like an actual home? With Evan sitting across from her, calm and perceptive for now, the place actually seemed different. More welcoming. "What's your apartment like in Washington?" she asked, wanting to know more about him before he left again.

His grin was quick and fleeting. "You wouldn't believe me if I told you."

Probably lawn furniture and takeout boxes filled a small one-bedroom that somehow still smelled good and like him. No doubt the lease was just for six months. She studied him, so big and strong and Evan. "It is good to see you." Maybe she could find final closure on him and stop comparing every guy she dated to her first love. It'd be a great help if her pulse would stop racing and her body rioting at having him near. She took a deep drink of the potent wine. Yeah. Like that was going to help. She ran a finger across the scar on his knuckles. "This is new."

He sucked in a breath. "Sharp blade." He lifted a wide shoulder. "I had my hand around the asshole's neck, so can't blame him too much." When she removed her hand, he leaned toward her. "It happened two years ago, a world away from here, Peaches."

Her phone buzzed and she yanked it from her back pocket, hoping it was Jayleen. She glanced at the screen and faltered before answering. "Hi, Mike." Evan's eyebrows rose again, and she tried not to squirm in her seat.

"Hey. I just finished work and was wondering if you'd

like to grab dinner," Mike said, traffic sounds around him as he no doubt drove away from the hospital.

She cleared her throat. "I, ah, can't tonight. How about I give you a call tomorrow?"

"No problem. Talk to you then." He clicked off.

She gingerly set the phone down on her leg.

Evan took a drink of his wine. "Mike?"

She swallowed. "Yeah. He's a physical therapist at the hospital. We met at a cooking class." Mike was a few years older than she, established, and stable. Plus he had a jawline like Jensen Ackles and the body of a lean swimmer. Not nearly as broad as Evan, but in great shape. On the down side, he'd invited her to go jogging with him, and she'd rather clean gutters than jog.

"Is it serious?" Evan asked, his voice just a mite too calm.

She fiddled with her wineglass. "Not yet, but it could be." Maybe. She'd never been able to get serious with anybody after him. Pushing her plate away, she lifted her gaze to meet his.

"I see." He stood and took his plate to the sink to rinse and place in the dishwasher.

She already knew that he wasn't dating anybody. A ding from her phone caught her attention, and she read quickly. "My boss said I can have the week off. It's the slow season at the restaurant, anyway." If it wasn't football season, it was the slow season at the sports bar and restaurant. She stood with her plate and handed it over silently to Evan. "I can check the other pawnshops myself tomorrow. You don't have to stay away from work."

He finished and turned to face her, crossing his arms. "I'm not leaving you until I know that Joey Bandini and his buddy are far from here."

Yeah, she'd figured. "Fine, but the couch is lumpy." Like he'd fit there.

"I've slept on worse," he countered, his stance relaxing. "You gonna tuck me in?"

Well after midnight, Evan kicked his legs over the end of the sofa, grimacing as he tried to awaken his tingling foot. The couch was made for a much smaller person. He tried to turn over and nearly face-planted on the coffee table. Muttering, he shoved the blanket off and sat up, rolling his neck.

Maybe he should go for a run and tire himself out. His skin felt too tight with Michelle sleeping in the other room so close to him. The scent of wild lilacs surrounded him, providing both an exhilaration and a comfort he'd missed more than he'd realized. If he left, he'd leave her unprotected, so that couldn't happen. Though he didn't think Bandini would return, he couldn't be sure.

So he flopped back down on the lumpy sofa and extended his legs over the armrest. His other foot started to fall asleep. Closing his eyes, he practiced deep breaths, the way the last shrink, an expert in PTSD, had taught him to do. One by one, he relaxed his muscles, head to toe. The base of the sofa protested beneath him. His shoulder hung off the side and he tried to press his body into the sofa back, ignoring the fact that Michelle was in a perfectly good bed. He'd peeked earlier. It was a queen, and his legs would still stick over the end, but it had to be more comfortable than the stupid sofa.

He finally dropped off to sleep, and the nightmare that took him was a scene that had actually happened.

"You don't have to go," Raider said to him, standing on the edge of the tarmac.

Evan looked at the closest thing he'd ever had to a big brother. Raider was tall with sharp features, his part-Japanese heritage giving him an intense look. "It's my team, Raid. They need me."

Raider nodded, looking toward the silent plane waiting. "I understand." Raider worked for the HDD and no doubt had missions of his own to handle. "I don't think she'll wait this time."

"I know." Evan turned to see Michelle step out of the truck and walk toward him, looking like any man's best dream with her round curves in a flowing blue dress, her hair wild around her stunning face. She walked toward him, her eyes bright, tears in them. "I haven't been all the way right in a while, and it's probably going to get worse. She needs better—she needs stability." He didn't have that in him right now

Raider pulled him close for a hug. "Call if you need me." Patting Michelle's shoulder, he strode back to wait for her in the truck.

Evan turned to face her, the smell of lilacs hitting him hard. "I'm sorry."

She smiled, a sad smile, and caressed her hand along his jaw. "Don't be sorry for being who you are. I'll miss you."

It was goodbye, and he knew it. Duty pulled him in one direction and love the other. His team was in trouble, and it was life-or-death. Leaving her like this felt the same. He couldn't ask her to wait—not again. His chances of making it back weren't good, and the mission was a long one, so he couldn't even give her a return date if he did survive. "I'll always love you," he murmured, leaning down for a kiss.

She opened for him, so sweet and giving. "Me too." Then she stepped away, her shoulders straight. "I'll wait for you."

The words filled him, catching him off guard. Filling parts of him he hadn't realized existed. His duty didn't fulfill her needs, and he knew it. She needed a home and a family and safety, after her unsafe childhood. If he could give her none of those things, he had to let her go. "No." The word nearly killed him. "I'm going on an extended mission, and it could be years, Michelle. There's no waiting for me." Then he hit her with the full truth. "I'm never going to be done."

Pain filled her eyes, but no surprise. "You're such a butthead. I'm going to do what you said—I'm going to move on."

He grasped her shoulders, pulling her close. "Make the life that you want and do it now. Don't wait around for anybody, ever again. You deserve everything." A part of him wanted to stay with her and turn his back on his men. But he couldn't do it. More than one of his teammates had saved his life, and now it was his turn to repay their loyalty and save them. "Go. Now." He turned her and gently pushed her toward Raider, who'd make sure she was okay.

Watching her walk away was the hardest thing he'd ever done, and he'd once had to hike five miles after being stabbed in a kidney. Even that was nothing close to the pain he felt saying goodbye to her. He'd gotten on that plane, flown across the world, and then faced hell.

He sat up, awake, before another nightmare could begin. Sweat dotted his bare chest and he wiped it off, twisting to sit on the sofa. There would be no more sleep tonight. Sometimes he could sense the worst nightmares coming and wake himself up, and here he was. Unfortunately, he couldn't go running, although dawn had just started to peek through the blinds in the kitchen.

Quiet surrounded him and he took several deep breaths to even out his system.

A noise caught his attention from the hallway. It was late for a neighbor to be arriving home. He partially turned his head, his body going on full alert.

Warning ticked through him just as the front door blew open, splintering so quickly one shard cut across his pinkie. He jumped up just in time to catch the glint of light off a silver gun.

Ducking his head, he charged.

Chapter Five

A loud crash awoke Michelle and she bolted from the bed, her heart pounding. What the heck? She removed the baseball bat from beneath her bed and ran for the door, yanking it open in time to see Evan tackle another man so hard they both flew into the hallway.

A second intruder, a blond male around forty years old, dressed all in black, slid by them, gun out, his gaze following the other two men. He was thin but held the gun with control.

Michelle barreled forward, already swinging the bat at his hand, fear making her movements quick. He turned at the last second to face her, but not fast enough. The bat smashed his wrist, and the gun flew across the room. His light blue eyes widened and he howled, grabbing his arm with his free hand and drawing it to his chest.

She lifted the bat, panting wildly and swung again, nailing him in the upper thigh. He yelped and went down to his other knee, inching away from her. "Evan?" she called, edging around the wounded man, panic rippling over her skin.

Evan and the other man crashed back through the doorway, landing on the coffee table and shattering the glass. Michelle turned away to protect her eyes, and the man on the floor went for her legs. She struck his rib cage with the bat, fighting, but he grabbed it with his unbroken arm and threw it into the kitchen.

She yelled as she fell, punching on the way down. Evan and the other man rolled across the glass and back into the hallway, striking and struggling for control.

The guy grabbed her hair and pulled, whipping pain along her skin. She smacked his hand away, quickly pivoting and aiming for his damaged wrist. He backed away, his gaze wild on her.

The ruckus in the hallway subsided and Evan, bare chested, with fury darkening his high cheekbones, strode back inside, his sweats loose and dotted with blood. A wound bled freely from the left side of his rib cage. "You okay?"

She nodded and pushed to her feet, her eyes wide on him.

He looked at the bat and then at the man kneeling on the floor. "Nice swing, slugger."

She couldn't breathe.

The intruder craned his neck to look into the hallway.

Evan narrowed his gaze. "Your friend isn't going to wake up anytime soon." Almost casually, he grasped the man by the neck and hauled him to his feet and up to his toes, making them almost the same height. "You have one chance to tell me who you are before I throw you out the window face-first."

Michelle stepped back, her body trembling as her adrenaline ebbed. The room spun crazily.

Evan shook the guy, still holding him by the front of his neck. "Well?"

The guy punched up with his healthy hand, and Evan slapped his fist down with an odd crunch. The guy cried out and tried to struggle, but Evan held him tight.

Evan leaned in, looking as lethal as Michelle had ever seen him. "Why. Are. You. Here?"

The guy gulped. "The girl. We were sent to get her. Something about her family owing money." He squeaked at the end of the sentence, his eyes bugging out, as Evan obviously tightened his grip.

Michelle sagged against the door frame to her room. "My mother?" It had to be the twenty-five grand Jayleen had wanted; apparently she'd been telling the truth for once. "Who does she owe the money to?"

The guy tried to shrug and then winced when Evan yanked him even higher up onto his toes. "I don't know," he gasped out. "Charlie just hired me tonight to make some money. He didn't say who the client was or where we were supposed to take you." He sucked in air, his jaw working furiously. "There wasn't supposed to be nobody else here."

A low sound, much like a growl, rolled from Evan's chest. "Jayleen owes money? Drug money?"

"Um, I think so," Michelle muttered.

Fury rolled off Evan in greater waves, heating the air between them. Great. Just great. Michelle gulped down nausea as the guy's face started to turn blue. "Um, Evan? You might want to lighten your grip."

Evan didn't twitch.

She couldn't have a homicide in her apartment, and right now she didn't feel all that comfortable approaching Evan. He looked like he'd relish killing the intruder. "You're a cop, remember?" she whispered.

"You're a cop?" the intruder gasped.

"Not at the moment," Evan said, his voice gravelly.

Michelle shifted her weight to see the feet of the un-conscious guy on the tile outside the apartment. Evan's easy violence shot anxiety through her. She'd known he was a marine, a good one, but she'd never seen him in action. "Any chance he'll be able to speak soon?" She needed to find out who Jayleen owed, since the bad guys were now after her, too.

"It might be a while," Evan said shortly. He nodded toward her room. "Call the police, would you? They'll have to question these two while I get you out of town." With a careless twist of his wrist, he tossed the intruder back down to the floor and faced her, his eyes blazing. "Don't even think of giving me a hard time about handling this yourself."

Her knees shook. "Are you nuts? Two guys, one with a gun, just broke into my apartment." Her voice rose and she tried to quiet it. Before, she hadn't really believed Jayleen and certainly hadn't thought drug dealers would come after *her*. Now things were different. Very. "You're a trained marine. No way in hell are you leaving me alone right now." Geez. She wasn't a moron.

Surprise flashed across his hard face, which he quickly suppressed. "Good. Get packed, Peaches. Guess you'll see my place after all."

Her belongings safely in the back seat of Evan's truck, Michelle walked out of the final pawnshop on her list with Evan behind her. They were in yet another dismal part of town, with hope slowly ebbing out of her. Even her toes hurt as she stepped up into the truck and sat, looking out at another rainy day, her eyes aching.

Evan stretched into the driver's seat and winced.

"I told you to get stitches," she repeated for the thousandth time that day. "A bandage from my apartment isn't enough."

"I'm fine," he countered—again. "Let's get out of here

and find dinner. Then we can head north." When she didn't answer, he looked her way, his face pale beneath his tan. "I'm sorry we couldn't find your tablet."

She nodded. "We tried." It was too much to hope that Joey Bandini had just thrown the tablet away. He had to have pawned it somewhere illegally.

Evan ignited the engine and drove away from the dirty establishment.

Her phone dinged, and she tugged it from her purse, gasping at seeing George's number. "Um, hi, George," she said, her voice hushed.

"Hi," George answered, his British accent clipped. "Would you care to tell me who Jayleen is and why she is trying to, as you Americans say, shake me down?"

Her stomach rolled. "I'm sorry. She's my mother. What did she say?"

"That she has your tablet with my newest comic on it. Either I give her a hundred grand—cash—to get it back or she uploads it for the entire world to see—free," George said, his voice sounding hoarse. "I don't have a hundred grand in cash."

Michelle winced. Darn it. Jayleen had somehow found the right pawnshop before Michelle could. Figured. "I know. I'll get it back—I promise."

"See that you do." George disconnected the call.

"Man, he's pissed," she murmured, her head swimming. George was the calmest person she knew, and for him to hang up without a goodbye meant he was furious. Scrambling, she dialed her mother's number, pressed the speaker, and set the phone on her knee.

"Hi, baby doll," Jayleen slurred. "I've found a way for us to get rich. Very rich."

Michelle's chest hurt. "You're drunk. Or high."

"Just had a little wine." Jayleen snorted.

Evan's hands tightened on the steering wheel, which protested with a squeak, but he didn't say a word.

Michelle clenched her fist near her side and fought to calm her voice. "Where are you?"

"Hotel?" Something dropped and Jayleen giggled. "Somewhere nice with clean towels. Big ones."

Could be anywhere. Michelle bit her lip and calculated the best way to find Jayleen. "I'd like to see those towels, too. Where are you? I could come and visit."

"I'm in Washington—away from Portland now, just in case. You should come and bring more wine." Jayleen yawned loudly. "I'm gonna make us both rich." Something else dropped and then the phone clanked against the floor. It scraped. "Sorry about that. Dropped it. Wait a minute. You can't come until I sell the tablet. You'll take it away."

So much for playing it cool. Michelle shook her head. "Jayleen? You can't blackmail George because he doesn't have money like you want. He really doesn't. Plus, he's my friend and I can't let you do that to him."

"He can ne-negotiate." Jayleen hiccupped. "Besides, that ain't what I'm talking about."

Michelle looked at Evan, who'd turned toward the phone, his brow furrowed. "Mom?" Michelle tried a new tack. "Two guys broke into my apartment saying you owe money to them. I know you're in trouble. Let me help."

"I don't owe money. Now they owe me the money," Jayleen snapped. "You have no idea what has happened, but I'm going to cut you in, I promise. A little from George will tide me over until I get the big payment. Trust me. I'm finally going to give you something."

Evan's teeth ground together loud enough that Michelle winced. What the heck was her mother talking about?

None of this was making sense. "Mom. Where did you get my tablet?"

"Tablet? Oh. There are a couple of good pawnshops east of Portland that I know about. They sell everything, and I figured that idiot would know about those places, too. It was kind of easy to find," Jayleen murmured, sounding like she was coming down from the wine and ready to sleep.

Apparently Michelle hadn't been given the names of all of the seedy pawnshops in the city. "I'll pay you for the tablet."

"Not like that famous George guy will," Jayleen countered. "I'll be in touch." She disengaged the call.

"This is crazy." Michelle slapped her leg. "What the heck do I do now?"

Evan took her phone, glanced at the screen, and then brought his phone to his ear. "Ian? Yeah. I need you to trace a number for me." He rattled off Jayleen's cell phone number. He paused and listened, and then his face cleared and he grinned. "That's great. It's about time you visited your dad. Yeah. Have your guys in Seattle do it. Thanks." He clicked off.

Michelle set her phone back into her purse. "Ian?"

"Yeah. Ian Brodie, a buddy who owns a private detective firm in Seattle, but he's home outside of Spokane, visiting the family ranch. He'll get the information for us." Evan turned and patted her hand, covering it with warmth and reassurance. "Don't worry. We'll find Jayleen."

Hopefully in time to spare George from having to pay.

Evan's phone buzzed, and he lifted it to his ear. "Boldon." He paused. "Anything else? Okay. Thanks, and keep me posted. I appreciate it." He clicked off and looked her way. "That was the Portland police. Charlie the intruder is awake and refuses to talk. Lawyered up right away."

Her chin dropped. "Well. Guess we have no idea who's after me, then."

Evan grimaced. "Not until we find Jayleen. For now, let's grab dinner and head north, since that's where she said she was, anyway."

North. To Evan's place. Her curiosity reared up and she tried to concentrate on the rainy dusk outside the car. Sleeping in the other room from him the night before had been more like *not* sleeping and thinking way too much about his hard and very able body.

Another night so close to him? A woman could only take so much.

He sped up and glanced her way. "You're flushed. What are you thinking about?"

"Cats," she murmured. "Definitely thinking of getting a cat."

Chapter Six

Michelle slowly awoke as Evan drove into Washington State, where the spring storm increased in force, making visibility difficult.

Evan's phone finally dinged, and he answered it, his chin lifting as he listened for about a minute. "Excellent. Thanks. Bye." He handed the phone over to Michelle. "Use Google Maps and find the Trailblazer Motel, would you?"

She sat up, groggy from a short nap. "Sure." She did so and read the results. "It's an hour and a half to the east. Is that where Jayleen is?"

He nodded. "Yep. We'll have to backtrack a little, but this is important, right?"

"Crucial." She couldn't let George down, and she needed to finish her comic. "If we found Jayleen, whoever is after her might have done the same thing."

"Affirmative." Evan switched lanes on the interstate so he could exit and circle around. "When we get there, I'm lead."

No problem. He was the guy with the gun and knew how to use it. "Fine by me," she murmured, wrapping her arms around her torso and trying to clear her head. Man, she needed some sleep. "How are your ribs?"

"Fine. The cut wasn't deep and is just a nuisance. I stopped bleeding a while ago." He didn't seem overly concerned about it.

What kind of injuries had he endured through the years that a knife to the rib cage was more of an annoyance than anything else? They'd gone such different ways in their lives. "Did you ever track your uncle down?" She remembered from their childhood that his uncle had raised him for a while after his parents had died, but then had become ill and had to give him to the state.

"Yeah. He died," Evan said quietly. "I don't remember much about him, to be honest. He was there and then not and that's the end of it." His tone was a little too matter-of-fact.

She reached out instinctively and grasped his hand, which was resting between them. "You're not alone."

He turned, those piercing blue eyes pinning her. "I haven't felt alone since I arrived at Miss A's. We have her, our friends from there, and I have my teammates. Now I have a whole town, one I hope you like."

Of course she'd like his town. That was the problem. "You can't seriously think you're going to stay in one place, Evan. It's not you."

His grin was somehow sweet with a hint of rueful. "After nearly getting blown up, a guy changes a little. Even a guy like me."

"Blown up?" Her heart rate kicked up.

He shrugged. "Close enough, and that's all I can say. It's in the past."

The rain splattered harder, spitting pieces of hail. He released her hand to use both of his on the steering wheel. "We might need to pull over."

She clasped her hands together and stared out at the nearly empty interstate. "Let's get as far as we can." Then she was quiet, humming along with the radio and letting him concentrate on the road. Every once in a while, she'd glance at the map on the phone and give him updates.

Finally, they pulled off the road to a nice area with multiple hotels, restaurants, gas stations, and a shopping mall. She sat up as he drove into the parking area of the Trailblazer Motel, which was two stories tall with wooden sides adorned with stone. "Stay here." He reached in the glove box for his gun and badge, leaving the engine running as he ducked into the rain and ran toward the front door. Seconds later, he was out of sight.

She looked around at the various cars in the parking lot but had no clue what Jayleen was driving these days. An old VW bug was parked away from the other cars; maybe that was hers?

Evan exited the motel and ran for the truck, jumping inside and turning the wheel. "She's in room twenty-four on the first floor around the building." He maneuvered past the other vehicles and parked in front of the clearly marked room, scouting the area. Few vehicles and no people were in the drizzling rain. He stopped the engine.

Michelle slipped out of the truck, shivering in the rain, and ran toward the door with Evan right behind her.

He reached in front of her and twisted the knob, which gave easily. "Step away from the door." He gently moved her to the side and rushed inside, going low with his gun out.

Michelle turned to see an empty room with wine bottles lined up on the counter next to a phone.

Evan swore and strode through the room, looking in the bathroom, shower, and beneath the bed. "There are no clothes or anything else. She's gone."

Michelle pushed wet hair out of her eyes, her stomach sinking. "She could be anywhere."

"Anywhere within three hours," he agreed, striding to a plain looking phone and picking it up. "Maybe we can find out what she's up to by going through this burner."

Doubtful. Jayleen had plenty of experience hiding things from the cops.

Michelle walked back outside the room. "All right. Where to now?"

Evan followed her, his gaze intense. "Nowhere. We both need sleep, and I got us a room on the second floor."

She blinked, and her body stilled. Then it warmed. Then it chilled. Then a whole lot of warmth and want and need that she so couldn't handle right now swept through her, making her voice unsteady. "A room?"

"Yeah, Peaches. Until we find the guys after you, I'm not leaving you alone for a second." His low rumble drifted easily through the sound of the rain.

Okay. She could handle this. The whole-body shiver that took her called her a liar.

This was hell. Pure, hot, devastating hell. Evan remained unmoving beneath the covers in his bed, all too aware that Michelle was in the next bed. Why did he get two queen beds? He'd been offered a king, but he'd wanted to be a gentleman.

Screw that.

Finally, he rolled over to face her, light from the outside street lamp glowing through the thin curtains and providing plenty of visibility. "Sorry we couldn't find anything on Jayleen's phone." The thing had been wiped clean.

"My friends in Seattle and Raider's contacts in DC are looking for her. We'll find her."

"I know," Michelle mumbled.

Not enough. He cleared his throat. "Are you still thinking of getting a cat?"

She rolled over on her bed, her hair flopping over her face. "That's the worst come-on you've ever used."

No, it wasn't. "Remember when I offered you peppermint schnapps and promised it'd make you want to get naked? That was worse." Although it had ended with them skinny-dipping in the river to cool off and then making love until dawn beneath the stars. He'd been smart enough to bring a blanket.

"Fair enough." She sighed, her pretty blue eyes clouded. "What are we doing?"

Not what he wanted to be doing, that was for sure. Guess it was time to get it all out in the open. "We broke up because of the uncertainty of my job for both of us. That's over now."

She swallowed, the delicate line of her neck moving. "I don't believe you."

Ouch. Jesus. Okay. For some reason, he hadn't expected that statement from her. "This is different from last time." The second he heard the words, they hit him in the chest. How many times had she heard that exact phrase from her drug-riddled mother as she'd once again gotten clean? Briefly. Another thought slammed him. "The physical therapist? Are you more serious than you said?" The man had a stable job; that was for sure.

"I don't think we need to talk about Mike," she said.

That wasn't an answer. Definitely not the answer he wanted.

"What do you want?" she murmured.

"You." It was the damn truth. He'd always wanted her and would always want her. It had taken him a couple of years to get straight and healthy, and at the end, somewhere deep inside, he had known she was his goal. He'd also known that some goals were out of reach.

Michelle, at the moment, was way out of reach.

The proof, as Miss A always said, was in the pudding. He didn't have pudding, but he had time to convince her. Time to reassure himself that their past wasn't just a dream he'd created to survive some horrible situations. "I could make you forget Mike," he drawled.

She pursed her pretty lips. "That's an immature challenge."

Yeah, it was. "You gonna take me up on it or not?" He held his breath, wondering how much of the kid she'd been was still inside her. They'd grown up together, and sometimes, those urges didn't completely dissipate. Man, they'd had fun falling in love. That time was the best in his life, without question. "Well, Peaches? Are you scared?"

Temptation glimmered in her intelligent eyes. Yeah. She was tempted. "You're a moron," she whispered.

That was not a no. Wasn't a yes, either. But definitely not a denial. "Come on. Don't you want to see if it's the same between us? Out of curiosity, if nothing else?" He couldn't make the first move —it had to be hers. But he could tempt her from across the room.

"I am curious," she murmured.

His body went from interested to full-on aroused in a flash. "What are you going to do about it?" His voice had gone hoarse.

Keeping his gaze, she slowly glided from her bed and moved to his.

Holy hell, this was not happening. He began to move.

"No." She held up a hand. "You stay right under the covers—all of you."

He held still, watching her while his entire body fought to jump up and grab her. "No problem."

Her smile was one of a siren—dangerous and thrilling. Placing a knee on his bed, she shifted over until she straddled him, her knees on either side of his waist. She looked like an avenging angel bent on destruction. "Am I hurting you?"

Oh, she was killing him. "My ribs are fine," he rumbled, not feeling anything but the ache in his groin. For her.

"Good." She set her hands on either side of his head and leaned down, her hair falling over his shoulder. The scent of wild lilacs wafted from her.

"You're playing with fire, baby," he whispered, knowing he was the one who had challenged her. Maybe challenged both of them.

Her tongue flicked out to lick her pink bottom lip. "I've always liked fire, and you know that." Her movements were too slow, but she finally lowered her head more, that lip brushing his. "Maybe I'll make *you* forget every other woman in existence."

"You already have," he said, his lips moving against hers.

Her sharp intake of breath nearly did him in. Instead, he drew on every ounce of training to remain still.

"Well?" It was shocking his voice remained level, albeit rough.

"Okay," she whispered, her lips finally curving against his in a seeking kiss. Tentative, intriguing, soft, she kissed him. Shocking desire spiraled through his entire body. Murmuring, deepening the kiss, she pressed down on his aching cock, awakening him from a sleep he hadn't realized he was in.

Then she lifted her head, just slightly, a pleased smile curving her mouth. Oh, she knew exactly what she was doing. "That was nice."

Nice? Oh, hell no. "My turn." When she didn't object, he lifted one hand and slid it through her curly hair, taking his time to enjoy the soft texture, the pure pleasure of finally touching her again. Then he pulled her down, his other hand cupping the side of her jaw. She drew in her breath, and he kissed her.

Full and deep, he took control, holding her tight and delving into heaven. A moan whispered up from her chest, filling him, prodding him on. He released her jaw to run one hand down her side, gripping her hip and settling her against his aching cock.

She gasped and rubbed herself over him, returning his kiss with an urgency he'd forgotten. So wild and free.

Finally, she wrenched her mouth away, gasping for breath, her body all but vibrating against him.

Out of instinct, he rubbed her lower back, trying to ease her. "It's okay, Peaches." Was that his voice? It sounded like he had eaten a bucket of broken glass. "Take a deep breath."

She did so, perched on top of him, her hardened nipples pressed against her T-shirt. "I'm not ready for this."

Damn it.

"Not again." She moved to get off him, and he let her, staying quiet until she'd settled back into her own bed.

His entire body hurt like he'd been run through a wood chipper. He turned toward her. "I'm home for good this time, Michelle. You'll see."

She didn't answer.

He cleared his throat. The only way he could get through the night was to go for a run—a long one. He moved from the bed. "I need to jog. Nobody knows you're here, but I'm leaving my gun, just in case." He moved for his bag and running shoes.

"I'm sorry, Evan," she whispered.

He turned to face her, his chest settling. "I'm not." He was a marine, and he could handle any campaign. Even one for the stubborn artist who still held his heart. "This is just the beginning, baby. Trust me."

Chapter Seven

An unfulfilled ache bothered Michelle for the entire drive north, but she still enjoyed watching the city turn to farmland, forest, and wilderness for the next several hours. As the rain disappeared and the sun began to shine down, highlighting roaming cows in pastures, her muscles began to loosen. Why in the world had she kissed Evan the night before?

Curiosity, maybe. Perhaps to show them both that she could. If anything, Evan was a better kisser than he'd been before, all man now. Yeah, she'd forgotten about not only Mike but every other man when kissing Evan. She and Mike had just started dating and there was no commitment yet, but she still wasn't comfortable dating more than one person at a time. It just wasn't her.

Could she take the risk with Evan again? Plus, she'd always felt like she'd let him down, even though he'd told her to move on. Maybe it was because she never had truly moved on.

She was older and stronger now. Maybe she could take a second chance with him, even knowing that he might not return from a mission. He'd been right the other night. No matter what, Miss A would always be there for them, and so would the other kids they'd bonded with in her home.

That was family. If something happened to Evan, she would still have family.

Evan drove along the country road, and soon houses and then small businesses lined the way. It was approaching dinnertime, and her stomach complained. She perked up as they crossed under an archway of what looked like deer antlers.

"Welcome to Doe City," he said, turning right and heading down what appeared to be Main Street as he rolled down his window.

Quaint little shops lined the way, some built of brick and others of painted wood. Several folks on the street waved as they passed, and he waved back. He pulled into the parking area of a larger brick building. "Do you mind if we pop by the office?"

"Um, no. That's fine." Had she fallen down the rabbit hole, or what? "You're the sheriff in Doe City."

"Yep." He got out of the truck and stretched his back as she took her time jumping out and walking around to him.

There was no way Evan Boldon could be content in this sleepy town. Almost in a daze, she let him take her hand and lead her up the steps and through the front door to a comfortable waiting room facing a long reception desk manned by one older woman.

In a nanosecond, the woman's gaze dropped to their joined hands, her smile widened, and she stood with her hand extended over the desk. "Well, hello. You must be Michelle."

Michelle stumbled but moved forward to shake hands. "Um, yes. Hi?"

"I'm Verna Templeton, the station manager. It's a nice way of saying receptionist, and the title came with a handy raise." She pumped Michelle's hand, her purple eyeshadow a shade lighter than her bright shirt. Streaks of matching purple threaded through her thick gray hair, complementing her purple lipstick. She had to be in her early seventies, but she had a nice firm grip despite her small hand. "The sheriff said he had to help a friend named Michelle, but it's nice to see you holding hands."

Evan sighed from behind her. "I don't suppose we could keep this between us, just for a few days?"

"Days?" Delight filled the older woman's brown eyes. "Of course, Sheriff. My lips are sealed." She eyed the cell phone on the desk.

"Right." Evan reclaimed Michelle's hand and tugged her through a doorway. "I do like the purple theme, though," he called back.

"Next week is green," Verna yelled.

"She's nice," Michelle mumbled, trying to get a grip on reality.

Evan snorted. "Listen. We have about ten minutes to check in and get out of here before people start descending on the station. I'm sure Verna is already calling folks."

It was that big a deal that the sheriff was holding her hand? She tugged it free and tucked her hand in her pocket as they passed two offices and then entered a much larger one with a view of a creek out back. Papers covered the desk and were tacked to a board on the wall, and the entire space smelled like Evan.

"Hey, boss." A portly man with gray hair and a thick beard strolled their way, wearing a brown sheriff's uniform.

"Hi," Evan said. "Michelle Peach, meet Deputy Francis O'Donnell."

"Call me Frankie," the deputy said, holding out a hand

to shake. He glanced back down the hallway. "You have about eight minutes, you know."

"I know," Evan said. "Anything interesting going on?"

Frankie tucked his thumbs in his wide belt. "I delivered a baby yesterday on the side of McKlerny Road."

Evan grinned. "Melissa Jordan had her baby? I chose girl in the drawing."

"Nope. Was a boy," Frankie said, smacking his lips. "I chose boy *and* the correct date. So, drinks are on me."

"Where am I?" Michelle murmured.

Evan chuckled. "Let's get you home, Peaches. Frank? Call me if you need me."

"Sure thing, Sheriff." Frank looked at his watch. "Five minutes."

Evan grabbed Michelle's hand. "Back door. Let's make a run for it."

Who was this man? Michelle stumbled behind him, trying to reconcile this new Evan with the wild kid and then determined marine she'd known long ago. This guy seemed to fit here.

She'd have to take a look around his apartment and see just how settled he'd become. Was he doing this for her? If so, was she holding him back? They emerged into the parking lot. "This life? Is it what you want?" she asked.

He lifted her into the truck and ran around to the other side. "I'm here, aren't I?" He drove away from the station quickly, heading toward the other side of town. "I always wanted to settle down someday, and now that I can, I like it here." He waved at a couple of kids playing catch on a front lawn. "One of my teammates is from here; we visited once, and I liked it. He's still deployed."

She didn't want to sound self-involved, but she had to ask. "Is this for me? You said you were going to track me down. You didn't give up your life, the one you loved, for me, did you?"

He glanced her way, his eyes bluer than any sky she'd ever seen. "You'd be worth it, Peaches. But I want this, too."

Was he telling the truth? She wasn't sure.

Evan was known for having nerves of steel, but now, his palms were almost sweating. Not quite, but close enough. Would Michelle like his place? He drove out of town through forests filled with pine, tamarack, and spruce, by a windy river, and finally down the newly paved road to his cabin.

Michelle stilled. "You live here?"

"Yeah." He couldn't help the pride in his voice. The hand-sawed log cabin sprawled along a curve in the river with stunning views of mountains on three sides. "There are four bedrooms, five bathrooms, a couple of living areas, a couple of offices, and a wide porch out back." He looked over at her. "One of the offices faces the west with big windows. It'd be perfect for a studio."

She paled.

Ah, crap. He'd pushed too hard. "I bought the land and had the house built because I wanted it, Michelle. This is exactly what I want, even if you and I go our separate ways for good." Of course, his perfect picture, when he'd allowed himself to dream, had included her. He had to go slow here.

She gulped and stepped from the truck, waiting until he crossed around to her. "How could you afford this?"

He chuckled. "One of the guys in my unit is a financial wizard. I gave him most of every paycheck I had, and he invested wisely. Very."

Apparently. This had to be a dream. She followed him

up the long stone path, across a wide porch, and into a comfortable-looking living room with floor-to-ceiling windows facing a stunning view of the river. The sofas in front of the stone fireplace held colorful pillows.

Wait a minute. "You said you weren't dating anybody." Something hurt inside Michelle. Deep.

He frowned. "I'm not. Why?"

She breathed in and out, not having a good reason to be upset but struggling anyway. "There is no way you decorated this. You wear the same color clothes so you don't have to match anything."

Evan winced. "It's that obvious?"

"Yes." Her stomach settled.

His ears turned a little red. "Fine. Verna helped me with the decorating." Evan shut the door behind them. "There are splotches of color everywhere, but I think it works. Maybe. Not sure."

Oh. Of course. The colors were all over the place, just like Verna, but the scheme worked. Definitely. "I don't know what to say."

"You don't have to say anything," Evan said. "How about I grill some steaks, and we can eat out on the deck? Maybe come up with a game plan on how to find Jayleen?" He led her into a sparkling kitchen with dark granite countertops. "Do me a favor and get out stuff for a salad, would you?"

She moved as if in a dream, grateful for the distraction. Evan Boldon was eating salad? Like *salad*, salad? What universe had she dropped into? Darkness began to fall as she mixed the lettuce with other veggies and he grilled steaks. They ate quietly on the peaceful deck, and even though she was still worried about Jayleen, she couldn't help but relax a little bit. "Your home is lovely, Evan."

He glanced up from his steak and smiled, looking like the carefree kid he'd once been. "Thanks."

This felt good. Too good? She set her napkin aside and decided to enjoy the moment. Why not? She grasped her wineglass, swirled the rich cabernet around and watched it glimmer. Her first glass had already warmed her, and this second one was finally relaxing her completely. "Thanks for dinner."

"Sure." His smile froze and he turned his head slowly, scanning the trees by the river.

"What?" She couldn't see anything but darkness and trees, but her heartbeat quickened in response to his expression. She set down the glass.

He grasped his steak knife, twisted it around in front of his chest, and stood, facing the trees. "Get inside. Now."

"Gun beats knife." A gigantic man, tight with muscle and wearing a leather jacket, strode out of the trees with a gun in his hand and a dog at his side. He had short hair, a faded scar from his temple to his jaw, and topaz brown eyes.

The German shepherd kept his gaze on Evan's knife and moved with strength and purpose, the fur on his back standing up as if he was just waiting for the command to strike.

Evan gestured her behind him. "Start backing up, and I'll cover you," he hissed.

The dog barked once.

Michelle stood, her lungs seizing, and moved backward toward the sliding glass door.

Then a white kitten popped his head out of the man's jacket pocket, one damaged ear flicking back and forth as his pretty eyes blinked sleepily.

Michelle composed herself. The man had a kitten in his pocket?

The guy sighed. "Kat, dude. You totally take the fierce out of my entrance." He tucked the gun in the back of his waist and leaned to the side to better see Michelle beyond Evan. "You Michelle?"

She nodded, a lump in her throat.

"You okay? Not harmed?" he asked.

Energy vibrated off Evan, and his stance didn't relax. "Who the hell are you?"

The guy's eyebrows rose in surprise. "Oh, sorry. Forgot that part. I'm Clarence Wolfe. Call me Wolfe. Not Clarence. Don't like that." He stroked the dog's head. "This is Roscoe, and Kat is in my pocket. Not because I make him but because that's where he likes to be." Wolfe looked down at the kitten. "Of course, there are goldfish in there, so that might be why." He looked up. "Crackers not bait."

Evan's muscles bunched. "Inside, Michelle. Now."

"Wait a minute. Wolfe from Raider's unit?" she asked, stepping to the side. Raider had mentioned the man but not the nuttiness.

"That's me," Wolfe said cheerfully. "Raider sent me to your place and I saw the damaged door, so I hustled up here to make sure Evan was okay. I was hoping you'd be here, too. I can't take Raider off his case, so I haven't called him yet. If you weren't here, I was gonna, though."

Evan relaxed slightly. "Call off your dog."

Wolfe's expression cleared. "Oh yeah. Roscoe, at ease."

The dog sat and cocked his head. Man, he was beautiful, his markings perfect. His gaze scanned the deck and then stopped on the table.

"No!" Wolfe grabbed for him, but Roscoe was too fast. He leaped over the edge of the deck, right over a rose bush, and landed on Michelle's vacant seat. In less than a second, he jumped onto the table and stuck his whole snout in her wineglass, sucking down the liquid loudly before turning and finishing Evan's. Then Roscoe licked his lips and eyed the steak remaining on her plate. With a doggy shrug, he gulped the entire thing.

Evan turned and gaped at the dog. "Seriously?"

Wolfe sighed and strode forward. "He has a drinking problem and is way too fast. I should've checked out the table before releasing him." He walked up the steps. "Bad, Roscoe."

Michelle could swear the dog rolled his eyes.

Wolfe clapped Evan on the back, and the sound echoed back to the trees. "So. Which room is mine?"

Chapter Eight

A nightmare jolted Evan wide awake. Or maybe that was thunder. Rain pummeled the roof. He sat up and rubbed his eyes, his heart still pounding. Nope. Definitely a nightmare. Silently, he slipped from his bed and drew on sweats and tennis shoes. Michelle was in the guest bedroom; she'd be safe with Wolfe in the house if Evan took a run.

Raider had called earlier from a burner phone, having to whisper but needing to make sure Michelle was okay. Once Evan had reassured him, he'd said that Wolfe might be a little off, but he was a dedicated soldier and excellent backup and Evan could trust him.

Evan trusted Raider's judgment, always had.

He quietly made his way down the stairs and out the front door, shutting it quietly and hurrying almost eagerly into the rain. The water drenched him, instantly cooling the unreal desire he'd been fighting since seeing Michelle again. He stretched his torso one way and then the other.

"I was going running, too," said a low voice from near his truck.

He moved forward. "Wolfe?"

"Yeah." Water ran down the soldier's hard face, and his eyes glowed with torment. "You need to run?"

Evan took in Raider's friend, noting his quick breathing and dilated pupils. "Not as bad as you seem to. Nightmares?"

"Always." Wolfe looked back at the quiet home. "You think they ever go away?"

"Probably not, but I think they get easier to live with," Evan said, his senses on alert. "Running helps."

Wolfe nodded. "Yeah. I run a lot." He turned back around. "I can stay on the porch to protect her while you go."

She was Evan's to protect. "No. You go ahead." He pointed toward the trees. "There's a nice trail along the river where you'll find some peace."

Wolfe's smile lacked humor. "There's no peace, man. But I do like a good run. Kat and Roscoe are sleeping in my room and will be fine, although make sure your booze is locked up."

He'd already taken care of that. "Have a good run."

"Thanks." Then Wolfe was gone. Silently and surprisingly fast.

Evan shook his head and moved up the stairs and out of the rain, slipping back inside the house.

Michelle hovered at the bottom edge of the carpeted stairs, looking delectable in a pink tank-top and matching shorts. "I heard voices. Is everything okay?" Her hair was mussed and her eyes sleepy, and she was the most desirable woman he'd ever seen.

"No. Hasn't been since we broke up." His hair dripped water onto his bare chest, but he didn't care.

Her chin lifted. "Evan."

It hurt to be around her and not with her. It was that plain and simple. "I went outside to go running, but Wolfe beat me to it. Go back to bed, Peaches. We'll talk in the morning."

"What if I want to talk now?" She reached out, her palm caressing across his upper chest, spreading droplets of the rain.

Heat slammed into his balls. "I don't want to talk."

She took the last step down and placed her other hand on him, looking up. "I don't want to talk, either."

Blood roared through his veins, pounding in his ears. Was she saying what he thought she was? "What? Why?" Now he couldn't even speak in complete sentences.

"I can't sleep, either." She leaned in and kissed his chest. "Last night. That kiss. It was good, and I want to know if my memories are real. If we feel as good as I think we did." She wiped water down his bare arms, tracing each ridge and valley of his biceps. "I've wondered all of these years. Haven't you?"

"Yeah." This was too good to be true. But if he had her and she left him, it might kill him. Death might be worth it, though. He brushed his knuckles along the smooth line of her stubborn jaw. "Are you sure?"

"Yes. I don't want to fight this any longer. I think about you a lot and I dream of you sometimes." When she decided to be honest, she opened herself with a vengeance, always had. It was one of the things he loved about her. "Being with you the last few days has brought everything back, and well, I just want you."

"I want you, too." For more than one night, but he didn't want to push her again.

Her smile was stunning. "I know, Evan." Levering herself up, she nipped his collarbone, her lips soft and her teeth sharp. "I learned to take what I could with you a long time ago, and right now, we have this night and maybe a few more. Staying apart when we don't want to is silly."

His body rioted; he tried to concentrate on her words, but they blurred together. There was only her soft touch on his skin. He ducked and swept her into his arms, carrying her quickly up the stairs, her soft laugh tunneling inside him and landing in his heart, where she'd always been. He walked by Wolfe's open door, where the dog was lying in the entry, nose on paws, eyes somber. Waiting for Wolfe? Or judging Evan? Evan grinned and kept going, carrying Michelle into the master bedroom to set her gently on the bed.

"I've missed being carried by you," she said, her eyes luminous in the darkened room.

"Any time," he said, meaning it.

She reached for him and pulled him down. "Thank you for coming for me when I needed help."

His bare chest met her hardened nipples, and he groaned. "Tell me this isn't a thank-you."

She grinned. "Please. I'm not *that* grateful."

Thank God. He kissed her, letting her sweet taste go right to his head. "It's been a while, Peaches."

She tugged her hands through his wet hair, spraying water. "Is that your way of saying we're going to go fast this time?" Her voice had dropped to breathy, brushing across his skin.

"I'll make sure you're ready," he promised, kissing down her neck to lick the hollow of her collarbone.

She moaned and tugged his hair back, shooting erotic pain down his spine. "Honey? I've been ready since you burst through my door the other night."

Michelle had completely lost her mind, but nothing inside her cared. She was in a cozy home in the middle of the woods during a storm with Evan Boldon for the night. As much as she'd like to blame her actions on inevitability, the truth was she wanted him. Always had and probably always would.

Why not take the moment and hold it close for years to come?

His easy grace lifting and carrying her up the stairs to the bedroom emphasized their differences, only increasing her desire. He was all strength and muscle, and she was definitely soft. She'd never been a small girl, but he made her feel feminine, even delicate. Protected and cared for.

There was nothing wrong with enjoying that feeling.

Until it was swept away by a more powerful force when he set her down and kissed her. Then there was only Evan. The hint of wildness always in him was fully unleashed in the bedroom, engulfing her in a fire just as hot, if not hotter, than it had been before.

Kissing her deeply, he somehow managed to grasp her hips and move them both farther up the bed until her head rested on a pillow. He kicked off his shoes and they thumped on the floor. She ran her hands along his shoulders and arms, wiping away the rain and humming at the feel of solid muscle warming her palms. There were new scars, some long and some round, that she'd explore later. She wanted to know everything that had happened to him the last six years. Everything.

He released her mouth, pressing kisses along her jaw to nip at her earlobe. "Ah, baby. I've missed you," he rumbled.

Her blood heated and her nipples hardened. "Me too." She dug her nails into his shoulders, gently scraping down his marvelous chest. So much power right above her.

He grinned and yanked off her top with one smooth motion. His eyes flared and hunger replaced the amusement. His touch was gentle as he brushed his fingers across her breasts, sending tingles straight to her core. "I've missed these."

Even aroused, laughter bubbled through her. "You can't miss breasts."

"Wanna bet?" He ducked his head and captured one nipple in his heated mouth, flicking with his tongue.

Electricity jarred through her and she gasped, arching against him. "Okay, maybe you can," she murmured, her eyes shutting from the raw pleasure.

He chuckled, the vibrations spreading beyond her chest.

It was almost too much. She reached down and shoved at the waistband of his sweats, pushing them down as far as she could. He lifted and helped her, pushing them all the way off. As he settled against her, his cock hard and throbbing against her core, her eyes almost rolled back in her head.

Thunder ripped apart the sky outside and rain smashed pine needles into the windows, not coming close to matching the storm brewing inside her.

She needed him. Now. "Evan," she murmured, scraping his flanks, his superb ass.

"I know." He kissed his way down her heated abdomen, his thumbs smoothly removing her panties. He kissed her right on her clit.

She couldn't breathe, so much need swept her. She craved. "Evan. I don't need—"

"I do." He licked her, knowing exactly how much pressure to apply. His tongue was rough, and when he slipped one finger inside her, she detonated as if she'd been on edge for a week. The orgasm hit hard, rolling through her, stealing her breath. She stiffened and let the energy take her, closing her eyes against the onslaught of scalding pleasure.

When she came down, he chuckled against her, his breath warming her even more.

That was so fast, it was almost embarrassing. But she didn't have time for awkwardness. Right now, she was empty, and she needed him. She grabbed his ear and tugged him up, reaching down for his length. Holy crap on a double cracker. She hadn't enlarged him in her memories.

The guy was huge.

She stroked him, and he jerked against her hand. "What's the hurry?" He sounded pained.

God, he felt good against her hand. "We can go slow later," she whispered, licking along his strong jugular.

"Good plan." He reached to the side and pulled open the bed-table drawer, smoothly extracting a condom. A quick rip with his teeth, and he freed it, reaching down to put it in place.

She widened her trembling thighs and curved her hands over his broad shoulders, waiting until he paused, his blue-green eyes devastating. "You sure?" she asked before he could.

His lips curved. "Yeah. You?"

"Definitely." Oh, it was probably a mistake, but who cared? This felt right and incredibly good.

He entered her slowly, stretching her, giving her time to take all of him. She sucked in her breath several times when pain and pleasure mixed, completely overtaken by him. Finally, a zillion years later, he was fully inside her. Filling her completely, beyond what she remembered.

Balancing himself on his elbow, he pulled out and gently pushed back in, hitting so many nerves on the way she could only gasp.

"You're ready," he murmured, reaching down to grip her hip.

Anticipation licked through her with heated flames.

She nodded and lifted her knees, allowing him to go even deeper. He groaned and then started to move.

Hard.

Fast.

Wild.

Evan took her, pressing her into the bed, kissing her deeply. She kissed him back, caught up in the vortex of passion he created so easily.

Sparks uncoiled inside her, and she fought them, wanting this to last forever. He shifted his hips, caressing her clit, and she cried out, falling over the cliff as the entire room flashed bright and then went dark. The waves ripped through her, raw and deep, taking her breath as she tightened around him, prolonging her ecstasy until lightning flashed behind her closed eyelids.

He pounded harder, his face a fierce mask, making it last even longer, until she went limp with a soft sigh.

His head dropped, he pressed a hard kiss to the crook of her neck, and then his powerful body shuddered as he came.

Whoa. She gentled her hold and caressed his back, her eyelids growing heavy.

He withdrew and did something, she didn't care what, with the condom before gathering her close and cuddling her to him.

Words. Should one of them say something? She could barely think much less speak.

His phone buzzed, and it took a moment for her to recognize the sound.

Swearing softly, he grabbed it from the table. "What?" he barked. "Shots fired? You sure?" He listened. "All right. I'll be there in a minute." Kissing her softly on the head, he rolled from the bed to get dressed.

"Shots?" She sat up, her brain still fuzzy.

"Yeah, baby. It'll be fine. I'll make sure Wolfe is here and then I'll run in to work." He quickly dressed and then was gone.

She shivered in the chilly air and pushed her way beneath the covers. He might not be a marine any longer, but he was a cop, and that was a dangerous job, even in a small town. Could she handle the uncertainty this time? Was there a "this time"? She'd promised him a night, and he hadn't pushed for more.

Her body felt satiated and sore already, yet she wanted him again. The door opened a crack and a plaintive meow echoed before Kat leaped onto the bed and tiptoed his way up her chest to rub against her chin.

Surprising tears pricked her eyes. She sniffed. "You know? I'm thinking of getting a cat."

The kitten purred.

Chapter Nine

Evan stared through the jail bars of one of three cells in the basement of his station, beyond pissed. "You two assholes have no idea what a problem you created for me tonight." Yeah, he'd seen the panic in Michelle's eyes. Why had he said "shots fired" out loud?

Ezekiel Devlin shuffled his size fourteen feet and hitched up his overalls, his eyes bloodshot and his thick gray hair mussed up. "Ah, shit, Sheriff. We're sorry. We was just goofin' around."

His twin brother nodded from his seat on the bench and then belched, smoothing down his gray flannel shirt. "We got into the moonshine a little bit, and then it was just a contest. I won." He rubbed his square jaw, the liver spots on his hand darker than they had been the year before. "Nailed that old birch tree like it jumped in front of me."

The two farmers were usually well behaved, but once in a while, they were just morons. Evan snarled. "How many times have I told you not to fire your shotguns within city limits?" True, they had been in the forest, but there were still homes nearby, and the young Jordan family, a mile away, didn't need to hear shotguns being fired in the middle of the night.

"Twice," Ezekiel muttered just as Sonny said, "Five times."

Evan pinched the bridge of his nose. "I'm gonna let Louise charge you two this time." The prosecutor had mentioned wanting to really teach them a lesson last time.

Sonny's eyes widened. "Come on, Sheriff. We only aimed at a tree that was almost outside of city limits, which aren't designated well, anyway. We're sorry we interrupted your night with your new lady."

Ezekiel nodded. "Heard that Michelle is a real looker. You could go back to her now. It's barely light outside."

For Pete's sake. There were no secrets in a small town, were there? Giving the men another look, he turned and strode up the steps to the main hallway, where he entered his office and sat at his desk. He liked his job, and it wasn't usually dangerous, but as a cop, there were always risks. More and more people visited town, drank, and floated on the river in the summer, and he'd busted several with drugs the previous year.

He'd dated a psychologist briefly once, and she'd said he had a protector's nature, whatever that was. Probably meant he was supposed to be a marine or a cop; he couldn't imagine doing anything else.

Could Michelle handle the risk now? If not, could he find another calling?

Not that she'd agreed to anything more than a few nights. Apparently they had a talk coming, because guessing wasn't his style. First he had to figure out exactly what he wanted and what to say. He glanced at the cell phone on his desk and then dialed, figuring if Raider couldn't talk, he wouldn't answer.

"Hey, brother. You okay?" Raider answered on the first

ring, the Southern accent he allowed few people to hear in full force.

"Yeah." Relief filled Evan. Raider's last year at Miss A's had been Evan's first, but they'd bonded quickly and stayed in touch regularly. "Sorry to bug you when you are undercover. Is it okay to talk?"

"Yep. I'm here at the office briefly but need to go back under tomorrow. Things are fine. What's going on with Michelle?"

Evan gave him the lowdown. "So Jayleen is out there, causing problems, and I don't know who's after Michelle yet."

Raider sighed. "I've had my guys trying to track Jayleen, and so far, no luck. My unit here isn't exactly in the good graces of the HDD, so I'm sure it's not a priority."

Evan had heard they were the misfits of the HDD, which he kind of liked. "I appreciate the attempt."

"I'm making the offer again, brother. You have a job here if you want it," Raider said. "It's exciting, which you like. We never know what's going to happen next."

"That's not me anymore, Raid. Plus, you wouldn't believe the excitement here." Somewhat true.

Raider cleared his throat. "Well? Why did you really call?"

Evan winced. "Michelle. I mean . . ."

"Be square with her. You're both all grown up now, and either it'll work or it won't. Depends how bad you two want it," Raider said.

Good advice, but not a lot of help. Fine. Evan could figure this out on his own. "By the way. Wolfe? Just how nuts is he?"

Raider chuckled. "The jury is out on that one. He's solid, and if you get in a bind, the guy can fight."

Well, at least that was something.

"But," Raider finished, "he's a total hound dog, and if you leave him alone with Michelle, he'll definitely make a move."

Wonderful. Just wonderful.

Michelle walked down the warm steps in her bare feet after having dressed in comfortable jeans and a pink sweater. Her hair was in a ponytail and she'd put on light makeup in case Evan had returned. The smell of coffee drew her to the kitchen, and she poured a cup before heading out to the back deck. The sun sparkled on the bluish river and was starting to dry the grass.

"Mornin'," Wolfe said as he leaned back in a wooden deck chair with his bare feet extended and crossed at the ankles, the dog snoring at his side. The soldier had dressed in a black T-shirt and ripped jeans, and in the daylight looked even deadlier than he had coming out of the darkened forest the night before.

"Morning." She self-consciously moved to the adjacent chair and sat, looking out at the river. "Pretty place."

"It really is." Wolfe dropped a hand to the dog's head and petted him gently. "Is Kat still sleeping?"

"Yeah. He's in my bed. I hope that's okay." She took a drink of the coffee and nearly spit it out before swallowing. "What's in this?"

Wolfe glanced over. "Oh. After I brewed it, I sweetened it a little. There was only syrup and sugar in the cupboard. No whipped cream or sprinkles, I'm sorry to say. Real tragedy, if you ask me."

Was he serious? She studied him, noting both intelligence and humor in his light brown eyes. "All right."

Wolfe looked back at the river. "I can go to town later and get better supplies."

"Speaking of which, you came from the direction of the river last night. Do you have a car somewhere?" The guy moved like a ghost.

He nodded. "Yeah. I went for a run last night and drove it back here. It's the rental in front of the house." He sipped his coffee with a happy hum.

Her face warmed. Hopefully Wolfe had been gone a long time on his run. She'd been pretty loud last night. Had he heard them? The idea of the burly soldier hearing her have sex burned her cheeks hotter.

He glanced over. "You okay?"

"Um, yeah. Sorry. Speaking of Kat, I was thinking of getting a kitten." Okay. She had to find a new excuse for her mind wandering.

"You really should." Wolfe stretched his neck. "I was telling you about my rental car. It's an SUV. I like states where you can rent an SUV instead of some tiny compact. Washington State seems okay, but didn't they legalize pot here?"

"Um, I think so?" She hadn't kept up with Washington State politics. "You like pot?"

"No. I have enough brain issues. They're finding daily pot intake leads to increased instances of schizophrenia. I have enough problems." He took another big gulp of his coffee, apparently well read-up on the brain.

She took another swallow, letting the warmth and sugar awaken her completely. "You ever make coffee for Raider? He likes it strong and dark with no sweets."

Wolfe chuckled. "His tastes have changed, then. He really likes sprinkles and extra caramel in his lattes now."

She doubted that, but arguing with the huge soldier seemed like a bad idea. "I haven't seen him for a while. How is my big brother?" Or the closest thing she had to one, anyway.

"Good. Undercover with the Irish Mob right now," Wolfe said.

She twisted toward him and her body chilled. "Are you joking?"

Wolfe turned her way. "Ah. Oh. That probably is a secret. Don't say anything, okay?"

She opened her mouth, but no words emerged. Raider was dealing with the mob? That couldn't be good. "Is he in danger?"

Wolfe rubbed his chin. "It's the mob."

Great. "He didn't say he was doing anything dangerous." She shook her head.

Wolfe grimaced. "Well, maybe when Evan joins the team, he can go undercover instead."

Michelle grew still and then turned to more fully face him. "Evan is joining Raider's federal team? The one dealing with the Irish Mob right now?"

Wolfe grimaced. "We defused a bunch of bombs last month. It's a good gig."

Oh, Evan had forgotten to mention that little fact. "I knew he wouldn't be happy in this small town." For a moment, just a moment, she'd allowed herself to dream.

Wolfe shrugged. "I don't know. Seems like a nice place. Beyond that, if you love somebody, you take them as is."

Love? Who had said anything about love? Michelle took a deep drink and coughed. "Some people don't want uncertainty all the time."

Wolfe chuckled, a low rumbling sound that had the dog's ears perking up. "All of life is uncertain. Doesn't matter what you do or choose, you have no clue what's around the corner. None of us do." His eyes twinkled.

"Though if you're mad at Evan, we could make him jealous. Wanna go back inside?"

She studied him, amusement tickling her. "That's the most half-hearted attempt at seduction I've ever heard."

His grin made his intimidating face almost charming. "Yeah, I figured I should at least make an effort, but truth be told, I think you and Evan look good together. Like two parts to a tactical knife."

Interesting. "Is that all?"

He rocked in the chair. "Yeah."

Oh, he was lying. She could tell. "You have a girl back in DC, Clarence Wolfe?"

"Nope." He rocked more, scratching the dog between the ears. "I have a friend, who happens to be a woman, who's driving me batshit right now because she takes too many chances as a journalist without decent backup. Dana and I are just friends, though, and that's all we can be."

Right. Man, people were clueless sometimes. She really needed to talk to Evan so they could figure themselves out. For now, at least she had something to concentrate on. "I think you like this Dana."

"I do," Wolfe agreed.

"Why can't you be more than friends? Is she married?"

"No. I'm on a mission, and it's not going to end well." He stopped rocking, his chest settling. "Plus, I'm not quite right, as I'm sure you've noticed. Been through a lot, including a head injury. I wasn't like most folks before that, anyway."

The way he stroked the dog showed gentleness and affection. "Don't sell yourself short. You have a dog and a cat that love you," she said, finishing the coffee and feeling an instant rush. There was no way Raider had taken to drinking anything this sweet.

Wolfe nodded. "The dog is actually owned by the leader of our unit, but the pooch is more like one of the gang, you know? Kat just adopted me for now because he likes my pocket. I'm sure he'll switch his allegiance to a pretty lady at some point."

Michelle's phone dinged, and she tugged it out of her back pocket, wincing at the number on the screen. She put it to her ear. "Um, hi, George. How is it going?"

"Well, your estranged mother has agreed to lower the amount to fifty thousand. The twit thinks I have a private plane I can show up in and then let her borrow." George's British accent had thickened and become more high pitched than usual. "I'm sympathetic to your plight, I mean, family is a disaster for everyone. However, if she uploads my work before release date, we're both screwed."

"I know." Michelle's temples started to pound. "Do you have the number she called you from?"

"I do." George rattled off the number, which was no doubt from a burner phone. "Better yet, I agreed to meet her at some private landing strip she found in Idaho, where they probably ship organic potatoes or whatever. Here are the coordinates. She'll be there tomorrow morning, supposedly." He rattled them off. "Take care of this, Peach. Thanks." He disconnected the call.

Evan strode out of the house, coffee in his hand and a grimace on his face.

She set her phone down. "So. Anybody feel like going to Idaho?"

Wolfe nodded. "I've never been, and it's just across the border, right? Sounds like fun."

Evan's frown deepened. "Who made this coffee, and what in the world is in it?"

Wolfe snorted. "Love and sunshine, man."

Michelle chuckled. "I like you, Wolfe."

His eyebrows rose.

"Not like that," she hastened to add.

His grin coincided with Evan's low growl. "I like you, too," Wolfe drawled.

Chapter Ten

Evan kept his hands loose on the steering wheel of his truck and let the springtime breeze wash through the open windows. He really wanted to talk to Michelle, but he'd like some privacy to do so. He glanced in the rearview mirror, where Wolfe smiled at him, the dog sprawled across his lap and the kitten in his pocket.

Life had gotten too weird too quickly.

Michelle had been giving him the silent treatment through breakfast and then all during the drive, which had taken a couple of hours. His fingers itched to take her hand, but he gave her space instead. He checked his GPS again, frowning. "Are you sure these coordinates are right?"

She shrugged. "That's what George said. It's totally possible that Jayleen got them wrong, depending on whether she was drunk or high. Hopefully the other day was just a wine fest and she hasn't started using drugs again." There wasn't much hope in Michelle's voice.

Wolfe leaned forward. "Why would she go to Idaho? Is there any connection for her there?"

Michelle partially turned to face him. "I doubt it. She started driving in Washington and probably just kept on I-90 until she landed somewhere she could call George from. Obviously she isn't thinking straight if she truly believes he can jump on a plane and go wherever. He's in England, for Pete's sake."

"She doesn't know that," Evan countered. "Comic-Con is coming up. She probably thinks he's in California." If the woman was thinking at all, which was doubtful.

He turned down another road, scouting the pine trees on either side of the truck. They were in the middle of nowhere. Finally, a barely there landing strip became visible. "You have got to be kidding me." He parked the truck, looking around.

Wolfe snorted. "A plane couldn't land there. Maybe a helicopter, but the wind would have to be just right."

If they didn't find Jayleen, the people hunting Michelle would find her. Evan sighed. "Let's look around and make sure she's not in a tent around here somewhere. Then we can head into the nearest town and check out the motels."

"Good plan." Wolfe leaped out of the car with the dog. "Roscoe will find her if she's here."

Michelle sighed and exited the vehicle. "I'm really sorry about this, you guys."

"Not your fault," Evan muttered. He really needed to get her alone so they could talk. He shut his door and went on full alert as Roscoe stared at a cluster of trees to the west, emitting an angry growl.

Evan moved at the same time as Wolfe, both blocking Michelle from the trees.

"You armed?" Evan asked.

"Of course," Wolfe said, all business for the first time that day.

Two men strolled out of the forest, one with reflective sunglasses and the other with green eyes that were almost luminous. Both wore cowboy boots and black cowboy hats.

Evan conducted a quick scan. No weapons, but they both were muscled and in fighting shape and moved like they could cause serious damage. They exuded a casual grace and confidence another soldier could easily recognize.

"This ain't gonna be easy," Wolfe muttered under his breath.

Evan nodded. "Michelle? Get back in the truck in my seat. If things go south, get out of here."

Michelle didn't move, frozen in place.

The duo reached them, stopping about two yards away.

"Hi. You're trespassing," the man with the glasses said easily. "Why?"

Evan studied them. "Do you know a Jayleen Peach?"

"Nope," the green-eyed guy said. He had to be in his mid or late twenties, and a world of experience, probably not good ones, glimmered in his eyes. "Should we?"

Evan lifted a shoulder. "She said to meet her here with a plane."

The green-eyed guy's black eyebrows rose. "You can't land a plane here. Helicopter, maybe." He tilted his head and looked at Roscoe, who was rumbling with displeasure. "It's okay, puppy. You're safe."

Roscoe yipped once, snorted, and dropped to his haunches, now panting happily. He even seemed to grin.

Weird. So weird. Evan flashed his badge quickly. "Sheriff Boldon. Who are you?"

"Garrett Kayrs and Logan Kyllwood," the guy with the glasses said easily. "You're out of your jurisdiction, Sheriff."

How did he catch such a good glimpse? "The GPS shows this land as being owned by a couple of corporations. I take it you work for them?" He wanted to figure this anomaly out, but he had other worries.

"You could say that," Logan agreed.

Evan's instincts sparked, but he couldn't put a finger on why. "What are you gentlemen doing out in the woods?"

Logan grinned. "Truth be told, we were headed into town because there's a new band playing at Louise's who now is into country music, and we, ah, heard you arrive and thought we'd check you out."

That explained the cowboy hats and boots, which just seemed off on these two. "Yet you are guarding your territory?" Wolfe muttered.

Garrett shook his head. "Nope. Walking into town and wondered who was trespassing. In fact, we're going to meet—"

The roar of a motorcycle engine pierced the day from deep in the woods.

Garrett sighed, looking more resigned than irritated at this point. "I thought Mercy was meeting us in town."

"When does Mercy stick to a plan?" Somehow, Logan looked larger than he had moments before as he turned back to Evan. "Time to go, buddy."

Not a chance. Evan put on his best sheriff's face. "Tell me about your corporations."

"No," Garrett said easily. "Please leave."

Evan didn't have a right to stay, and he knew it. "Our friend might be around here somewhere, and we'd like to scout the area for her."

"Your friend isn't here," Logan said, no longer appearing as the friendlier of the two men. "Nobody is around for miles. We have excellent security, and there's no reason for us to lie to you."

They had found Evan rather quickly, now hadn't they? Evan looked around for cameras, seeing none.

A dirt bike flew between two spruce trees and skidded to a stop exactly between the two men. The petite rider yanked off a helmet, and a mass of curly red hair cascaded down. "Howdy."

Wow. "You must be Mercy," Wolfe mumbled, stepping closer.

"I must be." Mercy had one blue eye and one green, and looked like danger on a tiny stick. "What's happening?"

"Nothing," Logan said, his body moving toward the redhead in a way that pretty much bellowed "mine."

Ah. Alrighty then. Evan eyed Wolfe. He had to get the guy out of there before fists started getting thrown. Logan's good nature had completely disappeared with the appearance of the stunning redhead. "We should get going."

"You really should. We haven't had trespassers for a couple of months," Garrett offered helpfully. "Your friend hasn't been here, and if she shows up, we'll tell her you were looking."

Good enough. "What's the closest motel?" Michelle asked.

Logan lifted a shoulder. "There are several in Coeur d'Alene, which is the closest town. The ones right outside of town take cash, if that's what you need."

Helpful, weren't they?

"Thanks," Wolfe said, not really sounding thankful, his gaze not leaving Mercy.

"Any time," Garrett replied. "Please do pay attention to the now-shut gate and trespassing signs on your way out." He smiled, looking like a hungry panther. "Rather, I should say the locked gate."

"I'm surprised you didn't have it locked earlier," Evan drawled.

Garrett nodded, his obvious charm barely masking the fighter beneath his taut skin. "Good point. Some of the kids rode four-wheelers the other day and apparently forgot to relock the gate. With us heading into town today, it hadn't seemed like a big deal. It won't happen again."

"You have kids working for your corporation?" Evan asked. He'd checked out the satellite map of the area and hadn't even seen buildings. Maybe the map wasn't updated.

"Of course not," Garrett said, angling a little closer to flank the woman on the bike. "We have a nice subdivision over on the lake."

"A private one," Logan added.

Mercy waved at Roscoe. "Aren't you a beautiful puppy."

The dog happily wagged his tail, his ears perking right up.

Garrett's gaze reached Michelle and softened. "It was nice to meet you all, and I hope you find your friend."

If that wasn't a dismissal, Evan wasn't sure what was. "You too. I'm sure we'll see each other again," he said.

"Doubtful," Logan said. "Have a nice day, now."

"That was so weird," Michelle said, her voice hushed as Evan drove back down the long road. "What was up with those guys?" Besides being impossibly good-looking, a fact she saw no reason to share with Evan and Wolfe. The two strangers were like super soldiers, calm and masculine. Kind of like the two men in the truck but somehow different in a way she couldn't quite pinpoint.

Wolfe shrugged. "There's a private subdivision over on the lake, and apparently rich folks like privacy, which I totally understand. That Mercy was something, though. Right?"

Yeah, she was. Michelle nodded. "How do you think Jayleen even knew about that landing strip?"

Evan drove through the gate, eyeing the no-trespassing signs on both sides of the road. "She probably just asked locals, and they obviously didn't know about the security. I feel like Kayrs and Kyllwood were telling the truth about her not being around."

"They found us fast enough," Wolfe agreed from the back seat. "Still, I wouldn't have minded going a round or two, if Michelle wasn't here. No offense."

"None taken," Michelle said. Now that would've been a contest. "I'm glad nobody fought." The last thing she wanted to see was violence. "You guys have dangerous enough lives."

Evan eyed her. "You have something to say?"

She'd been banking her temper all day, and after the adrenaline rush back at the landing strip, holding on to it was too much. "Yeah. I'm surprised you failed to mention you were joining Raider's bomb-defusing, mob-infiltrating unit in DC."

His jaw hardened. "I guess we'll have this talk now, then."

Wolfe cleared his throat. "I can get out and jog to town, if you'd like."

Evan slowed down.

"No," Michelle blurted out. "There's no reason for you to leave. In fact, I wouldn't know a thing if you hadn't talked to me this morning."

Wolfe winced. "Sorry about that, Boldon. My bad. Hadn't had all of my coffee yet."

"No worries," Evan said, his voice a mite too calm as he drove onto the interstate. "If Michelle had questions, she should've asked me."

There hadn't been time. "Maybe you should've been more forthcoming," she said, her throat dry.

Evan craned his neck to read a sign and then exited near a ramshackle motel. "Let's check this place out while we're here." He drove around the cracked asphalt of the parking area and then pulled to a stop next to the front door. "By the way, I told Raider no. Not once have I intended to go work in DC."

Well. "You could've said so," Michelle snapped, knowing she was being unfair.

"When?" he snapped right back.

"All right," Wolfe said cheerfully. "How about you give me your phone with a picture of Jayleen, and I'll run into the office and scare whoever's there into giving me information?"

The dog whined as if he wanted out, too.

Michelle silently handed over her phone. "Don't hurt anybody."

"No promises," Wolfe said, jumping from the car with the dog on his heels and the kitten in his pocket. As soon as he'd shut the door, Evan pressed the gas and drove to the far end of the lot, backing up against a row of spruce trees. With slow, deliberate movements, he parked the vehicle and then cut the engine.

Michelle's skin started to hum.

"If you had concerns, you should've said something," he said, way too evenly.

Oh, he didn't get to remain calm while they were fighting. Well, kind of fighting. "There hasn't been time, for Pete's sake." In fact, since he'd barreled through her front door, she hadn't had a chance to even catch her breath. "We don't see each other for years, then you're here, then we're in bed, and now what? We're supposed to figure everything out?"

"No." He turned toward her, overwhelming the cab with heat and intensity. "We don't have to figure anything out right now, but we do need to talk about it. If you have questions, you ask them."

Did she have questions? She was so muddled, she

wasn't sure what to say. "Why aren't you taking the job in DC?"

"I don't want it," he said shortly, his eyes a heated blue. "I like my life and my town. I figured you'd like them, too."

"This can't be about me," she protested, her heart rate kicking into gear fast and hard.

"Everything is about you," he countered, turning to see Wolfe emerge from the office with the dog, gesturing wildly toward the motel. "Ah, hell. Come on. Let's deal with Jayleen and continue this discussion later."

"Fine." She jumped from the truck, somewhat grateful for the reprieve so she could figure out what to say. Last night had meant a lot to her, and maybe she should've started with that. Her emotions had always been all over the board with Evan, and apparently that hadn't changed. Or maybe it was just her indecision. It was time to own her life, to decide what she wanted.

Not taking risks these last years had led to a calm and rather boring life. She'd thought that's what she wanted, until Evan had stormed into her apartment.

For the first time in too long, she felt alive. Electrified. Like she was living again instead of just existing. It was both intriguing and scary as heck.

She hustled after Evan, her mind spinning, until they reached Wolfe.

He gave the dog a command to sit, and Roscoe just looked at him. "Whatever," Wolfe muttered. "Kid behind the counter said Jayleen is down in room ten."

Michelle exhaled and tried to look beyond the door. "Kid? You didn't hurt him, did you?"

"Nope," Wolfe said. "Kid is a girl, about sixteen, and I charmed her with my HDD badge and sweet smile." He pulled a wallet out of his back pocket and flipped it open to show a shiny badge. "I wouldn't scare a girl."

Somewhat sexist, but Michelle couldn't fault him for not frightening a sixteen-year-old. "Let's get this over with." Her mother had better have that tablet. She turned and stepped lightly over mud puddles that led right to the doors of the hangdog building. The paint was peeling, and yellowed curtains hid the contents of the rooms through the dusty windows.

Finally, she reached the door to number ten and knocked loudly. Before she could tell her mother to open the door, Evan tackled her to the ground, covering her with his larger body.

She hit hard, and the air blew from her chest. What had just happened?

Then the world exploded.

Chapter Eleven

Evan lifted Michelle off the wet asphalt, keeping them both low, and dodged to the other side of the door. "Stay low." He pressed her behind him, making sure Wolfe was all right on the opposite side of the one window. The soldier had slivers of wood in his hair from the shotgun blast through the door and a pissed expression on his hard face, but apparently he'd heard the cocking of the shotgun right with Evan and had jumped out of the way.

Evan leaned to the side and pounded on the destroyed door. "Jayleen? You there?"

The shotgun pumped again.

"Duck!" He turned around and covered Michelle as another blast blew the door completely apart. As fast as possible, he swirled. "Now, Wolfe!" Ducking, he went in fast, with Wolfe breathing down his neck.

One look confirmed it was a naked Jayleen with a gun. He reached her in seconds and yanked the shotgun free of her bony hands while Wolfe jumped into the bathroom and returned, shaking his head.

Evan emptied the shells. "You could've killed us."

The woman chortled and reached for a blue silk robe on the bed. Her body was overly thin and pale, with track scars on her arms. Her blond hair was wild, and her eyes, a dimmed blue compared to Michelle's, were almost blank. "Didn't know it was you." Red wine stained her cracked lips, and several empty bottles were lined up on the dingy dresser. "Man, you're as good-looking as I remember," she said, drawing the robe closed and tying the belt. "Your friend ain't bad, either," she slurred. "How about a party?"

Evan's stomach revolted.

"Hell, no," Wolfe mumbled, heading right back out the door.

Michelle came into view, hovering in the doorway. "Is she high?"

Jayleen snorted. "No. Just drunk. A lot of drunk." She raised a hand and then wobbled, staggering to the bed.

A quick pain glimmered in Michelle's eyes and she quickly banished the emotion. "Where's my tablet?" Without waiting for an answer, she grabbed a green backpack off the floor and scrabbled through it. Then she went for the dresser, opening and closing each drawer.

Jayleen blinked several times, swaying on the bed. "Not here. I wouldn't have it with me."

"Bull." Michelle went through the closet and then the bathroom before looking under the bed.

Evan watched Jayleen carefully. The woman had stiffened when Michelle had approached the bed. "Look between the mattresses, Peaches," he said.

Jayleen jumped up and then fell on her butt on the dirty gray carpet. "Stay away from my bed, dammit."

Michelle grimaced and looked at the lumpy bed.

"I've got it," Evan said, lifting the top mattress with one hand and flipping it over the other side of the bed, revealing a tablet, some cash, and what looked like a packet of cocaine. "I'll take this." Ignoring Jayleen's screech, he took the powder to the bathroom and flushed it all down the toilet.

Michelle clutched the tablet to her chest. "Don't you have to arrest her?"

"Not in my jurisdiction right now," Evan said.

"You're an asshole," Jayleen slurred, falling to the side and resting her head on the bottom mattress. Her body went limp, and she started to snore.

Evan had never wanted to punch another person this badly before. He exhaled several times before he could speak. "We need to get her out of here just in case she's being followed." He absolutely hated the thought of taking this woman to his home, but he couldn't handle the threat to Michelle until he knew who was after her.

Michelle was too pale for his comfort. "If she drank enough to pass out, she won't come to for quite a while. I don't want to take her to your place."

"It's okay." Evan plucked Jayleen off the floor. "Grab her pack and let's go." He paused. "Make sure there isn't a phone in the bag, and if there is, leave it here."

Michelle nodded and grabbed a phone out of the pack, dropping it on the floor. "I'm sorry about this."

He paused, meeting her gaze over the too thin woman in his arms. "Not for a second is this your fault, Michelle. Don't take this on yourself."

She nodded. "I know." Yet the sadness in her voice nearly tore him in two.

He carried Jayleen across the parking lot to the truck, where Wolfe stretched out of the back seat. "I'm not sitting with her," Wolfe muttered. "I'll go give the gal at the front desk money for the door, so maybe she won't call the cops." He jogged away.

"He can have the front," Michelle said, her shoulders down. "I'll sit in the back with her and the dog."

Roscoe whined and licked her hand as if offering reassurance.

Evan settled everyone in the truck and secured Jayleen with the seat belt so she rested against the door and not Michelle before Wolfe returned and they drove off. "We okay here?"

Wolfe nodded. "Yeah, but I'm out of cash now."

"I'll take care of it," Michelle said quietly, already typing on her tablet.

"I've got it," Evan said, his chest aching for her. He could protect her from any enemy out there except for the one next to her, and that inability frustrated the hell out of him. When that woman woke up, she'd tell him everything she knew about the people after her.

Whether she liked it or not.

Michelle finished tucking Jayleen into the guest room and returned to her room before calling George, who answered immediately. "Hi. I have my tablet and I've deleted your comic," she said, the relief she felt almost dropping her to her knees.

Silence met her statement for two heartbeats. "You deleted my comic?" he repeated.

She rolled her eyes. "Of course. Just in case. I think it's better I don't have a copy, don't you?" Sometimes he was such a prima donna.

"Still." He drawled the word out with his British accent, sounding like royalty. "Not many people would actually delete me."

She drew deep for patience. "I didn't delete you, just

the comic. I will definitely buy myself a hard copy just like the rest of the world, and if you're super nice, I'll let you sign it for me."

"You're impossible," he said, laughter in his voice now. "Fair enough. I shall think of just the right thing to say."

"Can't wait." She disengaged the call. Who the heck knew what George would come up with after the last several days.

Her phone buzzed again, and she paused at seeing the number. Then she winced. Might as well get this over with. Considering she'd slept with Evan, and wanted only Evan, she couldn't lead Mike on.

The phone call was short and surprisingly congenial. Mike wished her well, and she did the same for him.

She couldn't help but keep her tablet with her as she strolled out of the room, down the stairs, and onto the back deck. The moon was coming up over the mountains, already glowing across the curving river.

Evan sat in a wooden deck chair, facing the mountain. Roscoe snored at his feet, while Kat batted something on the table back and forth.

She sat in the adjacent chair and kicked her legs out. "Where's Wolfe?"

"He ran to town for supplies," Evan murmured, his gaze remaining on the river. "God knows what he'll bring back home."

Home. The place truly felt like a home, even to her. "I don't know what to do about us," she said quietly, wanting to talk while also needing to delve into her comic and finish the adventure.

He chuckled. "I'll do anything you want."

Desire flushed through her, tipping all balances in his favor. What comic? She grinned against the incredible pull she'd always felt toward him. "I'm not talking sexually."

"Neither am I." He took her hand, rocking softly. "Here's the deal. It's always been you and that's not ever gonna change. So I'll switch jobs if you want and move to Portland, or whatever you need."

It was more than she'd ever dreamed, but the last thing she wanted was for him to become anybody other than Evan Boldon. It was time to take a risk, and she was ready. "I'm strong enough, grown-up enough, to handle your job, Evan. Here as a sheriff or even if you go back into the military." It was a possibility for him, even if he didn't realize it right now. "But how do we do that? It's not like we've been together these last years."

"Ah, that's just details, sweetheart." His voice deepened and roughened. "You only live six hours away. We can date for a while, relax into it, and end up where I know we're going. I'm not going to rush you, and there's nothing to stress about."

Long-distance dating?

"Besides," he continued, "I like the idea of a good courting."

Humor attacked her and she laughed. "Courting? Did you actually just use the word 'courting'?"

"Yep." He rocked more. "I want flowers. I expect love letters and a box of chocolates once in a while. A guy likes to be wooed."

Evan Boldon had just used the words "courted" and "wooed." "Man, this small town is going to your head," she said.

"Yep." He finally turned her way, looking unbelievably handsome in the moonlight. "I'm even helping to coach the pee-wee softball team."

She jolted. "You are not."

"Sure am." He shrugged. "I've got a pitcher with an arm you wouldn't believe. I mean, they're still playing T-ball,

but one day Annika Jones is going to play college ball,
I'm telling you." ·

The guy even sounded like a pee-wee coach. Had she
dropped into an alternate universe or what? The image of
what life could be with him filtered through her mind,
warming her, tempting her.

Wolfe stomped his big boots out on the deck, whistling
softly, and handed over two large mugs of fragrant brew
adorned with a pile of whipped cream and multi-colored
sprinkles. "The grocery store is very well stocked. I'm
happy." He scraped a chair away from the table and sat
down, emitting a huge sigh of pleasure.

"When did you get back?" Michelle asked, looking
warily at the whipped cream in her overlarge coffee cup.

"Five minutes ago," Evan said, eyeing his cup in the
same way. "You didn't hear him banging around in
the kitchen?"

She'd been concentrating on Evan and nothing else, as
usual. "No. I was thinking about that cat I want." Tilting
her head, she took a sip, trying to keep the whipped cream
from giving her a mustache. The brew splashed into her
stomach, and she coughed. "More than coffee," she sputtered, trying to control her breath.

Evan gently patted her back. "More than coffee?"

"Yep," Wolfe agreed, sounding mellow and pleased.
"There's good Irish whiskey in there, too. Makes for a
great nightcap."

At least the alcohol might counteract some of the sugar.
She took another drink, this time mixing whipped cream
with the liquid. Yeah, delicious and decadent. "This might
be the best coffee I've ever tasted."

Wolfe smiled in pure delight, still looking like a hungry
animal. "That's sweet. Did you two get your act together

while I was gone? I stayed away as long as I could, but your stores close really early here."

She barely knew this guy, but something about him invited trust. "Yeah. Apparently we're going to court and woo each other for a while."

Wolfe shook his head. "That's fucking stupid."

For some reason, the statement had her erupting in laughter. Why, she wasn't sure. But darn, he was funny.

Evan lifted an eyebrow. "I don't believe we asked for your opinion."

"I'm a giver. Always happy to give it," Wolfe said, downing half of his coffee and whipped cream.

Evan rolled his eyes. "Did you make the call?"

"I did and we're all set," Wolfe said.

Michelle turned to face Evan. "What call?"

Evan took a drink of his coffee and grimaced, wiping whipped cream off his mouth. "Wolfe has a contact at the Ryerthton Rehab Center over in Seattle, and we're checking Jayleen in tomorrow. We'll drive over there in the morning, and she can give us all the information about the drug dealers on the way. We'll go from there."

A rehab center? "What if she won't go?"

"She doesn't have a choice," Evan said. "It's either that, or jail. She'll do it."

Maybe rehab would finally work. "Thank you."

"No problem. Now finish that drink so you can take advantage of me," he said, warmth cascading off him.

"Now that's more like it," Wolfe muttered.

Chapter Twelve

The following morning, Michelle tried to hide a yawn as she settled into the passenger seat of Evan's truck with Jayleen in the back, huddled beneath a blanket.

"Michelle, you can stay at the house and catch up on sleep," Evan offered, pausing as they were about to drive away from the cabin. "I'll get Jayleen settled in at rehab."

Man, that was tempting. After a wild night with Evan, she hadn't been able to sleep, so she'd worked on her comic until dawn arrived. When creativity struck, sometimes she could do nothing but draw and write. She couldn't let Evan take this on by himself, though. Jayleen was Michelle's problem, not his. Plus, after they dropped her mother off, they could talk some more about this whole courting situation. What she'd say, she really wasn't sure. The idea that they really did have a second chance almost made her giddy, and she wasn't going to stand in her own way this time. "I want to go with you," she finally said.

His lips curved in a way that made her want to kiss him. Again. "All right."

Jayleen stirred in the back seat. "Does anybody care if I want to go?"

"No," Evan said shortly, pressing on the gas pedal

and driving down the long lane. "I haven't looked into warrants out for you, yet. It's either rehab or custody. Your call."

Jayleen settled back down.

Michelle cleared her throat, partially turning in her seat to look at her mother. "This is your last chance with me, Jayleen." She'd never said those words before, always wanting the hope of having a real relationship with the woman. "If you fail this time, we're done. I can't do it any longer." Someday she'd have kids, and she didn't want them dealing with the mess Jayleen could create. "I've given you second chances my whole life. This is it."

Jayleen's eyes clouded, but she didn't answer, no doubt suffering from a heck of a headache. She closed her eyes, falling asleep almost instantly.

Evan reached over and took Michelle's hand, and she gripped his tightly. It was time to create the life she really wanted. If a sober Jayleen could be part of that, she'd be grateful. If not, she'd move on.

Her phone buzzed and she took it from her purse, reading a text and smiling. "George says he's sorry for being pissy last night." She chuckled. "Would you like to accompany me to Comic-Con this year? You should meet him."

"Now that's courting." Evan grinned, full out. "I would love to meet him and have him sign a copy. Not one of my unopened, plastic protected ones. I'd buy a new comic."

Her badass marine was kind of a geek. "Good plan."

The sunny day turned cloudy, and rain began to fall as they drove along country roads, avoiding traffic and making good time. Michelle dropped off to sleep at some point, lulled by the soft pelting of rain and the rhythm of the windshield wipers.

She awoke some time later, sitting up. "Where are we?" Fields stretched out to mountains around them, but large fluorescent orange cones blocked off the second lane for construction, although nobody was working on the weekend.

"You were only out twenty minutes, Peaches. We're in the middle of Washington State, where there's always road construction," Evan said, glancing to the back seat. "Jayleen? You awake?"

"No," Jayleen muttered, sitting up.

Evan's jaw firmed. "We have a couple of hours to go, and it's time you told us who's after you and why."

"Nobody is chasing me now. I took care of it." Jayleen pushed back her unruly hair and yawned widely. "Stop worrying about it and mind your own business."

Michelle winced.

Evan stiffened. "A bunch of goons came after your daughter. Who are they?"

"I took care of it," Jayleen repeated, her voice rising. "You have no idea what I know. We're safe now, and we're going to be rolling in cash soon."

Michelle shut her eyes and counted to five before continuing. "Tell me you didn't just blackmail a drug dealer." Threatening George was bad enough, but a killer?

"It's not blackmail if it's not in writing," Jayleen said.

"Jesus," Evan muttered, glancing at his side-view mirror. "Yes, it is. You have one second to tell me who you blackmailed before I drop you off at the nearest police station to be booked for that and whatever else they can find on you. How many warrants are out there?"

"None in Washington State," Jayleen shot back.

Michelle's temper soared, and she fought to keep from yelling at the woman. "Does this have anything to do with Joey Bandini and that huge bald guy?" Her memories were a little fuzzy from that blow to her head, but she had the glimmer of an idea.

"Not really. Maybe a little," Jayleen said, her voice muffled as she snuggled down in the blanket. "They said something, and it got me to thinking, and then thinking more, and sometimes two plus two does equal four."

"What is she talking about?" Evan asked, tilting his head to study the rearview mirror, lines of concentration cutting into his forehead.

"I'm not sure." Michelle tried to remember what Joey had said before he'd slapped her. There was something that had perked Jayleen up. What was it? She ran through the night, what she could remember, and her head started to ache again. "Wait a minute." Something about some computer geek? "Dooney Bourke?"

Jayleen snorted. "That's a purse."

True. That was a purse. Darn it. "I can't remember," Michelle muttered. The whole night was still too hazy. A lifted black truck careened out of a field ahead of them with a tall man driving, and Evan slowed slightly. "Wow," she said. "That guy could've waited."

Evan stiffened. "Is your seat belt on?"

She instinctively pivoted to look out the back window and spotted a green SUV rapidly approaching. "Yes." She partially turned to make sure Jayleen was still buckled in. "What's happening?"

"Not sure." Evan set both hands on the wheel, his concentration absolute. "Maybe nothing."

The truck in front of them began to slow down.

"Or definitely something," he muttered, scanning the area. "Jayleen? Are you expecting friends?"

"No." Jayleen sat up and craned her neck to look behind them at the oncoming SUV. "Not at all." Her voice lowered to a whisper on the last.

"Jayleen!" Michelle turned to more fully face her mother. "What did you do?"

Jayleen paled, her eyes wide. "Nothing. Well, not much. I mean, I borrowed your phone earlier and might've made one phone call. Honest. I just want to pay you back for everything."

"Turn back around, Peaches," Evan said, his tone gritty. "Face forward and try to keep your body as relaxed as possible."

Michelle flipped back around and clutched the dash.

"More than that," Evan said. "Trust me. If we crash—"

The truck hitched as it was battered from behind. Michelle gasped, panic seizing her lungs. The driver in front of them slammed on his brakes, which flashed bright red and fast.

Evan twisted the wheel to the right and sped up, the driver's side mirror hitting a round divider and breaking off to hang awkwardly. He punched the gas, sped in front of the black truck, and pulled onto the main road again. With a flick of his wrist, he turned up the windshield wipers as the rain splattered faster.

Michelle, her entire body tightened, pushed against the floor with both legs. "What's happening?"

"We need to stay ahead of them," Evan said grimly, speeding up more, well beyond the speed limit. "So long as—shit." He slammed on the brakes.

Jayleen screamed.

Michelle saw the spike strip positioned across the road a second before they drove over it. Evan swore, the tires blew, and the truck flew into the air sideways almost in slow motion. It flipped all the way, and Michelle had a second to breathe before the truck landed on its roof with a crunch of metal and a sputtering of air. Blackness grabbed her and she struggled to stay conscious, held upside down by the seat belt. "Evan?" she whispered, her ears ringing.

He was upside down, blood covering his face, not moving.

Somebody tore her door open.

Jayleen coughed. "Dooby Brown," she mumbled.

Oh yeah. That was the name. Hands reached for Michelle, and she tried to fight them, but finally the darkness took her.

Who in the world was Dooby Brown? That thought scrubbed through Evan as he fought the darkness.

Everything hurt. He shook himself awake and took in the scene in a second. Michelle. He turned and looked toward her open door. She was gone. No sign of Jayleen either. Grabbing a knife from his boot, he released himself from the seat belt, barely catching himself with one hand before he crashed down on the roof. Crawling over the glass and damaged metal, he pushed himself from the upside-down truck and stood in the rain, looking both ways. How long had he been out?

Nausea attacked him, and he grabbed a tire to stay upright. Dizziness blasted him next, and he waited it out, partially bent over. He was in the middle of nowhere, and it'd take hours for legal backup to arrive. When he could breathe again, he tugged his phone from his pocket and quickly dialed.

"Yo," Wolfe said. "You miss me already?"

"Michelle and Jayleen were taken," he gasped, the pain in his head nearly dropping him. "I'm about an hour from you on Old Highway 26, and my vehicle is a shitshow. Get here fast."

"Sure thing," Wolfe said, the sound of movement echoing over the phone. "You know where they went?"

"Either you'll see them on the road, a black Chevy truck or a green SUV with a dent in the front, or they headed toward Seattle, which would be my bet. Bring your gun and hurry." He disengaged the call and dialed Raider, who answered immediately. "We're in trouble and I need everything you can find on a Dooby Brown. He's some sort of computer geek, but there has to be more to him than that. Start in Seattle." Once Raider had agreed, Evan let himself sink to his butt after clearing away some glass. He leaned his head back against the upside-down tire and let the rain wash blood off his face and down his shirt. How badly had Michelle been hurt?

Why hadn't he told her how much he loved her? He'd figured there would be plenty of time for that, and he, of all people, should know better.

The world swirled around him again, and he coughed. Then more darkness.

"Evan? Dude. Wake up." The rough voice came from a long distance away. Very far. Then a kick to the leg. "Now. Wake up." Something rough licked Evan's cheek.

Evan blinked against the rain, opening his eyes. "Roscoe." He leaned away from the dog's tongue. "Stop it." Accepting Wolfe's offered hand, he let the soldier pull him up. "Crap. I was out an hour?"

"No," Wolfe said. "Half that. I drove like hell." Concern glowed in his dark eyes. "Didn't see a green truck or a black SUV on the way here."

"Figures." Evan turned and limped through the rain toward Wolfe's rented Jeep with the dog at his side, leaning against his leg as if offering support. Pain ticked through him, but he climbed into the passenger seat and let agony take him completely for a moment.

Wolfe opened his door and jumped inside, while Roscoe leaped into the back seat. "I left Kat at your place. He hates high-speed chases."

Evan closed his eyes and swallowed, trying not to puke.

"How bad you hurt?" Wolfe asked, flipping on the heat.

"I don't think anything is broken, but I'm banged up and bruised." Evan didn't open his eyelids. "Probable concussion, but I can talk and walk, sort of, so the damage has to be minor." Yeah, right. If he blinked too fast, his head might explode.

"Been there. Just take deep breaths and don't look outside, because I'm going so fast I feel dizzy." For the first time, Wolfe sounded all business. "Trust me. If they're on this road, we're gonna find them."

Dual planes buzzed above them. "What's going on?" Evan asked.

"When you called, I was in town. Nice town you have there," Wolfe said.

Evan forced his eyelids open and nearly cried when the dim light pierced his pupils. A dinged up red crop duster plane flew by. "Is that Ezckiel up there?"

"Yep. His brother has his crop duster, too. They're going to scout ahead and find the trucks."

Evan wiped rain and blood off his face. "I left them in a jail cell."

"Verna let them out early this morning. Something about needing to clean the cell." Wolfe looked his way. "Folks sure don't have any secrets once you head to town in the morning."

That was one of the things Evan liked about Doe City— usually. He leaned slightly to the side and stared up. "I hope they're not still drunk."

The planes zoomed ahead, flying low.

"They're sober enough to fly," Wolfe said, focusing back on the road and driving way too fast. "Were Michelle and Jayleen okay after the wreck?"

"Jayleen spoke, but I don't know about Michelle," Evan said, his adrenaline flowing freely. She had to be okay. If she was hurt, she needed medical assistance. He couldn't lose her now that he'd finally gotten her back. "Go faster, Wolfe."

Chapter Thirteen

Michelle blinked her eyelids, unable to rub them. What was going on? Her head hurt and her stomach felt like she'd been punched several times. She listened to the silence, and then sound came rushing in.

"You're awake. Oh, thank God." Was that her mother?

Michelle turned to see Jayleen next to her in the back seat of an SUV, her hands tied together beneath a secured seat belt. She looked down at her bound hands beneath her own seat belt, but her vision was blurry. "What?" None of this was making sense. She shook her head, winced at the pain, and then forced herself to focus.

"Are you okay?" Jayleen asked, blood dripping from a cut on her cheekbone.

"Yes. I think so." The memory of the car crash came flooding back, and she looked around. "Where's Evan?"

Jayleen shook her head.

Was he okay? Michelle started to struggle.

"Stop," commanded a male voice.

Michelle stilled and lifted her head, looking toward the passenger-side bucket seat. Her vision finally cleared to see a thirty-something man dressed in a monogrammed white button-down shirt with modern wire-rimmed glasses framing intelligent brownish-green eyes. He smiled. "I wondered if you'd awaken." Almost carelessly, he lifted his hand, revealing a black gun before dropping the weapon out of sight again. "Behave."

"No problem," Michelle muttered. She wasn't exactly in fighting shape. She looked toward the driver, a burly man with bushy brown hair who stared straight ahead as he drove through the rain. His thick hands on the steering wheel were hairy and bruised. Where was Evan? "The man who was driving our truck—was he still alive when you grabbed us?" She held her breath, her chest hurting more than her head.

The guy shrugged. "No clue."

Michelle tried to shift in her seat, and her abdomen protested. She winced.

The guy nodded. "Those airbags can hurt, right?"

Yeah. Right. Michelle held still to keep the pain away. "Who are you, anyway?" More importantly, what did he want?

"Oh. Figured you knew. I'm Dooby Brown." He smiled, revealing a gold tooth. "Or rather, Julian Dooby Brown, but you can call me Dooby."

Okay. "Listen, buddy. I don't know a thing about you, and truth be told, I don't care about you. At all." She needed an aspirin. Her head could take only so much. "What do you want?"

His smile sagged away. "Want? First, I want the twenty-five grand that your mother owes me. Then? Well, then I want to bury you both so deep even the ants won't find a piece of you."

The mental image made her stomach roll over. How could he sound so cheerful while making death threats? She stared harder, but he didn't look insane. Maybe just mean. Michelle turned toward Jayleen. "This guy is the drug dealer you owe?" If anything, he looked like a techie who subcontracted for the Geek Squad. Wait a minute. "I thought Joey Bandini said you were some sort of computer nerd." None of this was making sense.

Jayleen sighed. "Yeah. See, it's like this—"

"I am a computer nerd," Dooby said. "Lots of guys, small-time crooks like Bandini, hire me to hack or search or do whatever. You wouldn't believe the information I'm able to get from their systems when I do so."

Michelle gingerly prodded a bruise on her cheekbone. "But you're a drug dealer?"

Dooby shook his head. "You're as dumb as your mother."

"I have a concussion," Michelle shot back. "Excuse me if I haven't figured out your criminal enterprise yet." She wasn't thinking clearly, but she probably shouldn't yell at the guy with the gun. She exhaled slowly, trying to concentrate and add the pieces together. "Wait a minute. You're the guy in charge of it all."

"There you go," Dooby said, condescension rippling with his words. "Most of those guys work for me and don't know it. Or they don't work for me, I find out everything about them when they hire good ole geeky Dooby, and then I create situations where they do work for me."

Michelle tested the bonds around her wrists, trying to keep him occupied. "If even a few of those guys found out who you really are . . ."

He nodded. "They'd be pissed. Oh, I have friends who could take care of the problems for me, but right now, I don't need problems. More importantly, if any one of those assholes knew who I am, they'd give me up in a heartbeat. I heard Bandini and his buddy are in custody in Seattle, and if they had any info to bargain with, they'd do it."

Bandini was in jail? Michelle sat up. "Why is Bandini in jail?" Had he found Meri? Had he hurt her?

Dooby shrugged. "Who cares? The point is, a low-level hacker like Dooby Brown doesn't merit a trade. My friends want me to keep it that way."

Michelle looked toward her mother. "You figured it out and tried to blackmail this guy."

Jayleen nodded, tears in her eyes. "Sorry. I ran for a dealer named Jack-Jack for a while, and I was in his place when he met with Dooby a couple of times. Well, Julian, not Dooby."

"I didn't know she was there," Dooby offered. "Your dear mama was banging Jack-Jack, and he hid her when I dropped by to collect."

The bindings were tight, but if she kept working them quietly, she might be able to get one hand free. What she'd do then, she had no clue. "So when Bandini mentioned Dooby in my apartment, you put it all together, Jayleen?" It seemed her mother was smarter than she normally acted.

"Yeah," Jayleen said, her head down. "Dooby? I'm sorry I tried to blackmail you, and if you let us go, we won't say a word."

Dooby chortled. "Right. That was a cop we left upside down back there. Try again."

"I shouldn't have called and threatened you earlier," Jayleen said, her voice raw.

Dooby waved the gun. "I'm glad you did. We never would've found you without tracing the phone. Once we saw your trajectory today, we set up our trap."

What a creep. Michelle glared at him. If she could get a hand free, maybe there was a way to grab the gun. She'd have to take him by surprise.

"I'll get you the money," Jayleen whispered. "Maybe Jack-Jack will help me."

"Bull," Dooby said. "Jack-Jack has already forgotten you."

If he didn't think he'd get his money, why were they still alive? Or was he just trying to get far enough from Evan to take care of them? Michelle tried harder with the bindings.

Jayleen sighed, her shoulders dropping. "Fine. Set my daughter free, and I'll tell you how to keep the information from going out."

Michelle paused. "Information?"

"Insurance policy," Jayleen said, flashing her teeth. "If something happens to me, or to you, my friend is going to send Dooby's information to everyone in the contact list in my phone and then email the Seattle newspapers with a pretty darn good story."

Evan had Jayleen's phone. Michelle kept her expression bland. Her mother was a heck of a bluffer. "Well, then. I guess we're safe."

Dooby smiled again, and it wasn't a reassuring sight. "It's nice that you think that."

A plane buzzed by them, nearly scratching their roof.

Jayleen yelped and ducked down in the seat. A second plane did the same thing. Were those crop dusters? Michelle tried to look outside her window.

"They're crazy." Dooby rolled down his window.

The first plane circled around and came at them again, flying really low.

"Who the hell are these guys?" Dooby yelled.

Michelle shook her head. She had no clue.

Dooby edged toward his door. "If they want to play, I'm game." He angled his wrist out the window and fired toward the oncoming plane, which lifted up at the last second, nearly crashing into them.

Michelle tugged frantically on her bindings, rubbing her now raw skin against the rope and trying to twist a hand free. The pilots, whoever they might be, were trying to help her. She didn't know if a handgun could shoot that far, but the planes were incredibly low, so maybe it was possible?

The second plane followed the first, heading right for them.

Dooby yelled and fired rapidly. A bullet hit a wing, shredding the casing. The bright yellow plane kept coming, piloted by a gray-haired man.

The SUV driver swerved this time, running off the road and quickly yanking the wheel to the left. Dirt and weeds spun up behind them as they fishtailed and then regained purchase on the old road.

Dooby brought his wrist in, pulled another clip from the glovebox and shoved it into place.

Michelle almost had one wrist free. "If you shoot a pilot or even the plane, the heavy thing might land on us," she yelled.

"No, it won't," the driver hissed, ducking to look in the side mirror. "Boss?" He increased their speed until the trees blurred by outside. "We've got more company behind us."

Jayleen whimpered. "We're going to die."

No, they weren't. Michelle twisted her wrist and pain burned along her arm. She bit back a cry and kept trying. Why hadn't she told Evan how she felt? She had loved him since the first moment she'd met him, and pretending otherwise had just been cowardly. Oh, she had to get out of this.

Dooby fired up at the second plane and then turned in his seat and fired behind them, nearly hanging out the window.

Michelle partially turned to see Wolfe's rental SUV

gaining ground. Her heart leapt at seeing a second figure in the vehicle. It had to be Evan. She needed to see his face.

Dooby fired again.

She wrenched her hand free and quickly unbuckled her seat belt, launching herself toward Dooby, her nails out. She shoved herself between the two bucket seats and scraped his neck, punching him in the ear as hard as she could. The driver grabbed her by the hair and yanked.

She screamed and scrambled to stay in place.

Dooby dropped back inside, his gun swinging toward her. They drove over a bump in the road, and Michelle punched Dooby's wrist at the same time. He yelped and the gun fired.

Heat flared along her earlobe and she ducked, wincing at the loud noise. Blood spurted onto the side of her neck from a wound in the driver's shoulder. He bellowed in pain and fought the wheel, unsuccessfully, barreling through a field of weeds and slamming into a tree.

The impact threw Michelle against her mother, and she sucked in air, trying to rise.

"You're gonna die now," Dooby yelled, grabbing her hair and yanking her through the seats.

She turned, ready to punch, and faced the barrel of a gun.

Chapter Fourteen

Evan kept a firm hold on the handle above his window as Wolfe screeched to a halt and spun the SUV to the left, blocking any exit from the vehicle they were chasing. Bullets tinged against the metal as the passenger leaned out and fired at them.

Panic seized him. Michelle could get shot too easily. He shoved down all emotion and drew back on his training. No feelings. Only action.

"This way," he ordered, throwing open his door and letting gravity take him down. He landed, rolled, and came up behind a tire, keeping the vehicle between him and the shooter. Wet weeds covered his legs while the rain continued to pound down. Wolfe flew out of Evan's door and dropped to his knees, flipping gracefully behind the back tire. Giving a signal, he reached up and opened the back door. Roscoe bounded out, turning in midair to land behind Wolfe.

Evan levered himself up, his gun on the metal. "Dooby Brown? It's over. Come out and we won't shoot you."

"You know my name," Dooby called. He fired out his window.

"I know a lot about you," Evan replied, ducking for cover. "Julian Dooby Brown, computer geek, kingpin. Bet you didn't know the DEA has an open case on you. In fact, they're gonna make a move soon." Raider had come through with plenty of information, and now all Evan had to do was convince Dooby that his time was limited. "You probably have a couple of hours to get out of here." Though Evan would spend any time he needed chasing the asshole down, first he had to get Michelle free.

"Then I guess I'll take your car." Dooby sounded much closer.

Evan leaned up to look, and his heart stopped.

Dooby stood in front of his steaming SUV with a gun to Michelle's temple. She had blood and bruises on her face, but she was standing on her own. "Throw your guns over the vehicle."

"You got a shot?" Wolfe rumbled under his breath.

"Negative." Evan's angle was all wrong. "You?"

"No." Wolfe whistled and Roscoe dropped to his belly and shimmied beneath the SUV. "Get ready."

Blood dripped into Evan's eye and he wiped it away. "Ready."

Before Wolfe could direct the dog, Jayleen ran around the side of the vehicle, shoved Michelle, and grabbed the gun. They struggled, and it went off, a bullet pinging off the nearest tree.

"Now, Roscoe!" Wolfe bellowed.

The dog sprang from beneath the SUV, snarling and running full bore for Dooby.

Dooby yelped and shoved both Jayleen and Michelle toward Roscoe, turning his aim toward the dog. The women fell and landed on their knees in a puddle, spraying water. The second they were free, Evan and Wolfe fired simultaneously. Dooby flew back against his vehicle from the impact, a hole in his head and one in his chest, his eyes wide in death.

The dog skidded to a stop, barked three times, and remained at attention facing the dead man.

Evan ran around the front of the SUV and reached Michelle in seconds, grasping her arms and lifting her up. She was bruised and bloody but had never looked better. "Are you okay?" He hugged her close, inhaling her lilac scent and trying to slow his thundering heartbeat.

"Yes." She snuggled close, her nose pressed to his chest.

He reached over and tugged Jayleen up. "Were you shot?"

"No." She patted her chest and then grabbed her daughter to hug, even though she was still in Evan's lap. "Are you okay?"

Michelle turned her head. "You grabbed a gun and tried to save me."

Tears streamed down Jayleen's face, mixing with dirt. "I'm your mother, and while I've sucked at it, I'd give my life for you. I promise I'll be better."

Evan watched Wolfe circle the vehicle, gun pointed. "Get out," he ordered. When nobody moved, he opened the front door, and the driver fell out. Wolfe crouched out of sight and then stood. "He's out cold but alive."

"Everyone take a deep breath. Let's make sure we have no serious injuries," Evan said, holding Michelle tight.

"I'm fine," Jayleen said, spreading her arms. "I'm fine. I still had on my seat belt."

Michelle sagged against Evan and then started, leaning back. "Are *you* okay? You were knocked out." She wiped rain out of her eyes.

"I'm fine." Although his head felt like Jell-O. So long as she was all right, he was great.

The two planes landed on the empty road, one after the other, gliding gracefully down.

Evan examined a purple bruise spreading across her

temple. "How do you feel about a plane ride?" The faster they reached the small county hospital, the better. The woman had been in two car accidents in one day, and he wanted her checked out.

"I love you," she blurted out. "I don't want to court or woo. I don't want to put life off any longer. I love you and want to move to this crazy town and be together."

The words were a sledgehammer to his chest.

Rain splattered him, flowing down his face, but he had never been warmer. "I love you, too. Have since the first second you smiled at me. I always will, too."

She smiled, her eyes glowing. "Let's start our lives now. Stop waiting and start living."

He leaned down and kissed her gently, mindful of her bruises. "That's the smartest thing you've ever said, Peaches." In fact, he'd go ring shopping the next time he was in Seattle. Forget that. He'd go in his own town, even though their engagement would be public news within an hour. The key would be trying to figure out how to propose before anybody else told her.

He did like a good challenge.

Gently turning her, he nodded to Wolfe. "I owe you one."

"Okay." Wolfe motioned for the dog to be at ease. "I'm just glad you two figured things out. I knew you couldn't be that dumb."

Evan grinned, truly liking this new friend of Raider's. "I appreciate that." He waved at Sonny, who stood on the main road with his brother. "I'm taking my girl to the hospital, if you don't mind."

"Not at all," Wolfe said, grinning. "I'll wait here until the feds arrive. Give them a call as soon as you're in service, would you? The DEA will be more than happy to see Dooby dead, and then take down the rest of his organization." He paused and glanced sideways at Jayleen. "I can deliver you to the Seattle rehab place afterward, if you want."

Michelle partially turned in Evan's arms. "Mom?"

Jayleen nodded. "I do want that. I really do."

For the first time since Evan had met her, he almost believed her. Who knew? This brush with death might've scared her straight. Maybe it was possible.

Ignoring the pain in his side, he swept Michelle up and strode toward the planes, nodding at Wolfe and then Roscoe as he went. "I'm sure the hospital is somehow already waiting for us," he said dryly.

Michelle stared at the myriad of balloons, flowers, and homemade cookies covering every inch of the two counters in her hospital room. More people than she could count had visited her that morning, introducing themselves and bringing gifts. She eyed the wrappings around her wrists, which had been more abraded than she'd realized in the heat of the moment.

Evan strode in, with a male nurse pushing a vacant wheelchair behind him. "Darn it, Sheriff, you have to sit down," Larry muttered, his lips tight.

"Hi, Larry." Michelle waved a hand.

"Now that's how a patient is supposed to behave," Larry said, standing tall in his light blue scrubs. He was broad across the chest and had interesting tattoos down both muscled arms. "I'll put you in here if I have to, but I don't want to be arrested."

A bandage covered the right side of Evan's forehead. Combined with the bruises down his jaw, he looked more dangerous than ever. "Fine, Larry," he said, his grin charming. "I'll get off my feet." He tugged an orange visitor's chair away from the counter and plopped down. "Happy now?"

Larry removed the wheelchair from the room. "If you fall on your face, I'm not picking you up," he sniffed, disappearing.

Michelle smiled, holding out a hand for Evan to take. "He's in charge of your meds, you know," she said.

Evan tightened his hold. "I really pissed him off earlier when I refused meds. Wouldn't take a painkiller when the doc stitched up my side. You were right about my needing stitches, by the way."

Man, he was impossible. Somehow he'd even managed to get the doctor to let him wear sweats and a T-shirt instead of a hospital gown. Yet she couldn't help but return his smile.

"I talked to my friend Ian, and you're not going to believe this."

"What?" she asked.

Evan ran a gentle finger over the bandage on her wrist. "He and your friend Meri met up—apparently for good. He's the one who put Bandini and his pal in custody."

Michelle straightened. "Really? Meri agreed to settle down?"

Evan chuckled. "Ian can be very persuasive. He's a great guy, and he already sounds excited about being a dad to Meri's little one. I'm sure we'll get together with them soon."

That was fantastic news. "I guess sometimes things do work out." She settled more comfortably against the pillows, so happy she wanted to pinch herself, but she had enough injuries at the moment. "I assume Wolfe met up with the DEA?"

"Yeah, and he's on the way to take Jayleen to rehab. I invited him back after that, but he's itching to head to DC. Truth be told, I'm happy he'll be backing up Raider. We should get Raider to visit us with Wolfe after he's done with his current case." Evan scratched his whiskered jaw and then winced as he rubbed a bruise.

She nodded. "I think Wolfe wants to get back to his journalist, too. I bet there's more there than friendship."

Evan laughed. "Just because you're in love doesn't mean everybody else is."

"Who says I'm in love?" she drawled.

"You did." His gaze heated even more. "No take-backs."

Well, that was a fair rule. She took his other hand, comforted by his warm strength.

He looked around the room. "I was only gone a couple of hours for tests. I take it the entire town visited?"

She widened her eyes. "I am never going to remember everyone's name. Not a chance. Not all of those names."

He leaned in. "I'll tell you a little secret. Whenever you run into anybody, just say, 'It's nice to see you.' Never use the word 'meet.' You're covered either way—whether you have met or not."

She inhaled his scent of mint and man. Uniquely Evan. "That's brilliant."

"I know." His greenish-blue eyes twinkled. "Although you'll be surprised how quickly you really do learn all the names. They don't give you much of a choice."

"I like your town, Evan," she murmured, holding tight.

"Let me share it with you, then," he said, leaning over to kiss her nose, her cheeks, and her lips. "Everything I have is yours, Peaches."

Was it possible to be this happy? She had no clue what life would bring, but she wanted to face it all with Evan. He'd been her first and only love, and now she had a lifetime to enjoy with him. "I really do love you, you know."

He sat back, sobering. "I know. I love you more than you can imagine, and we both know your imagination is incredible. All of my life, I wanted a family. I found that with Miss A, Raider and the kids, and definitely with you. Wherever we are, no matter what happens, we're family, Michelle. You and me."

Tears prodded her eyes, but she didn't care. She'd always felt she had a home with him. "Family."

He leaned over again, kissing her with all the promise of their life to come. "I love you, my Michelle. Always."

ECHOES OF THE PAST

ALEXANDRA IVY

Chapter One

Few people whizzing along Interstate 5 noticed the blocky, white stone buildings. The structures looked like any other office complex in Seattle. It wasn't until you entered the front door that it became obvious it was a correctional facility that housed many of the city's most dangerous prisoners. Including Bart Kowalski.

Kowalski, or Ski, as he was known on the street, was a tough guy who had a long history of violence that'd recently ended when he was shot and arrested for attempting to kidnap Lily Jones, the newly adopted daughter of Ian Brodie.

Detective Gray Hawkins had been called in to assist in the takedown, arresting Ski along with the kingpin of the crime, Joey Bandini.

Gray had returned to Spokane after the arrest. Then, three weeks ago, he'd suddenly decided to move back to Seattle. He told people that he wanted to be closer to his family who lived in the area. A perfectly legitimate reason. Only the chief was aware of the true motive for his return.

Well, the chief and Bart Kowalski, who was hoping to avoid a life sentence by turning state's evidence. Not only against his partner Joey Bandini, but the dirty cops who were involved in trafficking drugs into the city.

Entering the jail, Gray allowed the uniformed guard to lead him to one of the conference rooms that were reserved for attorney-client meetings. It'd been arranged by the chief, since it was the only place in the jail where they could speak without being monitored.

The guard glanced over his shoulder, taking in Gray's casual jeans and flannel shirt with the sleeves rolled up to his elbows. He could sense the younger man's puzzlement. God knew he didn't look like a lawyer with his thick chestnut hair tousled by the stiff breeze and a five o'clock stubble on his lean face. And he suspected his silver-gray eyes were smoldering with frustration.

No doubt the guard was wondering if he was there to stage a jail break. Then, with a small shrug, the young man seemed to conclude that his unease about the unknown visitor was above his pay grade, and he shoved open the door.

Gray entered the small, windowless room to find a narrow table and two wooden chairs bolted to the tiled floor. Bart Kowalski was already seated and glaring at him with blatant impatience.

The man was as large as a mountain, with a bald head and heavily chiseled features. Most of the bruises he'd received during his arrest looked like they'd healed up in the past weeks. Gray couldn't see the bullet wound on the man's leg beneath the blue prison uniform, but he assumed it was healing as well.

Gray closed the door, moving to take the empty seat across the table from Ski.

"'Bout time you got here," the man groused.

Gray leaned forward, his expression hard with warning. "I shouldn't be here at all. You're going to blow my cover."

"I have to talk to someone, and you're the only one I trust."

Gray frowned. He was in Seattle because Ski was anxious to make a plea deal by ratting out those involved in the local drug trade. During his confession, he'd revealed that there were a couple dirty cops who were working with the cartel. Gray was there to ferret out the traitors.

"What about your lawyer?"

"No one but you," Ski stubbornly insisted.

"Why?" It was a question that'd been nagging at Gray since he received word that the man was demanding to speak with him. "As far as I can remember, we've never met other than at your arrest. Why trust me?"

"I shared a cell with Spider a few years ago," Ski said. "I overheard him telling the guard that he'd worked as your snitch and that you were a stand-up guy. At least for a cop. He said you even stopped by and checked on his mother while he was locked up." Ski lowered his voice, his eyes darting around the cramped room as if making sure they were alone. "Plus, you wouldn't have been the one picked to sniff out the dirty cops if you weren't squeaky clean."

Gray remembered Spider. A low-level drug dealer and street hustler who'd provided just enough information to keep himself from a protracted jail sentence. Not the finest character reference, but he'd take it if that meant Ski would open up to him.

"Did you remember something?" he asked.

The man muttered a curse. "How many times do I have to say it? I've told you guys everything I know."

"It's not enough," Gray protested. They needed names if they were going to root out the corruption in the department.

"I was at the bottom of the food chain. I didn't get invites to the secret meetings and carry-in dinners."

Gray narrowed his eyes. "If you want to be a smart-ass, do it on your own time. I have better things to do."

"Wait," Ski grunted as Gray started to rise from his chair. "I need your help."

Gray sat back down. He didn't miss the edge of panic in the man's voice. "What's going on?"

Ski did the looking-around thing again. Did he think there was a guard hidden behind the potted plant? Then, the man reached into the pocket of his uniform pants to pull out a piece of paper.

"I found this in my bed last night," he said, shoving the note across the table.

Gray read the scribbled words out loud. "'Talk and your kid is dead.' Kid?" He lifted his gaze to study his companion in confusion. "What kid?"

Ski looked oddly uncomfortable. "I have a boy. Donny. He's six. I haven't had much to do with him until a few months ago when my ex dumped him on my doorstep. She has a new dude and a new kid and no room for Donny," he said. "My mom's been taking care of the boy since he got to town."

Gray tapped his fingers on the table. He'd read through Ski's file a dozen times, and he didn't recall a mention of a child. Which meant . . .

"He wasn't living in Seattle until recently?" Gray demanded.

Ski shook his head. "He lived in LA, and I never saw him. My old lady said I was a bad influence." Ski made a sound of self-disgust. "She was right. But then Donny got in the way of her new life, and she suddenly didn't care that I get the trophy for the worst dad in the world. She just wanted to get rid of him."

Gray shuddered at the thought of a young child being in the care of this brutal man. With an effort, he forced himself to concentrate on the reason he was there.

"Who would know you have a son?"

Ski blinked, caught off guard by the question. "My ex and her new douchebag of a husband," he said. "And of course, my mom."

"What about Joey?"

Joey Bandini was a complete lowlife. He'd have bartered Ski's son to the bad guys in a heartbeat if he thought it could help him. Hell, he'd been willing to threaten his own daughter for a few bucks to buy drugs.

Ski shook his head. "I didn't want anyone to know about the kid. I might not be the father of the year, but I'm not completely stupid."

"What about school?"

"I haven't got him signed up yet." The man shrugged. "I don't even know when it starts, to be honest." He paused, his brow furrowing. "I think my mom takes him to some community center to help with his reading, but I doubt anyone there would know I'm his father."

Gray continued to tap his finger on the table. "So, no one in Seattle knows you have a son besides your mother?"

Ski started to shake his head, only to suck in a sharp breath. "Wait. I caught one of the guards looking through the letters that I have in my cell. A couple of them were from Donny."

Ah. Now they were getting somewhere. "What's the guard's name?"

"Butch." Ski held up his hands at Gray's impatient glare. "That's all I know."

"When did you catch him going through the letters?"

"Two nights ago."

A sudden unease cramped Gray's stomach as his gaze strayed back to the note on the table. It could be an empty warning, but if there was even a small chance the boy might be in danger, he had to act. Now.

"Where is Donny?"

"With my mom." Without warning, Ski leaned forward, his brutish face pale. "Look, I know I'm scum, and I'll probably die in this shithole, but the kid is innocent. You have to protect him."

"Give me the address," Gray commanded.

Ski rattled off the street number, watching as Gray grabbed the note off the table and tucked it in his pocket.

"You're going to make sure Donny's okay?"

"Yeah, I'm going to make sure he's okay." Gray shoved himself out of the chair. "Don't talk to anyone. I'll be back."

Without waiting for Ski to respond, Gray walked out of the room and motioned for the nearby guard to escort him to the exit. He wasn't sure why, but he had a sudden, urgent sense that the boy was in trouble.

He'd learned long ago never to ignore his instincts.

He jogged across the parking lot to climb into the mid-size car that he'd rented before returning to Seattle. It was the sort of vehicle that blended into the background, unlike his father's 1969 Mustang, which he'd recently rebuilt and painted cherry red.

Heading downtown, he passed through the industrial area into a neighborhood that had gone from depressed to derelict in the past ten years. He parked along the curb, studying the house that was crammed on a tiny yard and surrounded by a chain-link fence. At one time it had been painted a cheery yellow, but now it'd faded to a dull mustard, with sagging shutters and a roof that looked on the point of collapse. There were, however, a couple ceramic pots on the front porch that were filled with bright flowers, and lacy curtains in the window. As if whoever lived inside refused to give in completely to despair.

Switching off the engine, Gray instinctively touched the gun that was holstered beneath his flannel shirt before sliding out of the car. It was just after five o'clock, but the neighborhood seemed eerily silent.

Gray opened the gate and moved up the broken sidewalk. Then, stepping onto the narrow porch, he felt his gut clench as he glanced through the window to catch sight of a form sprawled on the floor. Moving to the door, he turned the knob, relieved when it swung open easily.

He rushed across the worn carpet to kneel next to the fragile old woman. She was lying on her side with blood trickling down her face from a deep wound on her forehead.

Pulling his phone from his pocket, Gray hit 9-1-1, his gaze making a quick survey of his surroundings. He couldn't let his concern for the old woman distract him from potential danger. Not when he had no idea whether the attackers were still in the house.

"I need an ambulance," he told the emergency operator, giving the address before returning the phone to his pocket. "Mrs. Kowalski?"

The woman slowly opened her eyes and made a sound of distress. "Get away from me."

"Easy," he murmured as she rolled onto her back, fear darkening the blue eyes that her son had inherited.

"Who are you?"

"Detective Hawkins." He didn't waste time digging for his ID card. The woman was barely clinging to consciousness and he needed information. "Can you tell me what happened to you?"

She licked her lips, her wrinkled face tight with pain. "There was a man. He knocked on the door. When I wouldn't open it, he busted the kitchen window and climbed in."

Gray glanced toward the arched opening that led to a small kitchen. He could see the shards of broken glass that littered the linoleum floor.

"Did you recognize him?"

"No." She paused, as if trying to recall the chain of events. At last her lips parted with a sharp gasp. "Donny. He was here for Donny."

Gray's unease solidified into anger. Shit. He was too late. "Did he take the boy?"

She cautiously shook her head. "No, I snuck him out the side door and then pretended he was hiding in the bedroom."

Smart woman. Clearly, she was capable of thinking during an emergency. "Where would he go?" Gray demanded. "Does he have a friend nearby?"

"He's too shy." Her words were becoming slurred as she struggled to stay conscious. "He doesn't ever leave the house. Except . . ."

Gray leaned close, lightly grabbing her frail hand. "Yes?"

"The youth center," she managed to force out. "It's just down the road."

"Do you think he would go there?"

"He has a teacher who's been helping him with his

reading." The older woman's eyes closed even as she struggled to speak. "He . . . he adores her."

Gray rose to his feet as he heard the siren of the approaching ambulance.

"Help is on the way," he assured Mrs. Kowalski.

"Donny," she whispered.

"I'll find him." Gray clenched his hands as he gazed down at the woman who'd sacrificed herself to save her grandson. He intended to make whoever was responsible pay a heavy price for hurting her. "Don't worry."

Chapter Two

Melanie Cassidy locked the doors of the Hummingbird Youth Center and scurried to her car, which was parked behind the building. She'd discovered since moving to Seattle from Chicago three years ago that the low-hanging gray skies could release anything from a drizzle to a biblical deluge without warning.

She wasn't worried about the rain ruining her appearance. She kept her dark hair cut short and she never wore makeup to enhance her pixie features or large green eyes. And she was wearing her usual jeans and T-shirt with a bright red raincoat. The kids she worked with felt more comfortable when she looked like one of them.

Nope, her only concern was the phone she had pressed to her ear as she jumped into her rusty Ford Taurus and slammed shut the door. She'd just spent a large chunk of her modest salary on the thing. She wasn't going to risk having it drenched.

Then again, she wasn't prepared to end her conversation with Remi Walsh.

The two had been best friends since they'd both worked at a youth center in Chicago. It didn't matter that they were complete opposites. Remi had come from a wealthy family and earned her graduate degree in education. Mel had bounced between her mother's crappy apartment and foster care, and she hadn't been able to afford more than a few classes at the community college.

But they both shared a fierce desire to help those kids who too often fell through the cracks, and that was enough to seal their friendship. Even after Mel had moved to Seattle, they'd stayed in contact.

Settling behind the steering wheel, she closed the car door and tried to mentally process the reason her friend had called.

"Oh my God, Remi. I don't even know what to say," she breathed, in shock.

"You don't have to say anything," Remi assured her. "You told me that you needed fifty thousand to expand the youth center, and I have the funds to help."

Mel shook her head, glancing toward the empty lot next door. It'd been her dream to create a community garden that could be shared by the neighborhood. Growing their own food would not only be a wonderful learning experience for the kids, but for many families it would be their only source of fresh vegetables. But their funding was constantly being cut. Without donations from the community, there was no way they could hope to buy the land.

"I can't believe you remember what I said about my silly dream for a garden."

"Why wouldn't I remember?" Remi protested. "I'm not in my dotage yet."

"Yeah, but we were at your reception when we were talking about my work and you were so busy lusting after your new hubby that I assumed you didn't hear a word I said," Mel reminded her, hoping that her friend couldn't hear the hint of envy in her voice.

Not that anyone would blame her for being jealous.

Remi had endured hell in the form of a serial killer who'd stalked her for years, but over the past months she'd married a gorgeous Chicago cop who blatantly adored her, and she'd tapped into an inheritance worth millions to create her new charity.

"I'm a very talented woman, Mel," Remi assured her. "I can lust after my husband and listen to my maid of honor describe her frustrated plans for a garden at the same time."

"Talented, indeed," Mel teased, not sure she could be so versatile. Remi's new husband was delectable, with a capital D. Perhaps not as sexy as . . . No. She slammed a mental door on her renegade thoughts of the man who had walked away from her two years ago. "Seriously, Remi, this is so generous. How can I ever thank you?"

"By continuing the fabulous work you're already doing." Mel smiled. "That's easy enough."

"Not easy, but satisfying," Remi corrected.

"True," Mel readily agreed. She loved her job. Not everyone was so lucky. "Okay, since I can only say thank you again, tell me how you're doing. Is that husband spoiling you rotten?"

"He is." Remi's voice softened, contentment almost oozing through the phone. "Along with all his brothers. Sometimes I feel like I'm drowning in Marcel men."

Envy once again tugged at Mel's heart. And once again she reminded herself that no one deserved happiness more than Remi.

"And you wouldn't have it any other way, would you?" she teased.

"Not for a second. And what about you?" Remi demanded. "Any excitement in Seattle?"

"Excitement? Hmm. I stayed up until almost ten o'clock

last night watching the Mariners play baseball on TV. That's about all the excitement I can take. I was exhausted this morning."

Remi clicked her tongue. "That's it. I'm flying out there next month and we're spending a girl's week together," she warned. "I think we can find more trouble than a baseball game."

"*Mi casa es su casa*," Mel told her friend. "I'll talk to you this weekend. And thanks again."

Ending the call, Mel shoved the phone into her purse and started her car. There was a *plop, plop, plop* as the first of the raindrops hit her windshield.

"Great," she muttered. Couldn't it have waited another fifteen minutes? That's all the time it would take for her to drive to her apartment.

Apparently not. The drops came faster and faster until she was forced to switch on her wipers. With a grimace she leaned forward to wipe the fog from the inside of her windshield. Her defroster was on the fritz. Just like her right turn signal and the horn.

Clearing away the thin layer of moisture, Mel froze as she caught sight of a tiny form appearing around the corner of the youth center. Behind it, a black SUV hurtled through the empty lot, halting next to the building so a large man could jump out of the passenger side.

"Donny?" she breathed, easily recognizing the small boy.

She shoved open her door and slid out of the car. Her heart skipped a beat as the man, who looked like he'd overdosed on steroids, reached to grab Donny by the arm.

"No, let me go!" the boy cried.

Mel stepped forward, her mouth dry with fear. "Hey, what are you doing?"

Clearly caught off guard, the man jerked his head around to glare at her through the gathering gloom.

"Get lost, bitch."

Mel took a step forward, refusing to be intimidated. "Donny, do you know this man?"

The boy frantically shook his head. "No, Ms. Cassidy."

"Let him go," Mel commanded.

The man narrowed his eyes. "This is none of your business. Get in your car and drive away."

"I'm making it my business," she warned. "Let him go."

The man wrapped his big hand around Donny's throat. "Leave now, or I'll break his neck. Got it?"

The air was squeezed from Mel's lungs. What was going on? What sort of monster would threaten a little boy? Her gaze flicked to the SUV, where the shadowed figure of another man was seated behind the steering wheel.

Confused terror slammed into her with the force of a freight train, making it difficult to think. She couldn't leave Donny with the violent stranger. But she couldn't reach him before the hideous man could hurt the boy.

She had no choice but to back off. Or at least, pretend to back off.

"Yeah, I got it. Just take it easy." She lifted her hands as she crawled back into the car.

She heard the sounds of Donny's cries as the man pulled him to the very back of the SUV and shoved him inside. Mel swallowed her surge of panic and reached for her phone. She had to call the cops. What else could she do?

But even as she started to press 9-1-1, the man was moving to climb into the passenger seat of the SUV. The cops would never get here in time to stop them. She had to do something. Fast.

With mere seconds to act before the men drove away, she refused to consider the stupidity of what she was about to do. Instead, she clenched her teeth and shoved the engine into drive before stomping on the gas pedal.

The car lurched forward, jolting over the rough ground. She aimed directly at the driver's door, sending up a prayer that she wouldn't injure Donny.

She picked up speed and braced herself as she plowed into the larger vehicle. There was a screeching sound of metal scraping against metal, and Mel slammed against the steering wheel with painful force. Crap. She should have put on her seat belt.

With a small groan, she peered through her broken windshield to discover that her aim had at least been accurate. She'd blocked the driver-side door. And as an unexpected bonus, the weight of her car had been enough to shove the SUV against the building to trap the passenger as well.

It was now or never. Leaping out of the car with her phone clutched in her hand, Mel darted forward. She heard the muffled sound of curses as she headed to the back of the SUV and pulled up the tailgate.

"Donny, come on," she commanded, reaching to grab his hand and yank him out of the vehicle.

The poor boy tumbled out, and barely waiting for him to get his balance, Mel was dragging him down the alley.

"You crazy bitch," a male voice called out, but Mel never slowed. She had to find a place to hide Donny until she could get hold of the cops.

They had just reached the side street when a car pulled to the curb. Mel skidded to a halt, shoving Donny behind her as she watched the driver window roll down.

"Get in," a male voice commanded.

She scowled. "Go away."

"Mel, it's me."

Mel frowned at the sound of her name. She didn't recognize the car, but there was something about the voice that was familiar. Cautiously leaning down, Mel glanced into the interior of the vehicle, catching sight of chiseled male features and smoldering silver eyes.

"*Gray?*"

Chapter Three

Gray had recognized the Hummingbird Youth Center from a block away. And as soon as he'd caught sight of it, he'd suspected which teacher Donny adored.

Melanie Cassidy had a rare talent for earning the devotion of the children she helped. And while it'd been two years since he'd seen her, he didn't doubt for a second that she was still just as popular with the kids.

Thank God for his hunch. Otherwise he might have driven past the woman who was heading out of the alley with a young boy in tow. After all, he was looking for a child being chased by a maniac.

Mel, however, was obviously shocked by the sight of him. Or maybe she was horrified. Hard to tell.

Luckily, her hesitation lasted only a few seconds before she was hurriedly bundling the boy into the back seat of his car and then sliding in next to him. He barely waited for her to slam shut the door before he was squealing away from the curb and down the street.

"Tell me what happened," he urged, casting a quick glance at Mel's pale face.

With shaky hands she pulled on her seat belt. "I was leaving the center and I saw Donny running around the corner." She stopped, sucking in a deep breath. Then, with an obvious effort she continued. "There were these men in a black SUV chasing him, so I rammed them with my car and grabbed Donny. Then we just ran."

He would have been amazed by the stammered words if they'd come from anyone but Mel. She was the type of woman who would always charge to the rescue of a child. No matter what the danger to herself.

"Are you hurt?" he demanded.

"I'm fine." She glanced over her shoulder. "Donny?"

The boy in the back of Gray's car was small and pale with short blond hair that was flattened to his head from the rain. He had his father's light blue eyes and he was missing his two front teeth. He was shivering beneath his too-thin shirt and wet jeans.

"I'm okay," he whispered.

Mel turned back to stab Gray with a suspicious glare. "Why are you here?"

"I was searching for Donny," he said, weaving his way toward the interstate.

She blinked, clearly startled by his response. "Why?"

"It's a story for later," he murmured, deliberately glancing into the rearview mirror to indicate he didn't want to talk in front of the boy. "I went to his grandmother's house and found her injured."

Donny made a sound of distress. "She told me to run away."

"How bad is she?" Mel asked, her expression concerned.

"I called for an ambulance," he assured her. "I'm sure the doctors will have her fixed up in no time."

Lifting the phone she had clutched in her hand, she swiped over the screen. He wasn't sure what she was doing until he heard the sound of a movie. She reached over the seat to hand the phone to Donny.

"Here you go, sweetie. Your favorite cartoon."

The boy reached to take the phone, his gaze locked on the screen as he curled into a tight ball in the corner. As if he was trying to make himself as small as possible.

Mel waited, clearly making sure the boy was completely distracted before she spoke.

"What are you doing here?"

Gray merged into the rush hour traffic on the interstate before he responded.

"I told you."

"I meant, what are you doing in Seattle?"

"I transferred back a few weeks ago."

"Why?"

He grimaced. He didn't want to lie. Not to this woman. But what choice did he have?

"To be closer to my family," he forced himself to say.

She made a sound of disbelief. "I thought you left to get away from them?" she questioned in tart tones, then released a hissing breath. "Sorry," she muttered. "It's none of my business."

Gray zoomed through the traffic as an awkward silence filled the car.

He had no idea where he was headed. Or what he was going to do with Mel or the boy. For the first time since he'd joined the force he was working undercover, which meant he didn't have backup. He was going to have to figure this out on his own.

Well, maybe not completely on his own.

He glanced to the side. Should he tell Mel the truth? Once upon a time, he wouldn't have hesitated. She would have offered her trust and assistance without hesitation. But he'd destroyed her faith in him when he'd walked away. Now he was going to have to earn it back.

"Actually, I'm afraid it might be your business now," he

told her, taking the closest exit to enter a quiet suburb. He couldn't concentrate on their conversation when he was battling traffic. Besides, he wanted to make sure they weren't being followed. "Those men aren't going to forget that you interfered in their business."

"What business could they have kidnapping a little boy? His family doesn't have any money."

"No, but his dad is about to testify that the local drug cartel has members of the Seattle Police Department on their payroll."

He heard her shocked gasp. He didn't blame her. No one wanted to accept that officers sworn to protect the law were using their power to corrupt it. Then her eyes suddenly narrowed.

"That's why you're here."

"Yeah," he admitted, already regretting his attempt to deceive her. She'd put her life in danger to rescue Donny. She deserved the truth. He slowed to a mere crawl as they zigzagged through the elegant streets lined with mini-mansions. "We know that the dirty cops work in vice, but we don't have the names. That's what I'm here to get."

She nodded, her delicate features tight with fear. "Were those men chasing Donny cops?"

Gray considered her question. He'd assumed that the men she'd seen in the SUV had been the same ones who'd attacked Mrs. Kowalski.

"I can't be sure, but I suspect they were common street thugs," he finally said. "The cops will want to stay in the shadows as long as possible."

She settled back in the leather seat, weariness settling around her slender body.

"Where are we going?"

"A good question." Gray grimaced. "The boy—"

"Donny," she interrupted.

"Donny," he readily corrected. He could sense Mel was already attached to the kid. She always did lead with her heart. "He can't go back to his grandmother. She'll be in the hospital at least a few days. And his father is obviously out of the question."

Mel lowered her voice to a whisper. "What about his mother? Donny never mentions her."

"Apparently, she dumped him on his father's doorstep when she remarried and had another kid."

"Oh." She bit her lip, her expression sad. "Poor Donny."

"He needs to be in protective custody," Gray muttered.

"Can't you arrange that?"

"Not without knowing who I can or can't trust."

She grimaced, glancing over her shoulder at the boy, who was still curled in the corner of the back seat.

"I suppose Donny could come home with me. At least for a few days."

Gray shook his head. "They're already searching for you."

"How could they know . . ." Mel pressed her fingers to her lips. "Oh no. I left my purse in my car."

Gray didn't bother to tell her that the cops could trace her car even if she hadn't left behind her purse. She was hanging on to her nerves by a thread.

"I'm sorry you can't go back to your house. Not until we've managed to expose the criminals responsible for threatening Donny," he said. "Even those who are hiding behind a badge."

"Are you telling me that I'm homeless?"

"I promise you won't be sleeping in the streets."

Frustration flared in her brilliant green eyes, but with an effort she bit back her angry words. Instead she returned her attention to the child.

"I'm more concerned about Donny," she murmured.

Gray's heart melted. "That's no surprise. You've always had an amazing way of caring for others."

"It's my job."

He shook his head. "It's more than your job and the children you teach," he insisted. "You care about your friends, your coworkers, and the street people you pass out sandwiches to every day." He chuckled as he remembered their time together. "You even cared about that awful landlady who was constantly complaining and threatening to kick you out of your apartment. You would get her groceries and drive her to the clinic for her physical therapy, no matter how often she insulted you."

A blush touched her cheeks. "Ruby is lonely, and the only way she knows how to talk to people is by nagging at them. She's harmless."

He arched his brows. When he'd known Mel, she was fairly new to Seattle and her job. It made sense for her to rent the rooms above Ruby's garage, which was just a few blocks from the youth center. But he couldn't imagine anyone staying in that shabby, cramped space for a day longer than necessary.

"You still live in the same apartment?"

"I'm comfortable there." Her eyes widened. "Do you think Ruby will be in any danger?"

Gray grimaced. As far as he was concerned, the bitter old lady could hold her own against any criminal. She'd once threatened to shoot him when he'd shown up late for his date with Mel. It didn't matter that he'd been busy arresting a murder suspect.

"No," he assured her. "They've already left behind a string of messes trying to kidnap Donny. The last thing the cops want is to attract attention. Harming another innocent old woman is going to be the last thing on their list." He sent her a rueful smile. "They're more likely to send one of their goons to watch your place in case you return there with Donny."

In the past she would have shared his smile. Maybe even snuggled close to his side. Now she pursed her lips, her expression hard.

"What are you going to do with Donny?"

"We," he corrected.

"What?"

"Right now, we're in this together."

She stiffened, her eyes flashing with unexpected anger. "There's no together," she snapped. "Not between us. Not ever."

Gray winced. He deserved her rejection. So why did it hurt so much?

"Okay, let me rephrase that," he said in low tones. "I'm sorry you're mixed up in this, Mel. More sorry than you'll ever know. But there's no changing the fact that both you and Donny are in danger. I need to find someone I can trust to help us."

"Surely there's some cop you know who isn't dirty," she insisted.

Was there? He hadn't been in Seattle for over two years. And many of his friends . . .

Friends. The word echoed through his brain, and he suddenly knew exactly who he needed.

"Of course," he breathed. "Ian."

It took her a moment to place the name. "Ian Brodie?" she finally demanded. "The private detective?"

"The one and only." Gray pulled his phone out of his pocket and scrolled through his contacts to find the private number for his friend. A second later he heard Ian's voice float through the speaker.

"What's up, Hawkins?"

"I need your help."

* * *

Detective Gwen Dobbs stood in the thickening shadows of the youth center. She was a tall, thin woman with bleached blond hair she kept screwed into a tight bun at the base of her neck. As usual she was wearing a tailored black slacks suit, although she'd noticed when she'd put it on that morning it was a size too large. Over the past six months she'd lost more weight. The price of her escalating addiction to heroine.

Holding an umbrella to protect her from the drizzling rain, Gwen frowned at Hammer, the oversized idiot who'd called to confess that he'd managed to allow Donny Kowalski to escape.

"How the hell can you screw up grabbing one little boy?" she mocked.

Hammer pushed out his bottom lip like a petulant child. "The grandma refused to open the door."

"She's ninety years old."

Hammer hunched his broad shoulders. "We had to break through a window. By the time we got inside, the boy had taken off." He nodded his head toward the SUV, which was now pulled to the center of the alley with a big dent in the driver's door. "Then when we finally caught up to him, the bitch rammed us with her car. It wasn't our fault."

"Of course, it's your fault," she snapped. "I should lock you and your brainless brother in a cell for being incompetent idiots."

"But—"

"Stop talking," she interrupted. One more word out of the imbecile's mouth and she was going to shoot him.

Instead she watched Leo appear out of the darkness with a woman's purse held in his hand. Her partner was a short, thick man with a square face and brown hair that was threaded with gray. His eyes were dark and hard, like a snake's. As he stood next to her, Gwen caught the stench of stale coffee and cigarettes.

"Well?" she demanded.

"I did a sweep of the neighborhood," he said. "There were no witnesses and I couldn't find any CCTV pointed toward the alley."

Her gaze moved to the purse in his hand. "Is that all you found in the car?"

He shrugged. "There were a stack of books and some files in the trunk. That's it."

"See who it belongs to," she commanded.

Leo obediently dug through the handbag to find the wallet. Flipping it open, he pulled out a driver's license and handed it to Gwen.

She tilted the card toward the security light above the back door to the youth center.

"Melanie Cassidy," she read out loud. She studied the picture of the dark-haired woman, a frown tugging at her brows. There was something faintly familiar about the delicate features. Had she arrested the female? Hmm. It was impossible to remember them all. With a shrug, she shoved the license toward Hammer. "Here. She only lives a few blocks away. Take the SUV and keep an eye on her place. If you see her with the kid, grab her."

Hammer scowled. "What if she turns up without the kid?"

Gwen stared at him in disbelief. Had his mother dropped him on his head?

"Then follow her, for Christ's sake," she snapped. "And stay out of sight. The last thing we need is another screwup."

Hunching his shoulders, Hammer turned to shuffle his way to the SUV. He climbed into the passenger side and his brother hit the gas, clearly anxious to be away.

"This is turning into a shit show," Leo muttered, tugging up the hood of his raincoat in a belated attempt to protect himself from the relentless drizzle.

"Only if we panic," Gwen said, pulling out her phone to send a text to her contact at a local chop shop. Within an hour, all traces of the Ford Taurus would disappear.

She wanted to get rid of as much evidence as possible.

Leo snorted. "You know that Cassidy woman is probably on her way to the nearest police station with the boy."

"Good." Gwen dropped her phone back in her purse. "Then we'll know how to get our hands on him."

"She'll tell them that someone was trying to kidnap him," he insisted.

Gwen rolled her eyes. Leo was ten years older than she, but he had the ambition of a slug. He'd spent most of his career seated behind his desk, counting down the days until his retirement. But last year his wife had walked out on him, taking the house, his savings, and a large chunk of his retirement. That's when Gwen had requested him as her partner. She'd known he'd been in minor trouble before, but now she suspected that he was desperate enough to man up and join her in the big league.

And she'd been right.

Still, he had an annoying habit of panicking whenever something went wrong.

"It doesn't matter what she says," Gwen assured him. "All we have to do is claim that the boy is connected to one of our investigations and that we need to put him in our protective custody. Who's going to question us?"

He shot her an annoyed glance. "Doesn't anything rattle you?"

Gwen flattened her lips as an image of herself locked in her bathroom with a needle in her arm seared through her mind.

"One of us has to have some balls. If it was up to you, we'd be stealing small baggies of pot and a handful of pills from crime scenes. Now we're making enough to keep us both happy."

"A good gambler knows when to walk away."

"You're as stupid as Kowalski," she spat out. "There's no walking away. Not for either of us. The only way out of our deal with the cartel is in a body bag. Got it?"

Even in the darkness she could see him turn pale at the threat. She might be a bitch, but the head of the cartel was a ruthless killer. If he suspected they were getting cold feet, he wouldn't hesitate to have them murdered and dumped in the gutter.

"Yeah, I got it," Leo muttered.

Gwen lowered her umbrella and snapped it shut. "We need to get back to the station."

Chapter Four

Gray stood next to Ian Brodie at a roadside rest area north of Seattle. It was late enough that his car and Ian's green Jeep were the only two vehicles pulled next to the brightly lit brick building. Inside, Mel was keeping guard on Donny as he used the restroom. He'd also heard her promise the boy that she would buy him a few snacks from one of the vending machines.

Ian was an inch taller than Gray's six-foot-one, with blond hair and piercing blue eyes. He was wearing a thick sweatshirt and heavy jeans to combat the chilly night air.

"Thanks for meeting me," Gray murmured.

"You were there when I needed you," Ian said. "Just tell me how I can help."

"I need you to take Donny and find somewhere to keep him safe for a few days."

"He can stay with us," Ian offered without hesitation. "Lily would love to have a friend to play with."

"There are some very dangerous people searching for him," Gray warned. The last thing he wanted was to put Ian's new family in danger.

His companion shrugged. "I'll make a few calls. The bad guys will have to go through an entire clan of Brodies to get to him," he said, referring to his cousins. Gray had met most of the men. Only an idiot would dare to challenge them. "What about Mel?" Ian continued. "She's welcome to stay with us."

Gray shook his head. "I'm going to need her help. She's the only eyewitness to the men who tried to kidnap Donny," he told his friend, not adding that he didn't trust anyone to protect her. No one but himself.

"Where will you go?" Ian demanded.

"The family cabin. There's a computer there and access to the Internet. I can tap into the police department and pull up the mug shots for Mel to look through."

Ian nodded. "Do you have security there?"

"State of the art," Gray assured him. "My mother brings clients to the cabin to discuss business mergers that are top secret. She insisted on the sort of security usually reserved for the Pentagon, despite the fact that the cabin's in the middle of nowhere."

"Smart woman," Ian said.

Gray resisted the urge to roll his eyes. He loved his mother, but she was a force of nature who flattened anyone in her path. "No one could deny that," he said in dry tones.

Ian cleared his throat. "What else can I do?"

"I suspect the bad guys are going to be watching Mel's apartment. It would give us some breathing room if you could keep them busy."

"Don't worry." Ian smiled with sudden anticipation. "I'll have them chasing from one end of the state to the other." His gaze moved to the door of the nearby building where Mel had appeared with Donny. The boy was tightly clutching her hand. "I'll need that red jacket she's wearing. And tell her to turn off her phone."

Gray studied Ian in confusion; then he realized his

friend was right. If there were cops looking for Mel, they could easily tap into the GPS on her cell to find her.

Gray's blood ran cold. Damn. He should have thought of that danger himself.

"Good point."

"I have a burner in the Jeep she can use for now," Ian told him. "What else can I do?"

Gray laid a hand on his friend's shoulder. "You've done more than enough."

"Just let me know if you need anything," Ian insisted. "I'll keep an ear to the ground. If I hear any chatter on the street about Mel or Donny, I'll let you know."

"Thanks." Gray gave his friend's shoulder a squeeze before lowering his hand.

There was a short silence. Almost as if Ian was considering his words.

"How is Mel?" he finally asked.

Gray glanced toward the woman who was patiently waiting for them to finish their conversation. Clearly, she didn't want to take the risk of Donny overhearing anything they might be discussing.

His heart squeezed with an aching sense of loss.

"Furious that someone would try to hurt a child," he told his companion.

"Typical Mel. I don't know many people who would take on a couple of thugs, let alone ram them with their car." Ian's voice was edged with an unmistakable admiration. "I'm sure she must be terrified."

Gray sucked in a deep breath. "She is, but she's determined to keep it hidden. At least from me."

"It must have been a shock when you appeared to rescue her."

Gray released a humorless laugh. "If she wasn't being

chased by kidnappers, I doubt she would have gotten in the car."

There was a short silence before Ian asked the question that had no doubt been on the tip of his tongue since Gray had called to say what'd happened.

"And you?" he demanded. "How are you dealing with being around Mel again?"

A wistful sigh whispered through Gray's lips. "I realize why I spent the past two years waiting for an excuse to return to Seattle."

Ian folded his arms over his chest. "Why did you need an excuse?"

A good question. It was a shame he didn't have a good answer. "Because I'm an idiot," was all he could say.

"You're not going to get an argument from me."

Gray arched his brows. "Some friend you are."

Ian shrugged. "We all get to be an idiot once or twice in our lives. The trick is to learn from our mistakes and not repeat them."

"I don't intend to, but first I have to make sure Mel is safe." Gray's gaze took a slow, thorough survey of the woman who'd haunted his dreams for years. "After that . . ."

"Anything can happen," Ian finished for him.

"Yes, indeed."

Mel watched the windshield wipers swish back and forth. The rain had eased to a fine mist that could barely be seen in the glow of the headlights. As they'd left Seattle, a thick darkness had settled around them, making it feel as if they were cocooned from the rest of the world. A sensation that was only emphasized when the traffic thinned to a mere trickle.

"You're quiet." Gray at last broke the silence.

"I'm worried about Donny," Mel said, her heart twisting at the memory of Donny's pale face streaked with tears as she tucked him into the Jeep.

It'd felt like the worst betrayal to walk away from him.

"You can trust Ian," Gray assured her. "He's trained to protect people. He won't let anything happen to the boy."

Mel turned her head to study Gray's chiseled profile, which was visible in the glow of the dashboard. It was shockingly familiar. As if she'd memorized every sweep and curve of his features before he'd abandoned her.

The realization was unnerving.

"I don't question Ian's ability to protect Donny, but the boy will feel as if he's been more or less dumped on strangers. He'll crawl even deeper into his shell," she explained. "I'm afraid he'll never come back out."

"Ian has a stepdaughter around the same age," Gray reminded her. "He'll be much happier playing with Lily in a comfortable home than on the run with us. Besides, I'm hoping it's only for a couple of days."

She slowly nodded. He was right. She trusted Ian. And there was no doubt Donny would be happier with a playmate to keep him distracted.

"Okay."

Gray cleared his throat. "Is there anything else bothering you?"

Mel frowned. Was he probing for something specific?

"Yes, I'm worried about missing work," she told him.

He sent her a puzzled glance. "I thought you'd texted the center before you turned off your phone."

"I did." She heaved a small sigh. "But my students will worry if I'm not there," she said. "Kids who live in constant chaos tend to cling to the routine that I try to offer them."

"I promise to get you back to the center as quickly as possible," he assured her, his tone serious.

Mel wrinkled her nose. She knew it was ridiculous to worry about work when she was being chased by street thugs and dirty cops. But it was something tangible to fret over.

"This is all . . ." Her words trailed away as she struggled to explain her inner fears.

"What?"

"It feels like a dream," she finally said. "Or a nightmare."

"I'm sorry."

"It's not your fault." Her lips twisted in a rueful smile. It would be easy to blame Gray, but she knew exactly who was responsible. "I knew there was going to be trouble as soon as I rammed that SUV."

Gray slowed as they veered off the highway to take a narrow road lined by trees. The sense of isolation intensified.

"Do you want me to have Ian tow your car to a garage?" he asked.

She didn't have to think about her answer. "No, I'm pretty sure it's totaled," she said. The hood had been smashed into the shape of an accordion. Which didn't seem fair considering she'd only dented the door of the SUV. "Not much of a loss, to be honest."

Gray turned his head to glance at her. "It wasn't that same old Taurus, was it?"

"Yeah."

He returned his attention to the twisty road. "That thing was ready for the scrap heap two years ago."

"It got me from one place to another," she protested; then she grimaced, recalling the numerous times she'd been stuck walking to work. There was a reason she lived so close to the center. "Most of the time."

"And you didn't want the hassle of shopping for a new car."

She glanced out the window, annoyed that he knew her so well.

"I don't like change," she muttered. As far back as she could remember, she'd been bounced from place to place.

Sometimes with her mother, who'd struggled with a drug addiction, and sometimes in various foster homes. The only constant in her life had been the small, battered suitcase she kept packed and hidden beneath her bed, no matter where she was.

"I always wondered how you ended up in Seattle," he murmured.

She didn't like to talk about the past—it was too painful. But right now, she was willing to do anything to keep her mind from dwelling on what would happen if those men managed to find Donny. "It was a deathbed promise to my mother."

Mel could sense his surprise. "She wanted you to move to Seattle?"

"Not exactly." Mel shook her head, blocking out the last, horrifying days of her mother's life. Whatever mistakes the older woman had made, Mel loved her. "She wanted me to travel away from Chicago before deciding where I wanted to settle down. I spent three months driving across the country."

"Why Seattle?"

Her lips twisted. "I could say it was the beautiful views. Or the friendly people. Or the best grilled salmon I've ever tasted. But the truth is my car broke down. I had to get a job to pay for the repairs."

"The Hummingbird Youth Center?"

"Yep." She shrugged. "Not a very exciting story."

"I don't know," he protested. "Perhaps it was fate that caused your car to break down at that precise time and in that precise place."

"Or a broken fan belt," she said dryly, although she knew that there had been more than just bad luck that had made her stay in Seattle.

It'd almost been as if the dark grief that had haunted her for weeks had slowly lifted as she settled into her job at the center.

Gray released a short laugh. "Maybe a combination of destiny and faulty belts."

She resisted the urge to share in his amusement. Instead she glanced toward the passing trees that were creeping closer to the road.

"Where are we going?"

"To the family cabin," he told her. "It's only another hour or so from here."

She stiffened. It hadn't occurred to her that he intended for them to stay under the same roof. Stupid, of course.

"Why don't we just get a couple hotel rooms?"

"The cabin is remote enough we won't have to worry about nosy neighbors, but fully equipped with the technology I need to continue my investigation." He slowed and turned onto another road, this one even narrower. "But first, we need something to eat."

Chapter Five

Kevin "Hammer" Hamil shifted in his seat, wincing as his stiff muscles threatened to cramp. He'd been watching the narrow white house built on a corner lot for less than three hours, but already his ass was asleep, and he had to piss. Next to him, his younger brother, Manny, was doing his own share of squirming.

They weren't the sort of guys who liked sitting around. Unless it was in a bar with a cold beer in their hands.

Not for the first time he regretted becoming involved with Detective Gwen Dobbs. Back then it'd seemed like the answer to a prayer. After all, she'd busted him and Manny with enough meth to send them to prison for years. It wasn't until she'd started ordering him around that he'd realized he'd made a deal with the devil. Jail didn't seem so bad compared to an eternity of being at the bitch's beck and call.

"I'm hungry," Manny abruptly groused. "And I need a beer."

"Tough," Hammer said.

"Why can't we go grab some food and stretch our legs?"

"Because we're supposed to be watching the apartment."

"Even felons get a dinner break," Manny muttered.

Hammer scowled as his stomach rumbled. He was starving, and talk about dinner wasn't helping.

"And what if the woman comes while we're gone and then disappears?" he snapped. "Do you want to be the one to tell Detective Dobbs that we messed up again?"

Manny shuddered. No one wanted to piss off the female detective. "Fine. You can stay here, and I'll go get some food."

"Forget it. The last time you promised to come back for me, I didn't see you for two days."

Manny muttered a curse. "Then you go. I need something in my gut. You know how I get when my blood sugar drops."

About to tell his brother to shove his blood sugar up his ass, Hammer sucked in a sharp breath as headlights sliced through the darkness.

"Duck," he exclaimed, wiggling down in his seat until he heard the tires crunch on the driveway across the street. Then, popping his head up, he glanced over the dashboard to see a slender woman slide out of the car, pulling the hood of her red jacket over her head.

"Bingo," he breathed.

"Is that her?" Manny demanded.

"Yeah, I remember her coat."

"There's no kid with her."

"She must have stashed him somewhere," he said. "Probably with whoever loaned her the new car."

"Now what?"

Hammer frowned as he watched the woman hurrying toward the stairs on the side of the garage.

"Now we wait."

"Shit," Manny muttered, squirming in his seat.

They sat in silence as the lights in the apartment flicked on. Was she staying? Pulling out his phone, Hammer was about to call Dobbs and ask the detective if they should grab the woman, when the lights were suddenly flicked off and the door to the apartment opened.

"She's coming down the stairs," Manny warned.

"Start the engine, but don't turn on the headlights." Hammer hit Dobbs's number. "Keep close enough to follow her, but don't spook her. If she takes off, our ass is grass."

Manny turned the key and shoved the SUV in gear. "I don't need you telling me how to do my business."

"Just drive," Hammer snapped, pressing the phone to his ear as it connected to Dobbs. "Yeah, we're on her trail."

Gray finished putting away the groceries he'd purchased after they'd stopped for dinner. From his vantage point in the kitchen he could watch Mel take a slow tour around the vast, sunken living room with its bank of windows on one wall and a massive stone fireplace on another. She moved into the library that was used as an office and then into the dining room that boasted a chandelier shipped in from Venice and a glossy table that could easily seat a dozen guests.

"You call this a cabin?"

"My mother never does anything small," he admitted, not surprised that Mel was overwhelmed by the place. It had the vibe of an elegant Swiss chalet that'd been plucked from the Alps and nestled among the thick forest of aspen and cedars. "Besides, she uses it for business. She brings potential clients here, to seal the deal. That's why the place is fully equipped with an office."

Strolling into the open kitchen, Mel tossed the bag

of clothes they'd bought at a local dollar store onto the breakfast bar.

"She's a lawyer, right?"

"Corporate lawyer," he said. "She specializes in mergers between mammoth companies."

"And your brother is a lawyer, too?" she asked.

"Yep. They formed a partnership a couple years ago."

"So he uses this cottage as well?"

Ah. Now Gray understood the reason for her questions. "You don't have to worry about either of them making an unexpected appearance."

"How can you be so sure?"

Gray tucked away the last of the groceries and leaned against the marble countertop. "Because Jarod's wife is expecting their first child any day. There's no way they would drive this far from the nearest hospital."

"Oh." Her eyes widened. "That must be . . ." She paused, as if searching for the appropriate word. "Difficult for you."

Gray hesitated, then with brisk movements headed to the wine cabinet to pull out his favorite chardonnay and two glasses.

"Mel, let's sit down." He nodded toward the leather sofa in the sunken living room. "I need to talk to you."

She stiffened in instant rejection. "Actually, I'm tired. If you could show me to my room—"

"Please, Mel," he interrupted in a soft voice. "This won't take long."

Her lips parted to deny his request; then she seemed to falter as he sent her a pleading glance. She heaved an audible sigh.

"Fine."

Together they moved to settle on the low sofa. Gray

filled the two glasses with the crisp white wine and handed one to Mel.

"Here."

She took it with an unreadable smile twisting her lips. "Am I going to need it?"

"You might want to toss it in my face," he admitted.

"I never waste good wine," she informed him, taking a sip.

He chuckled at her quick smackdown. "I always knew you were smart."

She grimaced. "Not so smart."

"The *not so smart* honor belongs to me," he insisted, pausing to taste his wine. It was dry and velvet smooth as it slid down his throat. "I want to explain why I left Seattle."

Her jaw tightened. "There's no need to discuss this, Gray."

"There's every need," he insisted. "Looking back, I'm ashamed of myself."

"Why?" She continued to sip her wine, her gaze moving toward the large windows. "You couldn't bear to be around your brother and his new wife. No one can blame you."

Gray snorted. The excuse he'd given for leaving two years ago sounded even more embarrassing when she repeated it back to him.

"Yes, it was all very Shakespearean," he said dryly. "The love of my life married to my brother. And now she's having his baby." He shook his head in self-disgust. "But, you know, the truth is that I couldn't be happier for them."

She hunched her shoulders, as if she was protecting herself from some unseen threat.

"You don't have to pretend with me. I know it must be tearing you up inside."

"Not even a little."

"But —"

"Listen, Mel," he once again interrupted. It wasn't that he didn't want to hear what she had to say. He could sit and listen to her for hours. She was an intelligent, fascinating woman with a wry sense of humor. It was just that he was desperate to confess his stupidity before he lost his nerve. "I need to go back in history to fully explain."

He leaned forward to grab the bottle and topped both their glasses.

"Well?" Mel prompted.

"I told you that my father died when I was ten."

She nodded. "That must have been very hard for you."

"It was." Even now there was a soul-deep sadness that haunted him. "I worshipped my father. The days I spent out on his fishing boat were magical for a young boy. My mother and brother hated the water, so it was just the two of us most of the time."

"I'm sorry."

"I believed our special bond meant that no one could possibly grieve as much as I did," Gray continued. "My mother and brother turned to each other for comfort, but I kept myself apart from them."

"Is that why you didn't become a lawyer?" She tilted her head to the side, as if genuinely curious.

"In part. Plus, I couldn't bear the thought of being stuck behind a desk." He shuddered as he thought of the hours his mother and brother spent in their office. He'd be hyperventilating before the end of the day. "Thank God. I would have made a terrible lawyer."

"You never considered becoming a fisherman like your father?"

"I enjoy the water, but I need . . ." His words trailed away.

"Excitement?"

"Yeah." It was a nice way of saying he was an adrenaline junkie. "My mother was horrified when I finished college and entered the police academy. She threatened to disinherit me."

"I'm guessing that only made you more determined."

"Of course. I'm nothing if not stubborn."

She rolled her eyes. "No crap."

"My brother, on the other hand, was happy to follow in her footsteps," he said. Jarod had decided on which law school he would attend by the time he was twelve. At that age Gray had been planning to play first base for the Yankees. "It only made me feel even more of an outsider."

Mel grimaced. "Families can be difficult."

Gray felt a small pang. Mel had been neglected and sporadically abandoned when her mom was using. It made his own childhood troubles seem even more petty.

"Looking back, I can see I was as much to blame for the tension between us as my mother or brother," he admitted. "At the time I only wanted to start a new family. *My* family."

Her face paled. "With Tori."

Tori Stockton had been a waitress at a local coffee shop near the police station. She'd been young and pretty and when she smiled, his world was brighter.

"We met shortly after I passed my detective exam. We both seemed to enjoy being together and I was ready to settle down."

"Did you love her?"

"I did," he said without hesitation. He had no desire to hurt Mel, but this time he intended to be completely honest. Even if it was too little, too late. "But it was more comfortable than all-consuming. I thought that's what I wanted so I asked her to marry me. Of course, my mother insisted on hosting a huge engagement party."

"That's the first time she met your brother?"

Gray nodded. "He'd just graduated from law school and returned home. I'm assuming that it must have been love at first sight. Three weeks after we announced our engagement, she eloped with Jarod."

"Why didn't you tell me that you'd been engaged to your sister-in-law?"

"They moved to Portland and it was easy to pretend that they didn't exist," he said, holding up his hand as a rueful smile twisted his lips. "You don't have to tell me it was childish."

"And when they returned to Seattle, you fled."

Gray swallowed his protest. He didn't like the word "fled." It made him sound like a coward. But maybe she had a point.

"I told myself that I was doing it because I wanted to make it less awkward for Jarod and my mother to establish the law firm they'd always wanted. I would make the great sacrifice so they could live happily ever after." He released a humorless laugh. "As I said, very Shakespearean."

Mel leaned forward to place her glass on the low coffee table. It also allowed her to hide her expression.

"No one could blame you for wanting to avoid the woman you love."

He battled back the urge to reach out and touch her. He had to be patient. Not one of his talents.

"I was hurt when Tori ran off with my brother, but it was my dented pride that sent me . . . fleeing, as you called it."

"And your broken heart," she insisted.

"No. My heart healed a long time ago," he told her. "In fact, the day I entered the marathon to raise money for a local charity and a clever, charming drill sergeant appeared to create order out of chaos."

He could precisely recall the moment when Mel had arrived at the start line. He hadn't realized at the time that the charity event was for the Hummingbird Youth Center. He only knew that he'd been fascinated by the young woman who was herding the large crowd with remarkable ease.

It wasn't just that she was pretty. It was how the sun brought out the burnished streaks in her dark hair. And the sparkle of intelligence in her bright green eyes. And her patient kindness as she helped an elderly couple fill out the necessary forms.

Then he'd asked her out for coffee, and she'd told him in tart tones that she was there to raise money for the children, not to be picked up by random strangers. He'd been a goner.

"You don't have to say that."

"I know I don't. It's the truth."

With a sharp movement, Mel was on her feet, her arms wrapped around her waist.

"I'm tired."

Gray bit his tongue. He wanted to tell her that he'd eventually realized he hadn't left Seattle just because of his brother and Tori. He'd been afraid of the emotions that she was stirring inside him. After all, love had made a fool of him once. He wasn't anxious to risk his heart again.

And he wanted her to know that he'd been waiting two years for an excuse to return.

Instead he forced himself to his feet. "I'll show you to your room."

Chapter Six

The sun was splashing the first golden rays over the mountainside as Mel leaned against the railing of the porch. Below her she could see the glitter of a large lake framed by trees.

Savoring the peace that was as much a part of the landscape as the wildflowers and chirping birds, she failed to hear the approaching footsteps. It wasn't until Gray spoke that she realized she was no longer alone.

"Mel?"

She jerked, turning her head to study the man who was standing next to her. He was wearing the cheap gray sweats they'd bought last night. She had on a matching pair, although hers were a dusty rose and a size too big.

"Oh, you startled me," she breathed.

"Sorry. I brought you this." He held out a ceramic mug with steam swirling around the top. "I remember you can be a grump before your first cup of coffee."

She gingerly tasted the hot liquid. It was strong, with two sugars and one cream. Exactly as she liked it. Mel clenched her teeth. She didn't want to be pleased that he'd remembered.

"Thanks," she muttered.

"Did you sleep okay?"

She grimaced. The vast bed had been a considerable upgrade from the pull-out she slept on normally. Still, she'd found herself tossing and turning most of the night.

"As well as could be expected," she said.

"Yeah." Gray turned to study the vista around them. "It's quite a view, isn't it?"

Mel eagerly turned her attention away from Gray to stare at the trees.

Last night she'd been too rattled to fully appreciate the power of his presence. Now she found her gaze wanting to cling to the dark beauty of his face, while her fingers itched to run through his thick chestnut hair.

Of course, even with her head turned she could still catch the warm scent of his skin and the hint of soap. As if he'd just stepped out of the shower.

She shivered, awareness curling in the pit of her stomach.

"Stunning," she forced herself to say. "I've always been a city girl, but now I understand why people prefer to live out here."

"I'm saving to buy some land next to the lake for when I retire," he told her.

"I can't imagine you ever retiring," she said, trying and failing to see Gray sitting in a rocking chair, watching TV.

He literally vibrated with suppressed energy.

"I love what I do, but my dad's death at such an early age has given me an appreciation for living life to the fullest. At some point I want to spend my days hiking through the woods and teaching my grandkids how to fish."

She flinched, not sure why she was so surprised by his words.

"Grandkids?"

"Someday." A wistful smile touched his lips. "What about you?"

"What about me?"

"You're so great with kids. I can't believe you don't want a few of your own."

Her heart twisted. She didn't allow herself to think about having children. Not when she was quite likely to spend her life alone.

"I already have my hands full." She cleared her throat. "Have you talked to Ian this morning?"

She thought she heard Gray heave a faint sigh, but he didn't protest the change in conversation.

"Not yet. I thought I'd get you set up with the computer to look through the mug shots first and then give him a call."

"I'm ready."

Cradling her coffee mug in her hand, Mel followed Gray as he entered the house and led her into the library. The room was as elegant as the rest of the cabin, with long shelves that held leather-bound books along with an open-beam ceiling and a stone fireplace.

Gray led her across the room and waited for her to settle in the swivel chair behind the glossy mahogany desk. Then, standing next to her, he switched on the computer and tapped on the keyboard. A few minutes later he was searching through the Seattle PD arrest records.

"We'll try to narrow this down," he murmured. "Can you give me a description?"

Mel closed her eyes, concentrating on her memories of the men who'd tried to kidnap Donny.

"They were both male, and both had pale skin. Almost as pale as mine. I didn't get a good look at the man who was driving the SUV, but the one who grabbed Donny was big," she said. "Over six foot and wide. Not fat, but thick like someone who's used to physical labor."

"Hair?"

"His head was shaved."

"Any facial hair?"

"No."

"Tattoos or piercings?"

"Not that I could see," she said, "but most of him was covered up."

"Eyes?"

She struggled to recall whether she'd gotten a good enough look to notice his eyes.

"I think they were brown, but he was too far away for me to say for sure."

Gray thankfully accepted her vague answer. "Did you notice anything about what he was wearing? Anything that might reveal where he works or a favorite bar?"

"He had on a black rain jacket and jeans. He could have bought them anywhere."

She made a sound of frustration as she opened her eyes. It'd all happened so fast, and she'd been so terrified, she hadn't paid much attention to the attackers clothing or the SUV. Now she bitterly regretted not memorizing a few details that would help ID them.

"We've got a good start," he assured her, typing on the keyboard before he straightened. On the screen were mug shots of large white men with bald heads. "Just hit the mouse when you're ready to move on to the next page. If you're not sure about one, mark down the number and we'll come back to it. Okay?"

She nodded, settling more comfortably in her chair. She had a feeling this was going to take a while.

"Okay."

* * *

The late morning sun slanted through the windshield as Hammer tucked the phone back in his pocket and reached to open the glove compartment of the SUV. They'd been sitting in the parking lot of the cheap motel nearly a hundred miles south of Seattle for hours. Ever since they'd trailed Melanie Cassidy to this location and watched her check into one of the rooms.

"What now?" Manny demanded.

Hammer grabbed his handgun and pulled it out of the compartment with a smile of anticipation.

"We go in," he said.

"About damned time." Manny stretched. Although they'd taken turns with bathroom breaks and grabbing coffee at the diner across the road, they were both feeling the effects of twenty hours stuck in the vehicle. "You're starting to smell."

"You ain't fresh as a daisy yourself," Hammer muttered, shoving open his door.

Crawling out of the SUV, Hammer angled across the gravel lot toward the back of the motel.

"Keep watch," he ordered, waving Manny to stand guard at the corner. "I don't want to be interrupted."

Manny nodded and Hammer headed to the door at the end of the long wing of the motel. He lifted his hand and slammed it against the door. He wasn't in the mood to be subtle.

"Open up," he barked in a loud voice. Nothing. He knocked again. "I'm coming in one way or another," he warned.

There was more silence and Hammer's patience snapped. The woman had been nothing but a pain in his ass. When he got his hands on her, she was going to regret screwing with him.

Lifting his foot, he kicked the flimsy door. There was

the sound of splintering wood as it swung open, revealing the cramped room with one bed and a dresser. Hammer held his gun outstretched as he cautiously stepped into the shadowed interior. There didn't seem to be any place for someone to hide, but he wasn't going to bet his life on it.

He frowned, glancing around. The room was empty, but worse, it looked as if no one had been in it for days. Maybe weeks. The bed was made, the open closet was empty, and there was a layer of dust over the small TV.

Had he kicked in the wrong door?

Hammer shook his head. No. He'd memorized the room number when he'd watched the woman enter the motel. This was it.

So, where was she?

A sour sensation curdled through him as he forced himself to move forward, peeking into the attached bathroom. No surprise to find it as empty as the other room. But then his gaze landed on the open window above the tub and he released a string of curses loud enough to wake the dead.

There was the sound of pounding footsteps as Manny rushed to join him.

"What's wrong?" he demanded, his head swiveling from side to side. "Where is she?"

"Gone," Hammer rasped between clenched teeth.

"Gone where?"

"If I knew that do you think I'd be standing here like a dumbass?"

Manny scowled. "She can't have gone far. Not on foot."

"Don't be stupid," Hammer snapped. "All she had to do was crawl out the window and head into town. She could have called a friend to pick her up and we would never know. She's probably been gone for hours while we twiddled our thumbs in the parking lot."

Manny paled. "It's not our fault."

"Do you think that's going to matter to Dobbs? She's going to have us castrated." Spinning on his heel, Hammer stomped out of the motel room. "You make the call," he told his brother, heading toward the street.

"Where are you going?" Manny demanded.

"To find a bar."

Gwen hissed in fury as she tossed her phone on her desk. A second later Leo entered her office and closed the door.

"Well?" he asked.

"She's not there," Gwen told him, her fingers tapping an impatient tattoo on the arm of her battered chair.

There was nothing she hated more than incompetence.

"Damn," Leo muttered. "How did she get away without them noticing?"

"She slipped out a bathroom window." Gwen shook her head in disgust. "If it was her at all."

Leo looked at her as if she was speaking a foreign language. "Who else would it be?"

"If she has any brains, she would know her place is being watched," Gwen told him. "She probably had a friend lead those idiots on a wild-goose chase before disappearing."

Leo fidgeted from one foot to another. Gwen could sense he was battling against the urge to run out of the police station and keep running.

"What about the trace we put on her phone?"

"Still nothing."

"So now what?" he demanded.

Gwen considered the question. She'd personally checked Donny's house, as well as the hospital where his grandmother was being treated. There was no sign of the boy. Melanie Cassidy was her only hope of finding him.

"We need to find out where the bitch went after she grabbed the boy out of Hammer's vehicle," she abruptly announced. "There has to be surveillance footage of her somewhere."

Leo frowned. "Even if there is, it could take days to get the warrants necessary to get our hands on them."

She sent him a scathing glare. Did he think she was stupid? Of course, she wasn't going to let anyone in the department realize she had an interest in Melanie Cassidy. Not when it was quite likely they were going to have to dispose of her. It'd been dangerous enough to trace her phone.

"I'm not going through official channels," she informed him. "I have a source who can tap into CCTV without the hassle of a warrant."

"What friend? A cop?" he demanded, his pudgy hands clenching and unclenching. It was obvious his nerve was about to snap. Gwen silently considered whether it was time to dispose of her partner.

It was possible that Detective Leo Blake's used-by date had passed.

A worry for later.

"Dooby Brown is a . . ." Gwen drummed her fingers, trying to find the words to describe the weaselly little man. She'd busted the tech genius a few years ago for credit fraud. "A free spirit," she at last said.

"Can he be trusted?"

Gwen snorted. "About as much as I trust you."

Leo jutted out his jaw, his expression peevish. "I don't like including another player. It increases our risk of exposure. We should just kill Kowalski like I wanted to do in the first place."

Gwen shoved herself to her feet, reaching out to poke Leo in the center of the chest.

"Kowalski dies and internal affairs will never, ever stop digging for evidence of corruption in the police force," she snapped. "Eventually they're bound to find some mistake we've made and we'll both be looking at a retirement that includes an eight-by-eight cell. Is that what you want?"

Leo managed to look even more peevish. "No."

"If we can pressure Kowalski to tell the judge that he lied about dirty cops working with the cartel, then all this heat goes away." She gave him another poke, wishing it was a bullet going through his cowardly heart. "Got it?"

He hunched his shoulders, his face pale. "Yeah. I got it."

Chapter Seven

Gray strolled back to the library, taking a second to appreciate the sight of Mel seated at the desk. It didn't matter that she was in a pair of cheap sweats, or that her hair was tousled from standing in the breeze before it was completely dry.

Just being able to walk into a room and see her there was enough to ease a hunger he hadn't realized was gnawing at him. A knowledge that would have unnerved him two years ago. Now . . .

Now it only deepened his determination to earn his way back into this woman's heart.

He cleared his throat. "Time for breakfast."

Mel jerked her head up in surprise. Obviously, she hadn't realized she was no longer alone.

"I'm not done," she protested.

"They'll be here after you eat," he assured her. "Plus, I have a fresh pot of coffee brewing."

Her eyes brightened at the mention of coffee. "I could use a break," she admitted, rising to her feet. "The faces are starting to blur together."

Gray waited for her to join him before he led her out of the office and toward the breakfast bar. She climbed onto a high stool, her eyes widening at the sight of the fluffy pancakes, eggs, bacon, and bowl of fresh fruit.

"You made this?" she demanded, not bothering to hide her shock.

"Yep." He poured coffee into a large ceramic mug and slid it in front of her. "I'm a handy guy to have around."

She filled her plate, dousing her pancakes with the maple syrup he'd warmed in a pan, and hungrily dug in. He'd always loved the fact that she had a healthy appetite. With Mel there was never any pretense. She was who she was. Period.

"I don't remember you cooking before," she said between bites.

He piled his own plate and started to eat. "I didn't. But after I moved to Spokane, I got tired of eating out," he told her. He'd also needed a way to distract himself from his regrets over his hasty flight from Seattle. "Surprisingly, I discovered I enjoyed spending time in the kitchen. It helps me de-stress."

"It's delicious," she assured him, finishing her meal and then sipping her coffee. "Did you call Ian?"

"I did. Donny is fine and currently being bullied into playing hide-and-seek with Lily. I could hear him laughing in the background." A smile curved his lips at the memory. There'd been something in the echoing laughter of the children that had tugged at his heart. "Plus, two of Ian's cousins flew in this morning to provide extra protection."

Relief darkened her eyes. "Thanks."

He held her gaze. "You're not in this alone, Mel."

"It feels strange. I've been taking care of myself for a long time."

"Yeah, me too. I called it independence, but if I was being honest with myself, it felt like loneliness."

She shoved away her empty plate, her expression impossible to read. "Independence isn't a terrible thing."

"No, not terrible, but nothing replaces a family," he said, thinking again of the happy laughter of children. "Even if it is messy and painful and occasionally infuriating."

She frowned, but before she could respond, there was a buzzing from the burner phone that he'd left on the counter.

Sliding off the stool, Gray crossed to grab the phone and pressed it to his ear.

"What's happened?" he demanded, knowing it had to be Ian. No one else had the number.

"I have a license for you to run," his friend said.

Gray rummaged in the drawers until he found a small pad and pen. "Go," he commanded.

Ian rattled off the combination of letters and numbers and Gray jotted them down.

"Who does it belong to?" Gray asked.

"Two men in a dented SUV who trailed one of my employees, Jillian Harmon, from Mel's apartment to a motel south of town."

"The kidnappers," he growled. It had to be them.

"Jillian waited for a few hours to see if anyone else would make an appearance, or if the men would lead her back to Seattle and the cops that you suspect are involved with the drug cartel," Ian continued.

"Anything?"

"She's still waiting." Ian squashed Gray's brief flare of hope. "Right now, the two men are in a local bar drowning their sorrows at realizing Mel managed to slip away. She's going to hang around and keep an eye on them."

Gray's first instinct was to race to the bar where the men were drinking so he could beat the truth out of them. Every man had his breaking point, no matter how tough he might be. But he quickly reined in the impulse. Not only would he destroy any hope of getting the men convicted of attempted kidnapping, but the cops would only fade deeper into the shadows.

Nope, his only hope was exposing them once and for all.

"Thanks, Ian," he murmured.

"I'll keep you updated," Ian promised.

Gray tucked the phone in his pocket and turned to meet Mel's worried gaze.

"Well?" she prompted.

"We might have a lead," he told her, heading into the office. Mel quickly followed behind him.

Gray settled at the desk and used the private account the chief had set up for him to run a trace on the plate.

A minute later he had a name.

"Manny Hamil," he murmured, then pulled up the mug shots and typed in the name. "Does he look familiar?" he asked as the photo appeared on the screen.

Mel leaned over his shoulder. "He might have been the driver. It's hard to say."

Gray leaned forward to read the note at the bottom of the mug shot.

"He was arrested with his brother, Kevin the Hammer." He typed in the name.

"Kevin the Hammer?" Mel repeated. "That's his name?"

"Thugs aren't hired for their clever wit," he said dryly.

The mug shot of Hammer filled the computer screen and Mel sucked in a sharp breath.

"That's him."

"You're sure?"

"Absolutely."

Gray felt a surge of grim resolve. They had the names and faces of the bad guys. It was the break they needed.

"I'm going to print off their rap sheets," he said.

"What are you looking for?"

"The top priorities are unearthing the officers who've arrested them, any history of being a paid informant, and any contact with the local drug cartel."

He tapped on the keyboard and there was a humming sound from the printer on a nearby shelf. Then a small window popped up on the computer screen that showed there were over a hundred pages waiting to print.

"That's just the rap sheets?"

"Yeah, this is going to take a while," he told her. He could have chosen the criminal record, which would have been shorter, but he wanted the notes from any prosecutions.

"Let's go," he said, rising to his feet and heading toward the French doors that led to the back of the cabin.

"Go where?"

He slid open the door. "It's too beautiful a day to be inside."

"I thought we were hiding," she protested, even as she followed him out of the house and down the short flight of stairs.

"We can hide in the trees," he assured her, crossing the paved patio to the narrow pathway.

Mel hesitated, glancing back at the house. Then, with a tiny shrug, she moved to join him as he strolled into the trees. They moved through the dappled shadows, angling down the side of the mountain.

For several minutes there was silence broken only by the shuffle of pine needles beneath their feet and the chatter of squirrels scrambling from one tree to another.

Then Mel sucked in a deep breath and released it on a soft sigh. "I love the smell of cedar."

Gray tilted back his head to admire the towering trees around them, savoring the warmth of the dappled sunlight that managed to sneak through the branches.

"I used to think nothing was better than the salty tang of an ocean spray on my face. But after spending a few weekends in the mountains, I discovered an appreciation for the scent of the trees and the song of the birds." He returned his attention to the woman walking at his side. "My dad would have hated it here."

Mel shot him a curious glance. "Your parents didn't seem to have much in common. How did they get together?"

It was a question that more than a few people had asked. Not just because his father had been a fisherman and his mother a high-powered lawyer. It was the fact that his father loved being out in the fresh air rather than fancy parties and was obviously uncomfortable when he was being hauled to the opera or the latest art exhibit.

"My mother was in law school and after her finals she went bar hopping with some fellow students," he told Mel. "She was leaving a cheap joint near the wharf when some guy tried to drag her into his car."

Understanding sparked in the beauty of her green eyes. "Ah. Your father rescued her."

"Yeah."

"Very romantic."

He smiled with wry amusement. "It was certainly better than asking a woman to have coffee when she's clearly distracted by her job."

Mel hurriedly returned the conversation to his parents. "Was your father already a fisherman?"

Gray nodded. "He'd just bought his own boat and was working twenty hours a day to stay afloat. Literally. I think my mom admired his grit and ambition."

"So do I," Mel said without hesitation. "I have great admiration for anyone capable of creating their own business."

Her words warmed his heart. All his life, people had

fawned over his mother. Understandable, because she'd created the sort of power and wealth that most people envied. Still, it annoyed him that they ignored his father's accomplishments.

"I think they genuinely loved each other," he said, recalling the way his father would hold his mother's hand when they left the house together, or how his mother would brighten when his father walked into the room. "It wasn't until my mother had reached the top of the corporate ladder that she started nagging at him to sell his boat and get an office job." A sadness tugged at his heart. Those arguments had been the only blight on his childhood until the death of his father. "I didn't understand at the time why they were always arguing. Looking back, I assume that my mother decided having a husband who was a common fisherman tarnished her image."

Mel considered his words, her brow furrowed as if she was sorting through them to find some hidden meaning.

"Maybe," she said at last.

"Maybe?"

She came to a halt as they reached a pretty glade filled with wildflowers. Turning to face him, she tilted her head to the side.

"There's another possibility."

He was confused. "Is there?"

She took a second. As if gathering her thoughts. "When I was young and my mother relapsed, she would tell me that she didn't have the money to take care of a kid, or even that she was too busy with her new boyfriend, and that's why I had to go back to foster care," she said, her voice so soft that Gray had to strain to hear the words. "She didn't want to admit that she was using again."

Gray struggled to disguise his fierce reaction. He'd

learned that Mel refused to condemn her mother despite the fact she'd utterly failed her daughter.

"How would having a new boyfriend be a better excuse to put you in foster care?" he demanded, his voice edged with disgust despite his best efforts.

Her expression was wistful. "Because she didn't want me to know that she was too weak to stay sober. It made her feel like a failure," she told him. "She wanted her daughter to see her as a smart, capable woman, not a junkie who would do anything for her next hit."

Gray took a step forward. He had been awed by this woman from the moment they'd met. He'd never encountered another person with such a kind heart combined with such unflappable competence no matter what turmoil was spinning around her. She not only cared about her students, but she would move heaven and earth to make their lives better.

"How did you ever turn out to be so amazing?" he breathed.

She blushed, as always uncomfortable when he pointed out just how wonderful she was.

"I have my issues," she insisted. "And it's taken time to accept that my mother did the best she could."

He bit back his opinion of her mother. Instead, he returned his thoughts to his own parents.

"I'm not sure what this has to do with my mother's insistence that my father sell his boat," he said.

"Fishing is a very dangerous occupation," she pointed out. "Maybe your mother was worried your father would get hurt." She studied him, a hint of regret in her voice. "Or worse."

Gray stiffened. "If that was the reason, then why wouldn't she just . . ." His words trailed away. He'd been so young when he'd overheard those squabbles that he hadn't considered inner motives. He'd listened to their words and accepted them at face value. Now he tried to look back with the wisdom of an adult. "Oh," he muttered, feeling as if the earth was moving beneath his feet. "She didn't want to admit that she was scared."

Mel shrugged. "It's just a thought."

"A very good one," he admitted. "My mother prides herself on being invincible, which to her means being in complete control of her emotions. It would be hard for her to admit that she was afraid."

"It would also explain why she was so opposed to your becoming a cop," Mel suggested, her tone gentle. As if she understood that the bitterness he'd nurtured for years was being ripped out and replaced with regret. "That's a job that would give most mothers nightmares."

Gray slowly shook his head, wondering how he'd been so blind. "My father warned me that I needed to think before acting. Or in this case, before leaping to conclusions."

She reached to place her hand on his chest, her expression one of sympathy.

"It would probably be best to sit down and talk to her. Communication is the only way to have a healthy relationship. I learned that too late."

"You're right, Mel." He pressed his hand over hers, rejoicing in the feel of her touch. It'd been so long. *Too* long. "I've never found it easy to discuss my emotions or what's in my heart. I just assume I know what other people are feeling and that they know what's going on with me." He allowed his other hand to settle at the base of her spine, gently urging her toward him. "A mistake I'm not going to make again."

For a blissful second, she snuggled against him. Gray groaned at the sensation of her soft warmth. This was what he'd dreamed of, night after long night. Breathing deeply of her bewitching scent, Gray lowered his head.

He had to taste her . . .

When he was a breath away from her lips, Mel abruptly panicked. Shoving her hands against his chest, she broke away from his light grasp.

"We should go back."

Gray felt a sharp pang of rejection as Mel turned to hurry back up the path. He logically knew he had to be patient, but his heart was desperate to wrap her in his arms and kiss her until she couldn't remember that she wanted to run away from him.

Then his disappointment was replaced with concern as he watched her foot catch on a loose rock and she pitched to the side.

"Mel," he called out, leaping forward.

He managed to wrap his arm around her waist, but as she knocked into him, he lost his balance. Locked together, they tumbled to the ground, rolling down the steep incline to land in the bottom of a deep ditch.

Chapter Eight

Mel wasn't hurt. Her breath had been knocked from her lungs, and she had a few scrapes and bruises. Her pride had taken the greatest injury.

She'd acted like a nervous schoolgirl, running away from Gray. Now, she was lying flat on her back, covered in dust, with the large man perched on top of her. No doubt it served her right, but that didn't lessen her embarrassment.

Gray gazed down at her in concern. "Are you okay?"

"I'm fine."

His brows drew together, something that might have been pain darkening his eyes to a smoky gray.

"You don't have to break your neck trying to get away from me, Mel," he said in a husky voice. "If your feelings for me are gone, I understand. It's no one's fault but my own. I promise I won't say another word."

Mel's embarrassment started to fade, slowly replaced by a far more dangerous emotion.

"It's not that," she rasped as a potent, ruthless desire spread through her.

She felt his muscles clench, almost as if he was expecting a physical blow.

"Mel?"

She didn't want to admit the truth. It exposed a part of her that she preferred to keep hidden. But she'd just lectured Gray on the importance of honest communication.

"I don't trust you not to hurt me again," she forced herself to confess.

Regret softened his chiseled features. "I'm sorry. So sorry." He lowered his head, lightly pressing his lips against her mouth. "I was an idiot," he breathed. "Is there any way you can ever forgive me?"

A sweet, sensual pleasure swirled through her. Warm and familiar and utterly addictive. *This* was what she feared. Her aching, soul-deep need for this man. It'd nearly broken her when he'd left. Could she survive if he abandoned her again?

"I don't know," she admitted with blunt honesty.

"Oh, Mel." His lips skimmed over her cheek, his touch light. As if assuring her that she could push him away at any second. "I've never forgotten how soft your skin feels beneath my fingertips." He nibbled the edge of her mouth. "Or the sweet temptation of your lips."

Mel shivered, her body instinctively softening beneath his solid weight. It felt so good to have him pressing her against the cool earth, his warm scent teasing her senses even as his tongue traced her lower lip.

"Gray." Her hands lifted to rest against his wide chest. Instantly she was blasted with memories of the nights she'd spent exploring those hard, sculpted muscles. First with her fingers, and then with her mouth.

"Yes?" he murmured, sweeping his lips down the line of her jaw.

"This is crazy," she muttered.

He lifted his head, staring down at her with eyes darkened by a fierce hunger that echoed deep inside her.

"No, the past two years were crazy," he said, his voice harsh. "This is . . ." His head once again swooped down to claim her mouth with a demanding kiss. "This is salvation."

Passion ricocheted through her. "It doesn't feel like salvation," she muttered.

"What does it feel like?"

Mel gasped, as if the air had been knocked from her lungs as Gray's lips found the pulse at the base of her throat. Only this man could make her head spin and her heart race with his kiss.

"It feels like danger," she admitted.

He lifted his head, allowing his smoky gaze to glide over her with a warm caress.

"I know it will take time to believe in me again, Mel," he said, his expression somber. "But I swear I'm prepared to do whatever is necessary to earn your trust."

She licked her lips, trying to clear her thoughts. Her body hummed with hunger, and desire pulsed between them, battering through the barriers she struggled to build around her heart.

"And after you've exposed the dirty cop?" she demanded. "Will you return to Spokane?"

His gaze lingered on her mouth, as if searching for inspiration.

"I'm not running this time," he assured her, reaching out to grasp the hem of her sweatshirt. "I'm staying in Seattle to fight for my family. My mother, Jarod and Tori, along with their little one." He deliberately paused. "And you."

Mel shivered as he slowly tugged the thick fabric upward. She told herself to push him away. She was still mad at being abandoned. Wasn't she?

Instead she lay there in silent approval, allowing him to peel the shirt off of her before he gently tucked it beneath her head.

"Gray . . ."

Her words trailed away as his fingers nimbly managed to unhook her bra.

The lacy undergarment disappeared as he smiled down at her with a smoldering anticipation.

"Yes?"

"What if someone is walking on the pathway?"

"Don't worry," he assured her in low tones. "This is part of my mother's property. If anyone tries to pass through the fencing, it will set off an alarm."

He stroked his fingers through her hair before they traced the shell of her ear and skimmed down her throat. A moan of sheer pleasure was wrenched from her lips. His smile widened as Gray lowered his head to trail a scorching path of kisses over her forehead.

"Wait," she breathed, trembling with an odd combination of alarm and intense yearning.

"What's wrong?"

She hesitated. She didn't know. Nothing felt wrong. In fact, it all felt gloriously perfect.

Still, there was a small, stubborn part of her that insisted she give some excuse.

"This is going so fast."

His gaze scorched over her; then he bent forward and allowed his lips to press against her furrowed brow.

"We can take this as slow as you want," he promised, moving his lips to nuzzle against the tender skin of her temple.

Her hands slid beneath his shirt, no longer able to resist the temptation.

A sinfully delicious excitement curled through her stomach as her fingers explored the bare skin of his chest before moving down the hard planes of his stomach. By the time she reached the waistband of his sweats she could feel the thick length of his erection pressing against her.

"Maybe not too slow," she managed to acknowledge, digging her nails into his skin as his lips found a tender spot just below her ear.

"Not too fast, not too slow," he murmured, his voice amused as his hands cupped her breasts. "Just right."

A raw, earthy bliss shuddered through her as his fingers stroked over the tips of her tightened nipples.

"I can't believe this is happening," she moaned.

"Me either," he admitted, his lips stroking down her throat. "I've dreamed of this so many nights, I'm afraid I'm going to wake and discover you're nothing more than a figment of my imagination."

She didn't feel like a figment.

Just the opposite. For the first time in two years she felt vividly alive as a rush of sensations cascaded through her. His lips paused over the pulse hammering at the base of her throat and her back arched as need created a damp yearning between her legs.

Overhead the sun peaked through the thick foliage, but they were hidden in the soft violet shadows of the forest floor. Mel released her reservations and allowed herself to be swept from her mundane world to a place of crisp, cedar-scented magic.

"And in your dreams did I tell you that you were a jerk for leaving Seattle?" she teased.

His chuckle was low and sinful. "Yes." His lips traveled downward, tracing the upper curve of her breasts. "And it wasn't until I swore that I would devote myself to your eternal happiness that you allowed me to hold you in my arms." His fingers skimmed down the curve of her body.

A sigh escaped her parted lips. Desire continued to

thunder through her, but it was more than mere lust. It was tangled with emotions that had never truly died.

His lips brushed the tip of her breast and Mel groaned. Oh yes. She felt as if she was melting from the inside out.

Her hands glided over his shoulders around his neck; then her fingers tangled in the silk of his chestnut hair.

Anticipation heated her blood, searing away the fear that had guarded her heart for so long.

Gray lifted his head to gaze down at the woman lying beneath him. Surrounded by the beauty of nature, she looked even more like a pixie. A delicate woodland creature who might disappear in a puff of smoke.

A growl rumbled in his throat as his hungry gaze slid over the soft swell of her breasts. He needed more. He needed to have her completely naked in his arms.

With more haste than skill, Gray rolled to the side, shedding his clothes. He took a second to grab his wallet from the pocket of his sweats and pulled out a condom that he quickly slid onto his aching erection. Then, with the same haste, he disposed of Mel's clothing.

It wasn't that he feared she would change her mind. The last thing he would want was for her to make love if she wasn't absolutely ready. But he hadn't been exaggerating when he'd claimed that this woman had haunted his dreams for two years.

His body was clenched with a need that was painful.

Stroking his fingers over her cheek, he gazed down at her with blatant hunger.

"Are you ready?" he asked in a low voice.

She quivered, a flush of arousal staining her cheeks. "For longer than I want to admit."

He lowered his head, brushing a kiss over her mouth.

"I've missed you, Mel," he murmured. "Your taste." He swept his lips over her cheek, savoring the heat of her skin. "Your passion."

Allowing his fingers to slide over her body, Gray caressed the soft skin of her inner thigh. At the same time, he kissed a path to the tip of her hardened nipple and captured it between his teeth. He relished the sound of her soft pants filling the air.

Such sweet music.

He feathered his fingers up her inner thigh, heading for his prize. "Is this still too fast?"

She shivered, her hands running an impatient path down his back.

"It's just . . ." Her breath caught as his finger dipped through the moist cleft between her legs. "Oh."

He laughed, using the tip of his tongue to tease her nipple, at the same time sliding his finger into the welcome heat of her body.

"It's just what?" he teased.

"Too slow," she told him in a voice thick with need.

"But don't they say that good things come to those who—"

He forgot what he was going to say as Mel reached to wrap her fingers around his arousal.

"Were you going to suggest that we wait?" It was her turn to tease as she explored him with a light grip.

"Nope, you were right." Gray settled between her legs and entered her with one deep thrust. "Too slow."

A sigh of ecstasy was wrenched from his throat. She was tight, her sweet heat fitting around him like a glove.

Paradise.

He forgot the reason they were hiding in the mountains, and the danger that lurked in the distance. Nothing mattered but the exquisite sensations that jolted through him as he pulled back his hips and plunged into her slick warmth.

Gray nipped at her lower lip. She tasted of spring air and wildflowers. His woodland pixie.

Awed by the intensity of the sensations that shuddered through his body with every thrust, Gray was vividly conscious of the sounds of Mel's soft moans. He'd promised to devote himself to her happiness. Which meant ensuring that she reached her climax first.

Framing her face in his hands, he sought her mouth as he kept his pace slow and steady. She returned his kiss, her body arching as she neared her release.

"Gray," she whispered.

"I've got you," he muttered in thick tones. "And I'm never letting go."

Increasing his pace, Gray urged her legs to wrap around his hips. He heard her gasp in startled joy, and he clenched his teeth, his hips surging until he was buried deep inside her.

The world seemed to shift beneath them as a shattering climax slammed through him.

Chapter Nine

Wrapped tightly in Gray's arms, Mel tried to gather her dazed thoughts. A task that would have been easier if his lips weren't still brushing soft kisses over her heated cheeks and his fingers trailing up and down the curve of her back.

She felt as if she'd been shattered into a thousand pieces by the intensity of her emotions. And she wasn't entirely certain she'd ever pull herself together again.

The disturbing thought sent a tiny shiver down her spine. Instantly, Gray sat up and studied her with a worried expression.

"You're cold," he murmured, quickly helping her to pull on her sweats and shoes.

Mel didn't correct him, as she covertly watched him tug his clothes over the hard temptation of his body. She needed time to process what had just occurred between them. And what it meant to her future.

Once they were both dressed, Gray reached to grasp her hand, sending her a wry smile as he plucked a cedar needle from her hair.

"I've really got to work on my timing," he teased. "I

can't seem to get it right around you. Probably because you make me a little crazy."

She sent him a stern glance. "We need to concentrate on who's threatening Donny."

The silver eyes sparkled with wicked humor. "I can multitask."

Mel's heart skipped. Or maybe it fluttered. Hard to tell the difference. And she found herself longing to lean against his side as they walked up the pathway. As if she couldn't get close enough to him.

Dangerous, dangerous, dangerous.

Once they returned to the house, Gray moved straight to the office, where there were stacks of paper waiting for them on the printer.

Gray carried the pile to the desk and sorted the pages into those pertaining to Kevin the Hammer or his brother Manny.

"How can I help?" Mel demanded, feeling the need to keep her mind occupied.

"I want to read through the rap sheets and make notes of arresting officers, and any deals with prosecutors that might have lessened their sentence," he said as he motioned for her to take the leather desk chair. He walked to grab another seat from a corner.

Mel sat and started skimming through Manny's rap sheet. Her brows lifted in surprise.

"Good grief," she muttered. "They must have been arrested a hundred times."

"Close," Gray agreed, settling beside her to examine Hammer's endless sheets of paper. "It looks like most of them are petty thefts or disturbing the peace." His brow furrowed as he shuffled toward the bottom of the stack. "It wasn't until they were picked up in a drug bust at a local crack house that they served more than a few weeks in jail." He continued reading through the file until he reached the last page. "Hmm."

"What is it?"

"I don't have access to any juvenile files, but from the day Hammer turned eighteen he was arrested on a regular basis," Gray said. "At least once or twice a month. Then, for the past three years he has nothing in his record." He shook his head in disbelief. "Not even a speeding ticket."

She considered the various possibilities. "Could he have been in jail?" she at last asked.

"No. His last incarceration was four years ago for possession with intent to sell."

"That means he went straight. Or . . ."

"Or someone is protecting him." Gray completed her thought. He nodded toward her stack of papers. "What about Manny?"

Mel shuffled to the bottom page. "The same. No arrests for over three years."

He frowned. "Who was the last cop to pick him up?"

It took a minute for her to find the officer listed among the information crammed onto the forms.

"Rick Houseman," she read aloud. "Do you know him?"

"The name is familiar." Gray hesitated, as if silently testing the name to stir a memory. Then he made a sound of impatience. "No. He couldn't be involved. I remember he retired before I left Seattle and moved to Florida." Gray muttered a soft curse. "Whoever the cops are, they made sure that there was no way to trace the Hamil brothers to them."

Mel shared his frustration. "What do we do now?"

Without warning, he reached to brush the back of his fingers down the curve of her throat.

"I have a few suggestions," he murmured, sending her a devilish smile.

Mel blushed, abruptly aware of how close they were sitting. "I'm talking about your investigation," she informed him.

He turned in his seat, framing her face in his hands. "I'd rather think about you," he said, his gaze lingering on her mouth. "I assumed I remembered how good it was between us. The explosion of heat. The scent of your skin."

"Gray," she protested in a husky voice.

He smiled with sinful satisfaction. "Your breathless voice when you're aroused."

She cleared her throat and tried again. One of them had to stay sane.

"Gray."

"But I was wrong," he continued, his eyes filled with smoky invitation. "Memories are pale imitations of the real you. Did I tell you that I've missed you?"

Mel's heart melted. "Yes."

"And that I'm never leaving you again?"

"Yes." His head started to lower, his gaze still on her lips. "Gray, you're losing focus," she warned.

"On the contrary," he protested. "I've never been so focused."

She reached to press her hand against the center of his chest. "We have to find out who's threatening Donny," she reminded him, her tone firm. "We can't keep him hidden forever."

He heaved a heavy sigh. "As much as I hate to admit it, you're right." He laid his hand over hers, pressing it against the steady thump of his heart. "Later?"

"Yes." The word slipped past her lips before she could halt it.

"Okay." He squared his shoulders and returned his attention to the papers. "Let's go through these again."

Mel rose to her feet. "I'll make coffee."

* * *

Leaning out of her office, Gwen gestured for Leo to join her. With a jerky motion, he rose to his feet and hurried toward her.

Gwen pressed her lips together. The older man was looking frayed around the edges. His skin was pasty and damp with sweat, while his hair looked like he'd forgotten how to brush it.

Anyone who took time to really study him would know he was a man under stress. Sooner or later she was going to have to deal with him. But first things first. She crossed to settle behind her desk.

"What's happened?" Leo demanded.

"We have the surveillance tapes from my contact," she said in clipped tones.

"That was quick."

It was.

"Close and lock the door," she commanded. "I don't want to be interrupted."

Leo did as she ordered, then moved to settle next to her. She wrinkled her nose at the smell of stale cigarettes, but she didn't demand that he move. The quicker they searched the video, the quicker they could clean up this god-awful mess.

Concentrating on her computer, Gwen clicked the mouse on one of the video files.

"This is from the convenience store across the street from the youth center," she said.

For ten minutes they watched the cars that pulled in and out of the store, but there was no sign of Melanie Cassidy.

"I don't see her," Leo muttered.

Gwen ignored the fool, clicking on the second video. "This is from the bar on the south side of the block."

The image of a narrow street lined by shabby buildings filled the screen. The road was empty for several minutes, then a car appeared from around the corner and screeched to a halt next to the curb.

Gwen leaned forward. "What's going on?"

Leo stabbed his finger at the screen as a slender female rushed from an alley, dragging a small boy behind her.

"There she is," he breathed. "And she has the kid."

A grim determination seared through Gwen. Finally.

"There has to be a way to zoom in." She stopped the video and used the mouse to enlarge the image of the driver.

"Is that Detective Hawkins?" Leo demanded.

"It might be." Gwen leaned closer, studying the grainy outline of the man behind the wheel. "Yes. That's him."

Leo sucked in a sharp breath. "Damn. If she told him what happened, then he's probably already filed a report."

Gwen fast-forwarded through the rest of the tape. The woman placed the boy in the back seat before climbing in next to Hawkins. The car sped off and disappeared down the street.

There was nothing after that.

She tapped her finger on the desk, her mind churning with various possibilities.

"If he intended to make a report, then why didn't he drive straight to the station?"

"How do you know he didn't?"

"I have a friend keeping a watch for the name Melanie Cassidy," Gwen grudgingly told him. She didn't like to reveal her various contacts. Not to anyone. "If it had popped up in the system, I would know."

Leo fidgeted in his seat, the sweat dripping down his face. "Then maybe she didn't tell him."

"Why wouldn't she? Especially after she found out that he's a cop."

"Not all people trust a badge." His tone was defensive. "Especially in that neighborhood."

She shook her head. Melanie Cassidy wasn't another perp who thought of the police as the enemy. She would instinctively seek the help of someone in authority.

"It doesn't make any sense."

"Is there any way we can ask?" Leo glanced toward her, clearly expecting her to solve their latest problem. "You know him, don't you?"

"Don't be an idiot," she snapped. "We can't ask. Not without exposing ourselves. Besides, I've never worked with Hawkins."

Gwen restarted the video, carefully watching as the woman emerged from the alley and crawled into the car. A frown tugged her brows. Had Hawkins flashed his badge? She couldn't see it. So why had the woman so quickly accepted his offer of help? Was it just because she was scared of the men behind her? Or did she recognize him?

"Shit." Gwen slammed her hand down on her desk.

Leo flinched. "What now?"

"I know why her face was familiar."

"Why?"

"I attended a banquet for the mayor a couple years ago." Gwen was infuriated with herself. Why had it taken her so long to remember?

Leo sent her a sour glance. "Am I supposed to be impressed?"

"Shut up and listen," she snapped.

"Fine." The word "bitch" went unsaid, but it flashed through his eyes.

"I was seated at the same table with Detective Gray

Hawkins and his girlfriend." Gwen pointed toward the computer screen. "Her."

"Melanie Cassidy?"

"Yes."

"You're sure?" Leo paled as Gwen sent him a sizzling glare. He lifted his hands in a gesture of apology. "Okay, okay. Don't get your panties in a twist."

"It's not going to be my panties twisting if you're not careful," Gwen warned, perfectly willing to put the man's nuts in a vise. Always assuming he had a set.

Leo licked his lips, hurriedly returning his attention to the true cause of her annoyance.

"Do you think Hawkins and the woman are somehow working together?"

Gwen considered the question before giving a shake of her head. "I think he suspects that there's a connection between Donny's attempted kidnapping and the police force," she announced in firm tones. "That's the only thing that explains why he didn't bring the woman and the kid to the station."

"How could he suspect anything?" Leo protested. "He only returned to Seattle a few weeks ago, didn't he?"

Gwen released her breath on a low hiss. She'd been so blind.

"Of course. That's it."

"What's it?"

Gwen shoved herself to her feet. The need for action vibrated through her. Not just because her police training urged her to take command of a situation, but out of a sense of self-preservation. Like a cornered badger, she intended to strike first.

"He didn't just decide to return to the Seattle PD," she said, pulling on the tailored jacket she'd left on a chair and adjusting her holstered weapon so it was in easy reach.

Leo was slower to rise to his feet, his expression confused. "I don't understand."

"He was asked to return by someone investigating police corruption." Her jaw tightened in frustration. "Obviously, Bart Kowalski's claim that there are dirty cops involved in the drug trade got the results we were hoping to avoid."

Leo swayed, looking as if he was about to piss his pants. "They know it's us?"

She sent him a glance of pure disdain. How had he ever managed to become a cop?

"Don't you think we would be arrested if they did?" she said, sneering.

He hunched his shoulders. "It's only a matter of time."

"Then we have to act quickly." Gwen grabbed her phone off her desk and punched in a number.

"Act?" Leo shifted from foot to foot. "Do you have a plan?"

"If Hawkins has the woman and kid with him, it will be the perfect time to silence them."

"Are you talking about killing a cop?" he stammered.

"Do you intend to spend the rest of your life in jail?"

"No."

"Then we do this." Gwen nodded toward the door. "You find out where Hawkins is living. Oh, and any place that he might use as a hideout."

Leo's face paled to a greenish hue. Was he going to throw up?

"What are you going to do?" he asked in a strained voice.

"Call Hammer," she said. "We need backup."

Chapter Ten

By four o'clock that afternoon, Gray was convinced he would have a permanent hunchback from leaning over the desk as he studied the rap sheets in tedious detail. How did anyone spend their days stuck in an office?

Outside, the sky had darkened as a fierce spring storm rolled in, breaking the silence with the distant rumble of thunder and the incessant beat of rain against the windows.

Just as he was on the point of conceding defeat, a small, niggling memory wormed its way through Gray's weary brain.

"Butch," he abruptly breathed.

Next to him, Mel gave a shake of her head, as if coming back from some distant place in her mind.

"Butch?" she repeated.

"A guard at the jail," he explained, using the computer to pull up the employment records.

"What about him?" she asked.

"I just remembered Ski mentioned that he caught the man in his cell searching through his private letters," he told her.

She leaned toward the computer, brushing against him.

Gray sucked in a deep breath, forcing himself to concentrate on the screen and not on the tingles of delicious heat that licked through his body.

"What do his letters have to do with anything?" she asked.

"They're the only way the cops could know he has a son."

"Oh." She sent him a hopeful glance. "Can you do some sort of background check on Butch?"

"It's going to be limited. But Ian has the software to do an expanded search." He stopped scrolling and clicked on the only Butch he could find in the staff records at the jail. "This must be him. Butch Schmitz." He read through the man's employment record. "He's been a guard for a year."

"Did he ever work for the Seattle PD?"

Gray sent his companion an approving glance. "Good question." He turned back to the computer to search through the man's file. "Hmm. No, but he has a couple arrests for minor drug offenses."

"If he's a criminal, how did he get a job at the jail?"

He found the section that listed Butch's references. "It looks like he went through a mentor program." Gray made a sound of satisfaction. "A program run by Detective Gwen Dobbs."

"Do you recognize the name?"

He settled back in his seat, racking his brain for anything he could dredge up about the female detective.

"I remember a few jokes when she requested Leo Blake as her partner," he murmured. It was the first memory he pulled up.

"What was the joke?" Mel demanded.

"Leo is the station's slug."

She frowned. "I don't know what that means."

"Every police department has that one officer who's lazy, moody, just riding out his time until he can retire.

Leo is ours. No one wanted him as a partner. In fact, if you got landed with him, it was because you were being punished." Gray absently tapped his fingers on the arm of his chair. "But Gwen Dobbs specifically asked to be put with him."

"Did she say why?"

"We assumed she wanted him as a contrast to her own abilities as a detective. Next to him she looked like the smartest, most ambitious cop on the force." Gray scooted forward and tapped on the keyboard. "But now, I wonder."

"What are you looking for?"

"I want to see how Detective Dobbs lives."

"How she lives?" Mel demanded in confusion.

"There were rumors that Leo had been caught taking bribes from a local politician to make his son's DUI disappear," Gray told her.

He'd forgotten about the older man until now. Partially because there was always gossip swirling around the station, and partially because these rumors had nothing to do with the drug trade.

"He wasn't fired?"

"The politician had enough power to get it swept under the rug." Gray grimaced. "It's unfortunate, but it happens. Money and power can infect anything, even the police force."

"What do you think this has to do with Gwen Dobbs?"

"If I were a corrupt cop, I would want a partner that I knew had sketchy morals and a willingness to break the law for his own gain," he murmured.

"Leo."

"Exactly." Searching through Gwen's finances, he found her address. He clicked on the map to pull up the image. "Here we go. This is her house."

Mel made a sound of surprise at the narrow home with peeling paint and a roof that was missing several shingles. The yard was barren except for a rusty trash can, and the windows had bars across them.

"It's a dump," Mel said.

It was. Even on a cop's salary Gwen should have been capable of buying a property that wasn't a breath from being condemned. Gray returned his attention to Gwen's financial report.

"Wait. She cosigned on a house for her mother," he said, typing in the address.

Immediately the image of a sweeping mansion with banks of windows overlooking Elliott Bay filled the screen.

"Wow. That's . . ." Mel allowed her words to trail away with a shake of her head.

"Way above her pay grade." Gray finished the thought for her. "Which means her mother is independently wealthy, or Detective Dobbs has another source of income."

Mel sent him a curious gaze. "Now what?"

"I can't do any further investigation from here," Gray decided, shutting down the computer. "We need to go back to Seattle and see what Ian can dig up."

"Do you think Gwen is the dirty cop?"

Gray rose to his feet, anxious for some action. He was done sitting behind a desk.

"I think it's a very good possibility," he assured her. "Let's grab our stuff and get out of here."

It took Mel less than a quarter of an hour to gather her few possessions and meet Gray in the garage.

"Ready?" he demanded.

"Yes." She climbed into the passenger seat of his car,

relieved that Gray was behind the wheel as they pulled onto the narrow drive.

The storm had intensified, along with the wind that slashed the heavy rain against them, making it almost impossible to see more than a few feet ahead.

"We'll take it slow," Gray said, as if capable of reading her mind. "These roads are dodgy under the best circumstances."

They passed through the gates protecting the property before Mel broke the tense silence.

"What happens when we get back to Seattle?" she asked.

"I'll contact Ian to start a background check on Gwen Dobbs and Leo Blake, along with the Hamil brothers."

Mel didn't doubt for a second that if there was damaging information to be found, Ian would manage to dig it up.

"And if we find the evidence we need?" she pressed.

A small smile eased the stark lines of his profile. "The bad guys go to jail. Donny returns to his grandmother. And we live happily ever after."

Her heart skipped a beat. That was what she'd wanted to hear, but now that he'd said the words, she felt a small flutter of panic.

"Do you believe in happily-ever-afters?"

"I do now." He paused before he asked the question that was obviously hovering on his lips. "What about you?"

"I'm trying."

"We'll take it as slow as you want."

She laughed at his ridiculous words. "You're the most impatient person I know."

"That's true enough. And I didn't promise that I wasn't going to push for more, but I will always respect your—"

"Gray!" Mel cried out as a familiar SUV screeched around the curve and headed straight for them.

"Hold on," he barked between clenched teeth.

Mel braced herself as the large vehicle smashed into the front of the car, sending them spinning off the road.

They hit a tree and then another before skidding down a muddy bank. When the vehicle finally came to a stop, they both scrambled out. Not only was there a fear the car would continue to slide down the steep slope, but the SUV had come to a halt on the road above them. The bad guys were already climbing out, along with a smaller female form. Gwen? Hard to tell from this distance. The woman was pointing her hand toward the trees, as if ordering them to finish the job.

Grabbing her hand, Gray tugged her at an angle along the side of the mountain. The rain continued to pour down, drenching Mel within a few seconds and making the ground perilously slick. On the plus side, it also created a thick fog that shrouded them from the searching eyes of their enemies.

"Are you okay?" Gray whispered, his voice so low she could barely catch the words.

"Yes," she whispered back. "Where are we going?"

Gray came to a sudden halt, turning to face her. "You're going back to the house. The master bedroom doubles as a safe room. It even has steel panels that cover the windows. Just punch the silver button on the wall next to the door."

She stared up at him. The rain had plastered his hair to his head and his sweats were soaked. He should have looked like a drowned rat. Instead his grim expression and the handgun he held clutched in his fingers warned this was a trained warrior on a mission.

This was Detective Gray Hawkins.

"I'm not going without you," she protested.

"There's no cell service here," he warned. "You have to get back to the house to call 9-1-1. Otherwise we're both dead."

Her brows snapped together. "Fine. Come with me."

He was shaking his head before she finished speaking. "I'm going to lead them down the mountain; then I'll double back." They both froze as they heard the sound of shouts from behind them. "Go, Mel," Gray urged in a harsh voice.

Accepting that the only way to assist Gray was to get to the house and call for backup, Mel went on her tiptoes to place a fleeting kiss on his lips before turning to scamper over a fallen tree trunk and along the low ridge.

Reaching the fence that surrounded the estate, she climbed over it. Inside the house the alarms would be blaring, but they weren't connected to the local authorities. She still had to get someplace where she had cell service to call for help.

She continued to battle her way through the underbrush, at last reaching the narrow pathway that Gray had led her down earlier that morning. A shiver raced through her. Right now, it seemed like a lifetime ago.

Stepping out of the trees, Mel gasped as she caught sight of two large men standing on the path, just below her.

"I thought I saw a little birdie flitting through the forest," the taller of the men drawled.

Hammer. The creep who'd tried to kidnap Donny. Next to him was the thug she recognized from his mug shot. Manny Hamil. Hammer's brother and partner in crime.

Her heart lodged in her throat, stark fear making her freeze like a deer caught in the headlights.

Hammer smiled in anticipation, waving his hand toward his brother. "Go tell Dobbs that I have the woman."

Manny frowned. "Why don't we just take her with us?"

"I intend to have a little fun with her first."

"But—"

"Go," Hammer barked, sending his brother a warning glare.

Manny muttered a curse, but obediently turned to head back into the trees. Hammer studied Mel, a cruel smile curving his thin lips.

"Well, well. I finally get to have you all to myself." His smile widened. "I've been thinking about how I intend to punish you."

Mel trembled, but his harsh threat stiffened her courage. She'd grown up surrounded by drug users who were always willing to abuse a young girl. She'd discovered how to be a master of the quick escape.

Clearing her mind, she concentrated on her surroundings. She could run, but she didn't doubt the larger man could catch her. Plus, there was every possibility he had a weapon beneath his rain jacket. Screaming would be a waste of energy.

Her only hope seemed to be finding a way to distract him. But what?

Her gaze darted from side to side, and distantly she realized where they were. They were standing at the precise spot where she'd fallen into the ditch.

Perfect. It was her best chance. She swallowed a hysterical urge to laugh. Not her *best* chance—it was her *only* chance.

"You don't have to do this," she said, not having to fake the fear in her voice as she moved toward the edge of the pathway.

Hammer smiled, walking toward her with cocky confidence. "Actually, I do, you interfering bitch. You ruined everything."

"Because I didn't let you kidnap a helpless little boy?" she demanded, her heels hanging off the edge of the drop-off.

"It was none of your business," he snarled.

She tilted her chin in a gesture sure to challenge the testosterone-bloated fool.

"I always make it my business when oversized bullies are picking on little kids," she mocked. "You should be ashamed of yourself."

Easily provoked by the chiding words, he lunged for her. "When I'm done with you—"

Hammer cursed as Mel quickly darted to the side. It wasn't until the idiot tried to turn back, however, that he realized the ground was crumbling beneath his feet. He grunted in surprise, his arms windmilling as he struggled to regain his balance.

Mel kept her wary gaze on the man while she bent down to grab a heavy rock. Then, as he tumbled backward to roll into the ditch, she leaped forward and landed next to him. Without giving herself time to consider what she was doing, she smashed the rock against the side of his head.

There was a terrible crunching sound and his eyes slid closed as his body went limp. Mel didn't bother to check for his pulse. Right now, she didn't care whether he was alive or dead. Instead she reached beneath his jacket, finding the weapon he had holstered at his side.

She clutched it in her hand and turned back to hurry up the pathway. The quicker she could call the cops, the quicker she could head back out to help Gray.

Lowering her head, Mel slogged through the mud. The wind and rain were deafening as she struggled forward, which meant that she had no warning anyone was behind her.

Not until a hand reached out to grasp her arm.

Chapter Eleven

Gray returned to where his car had slid off the road. Searching for the perfect spot, he waited for Dobbs to cautiously make her way toward the wrecked vehicle.

"I know you're there, Hawkins, show yourself," the detective called out.

Gray pressed his back against the trunk of a large tree, his gaze searching for any sign of the Hamil brothers or Leo Blake. Where were they?

The thought that they might be tracking down Mel made his stomach cramp with terror. It was only his years of training that kept him focused on the woman who was inching her way toward him.

He had to deal with the danger in front of him before moving to the next.

"The cops are on their way," he yelled, deliberately leading Gwen in his direction.

"The cops are already here," she taunted. "Come out and discuss this like a man."

"You can't call yourself a cop," he sneered. "You're a stain on the badge."

There was the sound of snapping twigs as the detective pushed her way through the undergrowth. Closer and closer.

"At least I don't spend my days spying on my fellow officers," she said, obviously hoping to rattle him. "Are you any less of a traitor?"

"We'll ask the chief when he gets here," he suggested.

Her sharp laugh echoed through the air. "If the chief was on his way, why would you be leaving?"

Good point. Gray searched his mind for a reasonable explanation. "I wanted to make sure he didn't miss the turn in the rain," he finally said.

"You must think I'm stupid."

"I think you've allowed your greed to overwhelm any morals you might once have possessed." Convinced that there was no one else nearby, Gray replaced his gun in the holster beneath his sweatshirt. "How much did your house cost? I'm guessing several million. Clever of you to put it in your mother's name in case anyone started snooping."

She was close enough for Gray to hear her muttered curse. She hadn't expected him to have researched her. As far as she knew, no one suspected that she and Leo were the dirty cops.

"I don't know what you're talking about," she insisted.

Gray reached up to grab the nearest branch. The tree was slick from the rain, but digging his fingers into the rough bark, he pulled himself upward.

"A pity you have to share the cartel money with Leo and the Hamil brothers," he taunted, carefully climbing to a higher branch. "Oh, and of course, Butch," he added. He wanted her thinking of anything but the fact that he might be leading her into a trap.

He heard her stumble, followed by more cursing. Then with a determination he might have admired if she wasn't a lying, greedy bitch who put every other cop at risk, her footsteps restarted.

"Butch?" She forced a laugh. "Never heard the name."

"He knows you. The prison guard has been singing like a canary for hours."

Gray could see the woman emerge through the trees. She halted next to a large bush that would act as a shield and pulled her weapon from beneath her jacket. Then, crouching low, she peered around the limbs and fired a shot at where he'd been standing just a minute before.

"Right now, you're facing drug charges and attempted kidnapping," he warned, his voice ricocheting through the trees. The echo made it impossible to pinpoint his location. "Do you want to add cop-killer as well?"

Lured by the sound of his voice, Gwen crept forward. When people lived in cities, they never remembered to look up.

"I'll take my chances," she said, releasing another shot.

Gray tensed his muscles, at the same time slowing his breathing. The world disappeared as he mentally prepared himself to attack. The sharp breeze, the incessant rain, the creak of the branch beneath his feet. It all disappeared as he concentrated with fierce urgency on the woman who approached with nerve-racking caution.

If she looked up, or even decided to turn back, his opportunity to gain the advantage would be lost. But even as the dark thoughts threatened to distract him, Gwen halted directly below him. Almost as if she could feel he was near.

Gray didn't even consider pulling his weapon and shooting the woman. Not out of pity. He would kill her in a heartbeat to protect Mel. But a bullet was no guarantee of putting down an opponent. He had a better chance of overpowering her with his superior size.

Gray waited for the detective to squeeze off another random shot before he shoved himself off the branch and plummeted downward.

As he'd hoped, he landed directly on top of Dobbs,

crushing her to the ground with enough impact to knock the gun from her hand. She made a strangled sound of fury, her hands reaching up to scratch his face. Gray didn't hesitate as he pulled back his arm and then slammed his fist against her jaw.

Instantly her eyes rolled back in her head and she went limp beneath him.

Gray didn't let down his guard. Scrambling off the unconscious woman, he grabbed the gun that had skidded beneath a nearby bush and rose to his feet. What was that sound? The crunch of pine needles? Someone had to be approaching.

Silently moving to crouch behind a thick bush, he tossed aside Gwen's gun and pulled his own. He couldn't be certain her weapon was as accurate as his.

Preparing to fire as soon as the prowler revealed himself, Gray stiffened as the sound of a familiar voice called out his name.

"Gray, it's Ian. Don't shoot me."

Soul-deep relief cascaded through Gray as his friend stepped into view, along with Mel, who was walking beside the large man.

Gray straightened, but held his gun ready as he moved toward his friend. "There are at least two others sneaking around here," he warned.

"Actually, there were three," Ian told him, his face barely visible behind the thick black slicker he wore with the hood up. "I managed to take down the other cop while my cousin took care of one of the thugs." He nodded toward the silent Mel. "I tried to rush to this damsel-in-distress's rescue, but she'd already wrestled the monster to the ground and smashed in his head."

Gray didn't bat an eye. There was a core of strength in Mel that he'd always admired. It ensured that she was perfectly capable of taking on any challenge and coming out the victor.

Even if the challenge was a two-hundred-and-fifty-pound villain named Hammer.

He held out his arms, his heart filled to the brim as she rushed to throw herself against him. He hugged her close, indifferent to the fact they were both soaking wet and covered in mud. Nothing had ever felt as good as the feel of her trembling body pressed against him.

Glancing over her shoulder, he sent his friend a grateful smile.

"Not that I'm not happy to see you, but why are you here?"

"The associate that I had watching the goon squad followed them back to Seattle. When they stopped at your house and then headed north, she gave me a call," Ian explained. "I feared that they'd managed to figure out that Mel was at your family cabin, so we headed up to warn you."

"Is it over?" Mel whispered against his chest.

Gray tightened his arms. There were no doubt months of investigations left to ensure that there weren't any others involved in Dobbs's and Blake's corruption. And then the takedown of the drug cartel.

But both Mel and little Donny were safe.

For now, that was enough.

"Yeah." He laid his cheek on top of her head and closed his eyes in silent gratitude. "It's over."

Epilogue

The next few weeks were a whirl of activity for Mel. She had to give a formal statement to the police. A nerve-racking experience considering she was condemning one of their fellow officers to several years in jail.

Next had been ensuring that Donny was safely home with his grandmother. The young boy hadn't seemed traumatized by recent events, but she knew that looks could be deceiving. Especially when it came to children who hid their emotions as deeply as Donny. Mel had made it her mission to visit the boy at his home, as well as continuing to tutor him at the center.

And then there was Gray . . .

He'd been equally busy as he'd assisted the police. Detective Gwen Dobbs had refused to speak, but Leo Blake had been eager to reveal everything he knew about the local cartel, including names and addresses. They'd arrested over a dozen suspects.

Still, Gray had managed to find plenty of time to stop by her apartment, going so far as to bribe her landlady with bottles of her favorite wine to keep her from calling a tow truck when he parked in front of her house. And he'd become a regular at the youth center, volunteering to coach the older boys' basketball team.

Mel hadn't tried to get rid of him. Why would she? When she'd been running through the woods to call for help, she'd promised herself that if they survived, she wasn't going to waste one more day. She loved Detective Gray Hawkins. And she wanted to spend the rest of her life with him.

She just hadn't told him that yet.

Perhaps today was the day, she acknowledged as she glanced around the large crowd that had gathered to celebrate the purchase of the empty lot next to the Hummingbird Youth Center. The sun was shining brightly, and they'd just completed the ribbon-cutting. A perfect occasion. There was even champagne being passed out in slender, fluted glasses.

Almost as if able to read her mind, Gray appeared at her side, wrapping his arm around her waist. Like her, he'd made an effort to dress for the formal event. But while her own yellow sundress was at least five years old, he had on a new white shirt with his sleeves rolled up to the elbows and a pair of silky gray slacks that perfectly hugged his gorgeous backside. He'd even had his chestnut hair trimmed so it lay smoothly against his head.

It was no wonder that every woman at the ceremony was eyeing him with a hopeful glance.

"An amazing turnout," he murmured, his silver eyes glowing with unmistakable admiration. "You should be proud."

She smiled. She was happy with the large crowd that was there to support the center, but the money had come from Remi. Along with a generous check from an unexpected source.

Mel's gaze drifted toward the clutch of VIPs who were standing across the lot. Among them were local politicians, doctors who donated their services, and a sprinkling of wealthy citizens. Plus, one surprising guest.

Ms. Veronica Hawkins, Gray's mother.

"Did you thank your mother for her donation?" she asked her companion.

A wry smile touched his lips. "You can thank her yourself," he told her. "We're having dinner with her on Friday night."

Mel arched her brows, not entirely surprised. She knew that after their return from the cabin, Gray had been spending time with his family. Including his brother, sister-in-law, and their new baby girl, Ariel.

"Are we?"

"Now that she's a grandmother, I think she's anxious to mend bridges. She plans to make us all one big happy family." He rolled his eyes. "Sappy sentimentality."

Mel chuckled, not fooled for a second. There was a part of him, deep inside, that was finally healing. The resentment over his father's death had eased, and he was able to accept the family he'd kept at a distance for years.

"You were pretty sappy yourself when you were holding your new niece," she teased.

His features softened at the mention of Ariel. They were all bewitched by the tiny girl.

"I like babies," he admitted without hesitation, his gaze sweeping over her face. "Especially when they're my own."

Mel felt a blush crawl beneath her cheeks. "Gray."

He leaned down to brush his lips over her forehead. "Something to think about."

She clicked her tongue even as the thought of holding her child tugged at her heart.

"Impatient."

"Yes," he murmured, his lips moving to nuzzle her temple.

"And pushy."

"Yes."

"And . . ." Her words trailed away.

"And what?" he demanded.

"Annoyingly irresistible," she finished.

His smile widened. "Ah, now I like the sound of that. It gives me hope."

"What do you hope for?" she asked in a soft voice.

"Us. Together." His expression was suddenly serious. "Forever."

She'd heard the saying about a heart melting. It'd always seemed silly. People's hearts didn't melt.

But that's exactly what happened as she allowed herself to sink into the love that smoldered in the smoky gray depths of his eyes.

"That's a big hope," she murmured.

"Am I wasting my time?"

"No." There was no hesitation. She didn't want Gray ever to doubt her commitment to their relationship.

She heard his soft gasp as he wrapped his arms around her, his gaze searching her face as if trying to assure himself that she wasn't teasing.

"Are you saying that you agree we belong together?" he pressed.

She tilted back her head to study his stark, male features. How had she survived without him?

"Of course we belong together," she told him. "I've loved you from the moment you asked me out for coffee."

He trembled, as if he was having difficulty accepting that she was truly admitting her feelings for him.

"And you'll marry me?" he demanded, no doubt hoping

to secure her agreement before she could come to her senses.

She smiled, wrapping her arms around his neck. She knew that they were the center of attention, but at the moment she didn't care. All that mattered was Gray Hawkins and a future filled with glorious promise.

"And they lived happily ever after," she whispered.

With a low chuckle, he swooped his head down to press his lips against hers.

"The End."

Read on for an exciting preview of Kat Martin's

AGAINST THE SKY,

available now!

ALASKA
*In America's last wilderness there are no limits
to what a man can do.*

For Detective Nick Brodie, that means keeping the perps
off the streets of Anchorage 24/7.
Nick has never backed down from danger, but after the
horrors he's seen, he's definitely in need of a break.

Samantha Hollis never thought she'd meet anyone like
Nick, especially in a place like Las Vegas. But after one
reckless, passionate night, she discovers the charismatic
stranger is everything she wants in a man. But can he
ever be anything more than a one-night stand?

When Nick invites her to Alaska, Samantha decides to
find out, never guessing the depths she'll discover in
him or the tangle of murder, kidnapping, and danger
about to engulf them both . . .

Nick helped Samantha into his black Ford Explorer for the drive back down the hill to his house. It had started to rain. This late in September, rainy days were a given.

"What do you think really happened to Jimmy?" she asked. "A fistfight with a schoolmate wouldn't explain why he hadn't come home all day." The teen was back now, but when he had failed to come home, his worried aunt had called Nick.

"Maybe he was afraid of what his aunt would say when she saw his battered face, but it's hard to believe. Jimmy's usually the kind of kid who tackles trouble head-on."

"Then what else could it be?"

Nick shook his head. "Worrying his aunt that way was really out of character." He ran a hand over the late-night beard along his jaw. "I don't know, it seemed like he was trying to brazen it out, putting up a tough front like the fight meant nothing, but I got a feeling he was scared."

"Of his aunt?"

Nick shook his head. "No." He sighed. "Hell, he's a kid. Maybe I was reading the whole thing wrong. I'll talk to him in the morning, see if I can get him to open up." He looked over at Samantha as he pulled into the driveway. "I've got a microwave. How about we heat up some of that chicken you cooked before we had to go looking for a runaway kid?"

"Good idea. I'm really hungry."

"Me too." But the kind of hunger he was feeling had nothing to do with food and everything to do with Samantha Hollis. He tried not to remember the last time they had been together, the softness of her lips, her small, feminine curves, her sweet cries of passion as she'd moved beneath him.

He tried to prevent it, but by the time he pulled the car into the garage, turned off the engine, and helped Samantha down from the SUV, he was hard as a frigging stone.

Samantha smiled as he led her into the kitchen. "I imagine after all the excitement, we'll both get a good night's sleep."

He cast her a thunderous look. "You really think so? Because I'll be lying there half the night aching for you, wishing you were in my bed instead of your own."

Her eyes widened. "But you said—"

"I know what I said. I said you'd be safe if you came to Alaska, and I won't break my word. Doesn't mean I don't want you." He leaned over and very softly kissed her, felt his arousal stirring beneath his jeans. Samantha returned the kiss, making him harder still. Then she pulled away.

"I-I'd better get the chicken out of the fridge and into the microwave." She started walking toward the refrigerator, stopped, and turned back. "I'm glad your friend Jimmy is safe."

"Yeah, at least for now." It took superhuman effort to force his mind off sex and onto the conversation he needed to have with the boy in the morning. The kid was important to him. The boy's father had just died, and Jimmy was convinced it was murder. It was crazy, but after what had happened tonight, it was clear that something was wrong. Nick needed to find out what the hell was going on.

* * *

Samantha couldn't sleep. Nick had said he'd be lying in bed aching for her, wishing she were there beside him. She hadn't thought she would be the one aching.

How could she have forgotten the magnetic pull of the man? The aura of masculinity that had so effortlessly seduced her before?

Just looking at that lean-muscled body as he walked around the house made her want him, those long, purposeful strides that had attracted her from the moment she had seen him in the hotel. And those amazing eyes, the most arresting shade of blue she had ever seen. Eyes that should have been cool, but instead seemed to burn with an inner heat.

Nick was the kind of man who touched easily and without conscious thought, the kind who made a woman feel protected and desired. She remembered the feel of his hard body pressing her down in the mattress, his muscles flexing as he took her, the pleasure he had given her. She remembered every moment she had spent with Nick.

She wanted Nick Brodie, had from the moment he had rescued her from a stranger's unwanted advances.

But now there was more at stake. So much more. She needed to know him, trust him. She needed time to be certain he was the kind of man he seemed.

She heard movement in the bedroom next to hers. Nick was awake, just as he'd said. How long could she resist the urge to go to him, to offer him her body as she had done before?

With a sigh, Samantha plumped her pillow, put it over her head, and tried not to wish Nick would storm through the door and demand a place in her bed.

Read on for an excerpt from Rebecca Zanetti's
thrilling new Deep Ops novel,
coming soon!

BROKEN

Chapter One

Clarence Wolfe strode up to the entrance of the super-secret sex club as if he had done so a million times before.

Down the street and partially hidden by branches from a sweeping cherry tree, Dana Mulberry ducked lower in her car and pressed her binoculars to her face so hard her skin pinched. What in the world was Wolfe doing at a Captive party?

She swallowed. Her heart rate, already thundering, galloped into the unhealthy range. It had taken her nearly a month to find out about the club, an additional two weeks to track down the location, and yet another month to finagle an invitation to the casual play night as a guest. And the ex-soldier, the beyond hunky badass who'd relegated her immediately to the friend zone, was walking inside like he owned one of the coveted million-dollar memberships?

She shook her head. Once and then again. When she could focus once more, there Wolfe prowled, through her binoculars, clear as day in the full moonlight.

He'd followed the rules for the night, too. Male Doms were to wear leather pants and dark shirts, females any leather outfit, and subs were to wear corsets and small skirts if they were female and knit shirts and light pants if they were male. Apparently, Wolfe was a Dom. Figured. She'd assumed she'd chuckle at seeing guys in leather pants, but there was nothing funny about Wolfe's long legs, powerful thighs, and tight butt in those pants.

In fact, he looked even more dangerous than usual, and she would've bet that wasn't possible.

Where in the heck had Wolfe found leather pants? Was he really some sort of Dom who went to clubs? He did not *like* people enough to spend time with anybody in a dungeon. She giggled, the sound slightly hysterical, so she cleared her throat.

What now? She looked down at her tight green corset and black skirt that was as long as she dared. At the very least, it covered the still healing knife marks on her upper thighs that she hadn't told anybody about. Not even her doctor. The guy who'd cut her during an interrogation had been killed in jail, so why did it matter?

Forget the nightmares. They'd go away soon.

Her more immediate problem was that Wolfe had just walked through the front door of the mansion that housed the latest Captive party. Her source was inside that place, and she'd spent a lot of time gearing up for this.

Would Wolfe blow her cover?

She'd been sitting in her car for an hour watching people arrive. Okay. She might've been gathering her courage. This was so outside her experience. She hadn't even known sex clubs existed until that movie came out about BDSM.

But her boss at the *USA Post*, where she used to work, had once said she'd do anything for a story, and he'd been right. Well, mostly. Okay. She could do this. In fact, why not look at the fact that Wolfe was inside as a positive? His presence gave her unexpected backup.

Yeah. That was the idea. Forget the fact that the sexiest man she'd ever met was in a sex club right now. Yep. Good plan. She slid from her car and pulled her skirt down as far as she could, which still barely covered her butt.

Her heels tottered on the uneven sidewalk as she clip-clopped alongside a high stone wall that no doubt protected another zillion-dollar mansion. Then she crossed the street, her head high, shivering in the chilly breeze as she reached the front door and knocked.

"Hello." A man in full tuxedo opened the door. He was about six feet tall with curly blond hair, and he was built like a linebacker. "Can I help you?"

There was no way anybody could get by this guy if he didn't grant access. She handed over her gold-foiled invitation.

He accepted the paper and drew a small tablet from his right pocket, scrolling through. "Ah. Miss Millerton. I see that you answered the questionnaire and have signed all of the necessary documents." He smoothly slid both back into his pocket. "A couple of quick questions."

She forced a smile, feeling way too exposed in her scant clothing. Hopefully the questions weren't about her fake name or cover ID. "All right."

"What's your safe word?"

"Red," she said instantly.

"Good. If you need help, who do you yell for?" His voice remained kind but firm.

She paused, thinking through the documents she'd read online. "For anybody, but especially the dungeon monitors." The words felt foreign in her mouth. Should she ask him about Albert? Or was that taboo? She didn't want to get kicked out before she found her source.

"Good." The guy opened the door to reveal a rather ordinary looking front vestibule with another wide door behind him. "Go ahead and have fun, sweetheart."

Fun? She nodded and tottered on her heels to the door, which, somehow, he reached first and opened for her.

"Thank you," she murmured, instantly hit by a wave of noise and heat. Music blasted from the ceiling, and in front of her, a palatial living room had been set up as a dance floor on one side and a full-length bar on the other. Bar. Definitely bar. She could have a drink and maybe talk up the bartender. A quick glance around the darkened room, highlighted by deep purple lights from high above, didn't reveal Albert's location. She didn't see Wolfe, either. Good.

She made her way through a crowd of people in leather and other gear, finally reaching the bar.

A six-foot-tall female bartender dressed in a full leather outfit leaned over, her full breasts spilling out of the tight V-neck. "What can I get you, hon?"

"Tequila. Shot," Dana said. Should she ask for a double? No.

"Sure thing." The woman poured a generous shot and pushed it across the inlaid wood. "You a guest tonight?"

Dana nodded and tipped back the drink, sputtering just a little. "Yes."

The woman grinned, revealing a tongue piercing. "You new?"

"Yes." Dana coughed.

"I'm Jennie." She tilted her head and poured another shot. "Mistress Jennie."

Oh yeah. Dana had tried to memorize the appropriate lingo from the online sites. She accepted the second shot, her hand shaking. "Thank you." Was she supposed to add the "mistress"? The website hadn't said.

"You bet. Just have some fun, and remember you don't have to do anything you don't want to do. The play rooms are all over the house, and if there's a red sign on the door, it can't be closed. You can just watch if you want," Jennie said, moving down the bar as somebody caught her attention.

Good advice. Definitely. Dana took the second shot and let the alcohol heat her body.

"Hello." A man appeared at her elbow. "We haven't met."

She partially turned. The guy was about fifty with shrewd eyes and an iron-hard body. He wore leather pants and a red leather vest that showed muscled arms. "Hello. I'm Dana."

"Charles." He held out a hand to shake and kept hers a moment longer than necessary. "You here to explore a little bit?"

Oh, crap. "I'm just here to ease my way in." She tried for a flirtatious smile, but her lips refused to curve. "In fact, I was looking for my friend Albert Nelson. Any chance you know him?"

Charles slid closer to her, his pupils dilated. "No. But I could make you forget him." He took her hand again, and she tried to pull back, but he just smiled. "How about we go check out some of the rooms? I could show you around."

"No, thanks." She forced her smile in place as panic began to rise.

"Come on—" Charles began.

"She said no." Charles's hand was instantly removed from hers, and he was tossed toward the dance floor, barely catching his balance before he collided with two people slow dancing.

Dana gulped, tasting tequila on her lips as she looked up, knowing the voice very well. "Wolfe." Only training kept her from blanching at the raw fury in his sapphire-blue eyes.

He leaned in, his full lips near her ear. "What the hell are you doing here?"

She shivered and dug deep for her own anger. Then she pressed her hands to her hips. "What are you doing here?" she snapped back.

His gaze swept from her revealing top, down to her toes, and back up to her blazing face. "Subs don't use that tone, baby. One who does ends up over a knee. Quickly."

Oh, he did not. She glared. "I am not a sub," she whispered.

"You're dressed like one." His dark T-shirt tightened across his muscled chest as he leaned closer again. His buzz cut had grown out to curl a bit beneath his ears, giving him a wild look.

"There weren't many options," she hissed.

"Wolfe." A man also dressed in leather, his brown hair slicked back, moved up beside Wolfe. He was about forty with tattoos down one arm. "I see you found a friend. Finally going to play?"

Wolfe didn't look away from Dana, his gaze going from furious to calm in a second. How in the world did he control himself like that? "I'm normally not a public player, as you know."

What the hell did that mean? Dana began to ask, but Wolfe subtly shook his head.

The man held out a hand. "In that case, I'm Master Trentington. How about I show you around tonight?"

"That's kind of you." Dana shook his hand, her lip trembling annoyingly. "But I was actually looking for a friend named Albert Nelson. Do you know him?"

Trentington reluctantly released her. "I do, but he's not here tonight. I'd love to play your guide in his stead."

"No," Wolfe answered before she could, angling his

body closer to her and partially blocking the other man. He glanced over his shoulder at Jennie. "Spare cuffs?"

Jennie grinned, reached under the bar, and tossed over a pair of bright pink wrist cuffs.

Wolfe snagged them out of the air and snapped them on Dana's wrists before she could blink. They were fur lined and soft, but felt restrictive nonetheless. "We've already reached an agreement," he murmured.

"Well. In that case, have fun." Trentington moved to leave.

"Charles was being pushy again," Wolfe said quietly. "It's time you kicked him out."

Trentington sighed and turned toward the dance floor. "Thanks."

Dana looked down at the pink cuffs. She kind of felt like Wonder Woman. "Why did you—"

"They show ownership," Wolfe said, clipping the cuffs easily together.

Her abdomen rolled, and her head snapped back. "Excuse me?" She tugged hard, but they wouldn't separate, effectively binding her wrists together. She eyed his shin. With her heels, she could do some damage.

He chuckled, the sound low and dangerous. It slid over her skin, burning her from within. "Right now, you're playing a sub, no doubt for a story. But I'm playing a Dom, and if you kick me, I'll toss your ass over that bar and beat it."

His words slid right through her to pulse between her legs. For Pete's sake. That scenario was not sexy. The idea of Wolfe's hand anywhere near her butt sent her already sensitive body into hyperdrive. Oh, she'd handle him later. For now, she had work to do, so she shook off emotion and leaned closer. He'd said "playing." "Are you on a job?" she whispered.

"Yes." He glanced around. "Who's Albert Nelson?"

"My story," she said, looking again. "I scared him off last week, but I know he's a member of Captive, so I came here to ask him questions." Definitely to pressure him into answering all of her questions this time. At this point, she didn't care. Finding out who'd killed her friend was all that mattered. "Your job?"

"Confidential. You know a guy named Clarke Wellson?"

"No, but I could do a background check later," she murmured. They'd helped each other on cases before.

Wolfe glanced down at her, his gaze warming. "You look incredible."

"Thank you." It was nice he'd noticed, although the outfit wasn't really her style. She was more a jeans and flannel type of girl. She shuffled uneasily in her heels. That way he had of switching topics had thrown her ever since they'd met. "Okay. I'm going to mingle and ask questions. You?"

He smiled, the sight daunting. "I just cuffed you. No Dom would allow a sub to mingle."

Allow? Oh, heck no. She blinked. "Then uncuff me."

"No. Last time you didn't have backup, you nearly died." He crossed his arms, somehow scouting the entire room while also watching her.

Her back teeth gritted together. "You're not in charge here, Wolfe."

"The cuffs say otherwise," he said, angling his head to take in the dance floor.

She couldn't help it. She really couldn't. For months she'd chased this story, and she was here pretty much tied up because of a guy who only wanted to be her friend. She kicked him, as hard as she could, right in the shin.

He stiffened, rapidly pivoted, and both hands went to her hips to lift her. She was halfway in the air to the bar before she even thought to struggle. A heavy thud sounded from behind Wolfe. A woman screamed.

Wolfe dropped Dana to her feet and shoved her behind him, angling toward the dance floor. He looked up to a balcony high above.

Dana craned her neck to see around him, staring down at the dead man on the ground with a bullet hole in his head. His eyes were wide open and frighteningly blank. Her stomach lurched, and she coughed. "That's Albert," she whispered.

Wolfe looked over his shoulder at her. "Well, shit. That's Clarke, too."

Sirens sounded in the distance. Wolfe grabbed her bound wrists. "We have to get out of here. Now."

ONCE, SHE GOT AWAY
The body lying on a cold steel slab bears all the
hallmarks of the Chicago Butcher. There's a cruel slash
across her throat, deep enough to sever the carotid
artery, and a small crescent carved into her right breast.
Her delicate features are painfully familiar to Ash
Marcel, once a rising star in the Chicago PD. But though
the victim resembles his former fiancée, Remi Walsh,
he knows it's not her.

BUT THIS TIME
Though Remi escaped a serial killer five years ago, her
father died trying to save her. Grief and guilt caused her
to pull away from the man she loved. Now Ash is back
in her life, insisting that Remi is still in danger.

IT'S A DEAD END . . .
Someone is targeting women who look just like Remi.
With or without a badge, Ash intends to unmask the
Butcher. But the killer isn't playing games any longer.
He's moving in, ready to finish what he started,
and prove there's nothing more terrifying
than a killer's obsession . . .

**Please turn the page for an exciting sneak peek of
Alexandra Ivy's**

THE INTENDED VICTIM,

now on sale wherever print and eBooks are sold!

Prologue

The sun was still struggling to crest the horizon when Angel Conway entered the small park next to Lake Michigan. Shivering, she hunched herself deeper in her heavy coat. Shit. Was there anywhere in the world colder than Chicago in the winter? She doubted even the North Pole felt as frigid. Especially this morning with the wind whipping the icy droplets from the nearby lake. They stung her face like tiny darts.

Unfortunately, she had no choice but to drag herself out of her bed at such a god-awful hour to brave the cold. It was the same reason she snuck out every Friday morning.

When she came to Chicago, she'd intended to have a clean start. No drugs. No men. Nothing that would screw up her one opportunity to climb out of the sewer she'd made of her life. But after the operation, she'd been given painkillers, and the hunger had been stroked back to life. Within three weeks of her arrival in the city, she was back to the same old habits.

Stomping her feet in an attempt to keep blood flowing to her toes, she scanned the shadowed lot. Where was her john? Usually she was the one running late. She did it deliberately to avoid being turned into a human popsicle. She wanted to arrive at the park, climb into the man's expensive Jag, do her business, and get her pills. No fuss, no muss.

And no frostbite.

"Come on, come on," she muttered, rubbing her hands together.

Maybe she should bail. She could sneak out this weekend and find a street dealer. Of course, what little money she had . . .

Her thoughts were shattered by the sharp snap of a branch. She frowned, glancing over her shoulder at the trees directly behind her. She'd chosen this spot because it gave her an open view of the lot, but at the same time gave her cover in case a cop decided to drive through the park. Now she felt a weird sense of dread crawl over her skin.

She was from the country. She knew the sound of a critter scrambling through the underbrush.

There was someone moving in the darkness. The only question was whether it was an early morning jogger. Or a pervert who was spying on her.

She never considered there might have been a third possibility.

Not until she felt the cold blade press against her throat . . .

Chapter One

Dr. Ashland Marcel entered his office on the campus of Illinois State University. It was a small, dark space that had one window overlooking the parking lot. An office reserved for a professor who hadn't yet received his tenure. Not that the cramped space bothered Ash. As much as he enjoyed teaching criminal justice classes, he hadn't fully committed to spending the rest of his life in an academic setting. Especially after a day like today.

With a grimace, he dropped into his seat behind the cluttered desk. A sigh escaped his lips. It was only noon, but he was grateful he was done teaching his classes for the day.

The students weren't the only ones looking forward to the end of the semester, he wryly acknowledged. Early December in the Midwest meant short, brutally cold days. A bunch of twenty-somethings trapped inside for weeks at a time was never a good thing. His classroom was choking with their pent-up energy.

But it was Friday. And Monday the students started finals. Which meant that in less than seven days he could look forward to a month of peace and quiet.

Pretending he didn't notice the tiny ache in the center of his heart at the thought of spending the holidays alone in his small house, Ash opened his laptop. He needed to get through his email before he could call it a day.

He'd barely fired up the computer when the door to his office was shoved open. He glanced up with a forbidding glare. His students were told on the first day of class that they could come to him during his posted office hours. He'd discovered his first year of teaching that they would follow him into the toilet with questions if he didn't set firm guidelines.

His annoyance, however, swiftly changed to surprise at the sight of the man dressed in a worn blue suit who stepped through the opening.

Detective Jackson "Jax" Marcel.

At a glance, it was easy to tell the two were brothers. They both had light brown hair that curled around the edges. Ash's was allowed to grow longer now that he was no longer on the police force, and had fewer strands of gray. And they both had blue eyes. Ash's were several shades darker, and framed by long, black lashes that had been the bane of his childhood. And they were both tall and slender, with muscles that came from long morning jogs instead of time in the gym.

Ash rose to his feet, his brows arching in surprise. It wasn't uncommon for his family to visit. The university was only a couple hours from Chicago. But they never just appeared in his office without calling.

"Jax."

Jax stretched his lips into a smile, but it was clearly an effort. "Hey, bro."

Ash studied his companion. Jax was the oldest of the four Marcel brothers, but since they had all been born within a six-year span they were all close in age. That was perhaps why they'd always been so tight. You messed with one Marcel, you messed with them all.

"What are you doing here?" Ash demanded.

"I need to talk to you."

"You couldn't call?"

Jax grimaced. "I preferred to do it face-to-face."

Fear curled through the pit of Ash's stomach. Something had happened. Something bad. He leaned forward, laying his palms flat on the desk.

"Mom? Dad?"

Jax gave a sharp shake of his head. "The family is fine."

"Then what's going on?"

"Sit down."

Ash clenched his teeth. His brother's attempt to delay the bad news was twisting his nerves into a painful knot. "Shit. Just tell me."

Perhaps realizing that he was doing more harm than good, Jax heaved a harsh sigh.

"It's Remi Walsh."

Ash froze. He hadn't heard the name Remi in five years. Not since he'd packed his bags and walked away from Chicago and the woman who'd promised to be his wife.

"Remi." His voice sounded oddly hollow. "Is she hurt?"

This time Jax didn't torture him. He spoke without hesitation.

"Her body arrived in the morgue this morning."

Morgue.

"No." The word was wrenched from Ash's lips as his knees buckled and he collapsed into his chair.

Jax stepped toward the desk, his expression one of pity. "I'm sorry, Ash."

Ash shook his head. "This has to be a mistake," he said, meaning every word.

It *was* a mistake. There was no way in hell that Remi could be dead.

"I wish it was a mistake, bro," Jax said in sad tones. "But I saw her with my own eyes."

Ash grimly refused to accept what his brother was telling him. He'd tumbled head over heels in love with Remi from the second she'd strolled into the police station to take her father for lunch. Ash had just made detective and Gage Walsh was his partner. Thankfully, that hadn't stopped him from asking out Remi. She'd been hesitant at first, clearly unsure she wanted to date someone who worked so closely with her father. But from their first date they'd both known the sensations that sizzled between them were something special.

That's why he couldn't accept she was gone.

If something had happened to Remi, he would know. In his heart. In his very soul.

"How long has it been since you last spent time with her?" he challenged his brother.

Jax shrugged. "Five years ago."

"Exactly. How could you possibly recognize her after so long?"

"Ash." Jax reached up to run his hand over his face, his shoulders stooped. He looked like he was weary to the bone. "Denying the truth doesn't change it."

Anger blasted through Ash. He wanted to vault across the desk and slam his fist into his brother's face for insisting on the lie. It wouldn't be the first time he'd given Jax a black eye. Of course, his brother had pounded him back, chipping a tooth and covering him in bruises, but it'd been totally worth it.

Instead, he forced himself to leash his raw emotions.

"It's official?" he demanded.

Jax gave a slow shake of his head. "Not yet. The medical examiner is overwhelmed as usual. It will be hours before they can run fingerprints, even with me putting pressure on them."

The anger remained, but it was suddenly threaded with hope. Nothing was official.

The words beat through him, echoing his heavy pulse.

At the same time, he continued to glare at his brother. "Why come here before you're sure it's Remi?"

Jax coughed, as if clearing his throat. "I wanted you to be prepared."

Ash narrowed his gaze. The shock of Jax's announcement had sent his brain reeling. Which was the only explanation for why he hadn't noticed his brother's hands clenching and unclenching. It wasn't just sympathy that was causing his brother's unease.

"No. There's something you're not telling me," he said.

Jax glanced toward the window, then down at the scuff marks on his leather shoes. Was he playing for time? Or searching for the right words? "Let's go for a drink," he finally suggested.

"Dammit, Jax. This isn't the time for games," Ash snapped. "Just tell me."

Jax's lips twisted before he forced himself to speak the words he'd clearly hoped to avoid. "She was found with her throat slit."

Ash surged to his feet, knocking over the chair. It smashed against the wooden floor with a loud bang, but Ash barely noticed.

"Was there a mark?" he rasped.

It'd been only a few weeks after he'd started dating Remi that Gage had put together the connection that a rash of dead women was the work of a serial killer. They'd tagged him the Chicago Butcher since it was suspected that he used a butcher's knife to slice the throats of his victims. Only the cops knew that there had been a hidden calling card left behind by the killer: a small crescent carved onto the women's right breast. No one knew if it was supposed to be a "c," or a moon, or perhaps some unknown symbol. But it was always there.

"Yes."

"Like the others?" he pressed.

Jax nodded. Ash reached into his pocket to pull out his keys. He'd gone from white-hot emotion erupting through him like lava to an ice-cold determination.

The Chicago Butcher had destroyed his life five years ago. If the bastard was back, then Ash was going to track him and kill him. He didn't care if he had a badge or not.

He tossed his keys to his brother. "Go to my house and pack a bag."

Jax caught the keys, his brows tugging together. "Ash, there's nothing you can do."

"I have to see her," Ash muttered, not adding his secondary reason for returning to Chicago. His brother was smart. He knew Ash would be hungry for revenge. "She was my fiancée."

Jax grimaced. "It was all a long time ago."

Ash snorted. It had been five years, not an eternity. And most of the time it felt like it had all happened yesterday. "We both know it doesn't matter how long ago it was, or you would never have come down here to tell me."

The older man hunched his shoulders. "I didn't want you to hear it on the news."

Ash didn't believe the excuse for a second. "Pack a bag," he commanded, reaching down to right his chair. "I'll be ready by the time you get back."

"What about your classes?" Jax tried a last-ditch effort to keep Ash away from Chicago.

"Finals are next week." Ash sat down and reached for the cell phone he'd left on his desk. He might be under thirty, but he held the old-fashioned belief that there was no need for phones in his classroom. Including his own. "I'll call the dean and warn him there's been a family emergency. If I'm not back by Monday, my teaching assistant can proctor the exams."

"Ash—"

"I can go back with you or I'll drive myself," Ash interrupted.

"Hell, I don't want you behind the wheel." Jax pointed a finger toward Ash. "Don't move until I get back."

Ash ignored his brother as he turned and left his office. He not only needed to contact the dean, but he wanted to make sure that his assistant knew he would be expected to take over his classes if necessary, as well as making his excuses to the dozens of holiday invitations that were waiting in his inbox.

He was just finishing his tasks when his phone pinged with a text telling him that Jax was waiting for him in the parking lot.

Grabbing his laptop and the coat that hung in the corner, he stepped out of the office and closed the door behind him. Then, using the back stairs, he managed to avoid any acquaintances. Right now, he would be incapable of casual chitchat.

Pushing open the door, he stepped out of the building and headed for the nearby parking lot. The sun was shining, but there was a sharp breeze that made him shiver. Like all his brothers he enjoyed being out in the fresh air, either jogging or spending the weekend camping near the river. But with each passing year he found he was less willing to brave icy temperatures.

Soon he'd be spending the long winters sitting in front of a warm fire with a comfy sweater and his favorite slippers.

Shaking away his idiotic thoughts, he stopped next to

his brother's car. Pulling open the door, he slid into the passenger seat and wrapped the seat belt across his body.

"Have you heard anything from the medical examiner?" he demanded as his brother put the car in gear and headed out of the lot.

"Not yet." There was silence as Jax concentrated on negotiating the traffic out of town. It wasn't until they reached the interstate that Jax glanced toward Ash. "Mom will be happy to have you home for a few days. She complains you never bother to come and see her anymore."

Ash pressed his lips together. It was that or snapping at his brother that this wasn't a damned social visit. Eventually, however, he forced his tense muscles to relax. He wasn't so far gone that he didn't realize that Jax was trying to distract him. And that there was no point in brooding on what he was going to discover once they reached Chicago.

"Mom's too busy planning Nate's wedding to notice whether I'm around or not," he managed to say.

Nate was the youngest Marcel brother, who'd moved to Oklahoma after leaving the FBI. He had proposed to his neighbor, Ellie Guthrie, a few months ago, and since she didn't have a relationship with her own parents, June Marcel had eagerly stepped in to act as her surrogate mother.

Jax released a short laugh. "She's been in heaven running around the city to find the perfect flower arrangements and sewing the bridesmaids' dresses," he agreed. "The poor woman assumed with four sons she would never get the opportunity to be so involved in all the froufrou nonsense that comes with a wedding." Jax set the cruise control and settled back in his seat. "Still, you must have been gone too long if you've forgotten Mom's ability to concentrate on more than one thing at a time. I remember her baking cupcakes for Ty's Boy Scout club while helping Nate with his math homework and at the same time making sure I raked every damned leaf in the backyard because I missed curfew."

Ash's lips curved into a rueful smile. His mother was a ruthless force of nature who'd occasionally resorted to fear and intimidation to control her four unruly sons. Mostly she'd smothered them in such love that none of them could bear the thought of disappointing her.

"True. She has a gift." He felt a tiny pang in the center of his heart. It'd been too long since he'd been home. "I could use her in my classroom."

"Lord, don't say that. She'll be waiting next to your desk with a ruler in her hand," Jax teased.

Another silence filled the car, then Jax cleared his throat, and abruptly asked the question that had no doubt been on his lips for the past five years.

"I never knew what happened between you and Remi." Jax kept his gaze focused on the road, as if knowing that Ash wouldn't want him to witness the pain that twisted his features. "One day you were planning your wedding and the next the engagement was over and you were moving away."

Ash's breath hissed between his clenched teeth. "The Chicago Butcher happened."

He expected his brother to drop the issue. His breakup with Remi was something he refused to discuss. His family had always respected his barriers.

But whether he was still trying to keep Ash distracted, or if it was the shock of seeing a woman he believed to be Remi at the morgue, Jax refused to let it go. "You both suffered when she was captured by the Butcher and her father was killed trying to save her," he pointed out. "I thought it would draw the two of you closer together."

Ash turned his head to gaze at the frozen fields that lined the road. The memories of that horrifying night were firmly locked in the back of his mind. The frantic phone call from Remi telling her father that she was being followed. Gage Walsh's stark command that Ash drive Remi's route in case the killer forced her car off the road on the way home, while he went to his elegant mansion on the North Shore. And then his arrival at the mansion to discover that he was too late. Gage's blood had been found at his home, but his body had never been discovered. No one knew why the Butcher would have taken it, unless he feared that he'd left evidence on the corpse that he didn't have time to remove. The killing, after all, wouldn't have been planned like the females he stalked and murdered. Thank God, Remi had been alive, although she'd been lying unconscious in the kitchen.

But while he wasn't about to go into the agonizing details, Jax deserved an answer. The older man had been an unwavering source of strength over the past few years. Whether it was to shut down his father's angry protests when Ash announced that he was leaving the police department, or driving down to the university and getting him cross-eyed drunk when he was feeling isolated and alone.

"After I brought Remi home from the hospital she started to shut me out," he said in slow, painful tones. "At first I assumed she would get her memories back, and that she would be able to heal from the trauma she'd gone through."

"But the memories never came back," Jax murmured.

"No, they never came back." Ash grimaced. He'd wasted a lot of emotional energy trying to convince Remi to get professional help to retrieve her memories. As if the return of them could somehow heal the growing breach between them. It was only with time and distance he could see that they were struggling with more than the trauma of her being attacked by the Butcher. "But it was the guilt that destroyed our hopes for the future."

His brother sent him a sharp glance. "Guilt for what?"

Ash gave a sad shake of his head. "Remi felt guilty for her father's death. She had a crazy idea that if she hadn't called to say she was being followed, her father would still be alive. And to be honest, it only made it worse that his body was never found. I think a part of her had desperately hoped that he would miraculously return. With each passing day, she blamed herself more and more."

"And your guilt?" Jax pressed.

"I should never have let Gage go there alone. I was his partner."

Jax muttered a curse. "His *younger* partner. Gage was your superior, and it was his call to split up, so you could cover more ground. Just as it was your duty to obey his order."

Ash shrugged. Easy to say the words, it was much harder to dismiss the gnawing remorse. If only . . .

Heaving a sigh, he leaned his head back against the seat and closed his eyes. He'd given Jax the explanation he demanded. He didn't have the strength to argue whether it made any sense or not.

Ash kept his eyes closed even as the traffic thickened, and they slowed to a mere crawl. He'd driven to the morgue enough times to know exactly when they were pulling into the side parking lot.

Lifting his head, he studied the long, cement block building with two rows of narrow windows. Nothing had changed in the past few years. Maybe the trees lining the street had grown a little taller, and they'd replaced the flags out front. Otherwise it was the same stark structure he remembered.

Jax switched off the engine, turning his head toward Ash. "I wish you wouldn't do this."

"I have to." Ash unbuckled the seat belt and pushed open the door before stepping out.

Behind him was the sound of hurried footsteps as Jax rushed to keep up. Not that Ash was going to get far without him. He was no longer a cop, which meant he would have to hang on to the hope that Remi still had him listed as an emergency contact to get past the security.

Much easier to let Jax do his thing.

Quickly at his side, Jax took charge as they entered the building. They were halted twice, but Jax flashed his badge and quickly they were stepping into a harshly lit room that felt ice-cold.

Ash shivered. He hated coming here. Even when it was a part of his job. Now his stomach was twisted so tight it felt like it'd been yanked into knots.

They were led by a technician down a long row of steel racks where bodies wrapped in heavy plastic waited for an official ID. Or perhaps for an autopsy. He'd tried not to really notice what was going on behind the scenes. Now he felt as if he was in a dream as the technician waved for them to stop and Jax wrapped an arm around his shoulders. No, it was more like a nightmare. One that wasn't going to end if it truly was Remi who was being slid out on a steel slab.

Taking care not to disturb the body any more than necessary, the technician slowly pulled back the plastic cover. Ash made a choked sound as he caught sight of the long black hair that was glossy enough to reflect the overhead light. It was pulled from a pale, beautiful face, just like Remi liked to wear it.

He swayed to the side, leaning heavily against his brother as pain blasted through him. "Christ."

"Steady," Jax murmured.

Ash's gaze absorbed the delicate features. They were so heart-wrenchingly familiar. The slender nose. The high, prominent cheekbones. The dark, perfectly arched brows. The lush lips.

"I didn't want to believe," he rasped, his voice coming from a long way away. As if he was falling off a cliff and was waiting to hit the bottom.

Would he die when that happened?

He hoped so.

What would be the point of living in a world without Remi Walsh?

"I'm sorry," Jax said, his own voice harsh with pain.

Ash's gaze remained locked on Remi's lips. It'd been five years but he still remembered their last kiss. He'd just told her that he intended to take a job at the university. Deep inside he'd hoped she would be furious at his decision. He wanted her to fight for their future together. Instead she'd offered a sad smile and leaned forward to brush her mouth over his in a silent goodbye.

He'd nearly cried even as he'd savored the taste of her strawberry lip balm . . .

Ash stilled. Lip balm. Why was there a warning voice whispering at the back of his fuzzy brain? Maybe he was going crazy. What the hell did her lips have to do with anything? He frowned, telling himself to turn away.

He'd done what he came there to do. What was the point of gawking at Remi as if he hoped she would suddenly open her eyes? It was time to go.

But his feet refused to budge. He knew Jax was staring at him in confusion, and that the technician was starting to shift from one foot to another, but still he continued to run his gaze over Remi's pale face.

Something was nagging at him. But what?

Then his gaze returned to her mouth and he realized what his unconscious mind was trying to tell him.

She was wearing lipstick. A bright red shade. And more than that, there was makeup plastered on her skin and what looked like false lashes stuck to her lids. The harsh lighting had washed everything to a dull shade of ash, which was why he hadn't noticed it the minute the cover had been pulled back.

"That's not her," he breathed.

"Ash." Jax's arm tightened around his shoulders. "I know this is tough, but—"

"It's not her," Ash interrupted, his heart returning to sluggish life.

How had he been so blind? Remi never wore makeup. Not even when her mother insisted on dragging her to some fancy-ass party. She claimed that it made her skin itch, plus she didn't feel the need to slap paint on herself to try and impress other people. If they didn't like her face, then they didn't have to look at it.

Her down-to-earth attitude was one of the things he'd loved about her.

Of course, as far as he was concerned she was gorgeous. She didn't need anything artificial to make his palms sweat and his pulse race.

"How can you be sure?" Jax demanded, his voice revealing his fear that Ash had gone over the edge. "Like you said, it's been five years. She could have changed in that time. Unless there's something you haven't told me?"

Ash jutted his chin. He wasn't going to explain about the makeup. Jax would tell him a woman might very well change her mind about cosmetics as she started to age. Or perhaps she had a boyfriend who wanted her to plaster her face with the gunk. Besides, now that he was looking at the dead woman with his brain and not his heart, he could start to detect physical differences. The nose was just a tad too long. Her brow not quite wide enough. And her jaw too blunt.

"I'm sure." His voice was strong. Confident. "It's not her."

"He's right." A new voice cut through the air, echoing eerily through the racks of dead bodies. "I just got the results from the fingerprints back."

They all turned to watch as Dr. Jack Feldman, one of the city's top medical examiners, stepped out of the shadows. A short man with salt-and-pepper hair and a neatly trimmed beard, he was wearing a white lab coat that didn't hide the start of an impressive potbelly. He'd been a good friend of Gage Walsh, and had extended that friendship to Ash when he'd become Gage's partner.

He'd also adored Remi, treating her like she was his own child. It must have been a hideous shock to have a woman who looked so much like her show up in his morgue.

"Feldman," Ash murmured, stepping away from his brother so he could pull the older man into a rough hug.

They shared a silent moment of tangled emotions, then the doctor slapped him on the back and pulled back to study him with a sympathetic gaze.

"Good to see you, Ash, although not under these circumstances."

Ash cleared his throat, his attention moving toward the electronic pad clutched in Feldman's hand. "Did you get an ID?"

Feldman held up a hand before he glanced toward the silent technician.

"I'll take it from here, Jimmy," he told the young man. They waited until Jimmy turned and left the room before

Feldman led them to a distant corner. His dark eyes rested on Ash's face. "I shouldn't be talking to you, but I'm pretty sure you'll get the information one way or another. Plus, you're one of us, even if you did jump ship for a while. Eventually you'll come back where you belong."

They were the words he'd heard from a dozen different lawmen when he'd announced his decision to leave the Chicago Police Department and take a job teaching. And in truth, a part of him had secretly agreed.

Being a detective was in his blood.

He shook away the thought, nodding toward the electronic pad. "Who is she?"

Feldman lifted the pad and touched the screen to call up a file. "Her name is Angel Conway. She's a twenty-five-year-old white female. Five feet, six inches tall. One hundred thirty pounds."

Ash frowned. "Is she local?"

"No." Feldman brushed his finger over the screen. "Her address is Bailey, Illinois. A small town fifty miles south of the city."

Ash glanced toward Jax, who gave a shake of his head. He'd never heard of the town.

"Do you have any other info?"

Feldman was silent as he read through the short report. Ash knew Feldman must have shouted and bullied and called in every favor owed him to get any information so quickly. The Chicago coroner's department was notoriously understaffed and overworked. It was only because of their dedicated staff they weren't completely overwhelmed.

"It looks like she worked at a convenience store and has a rap sheet for petty crimes," Feldman murmured. "Mostly stealing and one count of prostitution."

Ash tried to process what he was being told. Not easy

when his brain was still foggy from the extreme emotions that had battered him. Fear. Shock. Grief. Soul-shaking relief.

He did, however, tuck the information away so he could pull it out later and truly consider what it all meant. "Where did they find her?"

"Jameson Park," Feldman said.

Ash lifted his brows in surprise. Jameson Park was built along the shores of Lake Michigan, and popular enough to be crowded this time of year despite the frigid weather. Plus it would have a regular patrol officer who would do sweeps through the area.

A dangerous place to do a dump.

"That doesn't fit the pattern," he said.

"No. But everything else does," Feldman told him, turning around the pad so Ash could see the photos taken of Angel Conway's naked body.

For a second his stomach rolled in protest. It'd been a while since he'd seen death up close and personal. And the violence one person could inflict on another. Then he sucked in a slow, deep breath.

Shutting down his emotions, he studied the picture with a professional attention to detail. He'd learned as a detective it was too easy to get overwhelmed by death. He had to break it down to small, individual pieces to keep himself focused on what was important.

Leaning forward, he studied the cut that marred the slender throat. It was thin and smooth and just deep enough to cut through the carotid artery. There were no hesitation marks, and no ragged edges to indicate nerves or anger. It was a precision kill that seemed to be oddly lacking in emotion.

Next his gaze moved to the small wound on the woman's

upper breast. It was carved into a neat crescent shape. This was the one detail they'd never revealed to the public.

"Christ," he breathed as he straightened. "He's back."

Jax reached out to grasp his shoulder. "We can't jump to conclusions, Ash."

Ash understood his brother's warning. There was nothing more dangerous for an investigator than leaping to a conclusion, then becoming blind to other possibilities.

But he was no longer a detective, and his gut instinct was screaming that this was the work of the killer who'd destroyed the lives of so many. Including his own.

"There's more." Feldman cleared his throat, lowering the pad. "She's had plastic surgery."

"Not that unusual," Jax said, echoing Ash's own thoughts. "Lots of women, and men for that matter, think they need some nip and tuck."

Feldman grimaced. "This nip and tuck was for a particular purpose."

A chill crawled over Ash's skin. Not the frigid air of the morgue, but something else. Perhaps a premonition. "What purpose?" he forced himself to ask.

"If I had to make a guess, I would say it was to make Angel Conway look like Remi Walsh."

Books by Bestselling Author
Fern Michaels

Connect with